THE
LOCK
BOX

THE
LOCK
BOX

A NOVEL

PARKER ADAMS

CROOKED
LANE

NEW YORK

Copyright © 2024 by Joseph Reid

Published in the United States by Crooked Lane Books, an imprint of The Quick Brown Fox & Company LLC.

Crooked Lane Books and its logo are trademarks of The Quick Brown Fox & Company LLC.

Library of Congress Catalog-in-Publication data available upon request.

ISBN (hardcover): 978-1-63910-703-2
ISBN (ebook): 978-1-63910-704-9

Cover design by Nebojsa Zoric

Printed in the United States.

www.crookedlanebooks.com

Crooked Lane Books
34 West 27th St., 10th Floor
New York, NY 10001

First Edition: March 2024

10 9 8 7 6 5 4 3 2 1

1

ALTHOUGH NEITHER COP had drawn his gun yet, Monna Locke figured that'd be coming soon. That's how shit usually went down when police learned what she did for a living.

She'd been speeding when they pulled her. State Route 27, known by most as Topanga Canyon Boulevard, was a tight, twisty mess of blind curves and cutbacks that wound for fifteen miles through the Santa Monica mountains before making a final, graceful descent to the Pacific. Whenever she had to commute to Malibu, Topanga Canyon was the worst part—the most Locke could ever hope to average was twenty-five through the bends. This morning, despite knowing traffic wouldn't be an issue, she'd left home late out of habit. Once she reached the ocean, Locke still faced another twenty minutes on Pacific Coast Highway before she could start the job.

And Malibu jobs always took longer than you thought.

So she'd pushed it. Between flooring the accelerator and gravity's helping hand, she'd gotten the van flying down the home stretch. When the flashers lit up her side mirror, she'd been cruising at sixty-five easy.

Maybe seventy.

Locke released a heavy sigh as she pulled to the dusty shoulder. Then a groan when she saw both a motorcycle and a cruiser. The month was nearly up—quota time. With everyone locked in their houses the past few weeks, she imagined the Highway Patrol's collections were running a little light.

Mr. Motorcycle came to her window. His badge and helmet gleamed in the sun, forcing her to squint. While mirrored shades and a surgical mask combined to obscure his face, his name tag said *Choi*. Any hopes for sympathy seemed slim, as the heavy starch on his CHP uniform creases suggested he wasn't the just-a-warning type.

Locke passed him her license and registration, then rested her hands at twelve o'clock on the wheel. Just to show she could be a good girl when she wanted.

"How do you say this? Moh-na?"

"Mon-na. Like Donna with an *M*."

Although she could feel Cruiser lurking at the passenger's window in her peripheral vision, Locke kept her eyes trained on Mr. Motorcycle. Glancing over would look suspicious, and these two were already giving her the serial-killer treatment.

"You know you're supposed to be sheltered at home, right? Governor's orders."

"I've got a job to get to."

Mr. Motorcycle raised an eyebrow over his shades. "That why you're in such a hurry?"

"I don't want to be late." Locke smiled—the meekest, sweetest, please-teacher-I-didn't-mean-it smile she could muster. Then she remembered he couldn't see it behind her own mask. She supposed the gaping shark teeth printed on it, *Jaws*-style, didn't send quite the right message either.

"Who's the job for?"

"Dunno exactly," she said. "A lawyer hired me."

"You often do jobs where you don't know who you're working for?"

"All the time." Rich folks rarely dialed her themselves.

"Why don't you step down out of there, miss. Real slow."

Locke nodded. With exaggerated movements she extended her arm out the window, then used the outside handle to open the van door. The soles of her Wolverines hit the pebbled asphalt with a crunch. Seeing she had Choi beaten by nearly half a foot, even with his shiny leather riding boots, gave her a bit of a smile.

"Hands up, miss. Move to the other side of the vehicle, please."

Locke's coverall sleeves sagged against her shoulders as she raised her arms. She took deliberate steps rounding the front bumper.

When she reached the passenger's side, Cruiser was waiting. A young, powerful-looking Black dude, Cruiser had Popeye forearms and hands that threatened to split open his gloves if he made a fist. "Up against the van."

"Guys, I'm just going to work." The van's navy paint, blistered and rusted, scraped at her palms when she pressed her hands against it. The beat-up look helped camouflage her in certain neighborhoods, but out here it was a liability.

Mr. Motorcycle joined them now. "Exactly what essential function do you provide people in these troubled times, Monna?"

Locke took a deep breath, knowing what was coming next. "I open up safes."

Both officers' hands flew back to their pistols. Cruiser said something into the radio clipped to his uniform shirt.

Locke looked to the sky. "Legally, guys. *Legally.* I'm licensed and bonded."

"Riiight," Cruiser said. "Like those guys in *Ocean's Eleven.*" He stepped behind her and kicked her feet farther apart before starting to frisk her roughly.

"People lock up their important stuff," she said. "Then they can't get to it when they need it, so they call me. I'm basically a glorified locksmith."

Mr. Motorcycle grunted. "That's the thing. Nobody's locked out right now, everybody's locked *in*. This flu's got folks stuck at home watching Netflix."

Locke didn't really want to do it, but this was getting out of hand. If she didn't act now, she'd never make it to the job. "Check the glove compartment."

"Why?"

"My license is in there." That, and something else she wanted him to see.

Mr. Motorcycle glanced to the passenger side door, then back again.

"It's not booby-trapped or anything. Besides"—she nodded back toward Cruiser—"he'll shoot me if it is."

Mr. Motorcycle hesitated another moment. Then he stepped to the passenger door, opened it, and leaned inside. Locke heard a click and a clunk as he opened up the glove box.

"Holeeeeey shit!"

Locke smiled.

"Jimmy, you're not gonna believe this."

"Whatcha got?" Cruiser asked.

Mr. Motorcycle popped back out of the van, holding up a glossy eight-by-ten. "She knows the Terminator!"

In the picture, Arnold Schwarzenegger had his thick python of an arm wrapped tightly around Locke's neck and shoulders. His spiky hair was still dark back then, and he sported the sly grin and thumbs-up he'd flash in the movies right before killing someone. Unlike most actors Locke had met, Schwarzenegger was legitimately huge. At six two, he had only an inch on her, but even slimmed down from his bodybuilder days, he made Locke look petite and feminine. Hell, Cruiser would have looked small next to Arnold.

"Read what's clipped to the back," she said.

Mr. Motorcycle removed the envelope, then withdrew the single sheet of California governor's stationery from inside. He read the note aloud in a thick Austrian accent—they always did that, Locke noticed. By the time he'd finished, Choi had his sunglasses off and was smiling so wide it crinkled the skin around his eyes into crow's feet.

He jabbed the earpiece of the glasses at her. "You're a regular public servant, Monna. Helping out the governor like that."

She nodded at her hands, still flattened against the van. "Does that mean I can, uh . . ."

"Yeah, sure. Sure," Choi said. "I'm Dave. This is Jimmy."

Locke wiped her hands down her coveralls before taking back the photo and letter. As she tucked them away, she stole a quick glance at her younger self, fresh out of the army. The effects of daily PT showed in her face—her features had rounded, softened since then. But what she loved about that photo was her expression. *Ballsy.* Barely old enough to drink, yet standing next to one of the most powerful men in the world as if it were nothing.

It was a total act, of course. Her heart had been pounding like a stopwatch standing next to him, her hands trembling. But asking for the letter was one of the smartest things she'd ever done. Not least of all for moments like this.

As Locke closed the passenger door, Jimmy—Cruiser—removed his black Oakleys. "So, you're headed to open up a safe? Right now?"

"That's the plan. I just gotta get there."

The cops exchanged looks.

"C'mon," Dave said.

Locke figured the escort—sirens wailing, flashers blinking—saved her ten minutes. By the time Dave and Jimmy left her at the entrance to Serra Road, saluting as they U-turned back onto the highway, her dashboard clock read 11:22.

Serra Road looked small and nondescript, more driveway than street. A dozen yards in, though, a white guard shack hinted at something worth protecting over the rise. She pulled up to the little structure and found it uninhabited.

Apparently, even rich people's security got to quarantine.

The lawyer who'd called this morning had given her a gate code among his other instructions. Facing the keypad, Locke figured this was the moment she'd learn if he was on the level.

She'd been lured into wild-goose chases before—jilted spouses digging up dirt for their divorces, greedy grandkids hoping to get a jump on the family inheritance. In her profession, you never quite knew who'd hired you, or why, until you actually popped the box. But the prospect of eight thousand bucks—twice her normal rate—more than justified the drive.

She punched in six digits. After a moment, the system beeped and the wooden arm rose to let her pass.

Although she'd done dozens of jobs around Malibu, Locke had never been summoned to this particular . . . what was the word for a gated group of mansions, anyway? *Community* was what she guessed the real estate agents would call it. Cresting the hill, she saw this one was fancier than most. The first few houses were multi-wing affairs, built around pools with adjacent tennis courts.

As she continued inward, driveways lengthened and the houses became tucked out of sight. Locke checked her phone and saw its GPS had stopped working—you had to be pretty rich to switch off the satellites, right? That left her searching for street numbers, old-school-style.

After two miles of twisting and climbing, she figured she'd missed it. She followed a blind curve up and over a final ridge, hoping for a spot wide enough to three-point-turn the van.

That's when she spotted the house.

Locke batted her eyes.

This place put the *man* in mansion.

Carved into the cliff, it gazed out over its neighbors toward a thick blue line of ocean. Built almost entirely from rounded panes of glass, the house looked a bit like a UFO that had crashed into the hillside.

Locke double-checked the number on a gatepost at the street and found it matched the one she'd scribbled down during her call with the lawyer. Another keycode he'd provided caused the metal gate to slide open. She followed the snaking concrete driveway up to the house and parked at the base of the front steps.

After sliding down from the van with her tool bag, she paused and glanced to either side. Quarantine had forced everyone to become more comfortable alone—freeways stood empty, offices were shuttered—but the absence of people here raised the hair on her arms.

Part of it was the elevation. The house stood several hundred feet above its nearest neighbor, allowing cool, salty air to wash across the drive and spill up over the rounded structure on its way to the desert. With her raven hair tousled by the wind, Locke's exposed neck felt a chilly prickle in the breeze.

It was more than that, though. Locke had done plenty of jobs solo; like busted pipes, locked safes were most often discovered after hours. But the solitude here was . . . unsettling. She didn't know why. Only that her insides were clenching the same way as when she arrived at the dentist's office.

Maybe it was all the surveillance. Large cameras were mounted on the edges of the house, and instead of a bell, a smaller camera protruded from a panel next to the front door. Locke waved at the little lens in case someone was watching her from the other end of the internet.

The door—a dark, polished slab of metal that seemed extra imposing compared to the glass framing it—bore an electronic lock, one of those fancy ones that allowed owners to program one-time codes for workers and guests. Locke punched yet a third set of numbers and heard another beep. When she tried the chrome handle, the door swung open with a whispered swish.

Inside, there weren't rooms so much as spaces. The two-story entryway spilled into a living area to Locke's left and a dining area to her right. Both contained uncomfortable-looking, minimalist furniture and various pieces of East Asian art. The floors were some kind of shiny, off-white stone that caused her boot soles to make tiny squeaks. Sunlight streaming in had warmed the air significantly, and Locke switched the bag from one hand to another while pushing her coverall sleeves up over her elbows.

She didn't bother calling out. The lawyer had warned her the house would be empty, its residents having fled to Montana or Wyoming or something. The safe was suppos-edly waiting in an office on the second floor.

A glance upward showed a balcony overlooking the place, but no stairs to reach it.

Locke proceeded inward until she reached a large, open-style kitchen. Metal cabinets and counters matched the front door, while dark accents in the flooring led off to either side. Her eyes naturally wandered left, following the inlays to a set of open risers that spiraled upward.

A closed set of double doors greeted her at the top of the stairs. Figuring they marked the master bedroom, she avoided them and proceeded through an archway to the balcony.

Between the clear railing and views out the glass exterior, crossing the balcony felt a bit like traversing a narrow moun-tain ledge. Although Locke spotted a hallway with additional sets of doors at the far end of the balcony, a single open door awaited her midway along the expanse.

Poking her head inside, she found a squarish room: the office.

With four solid walls, most of the light filtered down from a vaulted skylight overhead. A rectangular, glass-topped desk and a black leather rolling chair dominated the middle of the room. Behind them, two sets of bookshelves bracketed a six-foot-tall framed painting. Like the rest of the house, the shelves contained various East Asian pieces, ranging from a samurai sword to ceramic urns and figurines. Locke didn't know much about art, but to her the stuff seemed mismatched from all over the region—China, Japan, maybe other countries.

Gradually, her eyes moved to the painting. Locke didn't care for modern, splotchy art, but this—this she liked. The tall, narrow image showed some kind of samurai warrior posed with his sword up over his head. No background, no scenery, just the figure. Different sections of the warrior's robes were portrayed in varied but vibrant colors and patterns, while his face was rendered solely in black and white. The warrior's expression was simultaneously calm and aggressive. But what really caught Locke's eye was how the painting had been created. Underneath the glass, the image looked like it was painted on silky, iridescent fabric instead of canvas. Even the paint itself had a unique sheen that reflected the light as you caught it from different angles.

After a second taking in the art, Locke spun on her heel and glanced around the room. No safe stood anywhere in sight. She replayed the lawyer's instructions in her mind— he'd clearly said the safe was in the office.

For a moment, her heartbeat accelerated, echoing her goosebumps on the way in. Her immediate thought was the crowbar buried in her bag—if she needed a weapon, that was her surest bet. She'd never liked guns, even in the army. Something she could swing, though . . .

Swing.

Locke turned back to the painting. Ever so gently, she tugged at the edge of the frame.

It swung back at her like a door.

She smiled. Mounted within a rectangular cutout in the wall was one of the sexiest safes she'd seen in a long time.

The face of the black metal box was buffed to a high shine. Fancy golden filigree was stenciled at each corner, while matching script letters spelled out *American Fortress* along its upper edge. A fat combination dial sat squarely in the middle of the door, just above the three-pronged wheel that served as a handle.

The lawyer had said the residents couldn't remember the combination. Locke heard that all the time. If you only opened a box once or twice a year, it was easy to forget. Plus, people felt paranoid writing the digits down.

The dial went from 0 to 100. With a three-number combination, that meant literally a million possibilities. The fastest way to open a mechanical lock like this would be to drill a hole and thread a scope inside, one that allowed you to see the tumblers—the wheels behind the dial. Each wheel represented one piece of the combination, and each had a notch cut into it. When you lined up the notches, a bar called the fence would drop down into them, releasing the bolt that held the door closed.

But everyone understood that trick, including the safe makers, who worked to make drilling the hole extraordinarily painful. They barricaded the wheels behind so-called "hard plates," of reinforced metal. They added "relockers," mechanisms that would sense tampering and deploy extra bolts to secure the door. In the end, the idea wasn't so much to stop a thief completely as to slow them down. If opening a safe took too long, no one would bother trying.

Locke knew this particular model included a glass sheet that would shatter on contact and snap six extra bolts into place. The safe's hard plate also featured a layer of ball bearings sandwiched between two sheets of tungsten steel that would snap even the hardest commercial drill bit. And, intentionally or not, whoever installed the box had made it even harder to attack by mounting it between the bookshelves. Built from solid oak, they were secured to the wall, probably to withstand an earthquake. Unless you tore them down, drilling in from either side would be impossible.

Eyeing all this, Locke needed less than thirty seconds to identify the path virtually every safe technician in the country would take. Anyone rational—anybody who valued their time—would throw up their hands, cut away drywall above the box, then drill a one- or two-foot hole in the top of the safe and pull the goods out that way. "Sorry about the mess," they'd tell the owner, who'd be left to clean a room coated in metal dust in addition to needing a new safe and a new wall.

But a small handful of guys would approach it differently. Guys like Jeff Sitar in New Jersey, Dave LaBarge in upstate New York, Scott Gray in Toronto. Legends. Rock stars. All had won the Harry C. Miller contest, the world championship of safecracking. Hell, Sitar had won it eight times.

Those guys wouldn't have cut this box. They were "manipulators," professionals who cracked safes with their bare hands by feeling the way the tumblers spun behind the dial. Those guys would decipher the combination and open the door without so much as a scratch. Those guys—all *guys*, mind you—had their profiles written up in newspapers and magazines. Television shows timed them breaking into bank vaults. One online video tested Sitar to see if he could feel a Post-it note attached to a particular tumbler.

No female safecracker—and you could count all of those nationwide on two hands—had ever garnered that kind of attention. No woman had ever won the Harry C. Miller contest either.

Of course, Locke knew, that was because she'd never bothered to enter.

Contests, newspaper articles, even social media—she imagined they all helped generate a certain amount of business. For the rest of their lives, Sitar and LaBarge and Gray would have *World Champion Safecracker* emblazoned on their websites.

But Locke didn't care about accolades like that. She'd learned early: when it came to cracking safes in LA, discretion mattered as much as skill.

When a Rodeo Drive jeweler accidentally reset its time lock on Oscar morning, trapping a ruby choker bound for the red carpet that night, they needed their rocks freed fast without word hitting the *Hollywood Reporter*. When a prominent producer's children worried what kinds of pictures were lurking in his office safe after he passed, they wanted no questions asked. When the world's most popular porn star planned to ditch her director husband, she couldn't risk losing the videos they'd made together. Locke had helped them all.

Locke had cracked safes for cops, crooks, and corporations. She didn't have a website; you couldn't Google her. If you were important enough, you likely had an equally important friend who had her number. That was how she got business, and she preferred it that way.

This morning's lawyer, a guy named Oscar Sakamoto, hadn't mentioned how he'd found her. Frankly, that was fine. She liked lawyers because they said no more than necessary and paid up front. Sakamoto had wired her half her fee during the three minutes they'd talked on the phone.

Locke rolled the desk chair over to the safe, eased herself into it, and set the bag between her feet. Although it contained the crowbar, a stethoscope, and several other tools, all she extracted from it was a small notepad and a pen. The lawyer had said the combination contained three numbers—that meant three wheels behind the dial. Several turns to the right cleared the lock, then she placed the dial at 0. From there, she started spinning to the left, one turn, a second turn, a third. With each turn, she could feel another wheel engage until all were spinning behind the dial. Locke continued the turn until she felt the slightest change in pressure against the dial. That marked one edge of one notch on one wheel.

She made a note and returned to the start.

Over the course of five minutes, Locke's fingers spun the dial several hundred times. This was what movies never showed about safecracking—the constant, back-and-forth testing of the wheels to learn where their notches started and stopped. There was no sound, no ticking. Just her fingertips against the dial, sensing how it spun.

Eventually, Locke had circled three numbers on her pad, 12, 48, and 97. Those were the components of the combination, she was convinced. She tried them lowest to highest, then highest to lowest. When she put 48 first, then 12, and finally 97, the three-pronged handle spun.

Jackpot.

Inside, the safe was divided into numerous compartments, but Locke only needed one item. Sakamoto had asked her to retrieve a small box from the lowest drawer. When she slid that open, a white wooden cube sat alone on the green velvet cushion. The size of a coffee mug and weight of a soda can, the only unique thing about the box was markings along its sides, Mandarin characters Locke couldn't read.

Although a pang of curiosity echoed in her chest, Locke didn't open the wooden box. Discretion—and besides, she had no idea how many cameras were watching her every move inside the house. Instead, she wedged the box down into her bag, resting the pad and pen on top. Then she closed the safe, spinning the dial several times to clear it, before replacing the painting and chair.

A glance back over the room from the doorway confirmed it looked identical to when she'd arrived.

Locke emerged from the office with more spring in her step than her Wolverines provided. She'd just manipulated a major-league lock in under ten minutes. Even if you counted her commute and the trip downtown to deliver the box to the lawyer, she'd still be pulling down eight grand for four hours' work.

Not a bad day, quarantine or not.

Smiling, Locke paused on the balcony. She inhaled deeply, letting the trace of salt tickle her nostrils as she gazed out toward the ocean.

They said this virus took your sense of smell, your sense of taste. She considered for a moment how weird that must be, then pushed it from her mind. Thankfully, she was healthy. They said this thing didn't affect younger people, or if it did, not as badly. Kids didn't get it at all, apparently. All Locke needed to do was make it downtown for a five-minute meeting, then she could head back to Val Verde and ride this thing out.

Hell, if the lawyer Sakamoto paid the second half in cash, she wouldn't need to visit the bank for weeks.

She turned for the stairs. As she took a step, her eyes dropped instinctively to the narrow balcony. Her footing was fine, but her peripheral vision ended up catching something else. Outside, a panel truck was easing up alongside her van. Painted white, with a toilet bowl and plunger painted on the side.

Made sense for the owners: get all the maintenance done while you were away. Especially these days, when you had no idea who might be sick. In the back of her mind, Locke wondered if the plumber had gotten half his fee up front. Probably not—they charged by the hour.

A driver slid down from the cab. Young guy. Taking his quarantine seriously, as he wore both a plain white face mask and rubber gloves. Even in baggy coveralls, though, you could tell he was a bruiser.

Then she noticed a second guy. Equally buff, circling round the back of the panel truck from the passenger's side.

She supposed a mansion this size must be a big job. Bring two guys, finish in half the time.

When they opened the truck's rear doors, though, two more guys hopped out. All similarly dressed, all Asian.

Locke had never seen a team of four plumbers before.

That was when they took out the guns.

2

SEEING THE GUNS changed everything.

The mansion, so open and airy, seemed to shrink around Locke's shoulders. The balcony might as well have been a balance beam. Although a million thoughts collided in her head, including whether the gunmen had already seen her through the glass, her overriding concern was that she was cornered. To have any chance of escaping—to have any options at all—she needed to get back downstairs.

Her rubber soles gripped the stone floor tightly as she took off in a dead sprint.

After three steps, though, she heard the front door's familiar beep-and-swish. At the noise, Locke dropped to the floor.

It had been a long time since she'd practiced a combat fall. Her drill sergeants from basic would not have been pleased at the result. The hard stuff in her bag—the crowbar, the other tools—hit first. Not only did they make a hefty clunk, but her ribs and stomach came crashing down on top of them.

Locke bit her lip to stifle a groan from the impact.

A tiny sound leaked out.

Had the gunmen heard?

As seconds ticked by and no one sprayed bullets in her direction, it seemed maybe they hadn't.

The arch at the end of the balcony loomed a couple of feet away. Close enough Locke could reach out, curl her fingers around the corner of the wall, and pull herself to it. But while part of her wanted to do just that, a voice inside warned to check the door first.

Locke hauled herself up onto her elbows and combat crawled to the base of the railing. Below, the four gunmen had fanned into a semicircle. Communicating with hand signals, they were advancing steadily into the house, the nearest ones passing under the balcony and out of view.

Her head whipped back toward the stairs. Although they seemed tantalizingly close, she knew she couldn't make it.

She needed someplace to hide. Fast.

Her eyes slid to the double doors she'd bypassed earlier. Like all the others in the house, they were wood framed, with a frosted glass panel in the middle. In her mind, Locke imagined a sprawling king-size bed and huge walk-in closet inside. But the truth was, she had no idea what lay behind the darkened glass, whether that room would provide any kind of shelter at all.

Worse, it stood alone at the top of the stairs.

The first place the gunmen would check.

And a complete dead end.

Locke gathered her feet beneath her, then spun back toward the office. With the gunmen below, she didn't run, exactly—she couldn't risk her boots clonking against the balcony. Instead, she rose up on the balls of her feet and used long, slow strides to cover as much ground as possible.

Avoiding the office, she made for the rooms she'd seen farther down the balcony. Now that she focused on them, she counted three doors, two singles on the left and a double set at the very end on the right.

She stopped at the first single door. Although no one should have been inside, she caught herself checking the glass inset anyway.

Dark and still.

As Locke reached for the handle, she cocked an ear back over her shoulder. Not a peep from below. These guys were dead quiet—more noise came from her chest, where her heart was pounding, than from downstairs.

Locke put steady pressure on the handle bar until it started to turn. The clock in her head screamed that she'd already taken too long, that the gunmen would be sneaking up behind her any second. Out of nowhere, though, one of the Mule's sayings from high school echoed in her ears: *Go quickly, but don't hurry.*

Once she felt the latch release from the frame, she eased the door inward. Slowly, smoothly—she couldn't afford any creaks or groans. After slipping through the opening, she eased it back closed.

The interior handle included a simple twist lock, and she considered turning it to slow down the gunmen.

But a locked door in an otherwise empty house would be a dead giveaway. Emphasis on *dead*. These guys would simply shoot out the glass, unlock the door, and finish her off, if one of their bullets hadn't done the job already.

Imagining a burst of hot metal spraying toward her, Locke retreated a step. Thankfully, the room was dark—no skylight here—and she didn't cast a shadow on the door's glass inset. When she turned into the heart of the room, she found it filled with fancy white furniture: a four-poster bed, a desk, and a dresser.

The bed seemed to be her best hope, but a quick flip of the skirt showed its frame was solid all the way to the floor. No hiding underneath.

Locke's eyes flew to the periwinkle walls. The spaces over the desk and the dresser were covered in pictures—concert posters, candids of a redheaded teenager laughing with her friends, a couple of posed shots with her parents. The final wall displayed a series of artfully arranged shots of the same girl in an equestrian outfit, riding a horse. Bracketing these pictures were doors, one a set of mirrored closet sliders, the other solid wood.

Locke beelined to the closet, thankful the thick carpeting absorbed her footsteps. As she was reaching for the slider's handle, though, two thoughts struck her. First, the memory of her own teenage closet—a tangled mess of clothes and shoes and every other thing she could stuff inside to convince her mom that she'd cleaned.

Second, the way those sliders rumbled across their tracks. Everyone in the house would hear.

She diverted to the solid wooden door. Inching it open, she saw a tile vanity and mirror, then a pair of sinks, finally another door at the far end.

Locke recalled the balcony layout and decided this must be one of those jack-and-jill jobs, connecting two bedrooms.

That gave her an idea.

Stepping into the bathroom, Locke drew the door closed enough to conceal all but her head, which she poked out through the narrow opening. She also fished into her bag and pulled out the crowbar. It wouldn't be much help against those guns, but it was better than nothing.

Then she waited.

What she really needed now was noise. Footsteps, gunshots—some kind of sign of where the four mystery men were. Anything to drown out the sound of her own breathing, and the pulse racing in her ears.

With nothing coming, though, Locke trained her eyes across the bedroom on the door handle and glass inset. If she was going to get any warning before the gunmen burst in, that's where she'd find it.

Seconds ticked by.

Still nothing.

Locke breathed through her nose. Hoping it was quieter, praying it would slow down her heart rate.

She was certain a minute had passed since she'd entered the bedroom.

At least a minute. Maybe two.

She imagined the men, moving through the downstairs. How long could that really take? Although she wanted to close her eyes to picture it, she didn't dare. She stayed locked on the bedroom door.

Gradually, the tension in Locke's jaw started to fade. She eased down onto her heels. As improbable as it seemed, the thought crept into her mind: maybe the gunmen had left.

Maybe they weren't after her, or the box, after all.

Locke released a long, deep breath through her nose.

Then she saw a flash.

At the glass. Nothing solid, nothing sustained.

Just a quick change in light, as if something had passed by.

Locke tensed again.

The door handle started to move.

Almost imperceptibly at first. But it kept going, rotating toward the floor.

Locke retreated into the bathroom and pushed the door closed. Three quick steps across the jack-and-jill and she slipped through a door on that side, shutting it behind her.

Another bedroom. Navy walls with white stars and rockets stenciled all over them. Bunk beds. Messier than the last one, but Locke paid little attention as she stepped through the clothes strewn across the floor.

Her eyes were on the glass inset of this bedroom's door. Watching for flashes, watching the knob.

Seeing no movement, she crossed to it quickly, staying an arm's length away to keep her own shadow off the glass. She gave a quick glance behind her, then stretched out her arm, curling her fingers around the door handle.

In one, smooth motion, Locke turned the handle and pulled it open.

The area outside the door was empty. As much of it as she could see.

She stuck a toe out, as if testing cold water.

No sound, no reaction.

Locke shifted her weight onto that front foot, drawing herself out of the bedroom.

Directly across the hallway were the double doors she'd seen earlier. Looking back down the balcony, she saw the bedroom door she'd entered, now ajar. Even farther down, the office door remained open, bright light spilling out.

Nothing stood between Locke and the far end of the balcony.

Fifty feet—maybe sixty—to freedom.

If she could make the stairs . . .

She took one, silent step in that direction.

That's when one of the gunmen stepped out from the office.

Locke saw him first. He was looking straight ahead—out over the balcony, across to the windows and the ocean view beyond them.

Not knowing if the bunk bed room was clear, Locke turned toward the double doors. She reached for the closer of the two handles, praying, *Don't be locked, don't be locked.*

Her hand slapped down on the metal, turning it and pushing inward simultaneously.

Don't look back, don't look back.

The door opened an inch. Then two.

Locke was thinking she just might make it when a voice shouted from behind her.

She didn't stop.

A roar ripped across the balcony. The sound of shots echoed through the cavernous space, but she ignored the noise and the heat and the worry whether some supersonic shard of metal might slice through her.

Her only thought was to get inside the room.

As soon as she'd cleared the door, Locke spun back to slam it shut. When she did, she caught the face of a gunman in the bunk bed room across the hall.

The mask obscured his mouth and nose, but the rage in his eyes was clear.

Thankfully, the gunfire from the office had him pinned. Before he could start shooting too, Locke slammed the door, flipped the lock, and sidestepped against the wall.

Several more shots rang out. One shattered the glass while others ripped into the wood frame.

She only had seconds.

But when Locke checked her surroundings, her heart sank.

This, not the double doors at the top of the stairs, was the master bedroom. Other than the largest bed she'd ever seen, the chamber stood completely devoid of furniture. No nightstands. No dresser. Only a giant portrait over the bed of the same old, white-haired couple from the teenager's photographs.

Even worse, no obvious doors. No closet, no bathroom.

They had to be here somewhere, but two whole walls were glass, while the others were paneled in reflective black stone with no obvious outlines.

More gunshots pushed Locke off the wall and farther into the room. Her head swiveled, looking for something, anything she could use.

The windows.

Outside, bent around the corner of the house, was a waist-high wall and railing.

Another balcony!

But how to get out there?

Locke dashed to where the glass walls met and started feeling around. Heavy curtains had been retracted into that corner from both sides. Behind one set, she found a handle.

She struggled with it. It seemed locked somehow.

A crash sounded behind her, more glass breaking.

Locke didn't turn around. She was cloaked in the curtains now and had to hope they'd buy her the few more moments she needed.

Although she considered taking a whack at the wall with the crowbar, the panels were thick, like aquarium glass. Instead, she wedged the bar between the door handle and the glass and hung her weight on it, hoping the extra leverage would help if it was rusted shut.

Finally, it gave way. After she managed to turn the handle ninety degrees, a heavy section of glass swung inward.

Opening the glass wall unleashed a violent wind that punched its way into the room with a howl. It twisted and billowed the curtains. It stabbed at Locke's eyes, forcing them shut.

Blind, she pushed through the opening.

Feeling for the railing in front of her until she found it with her fingertips.

The wind relented just enough that she could reopen her eyes. When she did, the exterior balcony had the most fantastic view she'd seen yet—a panorama of rugged coastline stretching in either direction.

More gunshots reminded her not to get too taken with it.

As she glanced down from the horizon, her heart sank again. This corner of the house pointed out toward the ocean. Mere feet from the foundation, the ground dropped off in a sheer cliff face that was fifty, maybe a hundred feet high.

Some choice, she thought. *Shot or squished.*

With the wind wrestling her dark hair, Locke peered farther out over the edge. Hoping she could hang down from the railing, she checked the base of the house and noticed something.

Water.

A pool had been built out to the edge of the cliff. She guessed it was one of those infinity pools, where the water blended with the ocean. Probably great for sunsets.

But how deep was it?

From overhead, it seemed impossible to tell.

She dropped the crowbar and watched it strike the surface with a splash.

The dark metal wavered several times on its way to the bottom.

That gave Locke hope, but also sent a new chill through her.

She couldn't swim.

She'd never learned as a kid, then figured the army would teach her, but it wasn't a requirement. It'd be awfully ironic to survive a two-story fall and drown at the bottom of a pool. Still, what choice did she have?

She hoisted one foot up onto the wall, then boosted herself the rest of the way.

Although she kept a hand braced back against the house, standing on top of the narrow wall was completely disorienting. The wind whipped her hair so violently she had to close her eyes again. The rushing air made her feel like she was already falling.

Locke's throat squeezed nearly shut. So tight she couldn't swallow.

She wasn't sure she could breathe.

Instinctively, she turned back toward the house, away from the wind. She wanted to see her hand and the solid structure to know where she was.

When she opened her eyes, she saw the windows. The doorway. The curtains, billowing.

And then, one of the gunmen, emerging from behind them.

He started to raise the muzzle of his weapon. Pointing it right at her.

Locke pinched her nose and stepped backward off the wall.

3

T HE FALL TOOK forever.

So long Locke wondered if she'd missed the pool completely. In her mind, she pictured herself splatting across the concrete deck. Or worse, bouncing down the rocky cliff face, each impact smashing her bones into tinier and tinier pieces.

She squeezed her eyes shut even tighter.

As she did, her lungs started to demand fresh air. She'd grabbed a quick breath as she stepped back off the railing, but she'd never expected to have to hold it this long. Figuring she'd better steal another before going under, she started to exhale.

She was only halfway done when her feet hit the water.

The pool wasted no time swallowing her; she was submerged instantly. Icy water stabbed her shins first, just above her boots. Then her face, her scalp. Finally, it snaked its way everywhere—slithering up her sleeves and down her neck, even trickling into her boots, where it tickled her toes.

Locke continued exhaling after she was under, assuming she'd pop back up to the surface. But when her lungs had emptied and ordered her brain to breathe again, she was still underwater.

And sinking.

Part of it was the bag, but she hated the thought of losing the box and all her tools.

Locke opened her eyes and tried to ignore the water's salty sting. Looking up, she saw her bubbles dancing toward the shifting surface overhead. More than anything, she wished she could grab them and take them back.

One, hard kick pushed her upward.

The surface loomed closer for a moment. Then it started to recede again.

Locke's lungs were furious now, burning hot. Her heart began to pound.

She gave several more kicks and thrashed downward with her free arm. She could see the surface approaching, inches from her face. The air she needed was . . . right . . . there. But each time she stopped moving, anytime she relaxed, it slipped away again.

Her stomach muscles tightened—she was *not* going to die here.

Locke fluttered her feet like she'd seen the Olympic swimmers do. The coveralls were leaden, and her boots felt like anchors, but she ignored the pain in her thighs and kept churning her legs.

When her face broke the surface, it was like being kissed by the sky. She pulled her mask down under her chin and sucked in several breaths as fast as she could.

The crack of gunfire reminded her why she'd jumped.

Glancing up, she saw two masked faces at the balcony railing, along with two flashing muzzles.

Locke took a final gulp of air and ducked back under. With every ounce of strength in her arms and shoulders, she pulled deeper and toward the house. Clutching the bag made her motions lopsided, but she did her best.

After three strokes, she resurfaced, and now the bullet splashes erupted behind her. She'd gotten far enough under the balcony that the gunmen didn't have an angle.

Invigorated, she kept pulling even as water sputtered from her mouth and nose. Her boots started to scrape at the bottom—she couldn't quite touch yet, but she was getting closer to the shallow end. A few more inches, and hopefully she could stand.

A weak smile started to form on her lips. Her next breath was more like a sigh.

But then she noticed: the air had grown quiet. No more bullets flying, no more splashes.

If the gunmen weren't shooting, that meant they were coming.

Locke's strokes grew more frantic. Her right toe got some traction. Then her left. As she drew toward the edge of the pool, she started to look beyond it—the front steps and her van sat yards away.

Every motion was like steering a spoon through honey. Her clothes were heavy, her arms and legs ached like she'd run a marathon. Still, she crept closer and closer to the edge, bouncing off the bottom and paddling as best she could.

When she finally reached the wall, Locke hauled herself out, tumbling to her back on the concrete deck. As much as she wanted to lie there a moment and catch her breath, she forced herself up onto her feet. With water pouring off her, she sprinted for the van.

Thankfully, she hadn't locked it. The door flew open when she yanked on the handle, and she tossed the bag inside ahead of her before climbing up. Her keys sat in a small puddle inside her pocket. As she pulled them out, her hand was shaking—cold or scared or both, she had no idea—but somehow she managed to fumble the little wedge of metal into the ignition.

She was turning it when the front door of the house opened.

The gunmen dashed out as the engine sprang to life. Seeing her behind the wheel, they skidded to a stop and started to raise their guns.

Locke shifted into reverse and stomped on the pedal.

Their first shots missed completely as the van lurched backward. When she cut the wheel and banked around the plumbing truck, metallic plunks started to sound against the van's passenger's side. She barely tapped the brake before dropping it into drive, flooring the accelerator and aiming for the street.

The driver's door slammed shut as the van rocketed forward. She heard more shots, more plunks against the rear doors, but she didn't glance back. Her eyes were locked ahead of her.

Down at the street, the gate had started to slide open, but it was moving slowly. Locke didn't think she could wait— instead of braking, she kept the gas pedal floored. The van gathered speed quickly, and she pointed the nose for the center of the growing opening.

It was going to be close.

The impact threw Locke forward, then back, but the van kept moving. A deafening screech of metal scraping metal ripped through the air, and the van burst onto the street.

Locke fought to control the wheel, then steered down the ridge she'd climbed earlier. She allowed herself a quick glance to the side mirror and saw that the white panel truck hadn't budged.

She didn't care. She kept the accelerator floored all the way to PCH.

* * *

Locke didn't stop till she got to Duke's.

With the road empty, she kept it at sixty, barreling through traffic lights at the Malibu Pier, Nobu, and Carbon Canyon Road. She half-hoped to get pulled for running the reds—she wouldn't have minded some armed reinforcements. Unfortunately, Dave and Jimmy seemed to have made off for greener speed traps.

Duke's Restaurant sat on the ocean side of the street. In normal times, its sprawling views and high-end seafood menu generated so much business that the valets carved the parking lot into separate lanes with cones to control the traffic. Under quarantine, though, the place was closed, the lot deserted.

Exactly what Locke was hoping for.

She bounced the van up over the driveway lip at full speed, then pulled a swooping turn through the lot. The tires chirped as the van screeched to a stop dead center, its windshield pointed back out to the street.

Although she put it in park, she left the engine running.

Her arms dropped limp to her side. All her muscles tingled from the extreme exertion, a sensation she hadn't experienced in years. Suddenly conscious of her breathing for the first time since the pool, Locke noticed the way her chest was heaving. Her heart still pounding.

She drew a deep breath through her nose, trying to slow everything down. Two or three inhales, and the adrenaline started to drain away.

But now the tingling changed, grew more powerful. She started trembling all over. Raising one hand, Locke saw it was noticeably shaking. Even her teeth were chattering.

Lying to herself that it was the cold, she forced herself up and out of the driver's seat. Water oozed from her boots as she stepped to the back of the van. Her socks felt like wet sponges. She stripped those off first, emptying the shoes and wringing out the socks. The metal floor felt frigid against her bare feet as she stood and stepped out of the soaked coveralls.

Drilling safes was often messy work. Boxes were buried in basements or wedged behind walls. More often than not, Locke emerged from a job smeared in some combination of soot, dirt, and dust. She'd learned to keep fresh water, towels, and spare clothes in back.

After semidrying her hair, she gathered it into a tight ponytail and corralled it with a scrunchie. She had no replacement for her tank top, spandex shorts, or underwear—she'd have to live with them damp after patting them down the best she could. Fresh coveralls left her feeling somewhat rejuvenated. And warmer. She brought one towel forward and draped it across the driver's seat. The cloth upholstery was already soaked, and she had a feeling her bottoms would continue to wring out water the rest of the way.

Which raised the question—the way where?

A voice from her belly said to head straight home. Make sure things at the house were secure and barricaded there.

Locke blinked several times. Although she'd stopped shaking, the fear was still palpable, and she didn't know that the instinct to run was wrong. But she needed to think through it, not just react.

The dashboard clock read 12:45. With empty freeways, she could dash downtown in twenty, maybe thirty minutes. A quick handoff to the lawyer, she could be home by 3.

Could she really risk that?

Did she want to?

Today wasn't the first time Locke had been shot at on a job. Six months after she'd started the safecracker gig, a single bullet had whizzed through a window while she was opening a Tann 4720 at Tres Tacos in Simi Valley. Two years later, she'd survived a full-on firefight at Firenze Ferrari in Long Beach. Going in to drill a hundred-year-old Herring-Hall-Marvin safe, she hadn't realized the auto shop belonged to Big Bo King, one of the baddest drug smugglers in California. After six hours sweating over the two-ton box, Locke finally got it open, only to get greeted by a spray of bullets pouring through the glass garage doors. To her horror, the mechanics around her produced guns of their own and returned fire. She'd been forced back behind the big black box, hoping its steel walls would shield her.

She had no desire to be anyone's target practice. Assuming the muscle-bound mansion guys were after the little box from the safe, a part of her desperately wanted to ditch it in the Duke's dumpster or chuck it off the cliff into the ocean.

As appealing as that sounded, though, she knew it wasn't a serious solution. Those attack dogs would keep coming as long as they had a scent. The question was whether she could sic them onto some other meat.

The lawyer, Sakamoto. She'd happily trade places with him in the gunmen's sights.

Unless he and the hit squad were in it together.

Those bruisers had gotten their access codes from somewhere. The gate house, the driveway gate—those were probably pinchable with a little patience. Watch them long enough, you'd pick up the code, or the pattern if they rotated it. But not the front door—that lock was primo new tech. Guest codes were one-time deals that expired automatically after twenty-four hours. That meant they'd either used her code or been issued one of their own.

Locke thought back to her own entry. Could the gunmen have been watching her somehow, seen the digits she pressed? Through a long-distance lens or something?

She guessed it was possible. That eerie feeling had shaken her at the start—had her intuition picked up on being watched?

There was no way to know for sure. But if the man who'd called her was in on the ambush, the downtown rendezvous would be bullshit. She'd arrive to find an uninhabited office, or more likely, a trap.

Locke pulled out her phone and checked her bank account online. The morning's $4,000 deposit was still there. If the mansion call was a setup, why not freeze payment? That was a lot of coin to blow as bait.

She glanced over at her bag, which had tumbled into the footwell. Her eyes lingered on it for a moment.

Once again, she shook off the pang of curiosity in her chest.

Instead, she ran a search on her phone. This morning, when the lawyer had identified his firm, Sakamoto & Kim, she'd pulled up their website. It advertised their practice as *Business's Bridge to Asia*. While it didn't contain pictures of individual attorneys, the street address listed on the webpage had matched the one he'd provided as the rendezvous. The entire twenty-fifth floor of a fancy skyscraper, it had seemed legit at the time.

Now Locke navigated to the building's website instead. Its tenant list included a firm named Sakamoto & Kim on the twenty-fifth floor.

If Sakamoto was on the level, his office would still be the gunmen's next stop. But if she could beat them there . . . Make delivery, get paid. Get rid of the box and give those goons no reason to care about her anymore.

Locke checked the clock again. Her costume change had taken only three minutes, and she hadn't seen any trace of the fake plumbing truck.

Hopefully that meant she still had a head start.

*   *   *

Locke found the entrance to the skyscraper's parking garage on Hope Street. She crossed her fingers that it was some kind of sign.

The garage stood eerily empty, though, both gate arms raised in surrender. She imagined that, on normal days, the suit set fought for end spots to protect their Beemers and Benzes. Today, she pulled right up to the elevator bay. The only other vehicle in the entire place was a white Volvo SUV, parked in a numbered spot.

No sign of the plumbing truck, which was even better.

Before leaving the van, Locke visited her toolboxes in the back. The crowbar she'd dropped in the pool had been her favorite. The way it fit in her hand, the heft of it—she'd searched for duplicates of that model for three years and hadn't managed to find one. Still, this wasn't an occasion to go empty-handed.

A large, heavy alternative went into the bag.

The garage elevator delivered her to a massive three-story lobby. Although she'd hoped her boots would have dried out, the soles squeaked when she stepped onto the marble floor. At the noise, Locke's eyes flew to the security desk, but it was unmanned. The lobby lights were dimmed, and as at the mansion, the lack of AC was noticeable.

The building was tall enough that three sets of elevators served different groups of floors. Locke found the correct one and boarded. As the car traveled upward—so quickly her ears popped—she replaced her face mask and dug the replacement crowbar out of her bag. She adjusted it a few times in her right hand, trying to get the feel of it.

When she stepped off on twenty-five, she found herself in a narrow hallway. The passage was lined in dark wood, with the firm's name mounted on the opposite wall in gold letters above a logo featuring the flags of the United States, Japan, South Korea, and China.

Although both ends of the hallway were capped by pairs of solid-looking doors, one set had a button mounted next to it, along with a sign: *After Hours, Please Ring*. Locke stepped over and pressed the button with the tip of the crowbar, creating a muffled buzz inside the office. She fidgeted a moment, pondering her next move if no response came. In the back of her mind, the clock was still ticking—she had no idea how long the gunmen might take to find this address, but she planned to be long gone before then.

Just as she was about to bail on the buzzer, she heard a heavy latch release. The right-hand door swung open, revealing a trim man in a finely tailored charcoal suit. To her surprise, he wasn't wearing a mask. Gray flecks dotting his otherwise jet-black hair, prominent cheekbones, and square jaw all screamed serious businessman, while the absence of a tie and his open shirt collar seemed his only nods to the office being closed.

"Ms. Locke," he said. "You work quickly."

"I try, Mr. Sakamoto," she said, trying to determine whether his deep voice was the same as this morning's call. "I felt bad, you having to be here at the office all by yourself."

After a humble shrug, he flashed her a slick, toothy smile that seemed to require a maximum amount of effort. "I prefer the peace and quiet. Please, come in."

As he motioned inward with one hand, the lawyer took a pronounced step back, creating a buffer of space. Locke smiled at the quarantine courtesy, but her grip on the crowbar tightened.

She'd been hired countless times over the phone. The client—or their lawyer—would call out of the blue, often late at night. No time to meet over coffee, to have a consultation. It was box first, questions later. So she'd learned to do her due diligence. Like this morning, she checked websites, she verified deposits.

And one other thing.

Locke's all-time favorite TV show was *Mad Men*, the drama about 1960s advertising execs. It had debuted right as she was leaving the army—part of her reentry to real life. One episode contained the best line of the entire series: a boss screaming at an employee, "That's what the money's for!"

So whenever a client hired her sight unseen, Locke instructed them to say that line when they met, like a code. This morning she'd told Sakamoto the same thing: "When I say, 'It's a shame you're here all by yourself,' you say, 'That's what the money's for.'"

Slick wasn't the one from the call.

CHAPTER

4

WITH SLICK HOLDING the door open on her right, Locke expected one of the gunmen would be hiding just inside on her left, weapon trained at the doorframe.

Tensing her right shoulder, she led with her left foot as she approached, preparing to duck and throw all her weight into an upward swing of the crowbar. Best case, she figured the steel rod would catch the guy's forearm and shatter it. If it merely nailed him in the balls, that'd work too.

When she crossed the threshold, though, Locke found nothing to her left but empty air. Trying not to show surprise, she sidestepped in that direction. That gave her more space and kept the wall behind her—one direction she didn't have to watch for an ambush.

As she shifted her gaze back to Slick, Locke got a quick glimpse of the law firm's reception area. Typical stuff: desk on one side, seating area on the other. The far wall was glass, with conference rooms behind it staring out on the city skyline. A hallway stretched to her left, and she guessed another would extend in the opposite direction, back behind Slick and the door he was holding open. Whenever Locke visited offices like this, they struck her as human hamster cages, circular tracks surrounding the elevators in the middle.

Those offices had been bustling and alive, though. This one stood darkened and dead. The whole place smelled warm and stale, same as the air that blew out the side of Locke's ten-year-old laptop if she left it running overnight.

Without warning, Slick shoved the heavy wooden door shut.

It relatched with a solid-sounding thunk that echoed around the room. Slick's eyes, which had dropped to the floor, now crept up over Locke like a spider. An electric prickle spread across her skin. Although she had him beat by six inches and twenty years—even though she was the one holding the crowbar—this guy caused a twinge of panic in her stomach.

When he raised an outstretched hand, she almost flinched.

"Shall we?" Slick gestured toward the conference rooms.

Locke decided she wasn't going anywhere with him. But strolling back out the front door obviously wasn't an option. Seeing she was correct about the hallway behind him gave her an idea.

"I hate to ask," she said, letting her voice slip upward an octave, "but could I use your ladies' room first?"

He cocked his head.

"Long drive, you know? And too many Monsters." Locke batted her eyes twice. She had no idea if the mystery man knew his energy drinks, but if she could have blushed on command, she would have.

"Of course." With a nod, he spun on his heel.

Locke followed at a distance as he moved down the hallway. After several steps, she spotted a pair of doors ahead on their right. In her mind, she could picture the restrooms running behind the elevator shafts. Most times, these skyscrapers were built that way, the plumbing stacked inside the core with the utilities.

When they reached the restrooms, Slick turned back to face her. She pushed her way into the ladies' room, saying, "I'll be quick."

Once the door shut completely, Locke sucked in a breath and hurried inside. Her heart leaped when she saw what she was looking for.

To avoid forcing workers to circle the entire office just to tinkle, the bathroom had been built with a second entrance that faced the opposite side of the building. Locke made for that, pulling a metal stall door closed along the way in case Slick was eavesdropping.

When she reached the rear exit, she inched it open, half expecting the creepy little man to be standing there somehow. But all she found were empty cubes.

Locke tiptoed out, cushioning the bathroom door as it closed. The back entrance to the elevator bay loomed just yards away. She crossed to it quickly.

As she reached for the door handle, though, its lock released with a loud clack.

Locke winced.

A glance up revealed a motion detector on the ceiling that had unlocked the door automatically. Thankfully, when she opened the door, the elevator bay stood as dark and deserted as when she'd arrived.

Dashing to the down button, she mashed it several times with her fist. Although she kept her eyes on the office's main entrance and raised the crowbar just in case, an elevator chimed open almost immediately.

Locke backed into the car and pressed the LOBBY button. Seconds later, the doors slid shut and the car plunged downward.

Despite releasing the breath she'd been holding, she warned herself against relaxing. Slick wouldn't wait forever. After a minute or two, the fake lawyer would barge into the bathroom, see she'd split, and come scrambling after her.

He might even radio reinforcements—gunmen might be waiting downstairs.

She watched the floor numbers until the counter reached 3. After securing the bag on one shoulder, she raised the crowbar in both hands like a Louisville Slugger. When the doors finally chimed open, Locke charged from the elevator and rounded the corner into the lobby.

A quick glance showed she still was alone.

Eager to keep it that way, she kept running, pumping her arms to accelerate toward the opposite end. The garage elevator seemed to take forever, even as she banged on the button. Once it came, though, it delivered her downstairs in a matter of moments.

Locke scanned the garage as she crossed to the van. Although she didn't see anyone coming, she climbed in quickly. A check of the back revealed nothing but her toolboxes and damp coveralls.

Tossing the bag down next to her, she keyed the engine. Its roar gave her a jolt of energy and relieved some of the tightness across her chest. She peeled back out of the spot, tires squealing against the concrete. Ahead, she saw the exit gate was still raised.

She dropped it into drive and gunned the gas.

The van burst from the garage, bouncing violently as she took the ramp at speed. Thankful for the lack of traffic, Locke used the entire width of Hope Street to pull her turn. The van leaned precariously to one side, but she accelerated through it. Once the van wobbled itself straight, she really started driving.

Downtown LA was a maze of opposing one-ways, but she zigzagged through them, tires chirping at each sudden turn. Her eyes spent as much time in her mirrors as on the road ahead. She searched for the white plumbing truck from the mansion. For the Volvo SUV she'd seen in the garage.

She watched for any other vehicle that might be tailing her.

Anything at all.

But she saw nothing. She was alone.

* * *

After ten minutes suspiciously circling, Locke decided she could cut to the freeway. She grabbed the 110 at 3rd Street and cruised north to the 5.

That stretch usually felt cramped, claustrophobic. Near Dodger Stadium, walls funneled inward until the lanes felt narrower than the van's wheelbase. And Locke had never liked the Figueroa Street tunnels—the concrete caverns were historic and all, but if she was forced to drive through holes dug in a mountain, she'd prefer construction from this century, thank you very much. Stuck in traffic, the two-mile drive could take an hour, leaving lots of time to consider all the things that could cause a cave-in.

With the roads empty, though, she sailed through all of it. She kept a wary eye on her mirrors, but cruising at seventy, she saw nothing suspicious.

If she was being followed, it was by CIA-level pros.

Still, there were more precautions to take. Following the 5 up through Burbank was the straightest path home, but Locke turned onto the Glendale Freeway and connected up to the 210. She preferred the long, steady climb through the foothills—not only was it a reliable traffic beater in more crowded times, but she found the exposed rock and scrub-covered mountains out east far more attractive than the strip malls and movie lots you passed farther west.

Even better, the lack of traffic had cleared the air. Normally, you glanced out and the second or third row of hills was shrouded in grayish haze that made you wonder if you were overdue for the optometrist. Today, Locke felt like she'd just washed the windows: a cornflower sky stretched to the horizon, every detail below it crisp and clear. On the hilltops, chaparral yucca had bloomed, their creamy white flowers looking like rows of candle flames in the distance.

The forty-mile detour took just thirty minutes, and soon Locke was pulling off the freeway into Sylmar.

Despite stopping in the little town whenever she went to work, she knew virtually nothing about it. Freeway signs proclaimed that a National Guard airport and a Metrolink station existed somewhere in Sylmar, but she hadn't visited either one. Her only landmark, a tiny strip mall containing a Dollar Tree and a smoke shop, stood adjacent to the off-ramp.

Tucked behind that, with an uninterrupted view of the mountains, was a self-storage lot. After the shootout at Big Bo's, Locke had checked every storage place north of the 101 and found only three with the kind of extra-large units she wanted. When one finally freed up here after a six-month wait, she'd pounced on it like one of the feral cats she'd since seen skulking in the bushes at the lot's eastern edge.

Locke pulled the van to a stop along that line of scrub and left it running. Throwing the bag over her shoulder, she crossed to her unit, the last one in the row. The lock showed no sign of tampering when she keyed it open. And while the rolling door seemed to rumble louder than usual, everything inside looked exactly as she'd left it this morning.

Particularly the Prius.

The silver-and-black hybrid couldn't have been more different from the van: quiet, clean, polished. The kind of car a suburban soccer mom might drive. And, just as Locke had allowed the van's paint to rust, she'd adorned the Prius with purposeful little touches. Decals in the rear window showed a stick-figure family of four with a dog and cat. The license plate frame proclaimed love for a German shepherd. One of those *Coexist* stickers, each letter formed by a different religious symbol, was mounted on the back right bumper.

All of it bullshit, but that was the point.

With the car parked against the right-hand wall of the storage unit, Locke could open the driver's side door enough to toss the bag in and slip through sideways. She backed the car out and away from the entrance, then returned to the van.

Squeezing that into the unit was a much tighter fit, but years of practice had taught her exactly how much room she could spare. Once she'd parked, she stepped into the van's rear compartment and stripped off her boots, socks, and coveralls. After draping everything to dry, Locke donned a pair of rainbow flip-flops and popped out the back. The unit's rolling door cleared the van's bumper by five inches, and the lock gave a satisfying click when she closed it.

The Prius's clock read 2:25 as she steered back out to the freeway. Once she'd navigated the ramp, Locke inhaled deeply through her nose. Inside the quiet hybrid, the sound of her breathing was even more pronounced. She held the air down deep in her lungs a moment, then let it slip past her lips in a near whistle. Although the *Jaws* mask reflected the hot air back against her cheeks, she felt her shoulder muscles loosen.

She peeled off the mask, then rolled her neck, listening to the crinkles and cracks. Climbing into the car always prompted a physical reaction—like slipping into her comfiest PJs, pointing the Prius toward Val Verde made her feel like she'd left work behind. That whatever dirty, heavy, difficult job she'd faced down was finally complete.

After today's craziness, though, her grip on the wheel felt like cradling a crowbar in her hand; she found safety and security in the firmness of it. Slick had looked for her, had found *her*. Monna Locke, safecracker. But he'd have a hard time connecting that name to anything else in her life. The deed to the house still listed the Mule as the owner. The storage unit, this hybrid—everything besides the van, her phone, and her business license—had been purchased or rented under her real last name, Maguire.

My legal *last name*, she corrected herself.

Maguire wasn't any more real because it had come from her dead mother. Or because it was the last remaining trace of her. If anything, *Locke* was the reality—she'd created that name, building it from scratch along with her business and her reputation.

Monna Maguire didn't sound as sexy as *Monna Locke*. It certainly didn't make anyone think of vaults or safes. But paranoia, she'd learned, had its place. Safecracking was a job about secrets, and the incidents with Big Bo and others had taught Locke to keep some of her own.

Her eyes drifted to the bag resting in the passenger's seat.

Whatever secret that little wooden cube was hiding sure had caused a ton of trouble. Enough that she'd need to figure out a way to deal with it. Destroy it, toss it, lock it away—something.

She'd look inside the box tonight, discretion be damned.

While she hated to wait that long, when she first got home she'd need to check on Constance, make sure Evan got dinner. Once they finally dozed off, she'd get a moment to herself. That's when she could peek inside the little box and decide what to do.

Locke's eyes returned to the road. She'd reached the 5 again, and as she merged, she checked her mirrors.

Nothing to see but six lanes of concrete.

CHAPTER

5

RATHER THAN TAKING the 126 as usual, Locke remained on 5 up to Hasley Canyon Road before exiting and turning west. She followed surface streets as they narrowed from three lanes to two, then one. The asphalt's condition worsened, the double yellow faded. For long stretches, civilization's only markers were telephone poles and ranch fencing, zigging and zagging with the road as it wound between ridges. Unlike the scrub-covered mountains she'd seen earlier, these hills glowed bright green, grown over with thick grasses. And there were no palm trees, only mature wild oaks and hearty cottonwoods casting shadows down from their branches.

This was Locke's California.

As beautiful as the beach could be, glittering sand and sparkling waves had never felt quite right. Locke was an inland girl, raised here in the valley where people preferred steak to sushi and sipped Budweiser instead of trendy microbrews. Out where "good rides" meant horses, not surfboards.

A final turn took Locke up a narrow street wedged between two steep hills. This portion of the drive always caused her heart to catch in her throat, and today was no exception. The first time the Mule had brought her here, she hadn't known quite what to expect. Since then, the little lane had become far more of a home than her childhood trailer had ever been.

No houses were visible from the street, only gravel driveways that spilled downhill through the tall grass. The only clues about who lived at the far end of each stony path came from their mailboxes. Years ago, long before Locke had ever visited, Carlos Crocker on the corner had built himself a fancy red-and-white mailbox shaped like a barn. Not to be outdone, Jaye McCracken across the street put wheels and windows on her polished silver box, making it look like a horse trailer. Soon, everyone had something special. The Carrizosas had a doghouse. Richie Narvaez, a fishing boat. The newest neighbor, Constance Rojas next door, had a black-and-white cow wearing a pink frilly tutu.

The Mule's mailbox, fittingly, was a rusty toolbox. Not a mailbox made to look like a rusty toolbox, mind you, but an actual rusty toolbox he'd carried down the driveway one day and nailed to a post.

In all the time she'd been back, Locke hadn't had the heart to change it.

The man she called "the Mule" was Karl Muehlenberg. Not that she'd come up with that nickname—growing up, every kid at Val Verde High School knew the Mule, whether they found themselves in his metal shop class or not. White hair shaved into a permanent high-and-tight, pencil wedged behind his ear, arms folded across his barrel chest, he roamed the halls each morning, barking at students like one of Locke's basic training instructors would later on. His raspy baritone was so loud, so distinctive, it bent around corners and echoed down halls. Everyone heard the Mule coming.

For some reason, though, his approach never scared her. While kids on either side frantically grabbed books and slammed lockers to scurry away, she'd always taken her time, waiting for him to toss out a wisecrack.

"What are you waiting for, Maguire? An engraved invitation?"

"Just letting rush hour die down a little. Miss Sarja said she'd save me a seat in English, so I figure I'm good."

Although the Mule's ruddy cheeks and forehead would redden and his brow would furrow, one corner of his mouth always turned up, betraying the smile he was holding back. And that was even before Locke had ended up in his class, back when all she knew about him were whispered stories of what the crazy old Marine must have done to end up teaching juvenile delinquents to use power tools and blowtorches. That's what metal shop was, after all: last refuge of the hopeless. Troublemakers, burnouts—they all ended up in shop with the Mule.

That was certainly how she'd landed there.

The Prius's front wheels hit the driveway with a loud crunch, and the gas engine kicked in, grumbling about the long, slow climb. When Locke crested the hill and saw the Mule's handiwork, she smiled. Upon returning from Vietnam, he'd built the single-story craftsman himself, setting the cobblestone foundation, then framing and paneling the dark-wood exterior. She thought it looked like the perfect summer camp cabin, the kind of cozy place she used to dream about at night in the trailer.

And she'd had plenty of time for that. Her mother's bartending shifts had started midafternoon and ended well after midnight, so the trailer was always empty when Locke returned from school. From age seven onward, she'd spent six nights a week fending for herself. Cooking, cleaning. Homework—if she did it—plus whatever list of chores her mom had left out. Putting herself to bed alone in the dark, hoping not to be stuck awake when her mom stumbled in at three, reeking of whatever she'd drunk on the way home.

Until the night it wasn't her mom who woke her. Sixteen-year-old Locke had answered banging on the trailer door and found two CHP officers. Once they realized she was alone, they urged her to call someone to meet her at the station. She refused—there was no one to call. Besides, she figured she could handle it. ID'ing the car was simple enough. The cops spared her from seeing the body, but she wasn't afraid. Didn't cry.

The next morning, Locke rolled into school in the same clothes as the day before on almost no sleep. She was already in the Mule's class by then, for breaking Bobby McCallum's jaw after he'd hassled one of the special-needs kids at lunch. McCallum was Val Verde's starting right tackle, so while the six-foot tub-o'-lard was forced to sip his liquid lunch during one day of detention, Locke got sentenced to two semesters of metal shop. Not that she minded. She found that she liked using the machinery, working with her hands. Compared to the other shop kids, she paid attention, and the Mule returned the favor, whether it was standing by her shoulder as she used the drill press or allowing her to use the welding rig that was supposed to be off-limits.

That was why the Mule's reaction the morning after her mother's death caught Locke off guard. It wasn't like she'd expected a pity party or anything, but a kind word would've been nice. Even some joking around would have helped. But all through first period, the Mule seemed sullen. Angry, almost. When the bell rang and everyone shuffled to leave, he called, "Not you, Maguire. You stay."

She slumped back down onto her stool, confused as to why he'd picked that day of all days to treat her like shit.

He marched to her table, checking over his shoulder for the last person to leave the classroom. Once the door shut, he faced her, arms crossed. "I heard what happened last night. And I have to say, I'm incredibly disappointed."

Disappointed?

The Mule's clipped tone sliced right through her. Although she searched frantically for some comeback, some wiseass fire in her belly that would make her stand up to him, she couldn't find any. Her eyes dropped to the floor. More than anything, she wanted to crawl under the table, dig a hole, and bury herself in it.

"Why you didn't call me," the Mule continued. "Why you thought you had to go through that . . . alone."

She glanced up to see him quickly wipe at his eye.

"If you didn't think you could reach out to me at a moment like that . . ." The Mule swallowed hard and shook his head. "I have clearly failed at communicating the way this relationship is supposed to work. But we're gonna fix that. You wait for me outside after the last bell."

With that, he spun an about-face and made for his desk. Locke sat dumbfounded until he called, "Don't you have history? March."

After school, the Mule had driven her here for the very first time. He didn't say a word until they reached the top of the driveway and he silenced the engine. "No more of that trailer for you—no one should be alone like that. I got an extra room, you can stay here."

So many emotions had filled her head, she didn't think to point out that the Mule had been living alone until that moment too. That realization didn't hit her until over a year later, when she was tossing her duffel into the pickup so the Mule could drive her to the airport for her trip to basic. She'd glanced back at him and the house. "You gonna be okay here by yourself?"

The Mule grunted. "Young lady, you seem to forget I outlived the North Vietnamese's best efforts to kill me. I don't think some quiet and California sunshine is gonna do the job." Then his eyes had narrowed. "You worry about you. Thinking of life back here's not gonna help where you're going."

Locke now pulled the Prius to the same spot where the Mule had always parked his truck, a pad of well-worn gravel directly in front of the craftsman. Despite being baked by bright sunlight, the house looked as cozy and welcoming as ever. A covered porch ran the length of the front, and she loved to sit in the shade and feel the breeze blow by. Particularly today, the idea of falling into one of the rocking chairs out there and sipping at a beer sounded heavenly.

Catty-corner from the house stood an aluminum toolshed she'd helped the Mule put up. It helped frame the front yard, a long, flat strip of land covered in knee-high golden grass. The field stood empty, which was no real surprise—Evan was likely inside, and, as Locke had learned, when Constance went anywhere, she walked.

Despite living next door to Constance Rojas for over a decade, Locke hadn't interacted with her neighbor much until the past year. A heavyset woman with deep dimples and a long salt-and-pepper braid, Constance had spent thirty-two years as a middle school librarian in El Segundo before taking early retirement to move out to the countryside. But her one-bedroom ranch left little doubt as to her former profession. There were no paintings in the house, no pictures; literally every inch of wall was lined with shelves. Each set had its own genre, alphabetized by author, except the biographies.

Locke didn't read books, but that wasn't the issue between them. Constance had moved in while Locke was stationed overseas. But when Locke finally got discharged and returned to the craftsman, Constance had been the one to greet her.

The one who'd delivered the news about the Mule.

Constance must have known Locke was coming somehow, must have been on the lookout for her, because Locke hadn't even made it to the front door before Constance's voice called to her from behind.

"He's gone."

From the top of the front steps, Locke turned to see who was speaking. And to correct the round little woman. The Mule's truck was sitting on the gravel pad. He couldn't—wouldn't—have gone anywhere without it.

Before she could argue, Constance had shoved the Mule's letter into Locke's hand. She opened the envelope and read it right there.

The word *cancer* forced her to sit down on the steps.

She couldn't read past that word.

Constance had put her hand on Locke's shoulder. Said consolations. Locke hadn't registered any of it. For the next three days, she'd wandered around the house in a fog. Every hour or two, she'd return to the handwritten pages, making it a little further each time. But inevitably the tears would come, and she'd drop the papers to the floor and stalk away from them again. Praying they might disappear.

Hoping she might round a corner and find the Mule standing there, like it was all a mistake.

Even after the tears stopped, Locke couldn't bear to look at or speak to Constance for a long time. Down at the mailboxes, over at the grocery store, if she spotted Constance coming, she'd turn the other way and flee. Simply seeing her made Locke's throat constrict and her eyes well up.

Constance seemed to get the message. For a while—a couple of years, at least—she stayed away, and Locke was quietly grateful for that.

Until Evan arrived.

Once he'd come home from the hospital, Constance started showing up again. Wanting to see him, hold him. Then, as he got older, offering to babysit.

While Locke tolerated Constance's unannounced visits, she deliberately avoided accepting any help. Pride was part of that—Locke had always promised herself she wouldn't end up like her mom. Alone, raising a kid. Yet, here she was, and she absolutely fucking hated the idea of the Library Lady judging her. Especially living next door—Locke didn't need dirty looks or raised eyebrows. She'd rather drop Evan at daycare than deal with that.

But it also ran deeper. The Mule had been special. One of a kind. Locke wasn't looking to replace him. If Constance thought they'd be BFFs just 'cause she lived next door and had worked at a school once, well, she was going to be disappointed.

So, even when it was hard—even when gathering Evan's toys and preparing his snacks made her twenty minutes late, and he still whined that she'd forgotten the most important race car or announced he no longer liked red apples—Locke ensured he was covered. If she had a job to get to, she delivered him to daycare and prearranged the pickup time. Hell, one weekend she'd even brought him along, letting him play video games on her phone and spin in an office chair while she opened a Sentry S6370 at a high-end accounting office in Century City.

Until about six months ago.

A whoop from a siren had woken Locke. Thankfully, Evan had slept through it.

She'd tiptoed outside and seen flashers through the trees. Blue-suited paramedics already had a pressure cuff on Constance's arm and a tube up her nose by the time Locke got next door. Despite the oxygen, her neighbor was gasping for breath like she'd just run a marathon.

Seeing Constance that way was almost too much for Locke to take. All she could think of was Kori—forty years younger and half Constance's size, she'd been hooked up the same way at the very end. Before they carted her off to the hospital.

Before . . .

Constance's EMT strode over and started talking. When he said the word *edema*, something clicked.

This wasn't Kori. This was . . . different.

Or, at least, she'd make it be.

From that night on, once Constance recovered, Locke accepted all the help she was willing to give. Locke found

reasons to run small errands or to do projects outside while
Constance played with Evan. Meanwhile, knowing Constance didn't have a cell, she trained Evan to use the old flip
phone she left in the kitchen for emergencies. Having the two
of them watch over each other worked out well.

A bigger test came when Locke got called to open a box
down in Santa Ana, a twelve-hour day when you included the
commute. She'd kept her phone pressed against her thigh the
entire drive and all through the job. But no calls came. When
she got home, she'd found Evan tucked into bed listening to
Constance read him a story, something Locke had meant to
do more often.

They'd repeated the process over and over after that.
Often enough, Evan had started calling Constance "Miss C."

When the lockdowns were announced, Locke worried
their system would fall apart. Older people were supposedly
the most at risk, and those with lung problems had it the
worst. Locke figured there was no way Constance would
want to watch a preschooler when she could be sitting safe
and sound inside her little library.

But the very next morning, Locke heard a knock and
found her neighbor at the door. Constance had come wearing a hand-sewn mask with Dr. Seuss's Cat in the Hat on it.
She'd even brought extras.

In the days since then, their system had evolved. Locke
masked and gloved up to do all the shopping and errands for
both of them so that Constance wouldn't have to go any farther than the end of the street. She also bought one of those
plastic pill sorters, filling the different slots with the medi-
cines Constance needed and confirming that she'd actually
taken them. Constance walked to and from her house, bringing Evan with her sometimes, but Locke made up the craftsman's second bedroom so she could stay over whenever it
was more convenient. And, with the groceries Locke bought,
Constance cooked.

Man, could she cook.

Locke's idea of gourmet was Progresso canned soup instead of Campbell's. Constance made chicken enchiladas that kept you warm all day. A pozole blanco with shredded pork that melted in your mouth without you even chewing. Cheese flautas.

Locke had probably gained ten pounds, but Evan was happy. So was Constance. And Locke slept better at night as a result.

As she stepped out from the Prius, her stomach rumbled. The mailbox flag was down—usually the mailman raised it, which meant Constance had likely grabbed the mail on one of her trips between houses. Hopefully, that meant she was inside cooking.

Locke inhaled deeply through her nose, searching for some sign of what delicacy might be waiting. The only odors that greeted her were fresh air and overgrown grass, but she had no complaints about that.

She started for the house, flip-flops clapping against the wooden steps.

Since she'd inherited the house, the only detail she'd had the heart to change was the front door. Oversized, the door contained a stained-glass inset an artist had made for her as an extra thank-you for a box well opened. The square pane was translucent, with a dramatic swirl of yellows and greens blown into it. The artist said he'd been inspired by the circular face of the safe she'd opened, a digital lock with glowing amber numbers, but the colors matched the scenery around the house perfectly. Locke liked that the idea behind the glass was so personal, so secret—it seemed appropriate. Even more, she appreciated how every time she came or went, light caught the inset in a different way. Details jumped out that she'd never noticed before.

Today, as she keyed the door, light from inside the house left the yellow looking like lemons and the green like limes.

The citrus swirl left a tang on Locke's tongue, even as her mouth was already watering at the thought of flautas.

"I'm home," Locke called while still turning the knob.

No answer came.

When the door swung open, Locke's hand flew to her mouth.

Five-year-old Evan sat on the floor in the middle of the family room, playing.

But not with Constance.

Seated across from him, cross-legged in loafers and suit pants, was Slick, the pretend lawyer.

6

"M s. LOCKE." SLICK wore the same forced smile he'd
displayed earlier. "We were starting to worry. You
didn't make nearly as good time on this leg of the drive."

Her mouth opened, not so much to speak as simply from
shock.

"Momma!" Evan set down the Matchbox car he'd been
maneuvering around a plastic track and jumped to his feet.
He rushed to her and wrapped his arms around her leg. "I'm
so glad you're home!"

Although she stroked the boy's hair, Locke didn't dare look
down. She didn't want him seeing her expression. She could
certainly defend herself—scars from Camp Taji and Chester-
field Square confirmed that. But this . . . this was different.

Locke's eyes scanned the edges of the room for other
threats, and for Constance. She didn't find either one.

"What . . . what time did you get here?" Locke tried to
make the question sound nonchalant for Evan, but she genu-
inely wondered how much time the fake lawyer had spent
inside her home.

Slick leaned forward and retrieved the toy car. He still
wasn't wearing a mask, but at least he'd kept a little distance.
"Long enough for Evan to show me his room and introduce
me to . . . what is this car's name?"

"Mr. Zoom."

"Yes, Mr. Zoom. Can you come show me how fast he is?"

Locke felt Evan's grip around her leg loosen.

"Actually," she said, scratching his scalp to get his attention, "before you play anymore, I need your help."

She squatted down to his level. "I'm thirsty. And I notice our guest doesn't have a drink either. Would you be a good host and make us some iced tea in the kitchen?"

"How many cubes, Momma?" The way he said it, it sounded like *coobs*.

"Lots of cubes." Whenever she was this close, Locke couldn't help but notice the flecks in Evan's otherwise dark eyes. That and his lashes—naturally long and perfectly curled, the kind most women would pay good money for. Remembering where he'd gotten them always caused a little tug in her throat. "Give both of us *lots* of cubes."

Evan's face turned serious, and he gave her a crisp salute before dashing toward the back of the house and disappearing around a corner.

Once he was out of sight, Locke straightened to her full height and locked her eyes back on Slick. Her teeth clenched as her voice dropped to a growl. "I don't know how—"

"How is not important," he said. "You have something of mine."

"I'm not dumb enough to bring it here." Her insides squirmed at the lie as she kicked herself for bringing the box home. "I left it in my storage unit."

He shook his head dismissively. "The box is in your bag, Ms. Locke. We both know that."

"I'll take you to it, but we leave the boy here."

"I have attempted to acquire that box for a very long time. It is only because of these"—he paused—"unique circumstances that it became accessible. I think you have likely developed a good sense for the lengths I am willing to go to procure it."

Her heart sank slightly in her chest—she needed to get him outside. "I'm saying I will *give* it to you. I just want to know Evan's safe. And Constance, where is she?"

"Your friend is at her house."

Locke knew Constance wouldn't voluntarily leave Evan with a stranger. And Slick wouldn't have just sent her away. She imagined the Malibu gunmen standing over her inside the little library.

Locke's fist balled tightly. "If your men hurt her—"

Slick leaned back on his palms as if he were relaxing on a beach blanket. "You are in no position to threaten, Ms. Locke."

"You said it yourself, I have what you need. I have the box."

His head cocked to one side. "The box is not all I require."

Enough.

Whenever Evan emerged, she wanted to be between them. She took a single stomp toward the kitchen.

Before she could take another, something collapsed around her neck.

Thick and powerful, pulling her backward at the same time it cut off her breathing.

Locke grabbed at it and felt the outline of an arm. Thick with muscle, like iron. It forced its way under her chin, shifting her vision up toward the ceiling.

Dumb, dumb, dumb, she thought as panic flashed across her skin. Focused on Evan, she'd remained standing in the open doorway. Asking to get attacked from behind.

Although safecracking left her no real nails to speak of, Locke dug her fingers into the meat of the arm as hard as she could.

It didn't budge.

Already she could feel her lungs burning.

Locke lashed backward with one foot, trying to nail whoever was holding her. She reached behind her head too, searching for the attacker's face. Eyes, ears, nose. Any soft tissue.

Feeling smooth skin, she raked at it.

A howl near her ear said she'd scored.

Before she could go back for more, the grip around her throat tightened, and her feet left the floor. She dangled weightless for a moment, then saw the floor rushing up to meet her. When she hit, what seemed like an added ton of weight fell on top of her.

A bright flash filled Locke's eyes, and she felt the impact everywhere at once—her chest, knees, and stomach. Pain echoed through her in dull throbs.

Before she could regain her bearings, the grip around her throat adjusted. Tightening even more. Raising her head off the floor.

Her cheeks and forehead flushed, hotter than any fever she could remember. She had only seconds left.

Locke flailed backward with her arms and legs, hoping to connect with something, anything. But they found nothing but air.

And then Evan appeared.

He rounded the corner from the kitchen, carrying a glass of tea in each hand. She saw his eyes spread wide, and she felt a stab of failure in her gut.

Then the blackness overtook her.

* * *

A vibration shook Locke's body.

Distant, like she was sensing only the echo of it. Gradually, though, it grew closer. Jostling her noticeably.

A rumble, like thunder.

She stirred, eyelids not wanting to open. When they finally did, she blinked at how dim things were.

At first, Locke assumed she was still emerging from unconsciousness. But then she felt and heard the rumble again.

She realized she was moving.

Pressure against her shoulder came from a seat belt. Cool smoothness against her forehead from a glass window. Outside, she could see darkened sky. Lights on the horizon.

And water.

They were driving over some kind of bridge.

In her mind, Locke scrolled through all the bridges around LA. Nothing matched what she was seeing.

Palm trees flashed by, fronds painted yellow by halogens hanging over the roadway. Beyond them, out on the water, she saw a different color.

A deep, neon purple.

Through the haze that still clouded her brain, Locke recognized the lights. She'd been here once—a lifetime ago, to celebrate her nineteenth birthday. On leave, with Kori. Bouncing from club to club. Despite wearing the shortest dresses ever, they'd sweated more those nights than through morning PT in 110-degree Iraq.

How the hell had she gotten from her living room to Miami?

She noticed the humidity now, sweat slicking creases in her skin. Her hair felt like it was being squeezed and kinked.

And another sensation.

Her left arm, a dull ache.

When she glanced down, her neck provided almost no support—her chin bounced off her chest. Still, she saw a thick bandage at the crook of her elbow, like she'd donated blood. She flexed the arm, and the pain sharpened.

That jab helped clear her head, just a little.

She was in a car.

No, bigger. Higher up.

SUV.

Passenger's seat, plush leather.

But who was . . . ?

Locke tossed her head to the left. Slick was handling the wheel, the center of which bore a Mercedes three-pointed star. The suit was gone—he wore slacks and a golf shirt. A thick Rolex hung at his wrist. AC from the vents made his hair dance.

"Ms. Locke," he said, glancing over momentarily before returning his eyes to the road. "I was starting to wonder whether you would wake up in time."

"Time?" Still hazy, she rewound her memory and confirmed that the midafternoon sun had been shining the last time she'd been conscious. Was it even the same day? "Time for what?"

"To reach our destination."

Locke pumped her arm in tight little flexes, grateful for the way the pain cleared the fog from her mind. She continued replaying what had happened, trying to remember.

Grabbed from behind.

Sleeper hold, blacked out.

Then she saw Evan's face. Recalled the shock in his eyes. In spite of the heat, an icy chill spread across her skin.

"Where is he?" she demanded.

"Your boy is perfectly safe."

Locke's eyes ticked to the steering wheel. More than anything, she wanted to grab it—to jerk it toward her, run them off the road. Then she could force Slick to answer exactly what the fuck was going on.

But she wasn't sure she had complete control of her body. Her brain reached out to her extremities, checking everything. She flexed her wrists, her fingers.

As if sensing her unease, he added, "I will take you to him. Following one stop."

The bottom of the bridge loomed ahead, the entry to South Beach, where glassy towers stood lit against the night. The water outside Locke's window was filled with bobbing shadows as backlit boats rocked in their slips.

"I don't know who the hell you are," she said, "or why the fuck you've kidnapped us—"

"My name is Huang," he said, glancing over again. "And the rest, I would think, is obvious. As you demonstrated in Malibu, very few people can do what you do, Ms. Locke. And even fewer know how to keep quiet about it."

She grunted. "If you wanted to hire me, you could have just called."

"As you will see, this opportunity is quite . . . unique. I was not in a position where I could tolerate being refused."

Huang steered the SUV to the right, following the road as it cut back behind the first row of buildings and tracked the shoreline southward. After straightening out, the street grew quiet and dark, divided down the center by an island lined with palms. Periodic streetlights were shrouded by lush trees, while the tall, bayfront towers looming on their right only seemed to make the night darker and more claustrophobic.

No other souls were visible on the street, yet Huang appeared content to drive the limit, puttering along at twenty like some rich retiree.

Now, Locke realized, was her best chance.

Throwing her whole body across the console, Locke lashed her right arm out as if it were a bullwhip. Her hand snatched the wheel, fingers curling around the smooth leather and gripping it tight. That feeling, along with the surprise on Huang's face, filled her chest with a puff of joy.

Until she heard a metallic *shing* and felt a knife blade against her throat.

"I'd let go of the wheel, Ace. Blood is fuckin' hell to get outta leather."

7

The knife hovered in the notch north of Locke's clavicle.

The blade didn't press inward—it stood there, motionless. So close the cold metal sucked heat away from her skin. Just enough contact that she could feel the razor's edge brushing against her.

The sensation might have tickled if she weren't worried that laughing would slit her throat wide open.

Locke hadn't thought to check the SUV's rear seat, but when her eyes turned that way now, she found three figures packed in the back. It was the middle one trying to behead her.

Leaning forward, left arm extended with the knife, the man's face was framed between the two front seats. Unlike Huang and the Malibu gunmen, this guy was white, and between long, curly hair swept back behind his ears, a neatly trimmed beard, and a sharp hook of a nose, he might have been roguishly handsome. But even in the dim light, Locke could read his cruel grin. He wanted nothing more than to see the contents of her carotids spilled all over the console.

She released the steering wheel, splaying her fingers but otherwise remaining motionless.

"Aaah." The man's brogue was even more pronounced on the groan than it had been on his words. He turned away as if disgusted.

Locke felt the metal fall from her neck, and she instinctively swallowed.

Huang spoke again. "The fastest way to see Evan is to allow me take you to him."

Stretched toward the wheel, Locke's head sat several inches below Huang's. He was glaring down at her, pressing with narrowed eyes and an angry scowl.

Slowly, she shifted back into her seat.

"Better," he said. "You have now met Jack. Our other two companions may be called King and Queen."

Locke twisted around to see. Wedged awkwardly in the middle of the bench seat, Jack was silhouetted except for his eyes and mouth, which seemed to glow Cheshire-like. He puckered his lips at her, miming a kiss.

Her stomach turned, and she focused on the other two figures.

The man on Jack's far side was nothing more than a burly shadow—she couldn't decipher any details of King's face in the dark, in part because he was so huge. Jack barely cleared King's shoulder, and the big man's head was bowed so as not to scrape the ceiling. King took up so much of the rear seat, Jack was forced to lean toward Locke's side of the car.

There was extra room on that side because Queen was so petite. Several inches shorter than Jack, Queen's first impression on Locke was that of a restless teenager. Staring into her lap, digging under one thumbnail with her opposite index finger, she seemed oblivious to everyone else in the car, unconcerned where they were going. Bubblegum-pink hair added to the effect.

Without warning, though, the girl glanced up, and bursts of yellow from the passing streetlights splashed onto her face. A spiky, punk-rock-pixie cut and a slit in her eyebrow suggested Queen was older than Locke had first thought. Her eyes said it too. The big, round baby blues probably fooled others—men likely drowned in them—but Locke recognized the hollowness hovering behind the irises. She'd seen that pain once before, the invisible scar left behind by the darkest kind of betrayal. A parent rejecting their child.

Queen gave Locke a sarcastic eye roll. The same kind Kori used to do whenever some newbie E-3s would roll up to hit on them at the gym or the commissary. *Can you believe these . . . boys?*

Locke faced forward and settled back down into her seat. The small sense of sanity Queen's presence provided didn't help explain any of this. With her mind still clearing, it took a moment to register that no one in the car was wearing a mask.

She felt at her own face and found it bare too.

"Masks are not required here," Huang said. "Wearing them would call attention."

Locke had never been much of a news watcher, but this disease had her paying more attention. Not that it helped— every state seemed to be reacting differently. She had no idea if the precautions she'd been taking were worthwhile, but now she had to wonder, and worry. Were any of these people infected? If she escaped this crazy car alive and got Evan back, would they end up in the ICU?

She tried to settle herself without taking a deep breath. "I don't know what kind of plan you've got going here, with the kidnapping and kooky card code names. But I don't steal stuff. I got a license, and I'm not looking to lose it. I need to—"

"You need to be *quiet*," Huang said. "You may keep a low profile now, but I know what happened in the army. And I know not every one of your jobs since then has been completely . . . scrupulous. Besides, we are almost there."

Locke's face burned at his words. Her mouth flew open instinctively, but she stopped herself and shut it. In the back of her mind, she wondered what exactly he knew. Or thought he knew. The truth and his imagination were likely spread as far apart as LA and Miami.

While the silence hung there, though, her eyes drifted down to the door handle.

Her brain started churning as fast as it could with the haze still gumming up the works. If she moved with both hands, she could unbuckle and open the door in one motion. The SUV was driving slowly enough she could survive a fall, especially if she rolled off the momentum.

Could she do it before Jack pulled his knife again? Could she clear the car before Huang hit the gas? Could she . . .

A voice in her head interrupted as her muscles were tensing. The Mule's voice. *Can you really find Evan alone?*

She needed to be smart.

And patient.

Although she relaxed, Locke balled a fist several times in her lap, digging her fingers into her palm and focusing on the squeeze.

Several blocks ahead, the dim street bore to the left. As they approached it, Huang slowed the SUV and flipped on the right-hand blinker. It flashed and clacked until they turned in before the bend.

The SUV's tires squeaked against tiles that lined the plaza spread before them. The center of the space was dominated by a dramatic fountain, water pouring up and over abstract shards of etched glass. Blue and white lights made the cascading water look like ocean waves, perpetually crashing.

Huang inched them around the fountain, nosing up to a line of granite spheres that separated the driveway from a small lawn. Spotlights at the edges of the grass pointed upward. Out beyond the landscaping, a concrete boardwalk stretched in both directions, tracing the waterline. Large boats were parallel parked along the seawall.

Although she couldn't make out all the details, the marina behind the yachts seemed huge. A horizontal line

of lights traced an elongated pier with an imposing building mounted on top, its several floors of open-air hallways lit
against the night. Locke didn't know what the equivalent of
a hangar for boats was called, but she imagined that might be
the building's purpose.

"We have arrived," Huang said. When he shifted into
park, the engine's idle rose even as cool air continued hissing
from the vents.

Locke leaned forward and peeked up through the windshield. On either side, twin towers jabbed their way into the
sky. Unlike other condos they'd passed along the strip, these
looked brand-new. Smooth cylinders with no balconies, each
tower seemed carved from a single shaft of glass.

Turning out her window, Locke's eyes slowly walked up
the seamless surface of the right-hand tower. Twenty-five stories, at least. Every floor would have either a panoramic view
of downtown across the harbor, or over South Beach toward
the ocean.

She'd originally assumed the marina and the buildings
were connected, that residents would walk right out to their
boats. But now she decided that was wrong. The sealed windows gave it away: the people living in these places didn't love
Miami, or the beach. They loved owning pretty things, and
they'd pay extra to avoid any accompanying inconvenience.
The kind who rode the elevator upstairs for a workout on an
air-conditioned StairMaster. If they wouldn't allow an ocean
breeze into their living room, she doubted they'd be motoring out to take on wind and waves offshore.

Now that she was thinking of transportation, Locke
noticed no cars were visible anywhere either. Gated ramps
on either side of the plaza led to covered garages, but she
wondered if any of their spots were filled. Like folks here
would drive themselves. These condos weren't for rappers
and athletes with tricked-out Bentleys and Lambos—mere

millionaires probably couldn't clear the HOA. This place was built for net worths beginning with *b*.

Still, plenty of lights poked out from the windows overhead. Some richy-rich up there had a box Huang wanted her to open. She wondered which one. And how nasty the safe would be—these people could pay for the best. All that meant, though, was more time and tools. Not every box could be manipulated by hand, but every one could be drilled, with enough equipment and effort.

As the car remained quiet, Locke stole another glance into the back seat. Queen was staring up at the tower, eyes wide. Jack, too, had leaned over for a view; he was nearly in Queen's lap. King's face was still obscured, his head pressed against his own window, gazing out at the opposite tower.

Huang snorted. "The buildings are not our target."

"We stealing fish from the fountain, then?" Jack asked.

Huang pointed with his whole hand. Straight out the windshield.

Locke's eyes scanned across the lawn to the boardwalk. She didn't see what he was talking about.

"The *yacht*," Huang said.

Squinting against the lights on the building behind them, Locke checked each of the boats moored along the seawall. Several were long, sleek bullets. Although she knew the motors were mounted in back, she couldn't help imagining their elongated noses hid tremendous engines—like muscle cars with extra-long hoods. Others along the wall had tall platforms on top that she guessed were for fishing. These filled Locke's head with the seasick sensation of rocking back and forth, high above the waves.

Her stomach twisted, same as it had at Jack's mimed kiss.

But, after inspecting each of the boats in line, Locke still wasn't sure which one Huang meant. All were "yachts" to her.

She turned back, and Huang jabbed his hand forward a second time.

When she looked out the windshield again, Locke searched for something, anything she'd missed before.

And then she realized.

The lit-up building behind the boats. Its lights were . . . *moving*.

Her focus widened, and she finally saw the shadow. The "building" on the pier wasn't some kind of hangar. No port structure or harbor facility.

The pier wasn't even a pier.

The horizontal row of lights traced the waterline of a ship. Probably the biggest one she'd ever seen. Once she detected the outline and began following it, she realized why she'd been confused—it dwarfed everything else in the harbor. Longer than a football field, tall as a five-story building. Each "hallway" was a deck on the otherwise enormous craft.

Recalling how she'd floundered in the Malibu pool, how easily she'd gotten sucked beneath the surface, Locke wondered how something that massive could float.

"It is called *Helios*," Huang said. "The second-largest yacht in the world."

"Who owns it?" Queen spoke for the first time. Her voice was deeper, more authoritative than Locke had expected.

"Stepan Glebov," Huang said. "Russian oligarch. He made his fortune in construction, but he is a collector of . . . antiquities. *Helios* carries art gathered from each of the great civilizations. More Van Gogh paintings hang inside the *Helios* than in the Metropolitan Museum of Art."

"Then lemme guess, it also carries a small army," Queen said. "Or . . . navy."

"It is meant for a crew of fifty-two. Glebov's personal security force numbers approximately ten men."

Jack let out a laugh. "You've got us carrying frames out from under the noses of sixty-some people? Good luck with that, boss."

"Not frames."

Locke glanced over at Huang, whose voice had dropped to almost a whisper, his eyes fixed on the behemoth yacht.

"The Van Goghs are beautiful. But our target is something smaller. And much more valuable."

8

Locke fell asleep on the drive from Miami Beach.

She warned herself to stay awake, that she needed to know exactly where they were going and memorize the route. But once they hit 95 north, the car's smooth motion and the remnants of whatever had been injected into her arm caused her eyelids to sag. Prying them apart became increasingly difficult.

Outside, there was nothing to focus on but the ribbon of concrete stretching into the darkness. She tried pinching herself, biting her tongue, crossing and uncrossing her legs. Nothing helped.

The dashboard clock said it was almost 1:30 AM. She tried to do the math on the time difference between here and home, but her brain couldn't make the numbers work.

Slowly, her neck began yielding to the weight of her head, letting it roll this way and that. Each time her chin dropped, she yanked it up again.

But soon the fog descending over her was simply too much to fight. She let her eyes close and her head hang.

Just for a minute . . .

She bolted upright as the SUV pulled to a stop.

When her eyes flicked open, the highway had disappeared. All she saw out the windshield were the headlights' bright circles against a lime-green cinder-block wall.

She checked the clock again: 1:55.

A cold wave of panic flashed across Locke's skin. How far had they traveled in thirty minutes? Which direction?

She had absolutely no idea.

Her head swiveled, searching for some sign, some landmark.

Nothing but empty parking lot and palm fronds.

Locke turned to Huang as he silenced the engine. In the haze of waking, her only options seemed to be launching herself at him or taking off running.

Before she could choose, he said, "Evan is here."

Evan.

Fatigue fell away. Locke bolted from the car before anyone else.

After the air conditioning, stepping into the South Florida night was like entering a pressure cooker—the muggy air hugged her everywhere at once. The headlights reflecting off the wall cast an amber hue over everything, blending with thick vegetation that surrounded the lot. Being sandwiched inside that layer of green between the blacktop under her feet and the starless sky above only added to her sensation of being squeezed.

The lack of any salt smell left Locke guessing they'd driven inland. A steady buzz hung in the air, but not a freeway rumble—natural, high-pitched static from unseen insects out in the bush.

How far inland did you need to go to get this rural?

She had no idea.

Cursing herself again for falling asleep, Locke turned back to the wall. Several stories tall, it formed one side of what looked like some kind of warehouse. Up above, she thought she could make out smokestacks stretching into the sky, black on black.

Huang rounded the car quickly. He stalked past her without pausing, twirling keys around his finger. Although

Locke was tempted to stab an arm out and clothesline him, instead she fell in and followed him along a concrete path that led around the corner. When the other SUV doors opened behind her, she ignored them.

Getting to Evan was her only concern.

Up ahead, Huang used one of his keys on a metal door. It groaned as he hauled it open and clanged shut after he ducked inside.

She guessed quarantine courtesy was over.

When she opened the door for herself, she found what might as well have been a cave looming behind it. As she stepped inside, the inky blackness swallowed her completely. Then the door banged closed again, firing off echoes around her in the dark.

Locke stood motionless, trying not to count breaths or heartbeats. The air was loaded with the heavy scent of mildew and decaying grass. It took supreme effort not to wonder what else might have died around her in the darkness.

Without warning, a sharp, metallic screech attacked her ears. A vertical crack of light appeared ahead—narrow at first, then wider as an unseen door slid to her left. Huang's silhouette stepped into the light and Locke sprinted after him, worried the entrance might disappear.

When she reached the doorway, though, she paused at the threshold. The cavernous interior stretched at least four stories overhead. Dim safety lighting illuminated what looked like a mighty factory gutted to bare cement. No windows, only cinder-block walls. A large wooden structure sat squarely in the center of the space, but enough shadows were draped over it that she couldn't tell what it was.

And there was no time to puzzle it out—Huang kept moving.

He strode to her right, tracing the front wall of the building. As her eyes followed him, she saw a series of small rooms had been erected in the near corner. Little bean-counter offices with plexiglass faces and flimsy wooden doors—clear cages for folks who'd escaped the factory floor only to oversee those they'd left behind.

While Huang seemed headed for those, at the last minute he turned and followed the right-hand sidewall of the building.

Locke took an angled approach to intercept him. Judging Huang's speed against her own, she glanced ahead. Midway along the sidewall, a small, one-story section jutted inward toward the center of the floor. Two matching doors stood on the front face of this protrusion—bathrooms, maybe?

She accelerated, and Huang reached the doors only a few yards ahead of her. She caught him on the back side of the protrusion, unlocking the door to a janitor's closet built behind the bathrooms.

Evan.

With two long strides, Locke reached the fake lawyer as he got the door open. She pushed past him and entered the little closet, ignoring the sound as the door closed behind her.

She only cared about one thing.

"Evan? Where are you, sweetie?"

Blinking to adjust to the dimmer interior, her eyes flew around the room. The closet was built long and narrow. The back left corner had a porcelain mop sink built into the floor, while a large rolling bucket and several waist-high metal trash cans stood next to it. A set of narrow aluminum shelves, stocked with cleaning supplies, were set against the opposite wall.

She didn't see Evan anywhere.

A quick pirouette revealed the rest of the room, but the result was the same.

Nothing.

Anger—or was it panic?—set her face on fire. Locke rushed back to the door and found it locked. She pounded it with her fist. "Where is he?"

Through a louvered panel at the bottom of the wooden door, she saw Huang's loafers turn and start to walk away.

"Damn you, *answer* me! Where the fuck is he?"

Locke took a half step back and scanned the door for some way to dislodge it. The hinges were mounted outside. She could probably knock out the slats, but that panel was too small to climb through, too low to let her reach up to the lock.

Her eyes darted to the knob. If she could pop the circular plate where it met the door, she could manipulate the latch. Before she could try that, though, a tiny sniffle reached her ears.

She spun around but still didn't see where the noise had come from.

"Mah . . . Mah . . ."

Locke rushed to the rear of the closet. While her first thought was to check behind the shelving, something moved in her peripheral vision near the trash cans.

"Evan?"

Peering over the lip of one can, she found the pair of eyes she recognized so well. He was staring up at her while crouched in the bottom of the metal vessel, arms wrapped around his knees.

"C'mere!" Locke managed to get the words out before her throat snapped shut.

Relief washed over her, turning her muscles to jelly. She didn't breathe. Her heart seemed to tremble in her chest. All the difficulties of the last five years—all the times she'd doubted her decision, or wondered if she was worthy; all the times she'd been ready to pull out her hair and longed for a simpler life—all of it suddenly evaporated.

Tears flooded her eyes, but as much as Locke hated crying, she did nothing to wipe them away.

Although she threw open her arms, it took several moments before Evan managed to stand. When he finally

did, she wrapped her arms around him and yanked him up
and out. His toe caught the edge and dragged the can over,
causing a loud gonging that echoed off the concrete walls.

But the noise barely registered. All she could feel was the
cinch of his arms around her neck and the solidness of him
inside her grip.

"Momma!"

Noticing that he was huffing and puffing, she rubbed
circles on his back. She lowered herself to her knees, even as
the cool concrete scraped at her shins.

"I . . . you . . ."

"Shh, I'm here now," she said. "I've got you."

Evan buried his face in her shoulder. Warm, wet tears
began spilling down her chest, matching those on her cheeks.
His chest heaved as he started to sob, a bellowing noise reverberating in his throat.

"It's okay. Breathe with me."

She inhaled deeply through her nose, then released it
through her mouth. After two or three breaths, Evan started
following her lead.

Gradually, his head turned on her shoulder. His breathing deepened, and he became dead weight in her arms.

Gently as she could, Locke leaned to the side. Bracing
one hand against the floor, she lowered both of them until
she was lying on her back and he rested in the crook of her
arm. Although she could feel the grimy tickle of dust and dirt
against her sweat-soaked skin, she didn't dare move.

She continued listening to him breathe until finally all
the tension left him. As she felt his chest rising and falling,
she too relaxed.

Her eyes closed.

And sleep descended over her again.

THE DOOR THUDDING open startled Locke awake.

"Get up."

Huang's voice.

She cracked her eyes but immediately had to squint against light streaming through the door. By the time she'd rubbed her vision clear, Huang had disappeared again.

At least he'd left the door open this time.

As Locke's extremities reported in, her arm wasn't the only thing aching. Her back, neck, and shoulders had stiffened. Her hip bones were so sore, she guessed they might be black-and-blue later.

And, now that she'd started thinking, a stab of pain shot through her head. Her tongue felt dry and cracked. Exactly like the last time she'd woken in Miami, only back then Kori and whiskey shooters were to blame.

Locke had started to stretch when Evan stirred.

He'd turned away from her at some point in the night. Now, facing the door, he started to say her name. Midway it became a screech: "Mom-maaaaaaaa!"

She rolled toward him, threw an arm over his side, and pulled him close. When that didn't help, she clamped a hand over his mouth and whispered into his ear. "I'm right here, baby. You're all right."

He trembled in her arms, no matter how tightly she squeezed.

"I'm gonna take my hand away, but don't scream, okay? We don't want to make these people mad."

One by one, she lifted her fingers. Thankfully, he remained quiet. Wriggling around to face her, Evan asked, "Wh-where are we, Momma?"

"Florida, sweetie." When the lockdowns started, Constance had shown him maps and explained where places were. "Remember down in the corner, the state that looks like a boomerang? With the oranges and alligators?"

He pointed at her elbow, where the bandage still clung tightly. "They gave you that shot, an' I got real scared."

"I bet," she said. "That scared me too."

"Who's the meam guy?" Evan still had trouble with his *n*'s." Often, they sounded like *m*'s, so *mean* came out *meam*.

"I don't know."

"Why did they put you to sleep?"

"I think they knew I wouldn't agree to leave home if I was awake."

"Do you think Miss C is okay?"

As Locke swept a lock of hair behind her ear, she felt a sharp stab in her gut. She'd been so foggy last night, so singularly worried about Evan, she hadn't considered her neighbor. "I hope so. But I didn't get to ask you: what happened when the men came to the house?"

"They knocked on the door, and she answered."

"How many?"

Evan raised four fingers. "Meam guy said you were gomma be late. That you asked him to tell us so we wouldn't get scared. Miss C went home to call you."

Constance clung stubbornly to her landline. The ex-librarian was the suspicious sort—she'd likely figured Huang wasn't legit and wanted to check. But Locke hadn't gotten any calls.

While she could imagine the Malibu gunmen walking Constance down the gravel driveway, she didn't want to consider what might have happened when they reached the bottom. If Constance was alive and knew Locke and Evan had been taken, she'd be hounding everyone from the Val Verde Police to the FBI for an immediate manhunt. Locke didn't think Huang would have risked that.

"I wish the police had come faster," Evan said.

"What do you mean, sweetie?"

"I called them from the kitchem. When I went for the ice. Like you showed me: mime, one, one." He mimicked pressing the phone buttons.

A huge smile spread across Locke's face, and for a moment she forgot about her aches and pains. She pulled Evan in close and squeezed him tightly. "Oh my god, you are *such* a good boy!"

"But . . . they didn't come."

"I'm sure they made it as fast as they could. You may have saved Miss C—they may have helped her." *And*, Locke thought to herself, *now they may be looking for us.*

The hope of help made her heart accelerate. She'd need to look for ways to signal their whereabouts. That, and to keep Huang happy. The police, the feds, whoever was searching would need time to track her and Evan to Miami—she had to buy as much of it as possible.

Locke's wheels were still turning when Evan spoke again. "What does the meam guy want, Momma?"

"I think he needs my help opening a safe."

Evan scrunched up his face. "Why didn' he just ask you?"

"I don't know."

"Are we gomma be okay?"

The more upset Evan got, the more his *n*'s disappeared. Locke locked eyes with him. "I'm not going to let them hurt you. That's for sure."

"Whem can we go home?"

"I don't know.'

"Why—"

Locke held a finger to his mouth. Although she hated to cut him off, his questions could go on forever. She needed to think, and his talking together with her headache made that difficult. It felt like a metal nail was stabbing her eyebrow.

She rubbed it with her knuckle, trying to work out a tight little knot beneath the skin. That was when the smell hit her.

Rich and fatty.

Bacon.

Her stomach groaned loudly. She racked her brain to remember her last meal, a protein shake she'd sucked down on the drive to Malibu. That had been . . .

She glanced around instinctively, but without a phone, she couldn't tell the time. It felt like weeks rather than hours.

"Hungry?" she asked Evan.

He nodded eagerly and hopped to his feet. Hauling herself off the floor took more effort. As they emerged from the closet, though, the sight of what she'd missed last night distracted her from her aches and pains.

She'd been wrong about the lack of windows. Up high, near the roofline, glass panels circled the building. Many were tilted open to allow airflow, while two giant fans circled the middle of the ceiling to encourage it. Together they reduced the heat from completely oppressive to merely intolerable.

When she and Evan rounded the corner by the bathroom doors, she could see that the plywood structure in the middle of the space was far more monstrous than she'd imagined—the fan blades nearly scraped the top of it. Essentially a giant wooden cube, it reminded her of the kind of clubhouse Evan and his friends might have constructed from a cardboard carton, but on a massive scale.

Before Locke could decipher the wooden box's purpose, Evan tugged on her hand. He was pointing to the far front corner of the building, where Huang and the others had gathered.

As they started that way, she worried he might run ahead. Thankfully, he hung close, matching her careful pace.

"When we get there," she said, "keep some distance between you and them, okay?"

"'Cause of the germ?"

"Yeah. That."

Huang, King, and Queen were seated on folding chairs around a large circular table. Huang held a paper bowl near his mouth as he slurped something off a plastic spoon.

Queen had her chair turned and rocked back on its rear legs. Despite a short plaid skirt, her feet rested on the tabletop—the high shine on her Doc Martens would have pleased Locke's drill sergeants. The Pink Punker held her phone in one hand as she scrolled with flicks of her thumb. Keeping her eyes locked on the screen, she stabbed chunks of strawberry off a nearby plate using a plastic fork, then plucked each one off with her teeth.

Locke's first clear look at King showed why he'd dwarfed Jack in the car last night. The metal chair beneath him seemed ready to buckle beneath his broad chest and shoulders. Although he wore an orange-and-white football jersey Evan could have used as a tent, King's frame stretched it to the limit. The fork he was using looked like a toothpick the way it disappeared between his fingers. Each time he raised food to his mouth, his bicep ballooned, threatening to split the seams of his sleeve.

A stack of newspapers sat next to King's plate, the uppermost one folded open to a page he seemed to be reading intently. Unlike the others, though, King glanced up as Locke and Evan approached.

Four scratches were carved down King's cheek, red and raw against his dark skin. Now at least she knew who'd grabbed her from behind. And why she hadn't been able to pry his arm off her throat.

King didn't say anything. He simply stared at her as he continued chewing. With his head shaved, each motion of his jaw showed off muscles flexing beneath his scalp.

Locke didn't like that.

Or the way his eyes narrowed.

But King's most unnerving feature was a wicked scar across his scalp. Located where his hairline would have been, the thick line started at the middle of his forehead and curved toward his right ear.

Tall as she was, Locke wasn't accustomed to hiding, but the Giant's gaze made her long for some kind of cover. She dropped her eyes and steered Evan toward the corner of the building.

When she looked up again, she was standing before a rectangular folding table with Jack on the opposite side. His long hair was pulled back into a ponytail, while a Union Jack bandanna encircled his forehead. Despite the heat, he wore a long-sleeved jacket buttoned over his clothes.

Was he . . . cooking?

Three hot plates were arranged in front of him like a deejay's turntables. Tins of ingredients, a cutting board, and other items were scattered on either side. Although he wasn't wearing a mask, his hands were covered by rubber gloves.

"Sleeping Beauty rises!" he said. "Too bad—another couple minutes, I was gonna ask the boss if I could wake you with a magic kiss."

Jack gave Locke a slick smile that made her rethink eating for a moment. Before she could respond, though, he leaned down to Evan. "And how are you, young man?"

The boy didn't answer. His arm wrapped around the back of Locke's thigh.

"Ah, that's good." Jack nodded. "Dinna talk to strangers. But you're gonna have to tell me what you want for breakfast."

When Evan still didn't respond, Jack reached beneath the table and produced a single egg. He placed it on the cutting board. "Do you like eggs?"

Locke felt Evan's head move against her leg.

"Scrambled?"

Another nod.

"Best way, I agree. But you've got to scramble them properly." With that, Jack pinched the egg between his fingers and spun it like a top.

While it was spinning, he reached back and drew a butcher's knife from a scabbard on his belt. Jack gave it a leisurely twirl around his index finger as he brought it forward, then laid the blade flat against the cutting board.

Locke couldn't help wondering if that was the same knife he'd held to her throat. She took a hard swallow.

Jack's eyes stayed on Evan, even as he slipped the blade beneath the spinning egg with a flick of his wrist. When he raised the knife off the cutting board, the egg went with it, continuing to spin furiously on the blade.

After giving Evan a wink, Jack flicked his wrist again, tossing the egg into the air. As it rose, Jack snatched a frying pan with his free hand and drew it over to the cutting board. Taking a half step back, he brandished the knife over the pan, blade facing straight up.

The egg fell across the razor's edge and split open. Yolk and white poured into the pan, while the empty shell hung on the blade.

Locke checked Evan's face. His eyes were wide, his mouth open.

Jack twirled the contents of the pan, then set it on one of the burners before turning to Locke. "And you? I'd offer you some congee, but that's strictly for the boss."

She had no idea what congee was, but behind her, Huang made the slurping noise again.

"You herbivorous, like that one?" Jack pointed over Locke's shoulder.

When she glanced back, Queen looked up from her phone and gave a little wave.

Locke's eyes returned to the table and scanned the ingredients. "Omelet. Bacon, onions, and cheese."

"Attagirl!" Jack said. "Drinks are over there."

Locke led Evan to a small table holding containers of juice and tea. While she'd have preferred black coffee, she told herself, *any caffeine in a storm,* and belted down one paper cupful of the hot liquid like a shot. Then she poured herself another, along with juice for Evan.

By the time she'd gotten the drinks, Huang had left the table. Locke steered Evan to the empty seat and stood behind him. Moments later, Jack slid a paper plate in front of the boy and passed her another.

Locke immediately ripped off a large chunk of omelet with her fork. Although it scalded the roof of her mouth, it was easily one of the best she'd ever tasted. Fluffy eggs, crunch from the onion, richness and salt from the bacon and cheese. As she quickly downed several mouthfuls, she could almost feel the calories and caffeine seeping into her blood. The knot behind her eyebrow loosened.

"Thank you," Evan said.

Locke tensed. Although they'd worked on his manners, this wasn't the time she wanted him calling attention to himself. "Yeah," she mumbled with her mouth full. "It's . . . good."

Jack, who'd begun circling the table, spun back and bowed theatrically. Then he continued to where Queen was sitting. Coming up behind her, he placed his right hand on her left shoulder and leaned down by her ear. "Told you my meat was tasty."

Queen sighed loudly and set her phone down.

"Anytime you want a sample, Queenie—"

Without warning, she grabbed Jack's wrist and let her chair fall forward onto all four legs. That yanked Jack toward her and off-balance. Using his momentum against him, she pulled his arm all the way forward, locking his armpit against her shoulder. Jack's head was left exposed, above and slightly in front of Queen's own.

From her own hand-to-hand training, Locke expected Queen to pop Jack in the face with her free hand. Instead, she kicked her feet up off the table. Keeping her legs straight, Queen folded herself into an impossible-looking V with her boots up over her head. Crossing her ankles behind Jack's neck trapped him in nasty scissor-hold headlock.

Queen might be small, but her arms and legs were wrapped in thick ropes of muscle. Although Jack pawed at her calves, Locke knew he didn't stand a chance of dislodging them.

Locke glanced over at King, wondering what the Giant would do. Setting his fork down, he simply crossed his massive arms and eased back to watch.

Jack sputtered now, gasping for breath. His cheeks and forehead turned bright pink.

His left hand dropped to his side. It started fumbling near the scabbard on his belt.

As if sensing what he was thinking, Queen wrenched her legs, making Jack yelp.

At that moment, Huang stormed back and slapped the tabletop with his hand. "Release him!"

When Queen didn't budge, Huang produced a prescription pill bottle from his pocket. Holding it out toward her, he shook it.

The contents clattering inside got her attention.

Queen eyed Huang's hand for a long moment.

"I said, *enough*." Huang gave the bottle another shake. "Or do you need a reminder of what it feels like to miss a day?"

Teeth gritted, Queen released Jack's neck. Still clutching his wrist, she wedged the toe of one boot under his chin. Then she kicked upward, sending Jack flying backward until he landed spread-eagle on the floor behind her.

Queen settled down into her seat as if nothing had happened. Red-faced and coughing, Jack rubbed his neck. When he finally climbed to his feet, he wore a sheepish smile, nodding as if he'd enjoyed the tussle.

Locke wasn't sure she believed that.

Huang gave hard looks to Jack, King, and Queen. "We have no time for foolishness. You three will come with me. Ms. Locke, we have a separate space for you to practice."

"Practice what?"

"What you do best."

With that, Huang started toward the rear of the building. When he marched out of sight behind the plywood structure, the others rose to follow him.

Seeing no other choice, Locke took Evan's hand.

Once they cleared the corner of the wooden box, she could see two areas had been measured off against the rear wall. One was defined by a small area rug spread across the concrete. Wooden sawhorses surrounded the carpet like fencing, while inside a beanbag chair sat near several unopened boxes of Legos.

"Toys!"

Evan made the word sound five syllables long as he dropped Locke's hand and dashed over to them. Although she started after him, Huang's voice called to her.

"Ms. Locke, over here."

Huang stood in another fenced-off area several yards away. This workspace contained a table and chairs, a large rolling toolbox, an old-fashioned oscilloscope like the one she'd used in the army, and some other, boxy container covered in a white sheet.

Locke stopped in her tracks and looked back at Evan. He was smiling for the first time, turning over a race car set. "Can I build this?"

"Yes, Evan, those are for you," Huang said. After a beat, his voice chilled. "Ms. Locke, your work is *here*."

Reminding herself that she needed to keep Huang happy for the moment, she started toward him. Still, she couldn't help glancing back several times.

Evan seemed oblivious, ripping open bags, spilling blocks everywhere.

Once Locke reached Huang's area, the group fanned into a semicircle around him and the sheeted container, which stood as tall as he was.

"This," Huang said to Locke, "is what you will be working on."

He grabbed fistfuls of fabric and yanked the sheet away like some odd magician.

When she saw what was hiding underneath, Locke burst out laughing.

CHAPTER

10

AFTER SEVERAL SECONDS, Locke realized she was the only one who saw the humor in what had been hiding under Huang's sheet.

"That's it?" She nodded at the nearly six-foot-high safe. "You want me to open that?"

Huang's eyes ticked back and forth from her to the box. The others' faces showed nothing but blank looks.

"I thought you could open *any* safe," Huang said.

"Damn straight. But that thing'll take a week."

Locke stepped to the door of the matte-gray box. She slid her fingers over its embossed chrome logo, the word *Colonial* written in tight script, underscored by a looping line that led to a kite and had a key dangling from the middle of it. Meant to make you think of Ben Franklin, it wasn't any kind of subliminal marketing bullshit. Colonial Iron Chest was the real deal.

She'd learned that firsthand.

Years ago, not long after starting the safecracking gig, Locke had traveled to Philadelphia for a Colonial-sponsored lock-and-safe convention. In truth, the trip had been a tax-deductible excuse to see Kori before she redeployed. The two women hadn't spoken in months, not since Kori had surprised Locke by reenlisting. So when Kori first texted about meeting up, Locke didn't want to make the trip. After what had happened, she figured it wouldn't be like before. Besides, Locke was busy building a new life in California—what was the point in going back east and pretending?

Kori's call changed everything. She tried to make the trip sound fun, like the old days. But in her voice, Locke heard something else. A wistfulness, almost. Since basic, the two women had always shipped out together. There'd never been a question about when they'd see each other next.

Never a need to say goodbye.

Locke had dialed the airline as soon as Kori hung up. And for forty-eight hours after she flew into Philly, it was like Camp Taji had never happened. She and Kori ate cheesesteaks, took selfies with the Liberty Bell. They laughed and joked, without a single mention of Newton.

While they'd been apart, Locke had almost forgotten how touchy Kori was. Despite their size difference, Kori had always been the one to give Locke a shove, to bump her with her hip, to squeeze her forearm. In Philly, every contact helped lift the heaviness that hunched Locke's shoulders. She caught herself smiling more. Enjoying the butterflies that danced in her stomach whenever Kori grabbed her hand to drag her to something new. Delighting in the electric sizzle Kori's fingernails caused when they scraped her skin.

When Kori's leave was over, Locke watched her go. The taxi door closing at the curb rang in Locke's ears like the door to the Camp Taji brig. And for three days afterward, the Colonial convention only made things worse. Rather than learning any safecracking tricks or finding new clients, she spent the time dodging sweaty middle-aged meatheads who hit the hotel bar by noon, then roved the lobby looking for fresh meat. The only worthwhile part of the work trip had been a tour of Colonial's facility, the front of which was done up like a museum.

Called *iron chests* back in the 1700s, safes hadn't just been a thing for kings and pirates, one sign explained. Colonial had opened four years before Lexington and Concord kicked off the Revolution, and Ben Franklin had stored inventions inside a Colonial chest in his workshop. The company had recovered the door to Franklin's box, which was now displayed in a glass case along with a kite and a key. And he wasn't their only Declaration-signing customer—William Paterson had installed a Colonial Iron Chest in his office as New Jersey's governor, then had the thing hauled to DC when he became a Supreme Court justice.

Signs around the museum explained how Colonial's first sales pitch was proximity. Delivering a thousand-pound box by boat and buggy from Europe could take months, so ordering your safe from Philly was way more convenient. As the world shrank, though, Colonial evolved. In the late 1800s, a Swiss immigrant named Dietrich Johannes Fromal joined the company. Trained as a watchmaker in Lucerne, Fromal brought a fresh, technical eye to safes—he ended up earning Colonial over a hundred patents on locks, timers, and other gizmos. More importantly, he instilled a culture of innovation. In 1968, Colonial stepped seamlessly into the electronic era, adding its first digital combination lock.

Colonial also kept up its ties with the US government. Pictures in the museum suggested that Colonial's boxes had secured both the Normandy invasion plans and the Cold War nuclear codes. Locke had since heard that every lockbox inside CIA headquarters was a Colonial.

All that history helped Colonial in the private sector. Maps at the Colonial plant showed it had installed vaults in Vegas casinos, on Seattle tech campuses, and at New York brokerage houses. Anyplace with something to secure. Locke herself had run up against a couple of Colonial boxes guarding film masters at Hollywood movie studios. With opening weekends measured in the billions, Disney wasn't about to store its new releases in anything but the best.

But that was the problem: Colonial's boxes sat out on the bloody edge of tech. This particular bitch that Huang had unveiled, the Ticonderoga TXTL-60x6, was their top-of-the-line. Locke had only read about it—given that they cost over a hundred grand each, Colonial probably sold only a couple of these beasts a year.

"There's three separate locks." Locke pointed to a traditional-looking dial on the right-hand side of the door. "This one's a five-digit combo. With a hundred numbers on the dial, you're talking ten billion-with-a-*b* possibilities, so good luck guessing. It's got probably the smoothest set of wheels in the world behind it. There's three, maybe four people who could manipulate that lock."

"And you're one of them?" Queen asked.

Locke whipped around, expecting a skeptical squint or a raised eyebrow. But the Pink Punker was smiling. No sarcasm, no doubt—just a *You go, girl!* flash of pride in her big baby blues.

"Yeah," Locke said flatly. "I am. But that's not gonna help with this." Her hand slid to a keypad on the opposite side of the door. "It's also a five-digit combo, but digital. No moving parts, nothing to pick. You either know it or you don't."

"So you pinch it," Queen said. "Figure out where some dummy wrote it down."

"Or find someone . . . persuadable." Jack drew the knife off his belt, twirled it around his finger once, then resheathed it.

Locke didn't like the bloodthirsty gleam in Jack's eye. But he wasn't wrong.

"There's still one more." Her hand slid down, past the master door handle, to a spot in the middle of the bottom third of the door. There, a small metal awning protruded over a panel of black glass. "Biometric scanner. Same one

Customs uses at the airport. It needs *four* fingerprints." She raised her hand with the thumb tucked in and wiggled the remaining digits, index to pinkie.

"You gotta open all three?" Jack asked.

"Worse," Locke said. "There's a timer. If you don't trigger each of the locks within a certain number of seconds, they all freeze for an hour. Plus, five misses on any lock, and that one shuts down completely. You need to fly someone out from the factory to override it."

"So blow the door off with explosives or something," Queen said.

Locke smiled. Movies made that look easy, but the *X* in this safe's product designation meant it was explosive resistant. "The door's seven inches thick, including a layer of heat-resistant ceramic. Plus it's got a glass relocker. Break the glass and you've got six spring-loaded bolts to overcome."

"Cut it open," Jack said.

Locke was surprised he didn't draw his knife again to demonstrate. But she shook her head. "They cast this thing out of a single sheet of metal. There's no seams, nothing to attack. They've added a layer of tar insulation and a cage of alloy bars inside the walls. You'd need a whole truck of acetylene to torch through."

"Can you drill it?" Queen asked.

Locke nodded. "That's your best shot. Go in through one of the sidewalls. You need an industrial drill, titanium bits. And you're gonna break a few."

A few dozen, she thought without saying it. The numbers in a safe's rating indicated the minimum minutes of resistance it provided, and on how many walls. Most commercial safes were rated 15x6 or 30x6, meaning fifteen minutes or a half hour on all six sides. This bitch was a 60x6, and Locke had a feeling the actual drill time would extend well over an hour.

Standing behind the others, King began pacing back and forth. The way his jaw was grinding, it looked like his scalp muscles were doing calisthenics.

Jack cocked his head at Huang. "Don't get me wrong, boss, I love coming to South Beach. And it's fucking fantastic listening to these lovely ladies talk about blowing and drilling. Really. But if Ace can't open the box—"

"Oh, I can open it," Locke said. "I just need time. You leave me alone with a drill—"

"You will not be alone," Huang said. "No tools. Nothing larger than a purse. You will have approximately ten minutes to open the safe."

"Ten minutes?" Locke gave Queen an eye roll.

Huang cut between them and started advancing toward Locke. His whole face reddened.

"You will open the combination lock."

It wasn't phrased as a question. Despite the Miami air, Locke could feel his warm breath, and every huff and puff felt like fire licking her skin. She began backpedaling, even though a growing part of her wanted to punch the fake lawyer in the face.

"Then, you will open the digital lock."

Another statement, another order. Huang kept coming, and Locke kept retreating until her back struck the cinderblock wall. He closed within inches of her, a drop of spittle flying from his lips. "You will find a way—"

Her insides clenched, even as her skin continued to crawl at the thought of what might be swirling in the air around her. "I told you," she said through gritted teeth, "the digital combo *can't* be picked."

"You have opened digital locks before, yes?"

"Sure, but not—"

"Then you will also open this one."

She looked up at the ceiling. "You don't understand—"

"No, Ms. Locke," Huang hissed. "I understand everything perfectly."

When he didn't say anything further, she glanced back down and found him gazing off to the side. Down the rear wall of the building.

Her eyes followed his and landed on Evan.

Locke nearly doubled over. "No! No, you can't—"

"You care about the boy," Huang said. "I care for what is inside that safe."

In the play area, Evan had already assembled the Lego car's wheels and now was building a bumper. He was like Kori that way—he could spend hours working on the tiniest projects. If his hands were occupied, Evan was happy.

Locke tried to swallow but had no spit left.

Still, she couldn't do the impossible. "Even if I got through both locks in time—and that's an *if*—I can't fake the biometrics. The only way—"

"*I* will handle the biometrics." Huang's head swung back toward her. The steely look in his eyes, the way his chin jutted forward, he really believed it. "To ensure Evan's safety, all you need to do is open the other two locks. And I have given you a duplicate on which to practice."

Locke took a slow, shallow breath. "How long?"

"Ten minutes," he said. "Not a minute more."

"No. I mean, how long do I get to practice?"

"The rest of today. And part of tomorrow."

Two days.

Locke now knew exactly how long she had to signal for help.

11

Locke watched Huang lead the others up rickety-looking stairs to a doorway cut into the plywood structure's side.

Although she stood at the safe, turning the dial, she paid no attention to the numbers. She simply spun the knob, pretending. Once the crew disappeared inside, she started counting seconds in her head.

When she reached sixty, she slipped off her flip-flops and tiptoed from her fenced-off workspace. As she started back toward where they'd eaten, Evan rose to his feet in her peripheral vision.

She stopped and signaled him to stay put.

He hesitated a moment, then sat back down. That let her exhale.

And then she was off again.

Locke jogged the entire perimeter of the building, scanning for anything that'd let her contact the outside world. But when she reached the safe again, she had nothing to show for the run other than embarrassment at how hard her heart was pounding. She'd seen no phones anywhere. The little glass offices contained suitcases and cots, not computers.

Escape seemed equally impossible. Although each wall bore a set of emergency exit doors, all were chained closed.

The links were quarter-inch steel, secured by iron padlocks; even heavy-duty bolt cutters might not slice through them. And it wasn't like she had a set of those anyway—a quick check showed the rolling toolbox contained mostly electronics equipment. No real tools beyond a couple of screwdrivers.

The sliding metal door they'd entered through last night was weird. Almost like a submarine hatch, its "handle" was a wheel mounted in the middle that slid security bars up and down into the ceiling and floor. While she didn't see any obvious locks, there was no sign the wheel would turn freely either. Remembering the piercing screech the door had made, Locke decided to avoid it for now.

The only place she hadn't checked was the bathrooms.

Locke eyed the plywood stairs again as she slipped on her sandals.

With no idea how long the crew would be working inside the wooden structure, she figured she'd better wait to make a pretend pit stop. Whenever Huang emerged, he'd want to know what she'd been doing all this time. She needed to take a crack at the Ticonderoga.

The traditional dial was bound to be the easiest part, so she started with that. After setting a random combination with her head turned, she tried to decipher it.

Big mistake.

The dial was supremely well-balanced. Although each of her first few spins picked up another one of the five combination wheels, she couldn't sense any difference. No extra weight, no increased resistance. Just a smooth turn, every single time.

It was totally disorienting.

She hadn't felt this lost on a dial since she'd been a teenager. The Mule had kept an old safe in the middle of his classroom, a waist-high Alpine box he'd recovered from some junkyard. At the start of every semester, he'd take a hundred-dollar bill, set it inside the safe, and lock the door—a bounty for anyone who could get inside. Kids tried everything, every tool available inside the shop. Which, of course, had been the Mule's plan all along.

But no one had ever beaten the thing and gotten the money. And, after weathering years of failed attempts, that box looked like it had survived Vietnam with the Mule. Most of its paint was long gone, replaced by pockmarked patches of rust. Every one of its walls was scarred, drilled, and dented.

Still, the box looked beautiful to Locke—and that Benjamin inside was more money than she'd ever seen. She could picture herself on a spending spree at the mall, rows of bags slung over both arms. To get there, Locke figured she needed to be smarter than everyone else. Brute forcing it wasn't gonna work—she needed to actually open the thing. So she searched *safecracking* online and found a bunch of old TV clips.

After watching those over and over, Locke waited till everyone was distracted by pizza day at the cafeteria, then snuck back to the metal shop at lunchtime.

The TV safecrackers all had stethoscopes or other gizmos to help them listen to their locks. Lacking anything that fancy, Locke simply pressed her ear against the door and started spinning the dial. But it wasn't like what she'd seen on-screen—no ticking or clicking to guide her.

After several fruitless minutes, she was ready to quit when the Mule's voice called out from behind her. "You got the right idea."

She'd whipped around to find him grinning at her.

"But you're gonna have to work a little harder."

Now, Locke took a deep breath and stared down the Ticonderoga. Time to get systematic.

Using a pad and pen she found by the toolbox, she began the same process with the high-tech safe that she'd used back in Malibu: feeling for changes that signified the start of a notch on one of the wheels, noting the number where it happened, then reversing direction.

After ten cycles back and forth, Locke glanced over the numbers she'd written down.

She was off.

Like, *way* off.

The notch on a combination wheel wasn't very big, so she expected to find five tightly packed pairs of numbers. Instead, the digits she'd scribbled were so random, she might as well have picked them out of a hat.

She needed to start over.

On a fresh sheet, Locke made notes through another ten cycles of the dial.

Same result—ten numbers nowhere near each other.

Two more tries went no better. Four manipulation attempts, four complete failures.

The knot behind her eyebrow returned, with a vengeance. At this rate, she wouldn't need to worry about the digital lock. She'd never even get to it.

Locke was about to try again when a clatter echoed through the warehouse. Huang emerged from the plywood box, followed by the others. He paused long enough at the bottom to say, "Lunch."

Locke collected Evan and started for the folding tables. But, seeing Jack bustling behind his hot plates and King scanning the *San Francisco Chronicle*, she got an idea.

"Potty break?" she asked Evan.

Outside the restrooms, Locke leaned down, as if giving him a peck on the cheek. Instead she whispered, "Look for windows or vents, okay? Anything that might lead outside. I'll meet you out here."

When she straightened, Evan wore his serious face again. He nodded once before marching into the men's room. Despite a small pang of worry, Locke headed next door.

In the women's bathroom, the only light came from a single fluorescent tube above the two-sink vanity. A pair of stalls and a single, curtainless shower stood on the opposite side. Locke ignored all that and stalked to the far wall. Scanning it corner to corner, she found solid cinder blocks the whole way along, except for one panel at the ceiling where a metal fan had been installed. As tall as she was, though, Locke couldn't reach it. And even if she could, the panel was no bigger than a single block.

She was still staring at it when a toilet flushed behind her.

Locke jumped at the noise, then turned to see Queen exiting the first stall.

A wicked smile was splayed across her face. "Plotting your escape?"

Locke's eyes darted back up to the fan. "Oh . . . no. I—"

"I don't think you're getting out through that little hole, hon." Queen stepped to the sink and ran her hands under the water. In the mirror, her pale-blue eyes remained locked on Locke.

The intensity of the stare made Locke's face flush.

"I mean, I don't know if *I* could even squeeze into something that tight." Queen ripped paper towels from the dispenser to dry her hands, then crumpled them into a ball. Without looking, she let it roll off her fingers into the trash. "Although I'd probably try. Just for fun."

As silence hung there, heavier than the humidity, Locke searched desperately for something to say. "I . . . I don't know how you did that move this morning. But he deserved it. Jack."

Queen chuckled as she turned toward Locke. "Probably more time than he's ever spent with his face between a woman's legs." Then she grunted. "At least he talks."

"King never . . . ?"

"Not that I've heard. The couple days we been trapped in here, he's just Frankensteined around, glaring at everybody."

"Trapped?"

Queen took a step toward Locke, causing her to retreat an equal amount.

"Huang told us when we got here, no one leaves. We're locked in, same as you." She glanced up at the fan in the wall. "I don't think you're gonna find a way out, hon. I already looked."

Locke forced a swallow down. She had a million questions, but the way Queen was staring didn't help her efforts to string words together.

After another silent moment, the Pink Punker spun on her heel and started for the door.

Locke's stomach dropped, and she called after her. "Hey! You're not gonna tell—"

"Nope." Queen glanced back over her shoulder and winked. "Chicks before pricks."

As the door swung shut, Locke released the remainder of the breath she'd been holding. The tiny bathroom, which had seemed to shrink around them, now widened just a little. Although she assumed Evan must be waiting outside by now, she stepped to the sink and splashed water on her face.

The cold liquid seemed to sizzle against her cheeks.

When she straightened, the confusion was still plain on her face in the mirror.

Locke wasn't quite sure what Queen was playing at.

And by *quite*, she meant at all.

Growing up, Locke had gravitated to guys. She'd found their company more enjoyable, not least of all because they were easier to understand. Like bulls, they always charged straight at whatever red cape waved in front of them.

Dealing with women was more like playing pool, all angles and bank shots. Stranding the cue ball so the other player had to scratch.

The guys Locke grew up with had never judged her Salvation Army clothes. They didn't think she was weird for liking sports or being outdoors. Girls were always preoccupied with things that didn't matter, communicating in some language Locke had never been taught.

That's why Kori was special.

One reason at least.

A female friend Locke could trust. And understand.

The first of those, like, ever.

Not that it started that way. One corner of Locke's mouth turned up, remembering how Sergeant Nunez had pulled Locke aside and asked her to be Kori's keeper through basic. Locke had been horrified. Over the first three weeks, she'd been killing it—maxing out her PT scores, winning the combatives competition. Why did she suddenly need to babysit the mousy girl who started every drill on the wrong foot? The one who could barely finish the short runs, let alone the long ones?

Locke had decided Nunez's request was the very worst thing that could have happened. But she had to comply or face Nunez's punishment.

Problem was, Kori wasn't exactly psyched to receive help. When Locke approached her in the barracks, you'd have thought Locke had come to kill her. Kori actually reared back to throw a punch.

Locke had turned and stalked away.

Not because she was scared—she would have knocked five-foot-nothing Kori into next week. Because she didn't want the trouble. Who was this little girl to give her any lip? And why the fuck was Nunez forcing her to help someone so utterly ungrateful?

The next morning, though, when Nunez discovered Kori had lost her canteen, it wasn't just Kori who had to run around asking inanimate objects—doors, lampposts, rocks—if they'd seen it. Nunez made Locke perform the punishment too.

She's started off steaming. Her first time in trouble, and it wasn't even her fault! The paranoid part of her brain imagined Nunez calling the Mule back home, telling him how badly she'd done.

But no matter how mad she was, when Kori saluted a small tree like it was a goddamn three-star, Locke couldn't help letting out a chuckle.

Kori looked over, that wild gleam in her eye. The one Locke had seen so many times afterward.

The one that meant, *Oh,* that *made you laugh? Just wait!*

They'd become fast friends after that, Locke helping Kori with her soldiering, Kori forcing Locke to keep it light. They looked so different standing side by side—the tall, muscular white chick and the tiny Aleut girl—that Nunez started calling them Grande and Pequeña.

Looking at herself in the mirror now, Locke longed for one of Kori's smiles to take the edge off. A joke to break the tension.

Deep down, though, Locke knew none was coming. And she'd kept Evan waiting long enough.

One last splash on her face, and she headed back outside.

Evan stood waiting at the bathroom door. Seeing his face, she couldn't help but give him a hug. While her mouth was near his ear, she whispered, "Anything?"

He shook his head.

Locke tried not to let her disappointment show. Instead, she steered him toward the corner where the others had queued up for food. Huang was being served first, while Queen stood at the end of the line.

As they approached, Locke's eyes zeroed in on Queen's back pocket.

The edge of her phone was peeking out.

Locke bit down on her tongue to keep from running over and snatching the cell. A minute with that handset could solve everything; 911 could trace an emergency call from the cell towers or something. Even a quick text might bring the cavalry—how many abandoned warehouses this size could there be?

Still, Queen hadn't let the phone out of her sight. The only time she'd even set the thing down was when she'd sparred with Jack.

Jack.

Locke glanced up the line. He was ladling something steamy from a pot into King's bowl.

Could she pit Jack against Queen somehow? Create some kind of distraction to get her hands on the cell?

Locke didn't have long to ponder it. Once King got served, Queen recoiled at whatever she saw inside the pot. She staggered around the far end of the cooking table to a small refrigerator against the wall.

As she crouched to rummage through it, Jack called over, "If you can't handle hot pot, Queenie, it's a good thing you dinna make it to Beijing."

Queen shot to her full height at the remark. Although Jack turned his back to her, she looked ready to pounce on him again.

Huang's voice rang out from the table, where he was already seated. "Queen. Come."

Locke glanced over and saw him holding the medicine vial up again.

Queen's eyes darted back and forth between them. Finally, she stomped over to Huang, who passed her a pill that she popped into her mouth.

"How about you, Ace? You brave enough to take a dip in my hot pot?"

Locke blinked several times. "Excuse me?"

"Sichuan hot pot." Jack pointed a pair of tongs down into the vessel on the burner in front of him. "Traditional

Chinese—you pick your meat, your veggies, and you drop 'em in here. They're done in a flash."

Locke peered down into the pot. Liquid the color of molten lava bubbled furiously inside. "Spicy?"

"Wee bit. If the boy kinna handle it, I'll make him something else. But you . . . I'm guessing you can stand the heat."

The look Jack gave her made Locke want to push the pot over and see how much heat *he* could tolerate. But she reminded herself she might need him later, without third-degree burns. She nodded down at Evan. "I'll have whatever you can make for him. Something simple?"

"Aye."

Moments later, Jack handed her a paper plate stacked with several grilled cheese sandwiches. Locke led Evan to the side wall and eased herself onto the floor. After giving him the most reassuring smile she could, she bit into her sandwich and watched the others.

With everyone served, Jack emerged from behind his cooking station. He beelined for Huang and squatted next to his chair. His voice rose when he asked, "Whatcha think, boss? *Wèi dào rú hé?*"

Huang's expression soured. "A passable imitation."

"Imitation. Really." Jack wiped his hand down his face, the disappointment obvious. "They loved that recipe at the Peninsula in Hong Kong."

"It is like your Mandarin—not bad, but obviously Cantonese. My own small village has better hot pots than this."

Jack pinched the tip of his beard between his fingers. "You know, Sichuan Sun won a Michelin star while I ran the kitchen."

"And yet you were relieved of your position." Huang grunted, then shoved a wad of food into his mouth with his chopsticks.

Jack's face paled at that.

Queen lowered her phone and turned her chair to watch.

Still chewing, Huang said, "Did you hear how many stars the restaurant won after you departed? They brought in a chef who was actually raised in Chengdu."

Jack's chin dropped to his chest. The muscles in one of his cheeks trembled.

Huang's lips spread into a mocking grin as he scooped up another bite from his plate. "You should be thankful. Hong Kong has the nicest prisons in China, but they are still dangerous for laowai."

Although Jack remained silent, Locke saw his shoulders shake beneath his baggy chef's coat.

After a long pause, he abruptly turned to King on his opposite side. "At least you like my food, eh, big boy?"

King, who'd been immersed in the *Miami Herald*, slowly looked over at Jack.

"Not that I imagine a fella your size misses too many meals. I prolly coulda cooked cow shit and you'da swallowed it."

The Giant gave Jack a look that would have flattened some buildings Locke knew.

Jack leaned down, hands on thighs. That put him at King's eye level, just inches from the Giant's face. "Best thing about you, even if you dinna like it, you'd never tell me."

For such a mountain of a man, King moved in a blur. Exploding straight up off his chair, he seized Jack by the throat, lifted him like it was nothing, then slammed him down on the table.

When King reared his right hand back to throw a punch, Locke's first thought was to applaud.

But the more her mind raced through it, she realized Jack getting his face flattened wasn't the most positive development.

At best, it'd limit Jack's ability to distract Queen.

At worst, King might actually kill him.

She had no idea what that would do to Huang's plan. Or his need to hang on to Evan and her.

By the time Locke's brain caught up with her body, she'd already bounced off the floor and dashed over to grab King's elbow.

When the Giant glanced back and saw her holding his arm, Locke realized she was in deep, deep trouble.

12

ALTHOUGH LOCKE SCRAMBLED to secure her grip, wrestling King's elbow was like trying to tackle a normal-sized person at the waist. She was still fumbling when he lashed his arm out and flung her away.

Locke flew several feet, landing hard on the concrete.

When she looked back to the table, King was winding up again. She eyed the distance and knew immediately she couldn't reach him before he threw the punch. She opened her mouth to yell.

Before she could, a different voice rang out.

"Stop it! Just stop—please!"

Evan had crossed over from the wall and now planted himself between her and King. From behind, she could see his shoulders heaving. His little fists clenched at his sides.

"You don't meed to hurt anyone!" Evan yelled. "Stay away from my momma!"

As warm as his words made her feel, Locke's stomach cinched at the thought of how they might provoke the Giant.

She scrambled up behind Evan and wrapped her arms tightly around him. With her head perched above his shoulder, she gave King a hard stare, her eyes announcing, *You'll have to go through me.*

King started to turn back to Jack.

But Jack took full advantage of the distraction. He slid off the table, dragging King's left wrist with him. Landing in a squat and spinning to the side, Jack hauled King's massive arm up behind the Giant's back, forcing him facedown onto the table.

"Not so mighty now, are you, big boy?"

Leaning over King's back, Jack yelled the question directly into his ear. He even twisted King's wrist to emphasize the point.

King's other arm flew back behind his head and seized Jack by his ponytail.

As Jack yelped in pain, Locke could see the steel bands in King's forearm flexing to flip Jack onto the table like a rag doll.

But another sound cut through the din this time. One Locke recognized immediately.

The metallic click-clack of a round being chambered into a semiautomatic pistol.

"Enough," Huang said. He'd moved behind them and pointed the gun at Jack's midsection. "Let each other go. Or I will shoot both of you."

Neither man budged.

The deafening *crack* of a gunshot ripped through the air.

Locke's heart froze at the sound. She clamped one hand over Evan's eyes, and as the noise echoed around the concrete walls, she tried to shield his little ears with her elbows. At the same time, she searched frantically for some sign of where the bullet might have struck.

A stream of red liquid began pouring out a hole in the side of the hot pot. Steam rose off the floor as the broth splashed and spilled.

"There is only one indispensable person here," Huang said. "And it is not either of you."

This time, the two men released each other—Jack pushing himself away from King as King popped up off the table and whipped around to face him.

As the two men glared at each other, Huang took his finger off the trigger and raised the barrel toward the ceiling. "No more childish fighting, understand?" He turned to each of them in turn. "You all stand to make lots of money if you do not throw it away on this . . . foolishness."

After a moment of silence, Huang addressed Locke specifically. "I'm glad to see you have not lost your . . . fighting spirit since departing the army, Ms. Locke. You will need it."

Huang's words sent a shudder down her spine.

He'd been calling her Locke, but if he knew about her service, that meant he knew her name, knew everything.

But how?

Personnel records like hers should have been sealed up tight. And what could he possibly have planned that was anything like Camp Taji?

Huang didn't provide any additional clues. Instead, he marched over to King and slapped the Giant's chest with the back of his hand. "Of everyone, I expected better from you. Perhaps you've forgotten where I found you, how much debt I assumed to procure your freedom. If I default, it is not me that your former employers will hunt down."

King's jaw clenched.

"Or perhaps you simply aren't as intelligent as I believed. Perhaps your mind requires as much repair as that lump in your neck."

After the way he'd tossed Jack around, Locke imagined King might pluck Huang off the ground and hurl him somewhere.

But, to Locke's surprise, the Giant turned and stormed away toward the offices.

A few seconds later, a boom rivaling the gunshot echoed around the warehouse.

Huang didn't react to the slamming door. He simply returned to his seat and resumed eating.

With the excitement over, Queen's eyes dropped back to her phone, while Jack started for the corner behind his cooking table. As he crossed Locke's line of sight, though, he glanced over at her. His face was etched with pain and fatigue, but he held her eyes for a moment, then gave her a pronounced nod.

Before she could decide how Jack's appreciation might help, Evan spun to face her. He wasn't crying, but his breathing was ragged. "I'm—I'm sorry . . ."

Locke smiled sweetly. "For what?"

"For getting . . . angry and . . . yelling, I just—"

"Oh, baby." She pulled him into a hug. "You were so brave."

His chin pressed on her shoulder, and he returned the squeeze. "I wasn't gomma let them hurt you again."

She rubbed his back and shushed him.

After another minute, Evan withdrew from the embrace. "Will we be okay?"

Locke closed her eyes and nodded. "Of course." She pulled him in closer and whispered, "I'll get us out of here. I'm already working on it."

*   *   *

Once Huang finished eating, he shepherded Locke and Evan back to their spaces.

As they neared the play area, Locke shooed Evan ahead, then veered for her own workspace to lead Huang away from him. At the safe, she turned and found Huang had stopped at the fencing.

He raised an eyebrow. "Success? Opening the locks?"

"Working on it."

His lips pursed. "By dinner, progress!"

With that, he marched up and into the plywood structure. Once the others joined him, Locke did another quick mental count before considering her next move.

She saw only two options now. One was the sliding metal door. Although part of her itched to run and try it, she imagined it had to be locked. And the noise still scared her. If Huang intercepted her attempting to escape, who knew what he'd do to keep her from trying again. The door seemed like her last-ditch.

Locke's other idea was to search the offices. Queen kept her phone with her, but King or Jack might have one. Or a computer, or a gun. Something useful in those suitcases.

The question was, did she have time?

As if in response, a rapid *clunk-clunk-clunk* sounded, and Queen appeared at the top of the staircase. She skipped halfway down the flight, then grabbed the railing and threw herself over.

When her feet hit the concrete floor, Queen tumbled into a forward roll. One full somersault deposited her back on her feet, jogging toward the offices.

She returned a moment later, carrying what looked like a small satin clutch. When she saw Locke watching, Queen raised the bag into the air. "A girl needs her purse!"

After she disappeared inside again, Locke told herself the suitcases needed to wait. At least for a while, to ensure the crew was preoccupied.

She might as well give the Ticonderoga another shot.

Given her troubles this morning, though, she decided to change strategies. Instead of guessing blind, Locke deliberately reset the combination to 20-40-60-80-00 so she could focus on certain regions of the dial.

After getting all the combination wheels spinning, Locke brought the dial around toward 20. This time, she closed her eyes as she passed 10, trying to sense even the slightest bit of difference.

Feeling nothing, she opened her eyes and found she'd gone all the way to 25.

She'd blown right past the notch.

With a frustrated sigh, she continued around past 10 again. This time, she slowed her spin to a crawl. Closing her eyes, she continued at the new pace until . . .

Was that something?

It sure wasn't much—just the tiniest little slip. Less disturbance than a mosquito made landing on your arm. An eyelash on your cheek.

Her eyes flicked open. The dial sat at 18.

She jotted that number down. Then she turned slowly again . . .

to 20 . . .

21 . . .

There!

She felt it again at 22—the tiniest little slip.

The wheel notch must be four digits wide. And she'd just managed to detect the bar moving against its edges.

Now she needed to see if the pattern held for the other wheels.

Knowing the next digit was 40, Locke spun back in the opposite direction. She sped along until the dial was ten digits away at 50, then slowed to a crawl.

Time to see if she could feel it.

Eyes closed, she nudged the dial forward one millimeter at a time.

There!

She sensed the slip again.

Locke opened her eyes and saw the indicator arrow pointing to 42. A beaming smile spread across her face.

Eat your heart out, Jeff Sitar.

Although she assumed the Colonial craftsmen would make things match, she methodically proceeded through the rest of the combination. Every time, the result was identical. Two digits before and after each combination number, she noticed the same, infinitesimally small change in the dial.

But she'd *felt* it.

After setting the final number, she turned the little handle located next to the combination dial. When it yielded, she pulled the door open for effect. A cool breeze might as well have been hiding inside the safe, as a wave of satisfaction washed over her, neutralizing the heat. She was still a long way from being able to decipher an unknown combination, but now she had something to work with.

Reward time.

Locke stood and motioned to Evan where she was going. When he returned a thumbs-up, she made like she was headed for the bathrooms.

At the matching doors, she paused and gave the plywood structure one last look.

Its walls were solid, no windows or gaps. No way for those inside to see her.

Tightening her toes, Locke took off, trying her best to keep the plastic shoes from flapping and slapping as she sprinted for the offices.

Even from a distance, the locks on the door handles looked cheap, meant to discourage lazy thieves or slow down stupid ones. When she reached the first office, though, she found the handle turned freely.

Locke slipped silently inside. Enough light poured through the plexiglass wall that she didn't bother with the wall switch.

Spacious compared to her janitor's closet, the office was still tiny. A suit bag on a hook covered nearly one entire wall. That, together with a thick textbook resting on an air mattress on the floor, tipped her that this must be King's room.

She hadn't seen anyone else reading, although she wondered why he was interested in cancer.

A canvas suitcase pushed into one corner didn't bear a name, only an address in Mississippi. Sweeping her palms through the bag, she found clothes similar to King's outfit—athletic wear in various combinations of orange, white, and gray. Most pieces had frayed seams or bore obvious holes.

Up near the handle, her fingers brushed something hard. When she pulled it out, she discovered it was some kind of shoulder holster. Empty, no gun to go with it.

Nice to know King might be carrying.

In the next office, a long garment bag hung from a wall hook. The opaque container didn't reveal much about the gown inside, but peekaboo plastic up top showed shimmery black fabric.

Locke ignored the dress and went straight for the suit-cases underneath it. Queen had two, a rolling carry-on like King's and a smaller chrome train case encrusted with rhinestones.

Dropping to her knees, Locke hit the sparkly bag first. Although she virtually never wore makeup, she recognized it from work around Hollywood as the kind of heavy-duty cosmetics carrier actresses and dancers preferred. The case didn't open so much as it unfolded—the upper half split in two, revealing cantilevered trays that lifted up and out to the side.

Locke's eyes scanned quickly over more lip glosses and eye shadows than she'd ever owned. Underneath, she found a tray filled with manicure tools. These looked like torture implements—spikes and scissors of various sizes—but Locke realized they might make perfect lockpicks. Thinking of the padlocks on the emergency doors, she selected several different sizes and wedged them into her waistband.

Another tray contained all kinds of hair fasteners, from berets and rubber bands to bobby pins. Locke grabbed a handful of those too.

After closing the train case, she turned to the carry-on. Again she slid her hands through, feeling for anything interesting.

Locke's internal clock was telling her to hurry now. Given the way Queen had already exited the structure once, she or one of the others might easily come back. And if she got caught—

A voice from behind interrupted her thoughts. "I don't think we wear the same size, hon. In anything."

13

Locke winced, then slowly peered back over her shoulder.

Queen was leaning against the doorframe, arms crossed. There was no way to know how long she'd been watching.

"I . . . uh . . ."

Queen took an exaggerated step into the room, then bent at the waist, hands on hips. The height difference put the two women nearly eye to eye.

"That's twice now. Those guys may not see it, but I know what you're up to. And what a woman like you is capable of."

The hair on Locke's arms was already standing at full attention. The way Queen said *capable* made her ears ring.

"Third time's a charm. The next time I catch you, you're gonna owe me something *big*."

If Locke hadn't been kneeling, Queen's stare might have dropped her to the floor. Rather than anger, or cruelty, her pale-blue eyes were laced with . . . something else. Something that shrank the room.

Locke's heart pounded against the inside of her ribs, marking time while her brain struggled to form a response.

"What is going on in here?"

Huang's voice hit Locke like the first splash of cold water from a showerhead.

Queen spun and straightened in one motion, revealing him standing in the doorway behind her. Before Locke could even worry what Queen might say, the Pink Punker shook her head. "Poor thing doesn't have clothes. It's not like you packed her a bag, and that closet's filthy. I was letting her look for something to borrow."

Huang's eyes narrowed.

Locke didn't think he was buying it. The tools digging into her hip became hot in addition to sharp.

But, after a long moment, he grunted and spun on his heel. "We must measure her anyway. Bring her out."

Once his head was turned, Queen glanced back and gave Locke a mischievous smile.

Locke exhaled. Her shoulders slumped with relief.

Until Queen offered her a hand up.

Queen's fingers hovered inches from Locke's eyes, providing a close-up view of her nails. Cut short and perfectly polished. Colored to match her hair exactly.

Normally, nails like that would have turned Locke green with envy, but these points reminded her of nothing more than upturned fangs—rattlesnake teeth, laced with invisible venom. Being within inches of any human being other than Evan right now made Locke edgy. The idea of deliberately taking someone's hand . . .

But what choice did she have?

Locke tried hard not to flinch as she reached out, anticipating some kind of shock when they touched.

None came.

She rose to her feet. When they joined Huang outside, he handed Queen a measuring tape.

The Pink Punker began stretching it across and around various parts of Locke's body, causing Locke to shiver. She hadn't been sized up like this since reception at Fort Jackson. And they certainly hadn't left the job to anyone like Queen.

Clamping her eyes shut, Locke tried to ignore the hands roaming over her. "What's this for exactly?"

"Never mind," Huang said.

"I might be more help if I knew the plan."

"You know what you require. Be quiet."

Locke waited through more measurements than she imagined could possibly be necessary. Once Queen declared herself done, Locke reopened her eyes to find Huang's finger jabbing at her again.

"We will bring you clothes. Back to work."

With that, he stalked away. When Locke's eyes darted ahead of him, she found he was headed for the sliding metal door.

Was he . . . *leaving*?

"Don't worry, I'll make sure he doesn't screw up too bad."

Locke turned to see Queen wagging a mocking finger at her. "You be good while we're gone."

Queen skipped after Huang, leaving Locke dumbfounded. Halving the number of eyes watching her was simply too good to be true. Although she tried to hide her excitement, she doubted her poker face would fool anyone— she pressed her chin to her chest and started back toward her workspace.

When Huang and Queen reached the sliding metal door, though, Locke made sure to watch them. He used separate keys to open locks on each of the security bars. With both hands, he turned the wheel in the middle of the door and retracted the bars. The door slid open with another ear-piercing screech, a noise that repeated when he shut it from the opposite side.

Locke didn't see any easy way to defeat that front door, but that didn't take the shine off her moment. Going from four guards to two had her positively giddy.

She accelerated from a walk to a jog. When she reached the side of the plywood structure, she pressed her ear against it. She could hear rustling—King and Jack were still holed up inside, doing whatever work Huang had assigned them.

No time to waste.

Locke dashed to the emergency exit closest to her workspace, a set of doors located in the rear corner of the building. By the time she reached them, her heart was fluttering. Although she dealt mostly with combination locks, Locke understood key-operated locks perfectly well. The key slot was carved into a metal cylinder that could turn and move the bar that blocked the lock from opening. But that cylinder was held in place by a series of spring-loaded pins called tumblers. When the key slid into the slot, its jagged teeth pushed the tumblers up and out of the way, allowing the cylinder to turn.

Slipping a narrow tool into the lock to bump the tumblers up was simple enough—the tricky part was holding them out of the way. Because each tumbler was spring-loaded, it wanted to pop right back into place. If you didn't keep enough pressure on all the tumblers you'd already cleared as you moved to the next one, you'd get to the end and the lock wouldn't budge.

Locke knew she needed to temper all the nervous energy coursing through her, so she forced herself to take a deep, cleansing breath. Then she squatted down to get a better look at things.

The padlock was the size of her fist and at least an inch thick. Judging from its dingy exterior, this wasn't something Huang had slapped on recently. Maybe the original owners, when they'd shuttered the factory.

Locke fished into her spandex and pulled out two of the bobby pins she'd taken from Queen's case. Prying one pair of tines apart, she measured it against the side of the lock—it looked the perfect length to reach all the way inside.

When she flipped the padlock over, though, her positivity drained away in an instant.

The lock itself might be old, but the clear lump of superglue blocking the key slot was fresh and shiny.

Locke poked at it with the tip of the Bobby pin, but the glob of glue covered the lock completely. No way to get through. And, if the liquid cement had spilled inside, the spring-loaded pins would be frozen in place.

She didn't stand a chance.

Although Locke knew the result before she started, she forced herself to check the padlocks on all the other exit doors.

Every one had suffered the same fate.

Locke trudged back to the janitor's closet. There wasn't any point in continuing to carry the picks and pins around and risking getting caught with them—she was halfway tempted to return them to Queen's case. Still, she decided they might come in handy later, so she deposited them on top of the highest shelf inside the closet. She couldn't see up there, and King was the only one taller.

As she returned to her workspace, Evan rose and called to her. "You okay, Momma?"

Locke nodded but avoided looking over—he read her expressions too well. Instead, she slumped into a chair, making sure her back faced him.

Without a phone, she had no clue how long Huang and Queen had been gone. Not knowing their surroundings or what they were shopping for, she had no way to anticipate how soon they might return.

Even though this was her single best chance of getting Evan and herself out of this crazy concrete lockbox, she had absolutely no idea how to do it.

"Fuck," was all she found to say.

CHAPTER

14

LOCKE SAT MOTIONLESS, trying to puzzle out her next move. Although her headache had returned, she did her best to ignore it.

She had plenty of other things to worry about.

Assuming the locks were identical on both sides of the sliding steel door, she had no hope of exiting that way, not now. Not until Huang returned and relocked it from the inside. But even then, her prospects of getting Evan safely through that screechy hatch seemed slim at best. How could she possibly open the door without the whole crew hearing?

With no other means of escape, Locke figured she'd better tangle with the Ticonderoga again. To keep Huang happy, if nothing else.

Having already discovered the secret slip in the dial, she now worked to perfect her feel for the wheel. Over and over, she practiced, first on combinations she knew completely, then with random digits thrown in. Eventually, she started setting the entire combination blind. She was so consumed, she barely noticed King and Jack descending from the plywood structure.

By the time sunlight slid from the floor up onto the side of the box, Locke could manipulate the dial to five unknown digits without a problem. And, for once, she figured Colonial's precision would work against it. With some lesser company, she'd worry about variation between individual safes—not Colonial. Their standards were so exacting, she knew the boat safe's dial would spin exactly like this one.

Of course, that wouldn't help her in the slightest with the digital lock.

Locke's eyes drifted to the keypad.

Mounted on a circular platform raised a quarter inch off the door, the keypad was surrounded by a ring of chrome that matched the Ticonderoga's embossed logo. Its black buttons and green screen reminded her of a calculator more than anything else.

To see what she was truly up against, Locke swung the safe door all the way open. Unlike the Malibu box, this one had been hollowed out—no drawers, no shelves. Cavernous enough that Queen could sit inside it. The back of the door was formed from solid steel except for two small access plates. Using a screwdriver from the rolling toolbox, Locke removed the plate behind the digital lock. Underneath, she found a shallow cutout containing a shiny gold circuit board.

This, she recognized, was the brains of the keypad lock. The circuit board bore two black squares. One was a memory chip that stored the combination, the other a processor to compare it to whatever numbers were entered on the keypad.

Adjacent to the circuit board, Locke spotted a compartment holding several AA batteries. Dead batteries were actually the most common problem with digital locks. Although factory manuals warned safe owners to replace batteries annually, nobody ever did. Like with your house's smoke detector—you only remembered the thing needed new batteries when the old ones expired. But where a smoke detector would chirp maddeningly until you fixed it, a safe just sat there silently.

Storing the batteries inside the safe wasn't particularly common, though—if they died, you couldn't open the door and replace them. That suggested Colonial had added a backup.

Locke closed the door and inspected the chrome ring more closely. A small section on the bottom looked different from the rest. With a little tinkering, it popped open, revealing a pair of wires. She teased those out and found they ended in a plastic cap meant to snap onto a nine-volt battery.

While that'd allow a technician to provide external power to the keypad, Locke didn't see how it helped her. It wasn't like she could reach up through those wires and control the lock. She still had to know the combination somehow.

The knot behind Locke's eyebrow cinched tighter.

She and Kori had hugged and high-fived the night they learned they'd be going from basic to advanced individual training together. But once they reached AIT at Fort Lee, their paths diverged. Kori tested into a job the army numbered 91F, small arms and artillery repairer, while Locke drew 91E, machinist. Part of that was their stature—Kori's slender fingers were perfect for tinkering with the tiny parts inside everything from rifles to radios, while Locke's broad shoulders were better suited to the lathes, saws, and presses in the machine shop.

But some of it was mental too.

Locke could follow an army manual's troubleshooting guide like any other dummy, but she never really got how the systems worked. Too much math, too many things going on you couldn't see. Kori understood all that technical mumbo jumbo like a second language; she'd scan the innards of something and start spouting off about voltage and current. At the time, it had made Locke laugh—the girl who started marches on the wrong foot had a knack for electronics.

This wasn't so funny.

As Locke tried to focus, the headache continued to flare. Her stomach grumbled too. When she ordered it to settle down, it protested even louder.

One reason, she realized, was a hearty smell in the air. Salty, and the slightest bit sweet.

Locke set down her tools and approached Evan, who sat cross-legged between a folded-open manual and a mountain of Lego bricks. Engrossed in the instructions, he gave her no reaction except "Hey, Momma."

"How's it going?" Although the car was as long as his arm, he'd finished the wheelbase and now was working his way up the sides.

Even at home, she marveled at how building absorbed him—he'd sit and do sets like this for hours. And the things his little digits could do, the tiny pieces he could place just so. Like Kori with her little baby hands. Locke often helped him with the bigger pieces at the start, but by the time it got down to details, it was all Evan.

"Pretty good." He snapped two pieces together without looking up. "What's for dinner?"

"No idea. Wanna go see?"

They found Jack working over a steaming flattop. No line had formed this time—she and Evan were the only ones in sight.

"What's on the menu?" Locke was hoping for something substantial. Burgers or steaks.

"Fried rice. Plus sashimi for the boss."

When she snorted, Jack's expression hardened. "I'm not talking food-court fried rice here, love. I know how to make the real deal." Then, under his breath, "Even if the boss man won't admit it."

Using a broad metal spatula, Jack folded the rice over itself as he poured and sprinkled ingredients into it. She had to hand it to him: it smelled wonderful. Not just soy-salty but succulent and rich. On closer inspection, she could see large chunks of shrimp and lobster meat scattered through the browned rice.

Jack looked at Evan. "How about you, young man? You willing to give it a try?"

"I . . . uh . . . okay."

From his expression, Locke could tell he'd prefer another grilled cheese.

"Attaboy. You won't be sorry."

"Does your back hurt?" Evan asked.

Locke flushed at the unprompted question. But when her eyes darted to Jack, she found him smiling.

"Wee bit."

"I fell on my back real hard once," Evan said. "I couldn't breathe."

Locke's insides clenched at the memory. Evan had discovered the old Alpine safe from the Mule's classroom, out where it had come to rest in the craftsman's shed. Compelled to climb it for some unknown reason, he'd slipped and landed square on his back. She'd walked in and found him gasping for air. One of her worst parenting moments, until now.

"Got the wind knocked out, did you? I bet your momma took good care of you."

Evan nodded vigorously.

Good care would have been not letting him fall in the first place.

"Like she tried to help me this morning," Jack said.

"Momma's super brave."

"I agree."

Jack gave Locke the first smile that didn't leave her nauseous. It also made her think she might have more of a shot to earn his help than she'd originally thought. But now she needed to lay on some charm. "Did you learn all this overseas?"

"Aye. But I been cooking my whole life. My uncle owned a small pub in Inverness, little town in north Scotland. I grew up working for him, making stovies and Scotch pie. For my seventeenth birthday, I took a holiday in London. Had my first dim sum, and I was hooked. Decided right then to get my arse overseas. Saved two years for the airplane ticket.

Barely spoke a word when I got to Hong Kong but worked my way up from a dishwashing job."

"How long—"

"Fifteen years."

She whistled.

"Long enough I don't know myself anyplace else." Jack twisted his wrist to build three connected circles of rice. Quick pops of the spatula created two eyes and mouth, leaving the rice pile resembling a smiling Mickey Mouse. When Evan giggled, Jack flashed him a grin, then looked back to Locke. "You been?"

She shook her head. While the navy ported in sexy international hot spots, the best she'd done in the army was a fifteen-hour layover at Ramstein Air Base. "I've heard it's pretty."

His eyes glazed over before dropping to the griddle again. "People talk about the neon lights here in Miami." He shook his head. "Hong Kong harbor? At night? Makes this town look like Inverness."

"So you wanna go back?"

"Aye, before there's no Hong Kong left. I gotta straighten out a few . . . misunderstandings first. But it's home."

Suddenly, all Jack's ass-kissing of Huang made more sense. Plus, he'd given her an opening. "Going home is what I think we all want."

Locke deliberately looked down at Evan and stroked his hair. She held her breath, hoping the point would register.

After a long pause, Jack spoke again. "Huang said something about you departing the army—what's that about?" His eyes lit up. "Lemme guess—you broke open one of those safes they keep the nuclear codes in."

Locke grunted. "Nothing that exciting."

He pressed her with his eyes.

Although discussing Camp Taji was the very last thing she wanted, she did need Jack to trust her. "I . . . got in a fight."

"From the soldiers I've met, that ain't a first." Jack grinned as he continued tossing the rice. "Course, I kinna imagine the other guy fared too well. 'Specially if you were angry."

"I was. And he didn't." Locke pushed aside the images that filled her mind—she needed to make this about Jack, not herself. "What kind of misunderstanding gets you fired from a five-star restaurant?"

"Let's just say I learned when the owner's son asks you to hold something for him, say no."

Locke watched to see if he'd elaborate, but his eyes remained on the flattop.

Finally, he took a deep breath and made eye contact again. "If you and the boy wanna go home, I'll tell you another lesson from Hong Kong: look up. Sometimes what you're missing down on the ground can surprise you."

Jack tilted his head back in an exaggerated way.

As Locke started to follow his eyes upward, something snagged her peripheral vision. Huang and Queen were approaching—they'd drawn to within a few yards of the cooking table. Worried by what they might have seen or heard, Locke froze.

Without warning, Jack pushed two bowls of rice into her hands.

"You're gonna thank me for that," he said, giving her a pronounced wink.

Figuring he didn't just mean the food, Locke took the bowls and hurried Evan to the sidewall where they'd sat earlier. After getting him settled, she checked back to the cooking table.

Jack was chattering at Huang in Mandarin while Queen stared at them blankly.

Thankful for the distraction, Locke glanced upward.

The most obvious feature overhead was still the pair of metal fans spinning above the plywood structure. Now that she paid them more attention, Locke could see their blades didn't quite overlap. Each fan was roughly centered over one wall of the plywood structure, leaving a gap of several feet between them even at their closest point.

The ceiling itself was striped by steel girders that crossed from the wall behind her to the opposite side of the building. In addition to the fans, the beams supported large bell-shaped lamps that bathed the floor in bright-white light. Tracing the girders to the far end, she saw the windows tilted open several feet below them.

Was Jack suggesting those as a way out?

The more she looked, the less she bought it. The girders themselves would be easy enough to scale—each girder consisted of two metal beams sandwiching a web of triangular trusses, meaning plenty of handholds if you needed them. But there'd be no easy way to descend from the girders to the glass. And, even if you made the transition somehow, the windows could shatter beneath you, or you might roll right off and fall four stories.

Confused, Locke plunged her spoon into her rice and took a large bite. Although it scalded her tongue, the flavor was fantastic—sweet, sour, and salty all at once. She swallowed several more spoonfuls, hoping the food would clear her head and let her understand what Jack was trying to tell her.

Huang and Queen moved to the round table, where they were joined by King. All three dug into their helpings of rice. At the cooking table, Jack carved strips off a block of blood-red tuna, which he delivered to Huang on a paper plate.

While the others were occupied, Locke continued carefully scouring the ceiling. Before long, though, Huang asked, "Ms. Locke, what progress have you made?"

Every set of eyes locked on her. Even Evan turned his head.

"I've got the dial down."

"And the digital lock?"

"Just started."

Huang jabbed his chopsticks at her. "After dinner, more practice."

"I was kinda hoping for a shower." With sweat slicking over grime from the closet floor, Locke's skin had been itchy all afternoon.

"Shower tomorrow." Huang dragged a slice of tuna through a puddle of soy sauce, then shoved it into his mouth. "After all, you got to swim yesterday."

"Tonight's better."

Huang's head whipped around to see why Queen had contradicted him.

"She needs to try the clothes on," she said.

Huang grunted. "The safe is more important. Have her try them as she is."

Queen cocked her head. "Are you kidding? She's filthy—she can't try on the dress like that."

Locke did a double take.

Dress? What dress?

"Fine," Huang said. "After dinner, quickly as she can. Then back to the safe."

Queen flashed Locke a smile like they'd just been granted parental permission for a sleepover. Locke resisted the urge to scratch her forearms, but she wasn't completely convinced this deal beat staying dirty.

Huang turned to Jack, who'd joined them at the round table. "Is your practice complete?"

"Aye. Tiny and I finished while you were out and about."

King scowled at Jack, then gave Huang a single nod.

"Good," Huang said. "Once events begin, you will need to have the layout memorized."

"Assuming the model's right," Queen said.

Locke tracked this back-and-forth as best she could. She'd suspected the plywood box replicated part of the yacht, but she had no way of knowing which part or why they needed to memorize it.

Huang chuckled softly. "You doubt the model?"

"If it's wrong, that's a pretty big deal."

Huang's eyes locked on Queen. "That model cost more than your share in this operation. More than your *freedom*. You are in no position to question—"

"Freedom?" Queen waved her hand around. "And if that model's crap, we're all fucked. No matter what it cost."

Huang's gaze narrowed. "The information was obtained from those who built the *Helios*. The model is unquestionably correct."

"That's putting a lot of trust in your employer," Queen said.

"Some of us are more loyal than others."

"Who're we working for, boss?" Jack asked.

Locke's ears perked up. What she'd seen so far suggested it was someone very well funded, but otherwise she had no idea.

Huang shook his head. "I am your employer. You need not concern yourself with the identity of mine."

"Then what's your cut?" Queen asked.

"Why would I possibly tell you that?"

Queen glanced around the table. "We're all risking everything—"

Jack and King nodded.

"—so it'd be nice to know you're as invested as we are."

"Everything? *You* are risking *everything*?" Huang paused for a long, solemn swallow. "I have been working toward this moment since before you were born, and three generations preceded me. It took a once-in-a-century pandemic just to create this opportunity. Had a lazy millionaire not hired Ms. Locke to retrieve what he mistakenly regards as an expensive trinket, we would not even be here. So, while you may be risking your pathetic little lives—"

"Pathetic?" Queen recoiled. "Twenty years with nothing to show for it but that stupid little statue—*that's* pathetic."

Locke assumed Queen was referring to the contents of the Malibu box. Part of her now wished she'd looked inside it at the very beginning, although she wasn't sure seeing some statue would have changed her mind on anything.

Huang chuffed and eased back in his chair. "The figurine is nothing you would understand."

"Oh, that's right, stupid girl." Queen twirled her index finger through her pink hair, then stabbed it down onto the tabletop. "I understand money."

Huang let out a single laugh. "Ah, yes, capitalism. The American economic system that has benefited you so handsomely."

When Queen's cheeks flushed, Huang turned to King. "And you."

The Giant remained silent.

"Let us not forget the way you two were both summarily discarded when your financial contributions ceased. I do not do this for money." Huang looked to Jack, presumably for support.

Jack winced. "That Rolex wasn't cheap, boss."

Huang's face reddened, and he turned back to Queen. "My motivations are nothing at all like yours. Righting wrongs, returning what was stolen—these are *noble* causes. I have spent my entire life—"

"Oh, please," Queen said. "You're a crook, same as the rest of us."

Huang's whole body shook as he stammered, "Of course someone like . . . like you cannot understand. My country respects history. We do not travel the globe, destroying and stealing the cultures of others. My family's *zupu* shows a lineage dating back thirteen generations—tell me, did you even know both your parents?"

This time, Queen had no snappy comeback.

Huang leaned toward her wearing a sinister glare. "Do not question my information again, *jiàn nu rén*. Of everyone here, your *bī* is most easily replaced."

Huang bolted upright, tipping his metal chair over with a clang. Seizing his plate, he stormed off toward the offices.

Locke was startled by the noise, and then again when Evan grabbed her arm. She wrapped it around him and pulled him close.

"That went well," Jack said under his breath.

"Fuck you," Queen said.

Jack batted his eyes at her. "Mine's not the cunt he called replaceable, dearie."

Queen shot him a furious look before stalking off toward her own office. A few seconds later, a door slammed.

Although Jack grinned, Evan flinched again.

Locke squeezed him tight. He ducked his head into her lap. "Why's everyone so angry? Why are they yelling?"

She kissed the crown of his head. "Grown-ups don't always act like it." When she looked up, Jack stood in front of them.

"Take your trash?"

She passed him the empty bowls. "Thanks. It was good."

"You know what always cheers me up, little man?"

Evan sniffled, then glanced up.

"Seeing the blue sky. Knowing the sun's still shining." Jack leaned back and raised his eyes skyward again. Then he smiled at Evan before raising his eyebrows at Locke.

As Jack walked away, she scanned the ceiling. She leaned over and whispered, "Do you see the sky?"

"There."

Evan pointed, and she craned her neck to follow his finger.

He was gesturing directly at one of the lights. She squinted against it, then blocked the bulb with her hand.

And that was when she saw the small patch of blue.

A skylight. Positioned so close to the light fixture she'd never noticed it before.

15

ALTHOUGH SEEING THE skylight made Locke want to jump for joy, she dropped her eyes to the floor. Only after confirming that Huang and Queen hadn't returned and King was still buried behind his newspaper did she steal another glance upward.

The skylight sat squarely between two girders. Suddenly, she could picture herself climbing up through the little window onto the roof. Finding a way to descend to the ground. Getting away—going home!

Locke chided herself for the idea almost as soon as it formed. Before planning some circus escape, maybe she ought to figure out how she and Evan could get fifty feet up in the air. Grow wings?

No, the little window stood tantalizingly close, but also desperately far away.

She sighed.

Her shoulders slumped, and her eyes ticked down from the ceiling.

They landed on the plywood structure.

And that was when she realized . . . it was tall enough.

From the top of the wooden box, you could grab one of the girders. Hand-over-handing it along the steel beam shouldn't be too hard—not much different than obstacles she'd cleared in basic.

The longer she looked, though, the more she realized one of the fans blocked the way. The girders closest to the skylight ran directly above its metal blades. To avoid the fan, you'd need to start on a different girder, travel out the right distance from the structure, and then cross back girder to girder somehow.

Locke tried to gauge the distance between beams.

Three, maybe four feet.

Wider than O-course monkey bars, but still doable. It'd only take a few transitions.

Or . . .

Maybe she could use the fan itself.

The blade tips swung within a few feet of the skylight. She could snag a fan blade at the edge of the plywood structure and let it carry her out. Hell, the ride might even be fun—the world's craziest, elevated merry-go-round.

Locke's heart soared at the idea.

Until Evan shifted in the crook of her arm.

If they stood side by side, he barely rose to her waist. He couldn't possibly do all the climbing and stretching necessary to reach that skylight.

Even worse, she didn't expect she could carry him. Evan probably weighed forty pounds—there was a time she could've run several miles carrying a forty-pound ruck, but not recently. If she tried that . . .

If he slipped, or she dropped him . . .

No.

Too risky. She couldn't possibly take Evan up there. And she certainly wouldn't leave him behind.

Dammit.

Her face burned at the missed opportunity. But, as angry as she was, Locke tried to push the skylight from her mind. There had to be some other way to escape.

The sliding metal door.

It was the only other exit, and now that Huang had returned, it was locked from the inside again. If she waited till the crew fell asleep, she could break her and Evan out of the closet. Then she could pick the locks and they could make a run for it.

Until the ear-piercing screech wakes everyone.

Locke glanced at King, who was riffling through his newspaper. She could picture the Giant bursting from his office, gun blazing. Huang would surely do the same.

Did she really think she could get Evan and herself through the door and get it closed before those guns ripped them to shreds?

Sneaking onto the roof would be so much quieter . . .

Locke drew a deep breath and blew it sharply out her nose.

There had to be a way to use the skylight. There just had to.

One of the Mule's favorite sayings had been *Don't let perfect be the enemy of the good.* Although she'd always hated the phrase, the longer she pondered the skylight, the more Locke thought maybe that was the answer here.

Maybe the secret was *not* escaping.

Instead of worrying about getting all the way free, maybe merely making it onto the roof would be enough. She could create some kind of signal—a fire, or a message. She imagined a helicopter flying over and seeing *H-E-L-P* spelled out. If nothing else, from that height she could search for landmarks. Knowing where she was might yield clues about who was located nearby and how to contact them. Then she could sneak back in before anyone missed her. No leaving Evan behind, but no putting him in harm's way either.

That settled it.

Having a plan allowed her muscles to relax. She rolled her neck until it snap-crackle-popped back into place. She felt so at ease that when Queen emerged from her office and waved her over, Locke didn't even mind.

"Go build some more," she whispered to Evan. "I'll see what she wants."

While Evan plodded back toward the Legos, Locke started for the offices. From a distance, she could see the Pink Punker holding several shopping bags.

Queen raised them above her shoulders and flashed a megawatt smile. "Wait till you see what I picked out!"

Remembering some kind of dress was involved, Locke felt no need to hurry. But her sluggish pace made Queen impatient—the Pink Punker fidgeted until eventually she set the bags at Locke's feet. As Locke drew closer, Queen eyed her up and down, and even her smile disappeared. She squatted and rummaged through the bags.

When Locke finally arrived in front of her, Queen stood and tossed something from inside the bags in Locke's direction in one motion.

Locke caught the object instinctively at her waist. Without looking, her fingers recognized the smooth plastic of a shampoo bottle.

Queen waved a finger at her. "You need that shower before we do anything else. You're—"

Locke's brain finished the sentence with *filthy*. But the word arrived an afterthought—her eyes were locked on Queen's fingers.

Her nails.

That was when Locke realized—she hadn't washed her hands after Queen helped her up earlier. She'd been so excited to go pick the padlocks, she'd completely forgotten.

Locke's stomach dropped, even as her mind raced.

How many times had she touched her face, her eyes, since then? Wasn't that what they'd been warning about on the news? Why bottles of sanitizer had been installed seemingly everywhere in the past few weeks?

Then a real flash of panic struck.

Evan.

They'd just been snuggling against the wall—had she brushed his face with that hand? Or wiped away his tears? She couldn't remember, even as she frantically replayed things in her mind.

Locke turned and sprinted away before Queen could say anything else.

16

As Locke dashed toward the bathrooms, she called to the play area, "Evan!"

He glanced up but didn't move.

She waved frantically at him.

He rose slowly. It took Locke jumping up and down before he started jogging her way.

When he finally reached her, Locke said, "I just remembered—you should have washed your hands after dinner."

"Aw, Momma . . ."

"It's *super* important." She pointed at the door. "Go wash your hands and face. Really well—scrub!"

The look he shot her made the back of Locke's brain cringe at the thought of Evan as a teenager. But for him to have the privilege of showing her that much attitude, he'd need to survive that long.

She *would* get him there. Kicking and screaming, over her shoulder if necessary. She'd sworn that the day he was born.

When Evan still hadn't budged a moment later, Locke felt her nostrils flare. "Go!"

Hanging his head, he trudged through the door.

Once he'd disappeared inside, Locke pushed her way into the women's room. A pang of regret sat heavy in her stomach, but there'd be time to apologize later. Now she just needed to get both of them clean and pray it wasn't too late.

She opened the shower's hot-water tap all the way. The pipes clanged and coughed, but eventually water began hissing from the showerhead.

With no curtain to contain it, spray ricocheted out of the stall and slicked her skin. Locke paid no attention. As fast as she could, she kicked off her sandals and stripped off her sweat-soaked clothes.

When she stepped under the water, it scalded her shoulders, but she resisted the urge to cry out. Biting her lip, she did her best to ignore the stabbing heat and sour metallic smell of the spray and plunged her head backward.

Once her hair was soaked, Locke let the hot water spill down over her forehead, cheeks, and chin. With an initial squirt of shampoo, she scrubbed her hands, forearms, then her entire face. After rinsing that initial lather, Locke repeated the process. Only then, with shampoo stinging her eyes, did she set about washing the rest of her body.

Confident she'd boiled and scoured every square inch, Locke remained under the scalding spray. Part of her wanted to stay there forever—it was the safest she'd felt since before the drive to Malibu.

Locke finally closed the tap. As a final puff of steam wafted to the ceiling, she appreciated Miami's climate for once. Anywhere else, she'd have felt chilled leaving such a sauna.

As soon as she'd congratulated herself on that stroke of luck, though, a new thought dropped her chin to her chest.

No towel.

She didn't know if Queen bought one with the clothes— she hadn't thought to ask before running away.

Stupid, stupid, stupid.

Locke continued kicking herself as she wrung sheets of water from her hair. Listening to the drops pepper the shower floor, she remembered Queen drying her hands earlier. She'd used paper towels.

How many remained in the dispenser?

Locke gazed across to the sink. Two, maybe three steps away.

With a deep breath, she stretched one leg out of the stall. Once she was sure her footing was solid, she shifted her weight onto it. As she considered where to step next, something caught the corner of her eye.

When Locke saw Queen standing there, she yelped and jumped back into the shower.

"Silly girl, you ran off without a towel."

Locke's face flared hotter than it had felt under the spray. She frantically tried to cover herself with her arms and legs, until she ended up squatting in a tight ball at the bottom of the stall.

Above her head, a piece of plush purple terry cloth appeared at the shower mouth. Nothing else visible, only the towel.

"My eyes are closed," Queen said.

Pulse pounding in her ears, Locke wondered whether she could trust the Pink Punker.

Ever so slowly, she stood.

The towel hovered there. Waiting.

"C'mon, take it."

Locke contorted to free her left arm, then inched it toward the purple fabric.

When the towel still didn't move, she shot her hand out and yanked the cloth back into the shower.

"Better?"

Locke covered herself as quickly as she could, then stormed from the stall. "What the fuck—"

Queen's left hand was covering her eyes. She split her fingers now, exposing one baby blue. "I didn't peek, I swear."

Although Queen raised her right hand Scout-style, Locke wasn't sure she believed it. Especially when Queen's mouth curled up in a clever grin.

"Not saying I wasn't tempted. Just that I resisted. Like a good child of the Lord." Queen pressed her hands together and looked skyward.

The saintly sarcasm knocked Locke off guard, and the Pink Punker didn't give her any chance to recover—she just kept talking. "You know . . . you're cute when you're mad. Your face gets all flushed. Now you need something to wear."

Locke stood there stammering, even as Queen shoved a shopping bag toward her with the toe of her boot.

"Hope you like the outfit."

Locke glanced down at the bag.

"Go on. Take a look."

Clutching the towel to her chest with one hand, Locke squatted down and reached into the bag with the other. Although she tensed as she peeled back the paper, the first thing she found inside was a sleeveless linen top. Beneath that, reasonable-looking denim shorts.

"See? I did good, right?"

When Locke glanced up, Queen wore puppy-dog eyes.

"Yeah. But that doesn't—"

The Pink Punker pretend-wiped her brow. "I'm pretty sure I got the sizes right. These were trickier."

She slid a second bag over. When Locke looked inside, she found two bras and multiple pairs of underwear.

"Vickie's runs small, so I got a bunch."

It wasn't the size that worried Locke so much as the style. Even the "conservative" panties were thongs, which she typically avoided. The rest were G-strings, which she absolutely never wore.

She pinched one between her fingers and raised it like a rotten piece of fruit.

"You're gonna want those with the dress."

Locke dropped the narrow slip of fabric back into the bag. "What dress—"

"In my office. Come try it once you're toweled off."

For a moment, Locke worried Queen might offer to help. Thankfully, she turned and strutted out.

Not taking any chances, Locke hauled the bags into one of the toilet stalls and locked the door. The thong she chose wasn't quite comfortable but not as bad as she feared. Certainly not as weird as she imagined the butt-floss would be.

After dressing in the shorts and tank, she combed out her hair with a brush she found with other toiletries in one of the bags, then wrapped the towel around her head. The simple acts of applying deodorant and brushing her teeth left Locke feeling almost completely rejuvenated.

She separated clean and dirty clothes into different bags and returned everything to the janitor's closet. From there, she could see Evan had returned to the play area.

But he wasn't alone.

King knelt next to him.

Locke started in that direction. At a jog that quickly became a sprint.

When the Giant saw her coming, he rose and stalked away. By the time Locke reached Evan, King had disappeared behind the plywood structure.

"Baby, are you okay?" she asked.

Evan nodded without looking up.

"Sure?"

"I'm *fine*."

Locke inhaled deeply. "I'm sorry I yelled before. I just . . ."

Evan's eyes remained glued to his Legos. Without seeing his face, she couldn't quite tell if her words were registering.

"Look, I have to go up front. But once I'm done, I'll come stay with you, okay?"

He still didn't respond. Not knowing what else to say, Locke started for the offices.

Queen greeted her at the door, tapping her palms together in mock clapping. "Fashion time!"

"Yay."

"C'mon, you gotta have a sexy dress for the big night." Queen moved to the back wall, where matching garment bags now hung side by side. She unzipped the right-hand bag, revealing a sequined, emerald gown. "I figured this color would set off your hair and your eyes. Oh, and wait till you see the shoes . . ."

Locke hadn't noticed how fast Queen talked until now, words spilling from her mouth in staccato bursts. "Why do I even need . . . that?"

While her high school classmates picked out prom dresses, Locke had learned to arc-weld with tungsten gas. Kori was the only person who'd ever managed to get Locke into a dress. Few enough times to count on one hand.

Queen raised an eyebrow. "You think Billionaire Guy is having us over for chicken wings on the pool deck? It's a *party*. A rich-people party. We've got to blend in."

Locke wondered how much blending she could do in a skirt that short.

"Try it," Queen said, passing the hanger over. "If it doesn't fit, I can alter it."

Locke stared back at her.

"What?"

"Um, privacy?"

Queen rolled her eyes. "You're wearing underwear. It's no different than seeing you at the beach."

"I don't go to the beach."

The Pink Punker bared her bottom teeth. "Fine. Call me when it's on."

Locke waited until the door latch clicked, then moved behind it for additional cover. Once she started messing with the dress, though, she wished she'd asked Queen to explain how to climb into the damn thing. Both sleeveless and strapless—did you put it over your head? Step in and pull it up?

Neither approach worked.

Finally, she found a small, underarm zipper. That bought her enough room to wriggle in.

Once she had the dress on, Locke thought about opening the door, but the knob sat several inches past her reach. Unsure she could move that far without splitting a seam, she yelled instead.

The Pink Punker reappeared in the doorway and let out a wolfish howl. "Do you know how hot you look?"

"All I know is . . . I'm scared to breathe."

"Girl, every person on that boat is gonna want to *devour* you."

"I thought we were supposed to blend in."

Queen snorted. "You and I are a distraction. And you are going to distract everyone in that."

The way Queen was staring made Locke even more self-conscious. "Is your dress this short?"

"No. But I've got stubby little legs." Queen's eyes slithered down to Locke's toes, then slowly worked their way back up. "Yours are like ten miles long."

Locke's cheeks flushed.

When Queen stepped the rest of the way into the room and shut the door, Locke became acutely aware of how cornered she was.

Forgetting about the dress, Locke tried to breathe. But all the oxygen seemed to have been sucked out of the room.

When Queen's hands reached toward Locke's face, her heart clenched.

Locke had only been kissed a half dozen times in her life, including once here in Miami. The only kiss that had ever mattered. The intense tingle on the back of her neck screamed it was about to happen again.

Every nerve ending fired at once, blurring her thoughts. Locke rocked a half step backward, but Queen's fingers— and those long, pink nails—kept coming.

Although she towered over Queen, Locke felt helpless. Paralyzed.

Queen's face hovered inches below her own. Close enough Locke could make out flecks of gray in her blue irises. The individual strands of hair on either side of her eyebrow slit. Every wrinkle and pucker in her lips.

When Queen's nails finally grazed Locke's temples, they delivered tiny jolts of electricity. Locke sucked in a tiny gasp.

"Nervous?" Queen asked. "Being this close?"

Locke couldn't decide whether Queen's voice had dropped to a whisper or her own ears weren't working. Either way, she found it impossible to respond.

Queen's lips spread into a confident smile. "Been a while, hasn't it?"

Locke guessed the Pink Punker meant the pandemic, but it had been far longer than that. Years longer.

Too long.

When Locke tried to swallow, she found her throat blocked.

Queen's fingers dislodged the towel, which tumbled to the floor. Then, gently, she worked them into Locke's hair. When her sharp fingernails traced Locke's scalp, the skin still sensitive from the scalding shower, it sent shock waves down Locke's spine.

Gradually, Queen smoothed Locke's tresses, separating one section at a time, sweeping it to one side, and draping it down Locke's bare shoulder. Each time another lock fell against Locke's skin, the impact echoed through her.

She told herself to breathe, not remembering the last breath she'd taken.

When Queen was done arranging her hair, she stepped back. "That's it—that's the look. Add a little wave, it'll be smokin'."

Locke's head was swimming. But even as Queen continued manipulating her hair, Locke saw an opening she hadn't noticed before. A ray of sunlight cutting through the fog.

She glanced around for effect. "Do you have a mirror?"

"Only one is in the bathroom," Queen said. "But you don't wanna—"

"No, not in this. I just wish I could see it. Can I borrow your phone?"

17

As Queen reached behind her, Locke's heart fluttered. She couldn't believe the Pink Punker might actually offer up the cell.

Now she needed time alone with it.

When Queen passed the phone over, Locke scanned herself with the selfie camera, searching for something she could use.

"Oooooh, you're right. This looks so . . . oh, crap."

"What?" Queen asked.

"Tangle." Locke raised a frizzy patch of hair.

"No biggie. Where's the brush?"

"In the closet." Locke took a half step toward the door. "I'll—"

"No!" Queen blocked her path. "That dress is not going *anywhere* near that . . . filth. I'll go."

"You sure?" Locke asked. "I hate to make you—"

"Back in two shakes."

Locke had to work hard to suppress her smile as Queen disappeared through the door. Forget climbing to the roof; this would make calling for help infinitely easier. But she'd have only a minute.

Exiting the camera, Locke scanned the home screen icons. But Queen had about a thousand apps, collected into folders with nonsense names. Finally, in one marked "Road Trip," she found the Maps application. When she opened it, the usual blue dot marked her location, but none of the surroundings filled in. No roads, no landmarks.

The dot stood alone on a featureless, unmarked grid.

Locke zoomed in and out, moved the map with her finger. Nothing helped.

A quick glance showed Queen had already reached the restrooms.

Locke tried one more trick, requesting directions to Miami Beach. But a spinning dial showed the program going nowhere.

Realizing she'd burned half her time already, Locke exited Maps and went to the phone. She dialed 911 and held the device to her ear.

Nothing.

Not a sound.

She waited several seconds, then checked it. An error message said the phone couldn't connect.

Queen reappeared now at the corner near the closet, hairbrush in hand.

Locke racked her brain—if the phone didn't work, maybe the internet would. She jumped into the browser and typed the website that hosted her work email, cursing her thick thumbs each time she made an error. When she finished, she pressed enter, but the browser remained blank. No page popped up.

At this point, every heartbeat was a clock tick. Another step bringing Queen closer.

Locke tried one final website: a veterans' bulletin board she sometimes visited. Again, nothing.

"Found it!"

Locke's eyes rose and saw Queen drawing up to the door, holding the hairbrush like a trophy. Without looking back down, Locke typed a few more keys, praying her thumbs would hit the correct letters for once.

"Whatcha doin'?" Although the question sounded innocent, Queen's gaze was locked on Locke's hands.

"Searching for a picture. I got to go to the Oscars once, and J.Lo. had her hair done over one shoulder—I wanted to show you."

Queen grunted. "You won't get anywhere with that. Huang fucked with my phone."

"What?"

"When I got here, he said I couldn't keep it unless I let him mess with it. I've got no cell, no Wi-Fi."

Locke blinked. "But . . . I've seen you . . ."

"I've been scrolling through old stuff. Photos, shit like that."

Queen extended an open palm.

After a long moment, Locke set the phone onto it.

* * *

Locke went through the motions of brushing out the tangle and trying on the remaining accessories. Although Queen was totally enamored with the shoes and the clutch, Locke didn't care in the slightest—she fidgeted through the end of the fashion show, then escaped the office as fast as she could.

On her walk back to the workspace, she stole a glance up at the skylight. For a minute there, she'd really thought she'd be able to dial her way out of this mess, but now . . .

Now that little window was her and Evan's only chance.

She wasn't completely convinced she could trust Jack—how could he possibly know the skylight opened? And, while she hoped she'd earned his trust by taking on King, was that really enough? The sound in Jack's voice when he'd talked about Hong Kong, that was real. If Huang was his ticket back there, would Jack really mess with that by helping her?

Huang had humiliated Jack several times. Hitting him where it hurt most—his ego about his cooking. Was that enough to get Jack to flip?

Ultimately, there was no way to know for sure. And the truth was, it didn't really matter—the roof had to be real, because she didn't have any other choice.

When she reached her workspace, Locke looked over to Evan. He was sprawled across a beanbag, flipping through comics. Part of her said she should go apologize again. She didn't want them fighting, not now. But remembering how upset he'd gotten, she decided to give him more space.

That meant taking another run at the Ticonderoga's digital lock.

Locke decided to focus on the external power connector she'd found before dinner. In an upper drawer of the rolling toolbox, she found a pen flashlight. Realizing that might come in handy, she slipped it into her shorts pocket. Two drawers down, she found all manner of batteries. The safe's connector cap needed a nine-volt—she was relieved to find a two-pack of those at the back of the drawer.

Before connecting the battery, Locke set a combination on the digital lock. Another easy one, 10-20-30-40-50. She also pulled out the AAs to make sure her nine-volt was the only power source. Then she turned to the oscilloscope.

Oscilloscopes reminded Locke of Dr. Frankenstein's laboratory. Roughly the size of a dresser drawer, encased in a thick metal shell, the box weighed a ton. Half of its face was consumed by a green-tinted screen, while the rest was covered in more dials and buttons than you'd find in an airplane cockpit. A pair of cables extended from the base of the machine, ending in probes that looked like miniature knitting needles—long, thin, with a tiny metal hook on the end.

Back in the army, Kori had taught Locke to connect probes like these to tiny wires inside radios and other gizmos that needed fixing. By attaching the little hooks to two different places in a circuit, you got a glimpse of the electrical activity between those points. A glowing white line would appear on the screen, tracing a shape to show how voltage or current was changing over time—like one of those heart monitors in an old-fashioned movie that slowly ticked down as someone died, *beep . . . beep . . . beep . . . beeeeeeeeeeeep.* Thankfully, this scope not only let you zoom in and out, but it also had a memory feature, so you could record traces and look back at them later.

Locke hooked the probes onto the wires leading into the Ticonderoga's battery cap, then snapped the cap onto the nine-volt. When she touched the keypad screen, it lit up, ready to go.

At least the battery worked.

To see what kind of signal a correct combination entry generated, she pressed a 1 and then a 0. Then, to compare that with a wrong number, she deliberately entered a 2 followed by a 5.

On the oscilloscope, the trace of 10 looked like two heartbeats—the line started off flat, then jumped straight up, jiggled a little bit, and dropped back down before doing it all over again. But when she displayed the trace of 25, it looked awfully similar to 10.

By twisting some dials, she managed to superimpose the two traces—sure enough, the electrical patterns matched.

But if those signals were the same, then connecting to the external power port wouldn't help her decipher the combination at all.

Locke ran several more tests, adjusted all the scope's settings. Each time, the result was the same. Every button press looked identical.

Her head fell back against her shoulders. This was what she'd feared when Huang showed her the box this morning—there simply weren't many tricks to try.

I hate electronics.

Staring up at the ceiling, Locke's eyes drifted to the skylight again.

If she could get onto the roof tonight, her inability to open the safe might not matter. If she signaled for help and the cavalry came . . .

If Jack was on the level . . .

If she didn't get caught . . .

An awful lot of ifs.

Her head slumped to the right. In the play area, Evan had contorted himself further, his head nearly flat on the floor, feet straight up in the air. He was still looking at comics, holding the book up toward the ceiling. She wondered how that could possibly be comfortable, how all the blood didn't drain into his head.

Locke swallowed hard against a lump that swelled in her throat.

If Huang grew angry with her, if he sensed she was failing, Evan was the one he'd punish.

Images flashed through her mind—all the times Evan had gotten seriously hurt. Twisting his ankle in the yard, skinning his knee on the gravel driveway. The time he'd sliced open his finger trying to make her Mother's Day breakfast while she was still asleep.

Always the same expression on his face. Eyes scrunched so tight they disappeared. Mouth as wide as the entrance to the Figueroa Street tunnels. And the noise he could make—a shriek that stabbed your ears. That ricocheted around inside your skull.

Locke's lip quivered.

All this was her fault, every little bit.

She never should have brought that stupid box home. Never should have taken the Malibu job in the first place. She'd held on for several weeks without working; what was a little more time?

Besides, no good parent would have left their kid that morning, not midpandemic. Not when every minute of news the past few weeks had been plague and death. Really, how dumb could she be?

Locke broke her gaze away from Evan, but that didn't stop her eyes from filling. As she turned back to the safe, the keypad's green glow mocked her.

If she couldn't get it open . . .

If Huang started in on Evan . . .

Enough.

Back in high school, it had taken her three months after that first attempt to finally open the Mule's classroom safe. Twelve weeks of spinning that stupid dial every day. Tuning out taunts from the stoners and the rejects. Slowly figuring out how the wheel worked and what it was trying to tell her.

But she'd done it—what no one else had ever managed to do.

She could still feel the satisfying click of the handle as it turned. The stiffness and smell of the hundred-dollar bill as she picked it up and stuffed it in her pocket.

When she turned around, every mouth in shop class had hung wide open.

Except one.

The Mule was beaming.

The biggest, happiest, proudest smile she'd ever seen on anyone.

Picturing that now, Locke gritted her teeth. She wiped her eyes on her shoulders, leaving wet stains on the linen.

This fucking box is not *going to beat me.*

But she didn't have three months. What the hell else could she try *right now*?

This morning, she'd made progress by having access to the inside of the box. If listening to the electric signals from outside the safe was no use, maybe the back side of the door would help. She couldn't do that on the boat, but if she tried it here, maybe she'd discover something.

Leaving the nine-volt connected, Locke detached the oscilloscope probes and then swung the door wide open. She clipped the curled tips onto the circuit board, but that process took long enough that when she swung the door closed again, the keypad screen had darkened. She woke it by touching it, then repeated the tests she'd run earlier, entering a valid combination number followed by an incorrect one.

The traces that popped up on the scope didn't look much different than before.

Locke zoomed out all the way until she could see the tiny blip where she'd woken up the screen in addition to the heartbeat-type signal from the button presses. Once again, superimposing the traces showed they were identical. Each key used exactly the same amount of power, and that signal didn't change before it got inside the chips.

From what Locke understood, that meant the processor chip was doing all the work. Not just pulling the combination from memory and deciding whether to open the lock— these power readings meant the processor was also figuring out which buttons she'd pushed. Because she couldn't see inside the chip, she had absolutely no way to read the combination. It was impenetrable.

Although Locke had been standing throughout the testing, she dropped into one of the folding chairs. Her arms hung limp at her sides.

She sat motionless for several moments. Until something touched her back.

Locke's head whipped around to find Evan, who looked as startled as she felt. "What's wrong, sweetie?"

"I'm tired." He yawned as if to demonstrate. "When's bedtime?"

She rose to her feet. "Now's good."

"Yes, now is very good." Huang's voice.

Locke spotted him marching across the floor, followed by the others.

"We have come to see your progress, Ms. Locke."

18

HUANG WORE THE same slick smile as when he'd greeted Locke at the law office. The one she longed to remove forcibly from his face.

"Now?" she asked. "Really?"

"At this time tomorrow, we will be aboard the *Helios*."

"Evan needs sleep." She had no idea if the poor kid would be able to drift off, but he needed to try. And she needed to avoid answering too many questions about the safe.

Stopping at the sawhorses, Huang asked, "Evan, am I correct that there are things you do each night before bedtime?"

Locke had sensed Evan drawing closer to her hip as the crew approached. Now his arm slid around the back of her thigh. "Yeah."

"Like . . . brush your teeth?"

"Uh-huh."

Huang spoke over his shoulder to Jack and King. "Why don't you two get Evan started on his nighttime routine? Ms. Locke can join him once she demonstrates her handiwork."

As the two men stepped in front of Huang, Evan's arms clamped around Locke's leg. She looked down to find him staring up at her, shaking his head.

The fear in his eyes stabbed at Locke's heart. Especially after catching King near Evan earlier, she wasn't crazy about sending him away with the Giant. But given how angry Huang was likely to be, getting Evan elsewhere might be the safest thing.

She crouched down and pressed a kiss on his forehead. Then she hugged him, her head on the opposite side from Huang so she could whisper in his ear. "I know you're scared. But it'll be okay."

When she pulled away, he shook his head again. He seized the shoulders of her blouse.

The tears welling in Evan's eyes tightened Locke's throat.

"Come on, boy-o," Jack said. "Let your momma work."

Evan remained rooted to his spot. After another moment, King stomped forward, seized the back of the boy's shirt, and hoisted him up toward his massive shoulder.

Even in midair, Evan clung to Locke, dragging her along. With his face mere inches from hers, she had no choice but to look directly into his eyes.

They pled, *Don't let this happen*.

The look was painful enough. But remembering the last time she'd seen those eyes filled with such pain and fear nearly made her crumple to the floor.

Five years ago, when her heart broke.

She'd been just as helpless then. Only it was the doctors dragging her away.

Locke put her hands over Evan's and squeezed them. Trying to transfer whatever strength she could for what was about to happen.

Mouthing "I'm sorry," she pried his little fingers off the fabric.

Evan flailed his arms, but King raised the boy the rest of the way up to his shoulder. Then the Giant turned and started for the bathrooms, even as Evan writhed and kicked and screamed.

Locke squeezed her eyes shut and clamped her hands over her ears.

It didn't help. She flinched at every noise he made.

"You should teach the boy better manners."

Locke assumed Huang was making some kind of sick joke. But when she pried her eyes open, his nasty expression lit a fire inside her. "Gee, I'm sorry. We've never been kidnapped before. I'll be sure to work on that for next time."

Huang's eyebrows jumped. Behind him, Queen winced.

Locke continued glaring at him.

After a brief staring contest, Huang set his jaw and pointed to the safe.

Drawing a deep breath and ordering her pulse to slow down, Locke stepped to the box. "I'll set a random combination on the dial—"

"No." Huang turned to Queen. "You set it."

The Pink Punker's eyes darted to Locke.

She waved an open hand at the box. *Knock yourself out.*

As Queen stepped forward, Locke turned her head. She wasn't gonna let Huang accuse her of cheating.

He was already staring at his Rolex when Queen finished. Locke had barely a second to prepare herself before he called, "Go!"

She moved to the dial and spun right five times to pick up all the wheels. Sensing the others staring—she didn't usually have an audience—she closed her eyes to focus on her fingertips.

Within seconds, she felt the same slight disturbance she'd noticed earlier. The first notch. Checking the dial, she knew the actual combination digit lay two digits further. She made a mental note, then started back to the left.

Locke quickly found the remaining four notches. Although there were still 120 ways to arrange the five combination numbers, she knew most people went low-to-high or high-to-low. Especially in a pinch.

She tried those two sequences first. After high-to-low, the handle turned.

Locke turned back to her audience.

"Two minutes forty-two seconds." When Huang glanced up from his watch, he grinned so broadly his cheeks gathered into shiny pink apples. "Excellent. Now the digital."

"I haven't solved that one yet," Locke said.

His cheeks deflated. "We have less than twenty-four hours—"

"I know. I'm doing my best. But—"

"Are you? Or are you wasting time, thinking I am easily fooled?"

"You don't understand—"

"I *understand*"—Huang's voice rose to drown her out—"that someone of your skill should be able to accomplish this simple task. And I *understand* that if you are not properly motivated, I will find other ways to . . . inspire you."

The daggers his dark eyes shot sent a chill down Locke's spine.

That feeling only worsened when Jack reappeared. "Evan's asking for you, Ace."

Locke's heart rose into her throat. Her gaze fixed on Huang.

He seemed to revel in that. Huang crossed his arms and pushed out his lower lip. He stood that way for a long, silent moment.

Her hands fidgeted. Not because that's what Huang wanted, although she knew it was, but because she couldn't help herself.

Finally, Huang waved his hand dismissively. "Go now. Tomorrow, no more games."

Forcing herself to give a compliant nod, Locke started for the closet. After several steps, she felt someone nearby and turned to find Jack jogging to keep up with her long strides.

"He's okay. I got him calmed down."

Jack's words didn't relieve the uneasy feeling in her stomach. And when King's shadow moved in the closet doorway, she broke into an all-out sprint.

Locke pushed her way inside the tiny room, rushed to Evan, and wrapped him in her arms. "Are you all right? I'm so sorry I—"

"It's okay, Momma."

She pulled away and looked him over.

"I brushed my teeth. And I washed my face."

Only now did Locke realize he was sitting on an inflated air mattress like those she'd seen in the offices. "Where—"

"He gave it to us."

Locke's eyes followed Evan's finger back to the doorway. Jack was sliding in as King stalked out.

"Thank you," she said. Anything to help Evan sleep tonight was a godsend. And the way Jack had treated the boy gave her hope that he really did want to help them.

"No problem." Jack gave her another gentle smile.

"Momma—"

Evan tugged on her arm, but she gave him a sharp look that reminded him not to interrupt.

"I hope you both can sleep," Jack said. "Might be a bit noisy, but I imagine things'll calm down in an hour. Maybe . . . two." His eyebrows rose at the last word. Then he stepped back and shut the door. The handle locked with a click.

Although Locke picked up on Jack's signal, knowing how long to wait was worthless without some kind of clock. Two hours—she couldn't count that many seconds or minutes without losing track. And she didn't see any way Evan would let her concentrate that long.

As if to prove the point, he asked, "Do I *have* to go to sleep?"

Locke muffled a sigh. "You said you were tired."

"Not anymore."

"We both need rest. Lay down, close your eyes."

She returned to the door and flipped the switch to extinguish the overhead bulb. Evan's skin squeaked against the plastic as he shifted on the mattress in the dark.

Like the night before, enough light trickled through the louvered panel at the bottom of the door to keep the interior from blackening completely. Locke leaned against the wall and slid to the floor. From here, she could peek through the slats and know when the main lights were turned off.

To kill time, Locke started visualizing the tasks she'd confront on the way to the skylight. In her mind, she'd just begun picking the door lock when Evan said, "Momma?"

"What?"

"I can't sleep."

Locke took a deep breath. "I know it's hard. But you need to keep trying."

More rustling and squeaking let her return her gaze to the louvers.

"Momma?"

"What now?"

"We're gonma be okay, right?"

"We'll be fine. I've got a plan."

After another pause, he said, "There's something you should know. About the mattress. It wasn't—"

"Tell me tomorrow, okay? Go to sleep."

Locke regretted the clipped tone that creeped into her voice. But she didn't want to apologize and start another discussion. She just needed Evan to go to sleep. And stay that way, at least for a while.

Trying to make the room as quiet as possible, Locke held her breath the way she had when Evan was a baby. Praying the silence would continue one more second. Then another. And another.

Once she finally lost count of the passing moments, she allowed herself to exhale.

Sitting on the floor grew increasingly uncomfortable. No matter how she positioned her legs, her feet were getting tingly. Her back ached, her shoulders were knotted. Oddest of all, her butt was freezing after losing heat to the concrete.

Still, the lighting outside hadn't changed. And she didn't dare risk moving too much in case it disturbed Evan.

Locke leaned her head and shoulder against the doorframe. That took some stress off her spine and lifted one cheek off the ground.

Curious what she could hear, she pressed an ear to the door. The wood hummed faintly.

To focus on the sound, Locke closed her eyes. Once they were shut, though, she found them impossible to pry back open. Between the darkness and the steady humming, her thoughts started to drift.

Her mind slipped away for a moment.

When it returned, Locke bolted upright.

Her eyes darted to the mattress.

Evan lay still, breathing deeply. While she could still make out his silhouette, the dim lighting had changed. A quick look out the louvers showed the main lights were off.

How long had she been dozing?

No way to know. And no help from her body clock—it could be midnight or just before dawn.

Which meant she had no time to lose.

The concrete had stiffened her muscles, making standing a struggle. Once she was upright, she slipped out of her flip-flops and stepped gingerly toward the rear of the closet.

The air mattress lay at the base of the shelves, meaning she had to reach up and over Evan to retrieve the bobby pins. Unsteady on her tiptoes, she patted her palm along the top shelf, feeling for the clips.

Not finding them, Locke took a small step to the right. As she did, her foot grazed the side of the mattress.

She froze.

Beneath her, Evan shifted.

Locke held her breath, even as her lungs began to burn. She strained to see his face, whether his eyes were open.

When he finally snored, she exhaled. A few inches farther down the shelf, her fingers found the pile of metal clips.

She hurried to the door while flexing the tines of one bobby pin open and closed. After several bends, the narrow metal strip snapped like a wishbone, leaving her with a piece in either hand. She inserted the straight half into the base of the key slot. That let her turn the lock cylinder ever so slightly to pressure the spring-loaded tumblers. Then she started fishing the zigzag piece in and out of the key slot's upper edge. Each time she bumped into one of the metal teeth, she'd back off slightly, angle the pin downward, and push deeper. Once she got underneath the tumbler, she could nudge it up and out of the way.

After clearing a half dozen that way, the tension against the straight piece of bobby pin disappeared—she could turn the lock exactly as if she'd inserted a key.

Locke twisted ninety degrees. The lock gave way with a metallic clack. In the silence, it sounded like a sledgehammer.

She glanced back at Evan.

Although her own heart pounded, this time he didn't flinch.

She eased the door open. Finding nothing behind it, she stepped through on tiptoes. Compared to the closet floor, the polished concrete felt smooth and cool—almost slick. The space was much darker than it had been the previous night. The safety lighting had been extinguished; no moonlight leaked through the windows. That rendered the plywood structure a featureless black monolith in the middle of the floor.

Above it, she could see the motion of the fans more than the blades themselves. But a quick check of the skylight showed the little window still there, a patch of navy sky against the otherwise darkened ceiling.

As Locke started for the structure, she remembered the flashlight in her pocket. She'd only envisioned using it inside the box, but she didn't want to trip over something stupid getting there. Still, the light would be a huge giveaway out in the open. Even worse, white light would ruin her night vision.

Then she had an idea.

Sneaking back into the closet, Locke quietly rummaged through the shopping bags until she found the piece she'd remembered. Back outside, she eased the closet door closed. Then she pulled the flashlight from her pocket and stretched the fabric over the lens.

When she pointed the light at the floor and clicked it on, her plan worked perfectly—the red satin thong Queen had purchased was translucent enough that it acted like one of the filter caps they used to put on flashlights in the army. Red light didn't wipe your night vision, and a quick test confirmed she could look from its red circle on the floor to any other detail without losing focus.

Armed with the lingerie light, Locke started for the structure with delicate steps.

She paused at the corner of the bathrooms.

The offices to her left stood dark, doors closed. Locke cocked an ear but heard nothing.

If falling asleep herself had any upside, this was it— hopefully the whole crew was lost in dreamland.

With another quiet breath, she started forward again. Panning her light to the structure, she started to think through her climb to the top.

When the white light blinded her, it caught her totally by surprise.

19

THE LIGHT STRUCK Locke from the left, the same direction as the offices she'd just checked. The tight white beam caught her so off guard it seemed to pack a physical punch—it staggered her a half step to the right.

Otherwise, she froze. Picturing Huang and his pistol behind the light, she squinted and started to raise her hands.

Before they reached her shoulders, the white light disappeared. She was plunged back into darkness, her night vision completely erased.

"Enjoy your precious beauty sleep, princess?"

Even whispered, Jack's brogue cut through the darkness.

"You waited?"

"I'm the one who told you about the blasted skylight, ain't I? But my turn on watch was supposed to end twenty minutes ago—I kinna wait forever."

Locke blinked. Trying to get her vision back, wishing she could see his face.

"Don't just stand there," he hissed. "Move your arse!"

Still working to clear afterimages from her eyes, she shuffled toward the structure as best she could. The lingerie light helped—its glowing red circle created a target to aim for.

Jack's anger caught her off guard, but she took it as
another sign that he was on the level—if he hadn't cared
about her getting caught, why risk his own neck by extend-
ing his watch?

When Locke reached the corner of the giant box, she
pressed her hand against it. Although rough to the touch,
the massive plywood wall felt solid and reassuring. Counting
the seconds, she continued forward, following the structure
to her right and trailing her fingers along the wood to keep
contact. Eventually, the familiar staircase loomed as a jagged
shadow ahead.

Panning her beam over the steps, she found the wooden
risers looked sturdier in the dark. Not that it mattered
much—she'd have climbed a greased rope at this point.

As Locke started upward, she immediately regretted going barefoot. On each new stair, splinters jabbed at
her soles. When she finally reached the upper landing, she
allowed herself a deep breath before ducking into the box.

The door opened into a claustrophobic hallway that
stretched farther forward than the lingerie light could pen-
etrate. The walls were narrower than her outstretched arms;
the ceiling hung only a few inches overhead. Door-shaped
rectangles had been spray-painted on both sets of sidewalls,
the word CREW written over each one. The entire place smelled
of sawdust, adding to the sense that she'd been enclosed in
some kind of coffin.

As tight as it was for her, Locke wondered how King
shoehorned himself in here. Or how he managed to pry himself back out.

All the plywood panels had rough-cut edges, making
it easy to spot the seams between them. Worried equally
about noise and more splinters, Locke did her best to step
only where the floorboards were nailed down. She followed
the hallway like that—planting one foot on a safe spot, then
hauling the rest of her body over to it.

After several yards, the lingerie light revealed a left turn ahead. Locke approached the corner like she'd learned in basic, flashlight out front as if it were her old M9 pistol.

Quickly, she realized this wasn't another full passage, just an alcove. But inside it, stairs led up and down.

Locke started upward, testing each riser before applying her weight. At the top, she emerged in a room too large for her little lingerie light to fully illuminate.

Panning the beam around, she saw no other staircases, no markings to help identify where she was. Even weirder, the direction in which she'd been traveling was now blocked by a wall—all the open space stretched behind her, back the way she'd come.

As Locke backtracked, she discovered much of the room was filled with cartons shrink-wrapped together in various shapes. She assumed these were meant to represent furniture or fixtures—she navigated between them, alternating the light between what lay at her feet and what loomed in the distance.

Finally, the far wall came into view. She swept her light in both directions. After finding nothing to her left, she looked back right and discovered a hole in the ceiling.

A wooden ladder descended from it.

Locke wove her way to the base of the ladder. Although its rungs looked sturdy, the hole overhead was so dark she had no way of knowing what awaited her on the next level.

Pocketing the flashlight, she started upward. In total darkness, she had to find each new rung by blind feel, a painstaking process.

When she reached the top of the ladder, Locke hauled herself up to sit on the edge of the hole. She retrieved the lingerie light to check her surroundings.

Yet again, this level was constructed differently from those below it. She was sitting in a small alcove that opened into a hallway stretching to either side. Unlike all the right-angled rooms she'd encountered so far, the walls here were curved, creating the sense of a singular, undulating passage. Both the interior and exterior walls were painted with more door outlines. She quick-counted at least a dozen, but none bore names like those she'd seen below.

Although the plywood floor beneath her was solid, Locke felt like her head was spinning. The overwhelming darkness and inconsistent layout were disorienting. Eventually she would need to find her way back through this thing, but she worried whether she could.

Don't worry about backward. Just worry about up.

The problem was, the ladder ended at this level. She'd have to find another way. And the clock in her head was screaming now—she had no idea how long she'd taken to reach this point.

Drawing her legs up through the hole, Locke climbed to her feet and followed the passage around to the right. Although she kept the light trained in front of her, the curved walls kept her from seeing too far ahead. She moved faster, ignoring the splinters, until finally she spotted an upward staircase.

Eager to make up time, she ran right onto the risers, skipping steps as she went. Although she slowed at the top to get her bearings, for once the layout repeated—another curved hallway.

Even better, a ladder extended upward just a few yards away.

She dashed to it and shined the lingerie light upward. Through a hole in the plywood, she could see a black girder against the white ceiling.

The roof!

Something flashed across the opening, causing Locke to retreat a step.

A second later, something moved again. Then again.

All in the same direction.

The fan blades.

A small sigh escaped her lips. Only a few feet and several wooden dowels separated her from what she'd been eyeing all day. Still, she reminded herself that the hardest part of reaching the skylight remained ahead.

When Locke reached the top of the ladder, she poked only her head up through the hole at first. Although she expected the air to feel hotter here, the fans were more powerful than she'd realized—a blade swooped by overhead, its deep hum followed by a huge gust that tousled hair across her face.

Locke scurried the rest of the way up and knelt beside the ladder. After corralling her hair into a loose knot, she retrieved the lingerie light from her pocket and shined it at the edge of the structure.

Darkness made the five stories to the floor seem like ten. And while she told herself this wasn't much taller than obstacles she'd climbed in basic, whenever the fan sent a burst of air rushing past her, she felt like she might topple over the side.

Locke raised her eyes to the fan blades, then glanced out to the girders. Thankfully, the white background of the ceiling made the black beams more visible in the dim light. She'd be able to see where she was going, even without the lingerie light.

But now a new worry crept in: could the fan support her weight?

From below, she'd never questioned it—the metal blades looked strong and sturdy. Up close, though, they were awfully thin.

Still, with the motor positioned above the edge of the structure, riding one of the twelve-foot blades out to its farthest point would deliver her to within feet of the skylight. Once she transitioned from the blade to the girder, a couple of hand-over-hand passes and she'd be there.

Shortening the trip was a chance worth taking.

Locke shimmied along the wooden edge, measuring herself against the fan blades each time one swung by. Once she'd positioned herself beneath the very tip, she tucked the light away and began breathing deeply.

The extra oxygen didn't dampen the electricity crackling across her skin. After another fly-by, she jabbed her left hand straight up to await the next blade.

A deep hum forecasted its approach.

Locke tensed as the metal strip swung into view.

A moment later, she felt a sharp smack against her palm.

The blade hit much harder than she expected—the metal stung her hand, slapping it away.

Even after the impact, though, Locke kept her eyes locked on the blade. It was still so close.

Right there.

Rising up on tiptoes, she made a hook with her fingers and swung her arm up from below, figuring she could snag the front edge of the metal strip.

But the blade was turning too fast.

Her fingers found nothing but air and the metal sheet slipped away into the darkness.

When Locke realized she'd missed, time froze. She glanced down—although her toes still clung to the edge of the structure, her head, her whole body seemed to have slipped out past it.

As gravity grabbed hold, a wave of cold panic washed over her.

Locke did the only thing she could think of—she kept swinging her arm. With every bit of power she could muster, she forced it up and over past vertical, then back toward the structure.

The arm pulled her shoulders behind it, and Locke spun back toward the edge. She leaned as hard as she could in that direction, praying her center of gravity would end up somewhere safe.

The momentum saved her. Barely.

She wound up collapsed into a tight squat. Although the balls of her feet gripped the edge, she could sense exactly where the wood ended. And how her heels hung back into empty space.

Locke clenched every muscle just to hold herself in place. There didn't seem to be any room to breathe, no space for her heart to beat. Balanced so precariously, she could feel gravity alternately nudging her forward and back. A tug of war to see which way she'd fall.

As the tension in her chest grew unbearable, Locke threw her head forward as hard as she could.

That sent her tumbling onto the wooden roof. She sprawled onto her stomach before rolling flat onto her back.

Finally free to breathe, her lungs began panting uncontrollably. Her muscles twitched and shook with every thump of her pulse.

Oh my god, oh my god, oh my god.

The gust of air from the next fan blade spilled down over her skin and left Locke shivering. Only then did she realize she was soaked with sweat.

She watched several blades whiz by overhead, alternately thankful and amazed she'd survived.

Locke rolled onto her side.

Can't . . . do that . . . again.

The fan might be suicide. But she couldn't climb down empty-handed either. At this point, she had to get out that skylight onto the roof—it was her and Evan's only hope.

Evan.

Picturing his face pushed her back up to her feet.

Once she was upright, Locke tried to shake the heaviness out of her arms and legs. She inched her way back to the edge and then along it until she was well out from under the fan blades. Positioning herself beneath one of the other girders, she wiped her palms up and down the denim shorts, trying to get them as dry as she could.

Then she took two quick steps and jumped straight up.

The girder hung only a couple feet above her outstretched arms—an easy jump-and-catch without the fan interfering. The bottom lip of the girder was flat, though, which forced her to hook her fingers over the top of it instead of clamping around it with her thumb. It made her grip slightly less certain, and she knew her forearms would tire faster than she'd like.

To work her way around the fan, she'd have to hand-over-hand her way down this girder, transition to its neighbor, and then over one more. Twenty yards, maybe two dozen max.

Like monkey bars. Just swing back and forth.

Locke stretched forward with her right arm, made sure she got a solid grip with that hand, then let go with the left and brought it around.

Once she got moving, the fear from her near fall melted away. The Fort Jackson record for female pull-ups had been fifteen before Locke arrived for basic training and twenty-three when she'd left. She'd surely lost some shoulder since then, but her arms still packed plenty of power. And for once, the darkness worked in her favor—unable to see what lay below, she could keep her focus on her fingers.

After five or six hand passes, she'd made it about half-way down the girder. Locke was reaching forward with her left hand again, her fingers just inches from the catch, when white light bathed her from below.

It looked like the same beam Jack had shined on her before.

What the fuck?

Not looking down at the light, Locke wasn't blinded by it, not completely. But black shadows were suddenly playing all over the ceiling as she swung. They made it harder to aim—when her fingers grabbed at the girder, they only grazed it.

After missing the catch, Locke's left arm fell to her side. Her body, having swung all the way forward, now started to swing back.

Locke worried all that downward momentum might pull the rest of her with it.

She squeezed tighter with her right hand.

Her grip held. But even after her arm absorbed the impact, the realization that she was now hanging five stories up by four fingers caused her heart to slide into her throat.

Locke gritted her teeth and shook off the panic. She'd hung by one arm plenty of times. Making sure she had a solid grip with her right hand, she drew in a deep breath and shot her left hand upward.

Once that locked on, she felt better. Although now she could feel lactic acid starting to burn in her right shoulder and arm.

Locke swung her hips once, twice, and on the third swing, she flung her foot up to the girder. Hooking it through one of the triangular trusses took some of the pressure off her arms. Enough that she could finally figure out what the fuck Jack was doing with the flashlight.

Clamping her eyes shut to protect the remains of her night vision, Locke hung her head backward. "Stop it!" She tried to keep her voice down to a hiss. "Turn it off!"

From the way the inside of her eyelids continued to glow red, she knew the light wasn't going anywhere.

And then the whistle started.

Tweeeeeeeet, tweeeeeeeet!

The shrill noise sliced through the air, over and over.

Locke had no choice now—she opened her eyes. Through the glare of the flashlight, she could see Jack upside down on the floor below. The black whistle clutched between his lips was unmistakable. His shoulders lurched and the flashlight bobbed every time he blew it again.

Between the piercing bursts, she heard shuffling.

Building lights around her started to glow. As white circles began to appear on the floor, she could see Huang and the others, staring upward and maneuvering underneath her.

For the first time, she could truly see how high up she was. From this distance, even King looked small.

"Boss!" Jack was jabbing his finger up at her. "I caught her trying to escape!"

20

THE WATER CAUGHT Locke square in the face.

Cold jabbed sharply at her skin even as the wet trickled over her scalp and spilled down into her shirt.

"Wake. Up."

Locke blinked her eyes open to find Huang standing over her, clutching an empty cup. From the backlighting, she guessed it was well past dawn.

As she reached to wipe her eyes, the solid steel grip on her left wrist reminded her: she was handcuffed to the metal shelving. She used her right hand instead.

After Jack sounded the alarm, Huang had marched to the top of the structure and ordered her off the girder with the gun. Once she'd descended, he'd punched her square in the face. She'd seen stars the whole way down, even as he dragged her by her hair.

Then he'd locked her in the janitor's closet alone.

The moment the closet door shut, she'd reached for a bobby pin to pick the lock. Despite nearly dislocating her shoulder to reach it, when she finally felt along the metal shelf, it was empty.

They'd found her stash.

The rest of the night, she'd rubbed her wrist raw trying to squeeze free from the cuff. She must have passed out at some point, although the pain radiating from her face and scalp mixed with the fatigue to fog things up.

Huang squatted in front of her now. Close enough she could smell cigarettes and tea on his breath. "I said, wake . . . up."

"Where's Evan?" Before locking her in, they'd dragged him from the closet, kicking and screaming. Although the noise had rapidly subsided, she'd told herself he was okay—Locke wouldn't let herself believe anything else.

"He is eating breakfast. Or, should I say not eating, just as he did not sleep after your . . . escapade last night."

Locke took some comfort in the idea of Evan keeping Huang awake. "You should have left him with me."

"And you should have thought of him before trying to escape." Huang's eyes narrowed. "I have the opportunity—the privilege—to correct nearly two hundred years of injustice. I will not lose it because of you. I have treated you and the boy well—"

"Oh yeah. Totally a five-star kidnapping experience."

Huang's eyebrows rose even as his voice dropped. "If you will not cooperate, he will pay the price."

Locke's temperature soared at the threat. Her right hand, which had lingered near her face, now shot forward and seized Huang by the ear. Simultaneously, she jabbed her left leg out. Down in the squat, he didn't have much balance—she forced him over her leg onto his back.

She rolled with him, pinning his arms under her knees. While the cuff neutralized her left arm, Locke jammed her right forearm under Huang's chin until she felt the hard structures of his throat. Leaning all her weight forward, she pressed down.

Huang's mouth popped open. His eyes gaped even wider in surprise.

As his face flushed, Locke's strength surged. The heat coursing through her intensified, and she felt a familiar tingle in her chest.

She lifted her knees to apply even more pressure.

Tears spilled out the corners of Huang's eyes and rolled straight to the floor. He let out a couple of small gasps.

"Let him up, Ace."

Locke's head whipped around to find Jack in the doorway. Evan stood in front of him, pouting. Jack's right hand was clamped over the boy's shoulder while his left held the knife aloft, its point angled up at the ceiling.

"Momma—"

Jack's right hand shifted from Evan's shoulder to his mouth. "Seriously, Ace. Let him go."

Unlike that first night in the car, Jack's expression was as flat as the sound of his voice.

Locke's muscles clenched so hard that she started shaking. A tremor down in her gut vibrated up into her throat where it escaped as a frustrated growl. She rolled off Huang, who remained on the ground, sputtering.

Locke slid as far away as her cuffed arm would allow. Facing the rear of the closet, she pulled her knees to her chest and stared down between them. Her breathing turned ragged as her shaking continued.

She didn't dare check Evan's expression. She couldn't bear the thought of how he might be looking at her.

In her peripheral vision, she sensed Huang rising to his feet and maneuvering around her.

"Look at me."

Although Huang's voice was reduced to a raspy croak, she understood the words. She just didn't comply.

"I said, *look at me!*"

Locke started to look up.

Her eyes hadn't even reached his knees when Huang's open hand hit her cheek. Connecting right where he'd struck her the night before, this new impact seemed to set off a bomb inside her head. Everything flashed white, then black, as her brain exploded with pain.

"Mommaaaaaa!" Evan's howl cut through the haze that filled her head.

"Get him out of here," Huang shouted at Jack.

"No!" Locke tried to struggle to her feet. "He needs to be with me!"

Huang whipped back around in a blur—the fastest she'd seen him move—and clamped his hand around her throat. She'd never given him any credit for being strong, but his fingers felt like iron digging in beneath her jaw.

"You have lost that privilege."

Locke could see the rage in Huang's bloodshot eyes. The way his nostrils flared.

"Take him out," Huang barked again. "And keep the brat quiet. Ms. Locke has work to do."

*   *   *

Huang didn't move her himself.

She figured that, deep down, he knew he couldn't.

Instead, he sent King to do it.

When the Giant arrived, Locke considered putting up a fight anyway. Although the odds were crazy, she considered what kind of cheap shot might take him down. Everyone had soft spots. Eyes. Balls.

Her wheels were still spinning when he tossed her the handcuff keys.

Whether they were too small for his massive fingers or he sensed her plan, King remained standing at the door. Blocking the only exit.

As she undid the lock, Locke scanned King's face. It looked . . . different. For one thing, he wasn't scowling—his mouth merely stretched into a straight, unflinching line. His brow, so often furrowed, had softened.

After removing the cuff, Locke rubbed her wrist and started to stand.

He pointed back at the cuffs.

"We bringing those?"

King nodded. Then he jerked his head outside.

Locke watched King duck his shoulders to squeeze through the door. She didn't know whether to take him turning his back on her as a compliment or an insult. But even when she emerged from the closet, he didn't act aggressively. Standing several feet away, he simply nodded toward her work area.

As they walked, Locke's head swiveled. "Where's Evan? Where'd they take him?"

King pointed at the offices.

Locke's eyes scoured the plexiglass windows, but she couldn't make out anything.

A heavy weight dropped onto her shoulder. She looked over and found King's giant mitt. He pointed at the offices, then gave a thumbs-up.

"Evan's okay? That what you mean?"

He nodded.

"I don't trust—"

King made a sawing motion with one hand, then shook his head.

"Evan's not with Jack?"

King leveled his palm and lowered it toward the floor.

"Queen? Evan's with Queen?"

The Giant's bald head bounced.

When Locke checked the offices again, the windows didn't reveal anything more than before. She hated the thought of Evan being with any of these people, but she imagined Queen was the safest of the bunch.

Forcing a swallow down, Locke turned back the way they were headed. Ahead, she could see the Ticonderoga waiting for her. As King walked silently alongside, she noticed he wore a different jersey today, white with orange numbers. "Did you play?"

King blinked.

She pinched her own blouse, then pointed at his shirt. "Football?"

He set his jaw before giving a single nod.

Although she'd never enjoyed watching it, everyone around her—at home, in the army—was so preoccupied with football that she'd ended up following along. Locke tried to imagine how much more imposing King would look in a helmet and shoulder pads.

When they reached the work area, he stopped at the saw-horses. Once she'd slipped inside, Locke held up the cuffs. "Am I supposed to . . ."

King nodded.

Locke glanced around and wondered what she could get away with. She reached for the metal chair.

King shook his head. He pointed at the safe.

Locke scanned the Ticonderoga but didn't see how she could clip herself to it. She shrugged at him.

King circled behind the box. As tall as it was, the Ticonderoga rose only to the middle of his chest. He threw his arms across the top of the safe, hooking his hands over the front lip.

Then he flexed, and growled.

The Ticonderoga's front legs tipped back off the floor.

Locke took a half second to blink away her shock. But then she fastened one cuff around the safe's front leg. Once she was clear, King let the box go.

She'd felt smaller earthquakes than when that steel slammed down against the concrete.

After King emerged from behind the box, she clipped the other cuff to her ankle and twisted to show him.

He flashed her a thumbs-up before lumbering away.

The moment his back was turned, Locke's eyes flew to the toolbox. She started inventorying what she'd seen inside. Thinking what could pick the lock or saw through the chain.

As her pulse quickened, she ordered it to slow down.

There was no point in escaping now, not with Evan being held by the others. She'd risked enough by angering Huang. Better to be a good girl.

For now.

After a deep breath, Locke turned back to the Ticonderoga. She swung the door open and stared at the circuit board.

If she and Evan weren't getting rescued, she needed to figure out the digital lock in a hurry. That was the only way to keep them safe now. But after yesterday's frustrations, she really didn't see what else she could possibly try.

The information she needed was stored inside the digital lock's memory chip. But outside the safe, all she had access to was the keypad. As she'd learned yesterday, those two never talked directly—they each spoke only to the processor between them.

Locke stared hard at the little black square. Like a safe within a safe, it was tucked away, guarding its secrets.

So crack it. That's what you do.

Locke thought for a long time.

The processor chip took numbers entered on the keypad and compared them to the combination. But all she could see were the keypad entries themselves, not the action inside the processor. That was no help.

But.

The processor had known the combination somehow. Otherwise there'd be nothing to compare the button presses to.

So how did the processor get the combination?

Duh, Locke told herself, *the processor asks the memory chip for it.* That was the whole point of "memory"—it "remembered" things for the processor.

The memory had to tell the processor what the combination was.

Locke grabbed the oscilloscope probes and clipped them between the memory and processor chips. Then she activated the oscilloscope—with her ankle cuffed, it required turning and stretching backward like an odd game of Twister.

When she ran traces, though, the scope showed the weirdest result: nothing.

Absolutely nothing.

It didn't matter what she did with the keypad, the processor and memory never seemed to talk. No signals passed between them. Ever.

Locke rubbed her palms against her eyes.

What was the point of the memory chip if the processor never used it? And how the heck did the processor receive the combination if it never asked for it?

"I *hate* electronics." She said it aloud this time.

"Little chow might help."

Locke wheeled around to find Jack standing at the saw-horses. Dressed in his chef's coat and bandanna, he held a paper plate.

"Fuck you."

"You're angry, I understand—"

"What you should understand is that if my ankle wasn't chained to this safe, I'd be over there ripping your beating heart out so I could shove it down your throat."

Without realizing it, her fingers had curled into fists. Locke knew firsthand what it felt like when bones broke beneath their weight. The satisfying way resistance was there one moment, gone the next. More than anything, she wanted that sensation again, right now.

Jack gave a little shrug. "So you know, Evan ate—"

"Don't go near him. You so much as look at him, I'll—"

"—a full breakfast. I thought you might be hungry too."

"I'm not. I don't want anything from you." Locke inched toward the fencing. Far enough that her cuffed ankle started to rise off the floor.

"I'll leave it here. Just in case." He set the paper plate down and tucked it inside the fencing before turning to walk away.

Locke stretched to hook the edge of the plate with a fingertip. Dragging it closer, she scooped it up and hurled it after him.

When the plate struck Jack between his shoulder blades, he whipped around and reversed course. Brow furrowed, neck veins popping, he looked like he'd march right up to her.

The corners of her mouth turned up in a smile. *C'mon.*

Without warning, he halted at the fence line.

"What's wrong?" she asked. "Afraid another girl's gonna kick your ass?"

"You're tough as all fuck, you know that? But you're really not too bright."

Locke lunged at him, but the cuff stopped her short.

Jack shook his head. "Thinking I'll come in there and let you beat on me is about as dumb as thinking I'd skip the chance to turn you in."

"You lied—"

"No, I didn't. I never said I'd help you. I never promised you anything—I just pointed you at the bright, shiny object and let you chase it."

Locke's face flushed.

"That's your problem, Ace—you're too easily distracted. Haven't you noticed? How I run around like a hamster on a little wheel, making all the boss's favorites, speaking to him in Mandarin? The whole time I've been here, I've only had one thing in my mind." He flashed his index finger at her, then jabbed it against his temple. "One thing, from the start. Getting home. And if catching you red-handed for the boss man gets me one step closer, so be it."

"Selfish prick."

"Maybe. But I've been plenty nice to that boy of yours. Better than you've been, almost making him an orphan."

Jack spun on his heel and stormed away.

Her face on fire, Locke strained at the cuff. She stomped over to the metal chair, planted her cuffed leg, and fired her free foot against the seat back.

The chair rolled several yards, clanging and clattering the whole way.

Although a part of her enjoyed the noise, quickly Locke's eyes returned to the safe. Right now, what Evan needed most was for her to figure out that digital lock. That was the only way to keep him alive.

As she opened the door and stared at the circuit board, though, the only thing in her mind was Jack.

"One thing in my head this whole time." She said it out loud, mocking his tone and accent. "One thing, from the start."

Stupid boy brains only had *room* for one thing at time. Food, sex, violence.

Another growl formed down deep in her throat. She swung the safe door shut, letting it clang against the frame.

Her eyes settled on the digital keypad. Locke wasn't quite sure which she hated more: the little silver circle with the buttons or that arrogant Scottish prick.

She noticed the keypad screen had gone dark. While she'd been arguing with Jack, the system had turned itself off to save power.

Jack's words echoed in her head.

"One thing."

"From the start."

Suddenly, the digital lock made sense.

21

LOCKE MADE SURE the oscilloscope was ready to record before reactivating the keypad. Then she tapped the screen, woke the system up, and entered a combination.

All her button presses were wrong. Deliberately so. She didn't care about the button presses anymore—all she wanted to see was what the processor did when it first started.

The oscilloscope, connected between the chips, didn't show any activity when she was pressing buttons. But when she first woke the screen, a tiny blip appeared on the trace.

Doing her awkward Twister contortion again, Locke stretched to the scope and zoomed in on the blip. The small, singular spike split into multiple little heartbeats. Five of them, stacked closely together.

It couldn't be . . . could it?

Locke ran a series of tests, changing one combination digit each time while leaving the others constant. After each reset, she'd let the keypad fall asleep, then wake it again.

When she compared all the different traces, her fists shot straight into the air.

Four peaks on the oscilloscope trace never changed. Only one varied from test to test, the one corresponding to the digit she'd altered.

She was watching the combination being passed from the memory to the processor—it happened at start-up. The processor must hold on to the combination while awake, then forget it when turned off. Restarting the system caused the processor to ask memory for the combination again.

One thing in its head, from the start.

Locke glanced around—no one had witnessed her accomplishment. That didn't make it any less sweet. Her cheeks spread so wide they almost hurt.

Even as she beamed to herself, though, a voice in her head tamped down the enthusiasm. *Slow down, genius. You're not done yet.*

And she wasn't. She could only eavesdrop on communications between the memory and processor because the door was ajar. That wouldn't help her on the yacht, where the safe would be locked up tight. So how could she use her new-found knowledge to open the damn box?

Locke couldn't remember if she'd seen the start-up spike during her tests yesterday. And when she'd scrolled through the saved oscilloscope traces, the very first ones had disappeared. The scope must have limited storage.

She quickly detached the oscilloscope probes from the internal circuit board and reconnected them to the power port wires on the digital lock outside the safe. Then she repeated her procedure of setting a combination, letting the system fall asleep, and waking it up again.

As she entered numbers on the keypad, spikes appeared on the trace representing her button presses. But she didn't see any sign of the start-up spike.

Locke did another backward pirouette to the oscilloscope controls. When she twisted the amplitude dial, the spikes from the button presses grew into giant mountains on the screen. She scanned backward in time along the trace, looking for the moment when she'd woken up the system.

Eventually, with the amplitude dialed up almost as far as it could go, she saw it.

A blip.

Minuscule compared to the button presses—a speed bump next to mountains. But it was there.

When she gave the amplitude dial its final twist, the startup blip expanded into five little spikes. The same as she'd seen when connected to the interior of the safe, but this time on the outside.

Locke imagined that, as the processor woke and retrieved the combination, voltage changes echoed out to every part of the circuit, like ripples in a pond. Connecting to the external power ports was like standing on a distant shoreline—the ripples were tiny by the time they reached it, but they still arrived.

Over the next hour, Locke worked to determine how the tiny start-up spikes corresponded to digits in the combination. It took trial and error, changing the combination over and over. Eventually, though, she ended up with a hand-drawn chart showing how every possible number appeared on the oscilloscope. Deciphering the combination became a matter of looking up the shapes to see which numbers they represented, like reading old-fashioned Morse code.

As she'd done with the traditional dial, Locke practiced to get faster. After several dozen tries, she felt as confident about her ability to open the digital lock as she did about the manual one.

Locke allowed herself a satisfied sigh. She hadn't expected to decipher the digital combination at all. Conquering the Ticonderoga under the gun made the victory especially sweet.

Now she had to tell Huang the bad news that she needed the oscilloscope.

He'd said no equipment, and it wasn't like she could smuggle the giant scope under her skintight dress. Unless he had some magic shrink ray, she'd get the joy of telling him she could absolutely crack the safe, just not the way he wanted. Although she'd have to deal with the fallout, the idea of sticking it to him for once sounded nice.

Locke was still imagining what Huang's face would look like at the news when his voice sounded from her side.

"Ms. Locke, we are almost out of time. I trust you have progress to report?"

She measured her words, trying to decide what would be the most satisfying way of disappointing him. "Sort of."

Huang cocked his head. His confusion made her smile.

"I can crack the digital lock. But I need an oscilloscope and this pad to do it."

He pursed his lips and nodded. "Excellent."

Now her own face contorted. "You're . . . okay with that?"

"I expected as much."

"But you said I couldn't bring equipment. You said—"

"I said nothing larger than your purse." Huang produced a cell phone from his pocket. "I have installed an oscilloscope application we can use aboard the *Helios*."

Her face fell.

"We will also bring your notes." With the phone, he snapped several pictures of her chart.

When Huang finally looked up, he gave her an enthused smile. "Do not be disappointed, Ms. Locke—you are about to undertake an extremely worthwhile mission." He produced a small key from his pocket and tossed it to her.

She snatched it out of the air and unlocked her ankle. She was surprised at how red and raw she'd worn the skin.

As Locke straightened to her full height, Queen approached Huang from behind. "It's time," she said. "If we're gonna do this, I need to start making us pretty."

"Perfect timing." Huang beamed, rocking back and forth on his feet. "Ms. Locke has finished with the safe."

"Where's Evan?" Locke said.

"With the boys," Queen said.

Locke crossed her arms. "I'm not doing this if he's with Jack and King."

"Evan is fine," Huang said.

"Then I don't help. I don't do any of this if he isn't safe."

Huang lowered his head so that he was looking down his nose at her despite their height difference. "You are—"

"I"—she shifted her weight to her front foot—"am not doing *any* of this if Evan isn't safe. Let him play. Let him read. But if he's with those . . . animals, I'm done, understand?"

Huang opened his mouth, then shut it again. Finally, leaving his eyes locked on Locke, he told Queen, "Get him."

The Pink Punker shuffled away, then quickly returned with Evan in tow.

His face lit up when he saw Locke. She couldn't contain her own smile, even as she tried to blink away moisture welling in the corners of her eyes. "Hey, buddy!"

"The boy can play," Huang said. "But you must get dressed."

"No—Momma!"

Evan started for her, but Huang blocked his path.

"I'll go," Locke said. "Just give us a second."

Huang stared at her hard before moving out of the way. Evan sprinted to her and wrapped his arms around her neck. She felt her throat tighten, and not just from his grip.

"Hey, kiddo. I've gotta get cleaned up. But I made them promise you could play, okay?"

He pulled away slightly, shaking his head. "I don't wamma play, I wamma be with you."

"I know. That's what I want too." She tried to soothe him with her eyes. "But I have to get into a fancy dress for this job."

"Like when you wemt to Hollywood for the Ozarks?"

Locke chuckled. "The Oscars? Yeah, like that."

Evan squeezed her again. "I don't wamt you to go."

"I know, baby. You've been super brave, but you gotta keep it up a little while longer."

When she pried herself out of his embrace, his lip was trembling. Locke felt tears spilling down her own cheeks but realized she couldn't stop them. Determined not to let her voice crack, she forced words up from her belly. "I want to see how much of that car you can build while I'm getting dressed, okay?"

Evan blinked but didn't move.

She stood and gestured toward the play area. "Go on, now."

He hesitated another moment before finally hanging his head and trudging off.

* * *

Before either of them could reconsider, Locke hurried to the closet, where she grabbed her things and wiped at her face.

When she emerged, Queen was still several yards away. Locke rounded the corner and ducked into the bathroom without waiting. Racing to the vanity, she stole a sideways glance at the mirror. Thankfully, she saw no obvious signs of how upset she'd been. She turned to the door, steeling herself against whatever wisecrack Queen might be brandishing.

To her surprise, though, the Pink Punker's own cheeks were glistening wet when she entered the room. Queen disappeared into one of the stalls, returning momentarily with a folded triangle of toilet paper that she used to dab the corners of her eyes.

"Fucking pollen in here." Queen shook her head and gave a sheepish smile.

The brief show of emotion allowed Locke to lubricate her throat. "How are we doing this?"

Queen sniffled loudly. "I'm gonna need lots of time for your makeup."

"Gee, thanks."

"I doubt anyone's going to this party looking like an MMA fighter." Queen nodded at the mirror.

Locke spun back to the vanity. Her right eye, hidden during her quick check a moment ago, was underscored by a dark-purple mark. "Can you—"

Queen nodded. "I've covered worse. It'll just take time. I'm guessing you'll want to wash up first. We don't have a dryer, so don't get your hair too wet."

While Locke's scalp registered its unhappiness by itching, the rest of her thought a shower sounded heavenly. Still, she wasn't looking to repeat yesterday's . . . incident.

"I'll wait for you," Queen said.

Locke raised an eyebrow.

"In the office!" Queen raised her hands to demonstrate her innocence, then made a show of leaving the room.

Locke kept it quick—she was out of the water in less than two minutes. She grudgingly pulled on one of the G-strings along with a strapless bra before redonning her shorts and blouse.

When she reached Queen's office, the metal makeup bag was splayed open across the floor. An empty chair sat waiting in the middle of the room.

"Here," Queen said, patting the seat. "Lean your head back."

Staring up at the ceiling reminded Locke of the dentist's office, which didn't help her mood. Her heel started tapping, eventually matching the accelerated rhythm of her heart.

When Queen put a hand on Locke's shoulder, Locke's whole body flinched.

"You gotta relax," Queen said.

Locke nodded, drawing a deep breath.

No sooner had she exhaled, though, than Queen leaned closer.

Locke could see the gray flecks in her irises again, little islands of slate awash in a pale-blue sea. Queen's eyelashes, burnished and black, curved elegantly away from her lids, framing the baby blues perfectly.

But Locke was even more focused on Queen's fingertips. Moving strands of hair, they brushed her face, her scalp, and her ears. Light, feathery touches.

Locke tried not to shiver.

"Eyeshadow first," Queen said, "so close your eyes."

Locke obeyed, although blinding herself only heightened her sense that Queen was completely in control. "Were you a gymnast? That where you learned all this?"

"Yeah, hair and makeup are the show-pony skills the announcers never mention at the Olympics. Open?"

Locke lifted her lids to find Queen stalking back and forth, eyeing her from different angles.

"You were in the Olympics?"

Queen answered without breaking her concentration. "For Beijing, they took six girls and three alternates. I was number ten. Shut 'em again?"

"So that's what Jack meant about you not going to China."

"Yeah. I made the mistake of mentioning it."

"Still, tenth? In the whole country?" Locke thought about the Harry C. Miller Contest, the world championship she'd never entered. Her eyes popped opened again. "I've never been ranked tenth in the country at anything."

"The whole thing was a steaming pile of horseshit. Close 'em."

Locke deliberately disobeyed. Her eyes pressed Queen for more.

Finally, Queen sighed. "Two weeks before trials, we're at the National Training Center. This coach, he . . ."

Her baby blues glazed over. Then they dropped to the floor.

"He had a reputation. All the girls knew about him. I was taping myself up and suddenly I was alone, and . . . well . . ."

Locke held her breath.

"Let's just say he tried to put his finger somewhere. So I broke it."

"Good for you." Locke nodded vigorously.

"Yeah, everybody said that. Except, after finishing third or fourth in six straight meets, suddenly I'm tenth."

"They screwed you?"

"His brother was one of the judges on beam. My best event, and suddenly I'm scoring three points lower than usual."

"Did you protest?"

Queen shrugged. "All the judges knew what happened. The coaches knew. But there were thirteen other girls at trials, and like thirty more who'd've gone if they could. They didn't need some white trash like me."

Her voice hardened. "Now shut your eyes. I need to work on this color."

This time, Locke complied. Almost immediately, though, she asked, "How do you get a black eye in gymnastics?"

"I learned this little trick after I was out."

Locke grunted as the makeup strokes moved to her cheekbone.

"That hurt?" Queen asked.

"Not as much as getting hit."

"Yeah, this looks like it came from one of my dad's left hooks."

Locke wanted to open her eyes but left them shut. "Your dad hit you?"

"Toward the end. My mom split when I was real little. That's how I got into gymnastics—my dad needed someplace to park me while he was working. Once I started making elite teams, I was away a lot. He'd see me at meets and be all proud, and when I did come home, it was like vacation, you know? But once they bounced me out and I was home for good, he kinda couldn't handle it."

"Still, hard to believe he got mad at you for defending yourself."

"I mean, he said all the right stuff. But I think he always figured I'd go to the Olympics. Make a Wheaties box, get endorsements, you know? I fucked the whole plan up."

Locke let the pause linger.

"He paid a fortune for me to compete. Moved us to Texas to be near the big gyms. When I dropped out, he decided it was my turn to pay it all back. Said if I wasn't working in the gym, I needed to be working somewhere."

"How old were you?"

"Fifteen. I couldn't get hired legally, so he'd find me a job and they'd pay him under the table. But I couldn't miss a shift. If I missed work, or if I showed up with a giant bruise on one eye, they'd fire me. Then I'd have to go home and he'd take it out on my other eye. So I learned makeup."

"What about school?"

Queen let out a single laugh. "I stopped going to real school when I was eight. Gymnastics gave us, like, 'study time'—a couple hours between practices. But I always fucked around. If I'd gone back to some random high school, I'd flunk out in a minute."

She tapped Locke twice on the shoulder. "See what you think."

Locke opened her eyes. When Queen raised her phone with the selfie camera on, Locke couldn't believe it. Her lids bore a smoky green color and the bruise had completely disappeared. No matter how close she held the glass, the two sides of her face matched perfectly—she couldn't tell where the makeup started and her own skin began.

"Wow."

Queen smiled. "Not bad, if I do say so myself. We'll cheat a little and sweep your hair to that side. But first, lashes and lips."

She fished around inside the metal case for more supplies, then started applying mascara.

"When did you leave home?" Locke asked.

"When did I get kicked out, you mean? Three weeks after my seventeenth birthday."

"He was still mad?"

Queen grunted. "Oh, I'm sure he'll never get over me missing the chance to make him rich. But he kicked me out 'cause I was partying. I got wasted one night, overslept the next morning."

"He kicked you out over that?"

"Well, I missed work. And let's just say it wasn't my first time. I woke up as he was dragging my mattress out the front door with me still in it."

"Holy shit." Locke flashed back to the night she'd opened her door in LA and found Kori standing on her front step. She had no idea why parents could be so cruel.

"He dragged the mattress down to the gutter, rolled me into it, and told me that's where I belonged. Then he went back inside, locked the door. I never saw him again."

"Oh my god. What did you do?"

"I . . . survived. But that's why, when I see you . . ." Queen sniffled loudly and fluttered her eyelids. "The way you are, with him. It just . . ."

Queen's lips moved, trying to form the words. "Let's just say no one ever dangled off a roof for me. That boy out there, he's got a real good mom."

Locke felt a sharp pang in her chest.

"I'm . . . I'm not his mom," she said. "Evan's not my son."

22

"WAIT, WHAT?"

Although Queen had been hovering close to apply the mascara, now she retreated. "But he calls you—"

"He calls me Monna. He just doesn't always say his *n*'s." Locke recalled the effort to find a speech therapist and the appointment that ended up being scheduled a week after the lockdowns went into effect. A lifetime ago now.

"So . . . he knows?"

Locke nodded. No holiday passed without Evan asking about his mom, checking to make sure she was still in heaven. "His mother was . . ." Her voice trailed off as she weighed how to describe it. "She was my best friend."

"Dad a deadbeat or something?"

"He's scattered across Anbar Province."

When Queen's glassy eyes said she had no idea what that meant, Locke added, "Iraq. An IED killed him."

"Oh. So he was a good guy."

Locke shook her head. "No, he was a lying, stalking scumbag piece of shit. But he happened to be a soldier, and he died soldiering."

"I still don't get it. Why would you sign up for . . . all that?" Queen jerked her head toward the door.

Locke's eyes dropped, and she poked at her teeth with her tongue. "Kori was . . . kinda like you, I guess. When she got pregnant, the army was done with her. Her parents wouldn't take her back. She had no place else to go. I was the only one who ever really . . . loved her. So, when she showed up one night, I wasn't gonna say no. I just wasn't thinking she'd die a couple weeks after Evan was born."

Sixteen-year-old Locke hadn't cried when the cops came about her mom. A decade later, she hadn't been so steely with Kori's doctors. Even now, five years on, her skin seemed to hum when she thought about that night. The doctors used a bunch of words she hadn't understood till later—*preeclampsia* was one—but Locke surely knew what *expired* meant.

Queen's loud sniffling interrupted Locke's thoughts. When she glanced up, the pools gathered in Queen's eyes made her own eyes moisten.

As if she could read Locke's mind, Queen blinked hard and shook her head. "Oh, no." She pointed a sharp-nailed finger at Locke. "Don't you dare cry! If you mess up that perfect fucking makeup job, I swear . . ."

Queen chuffed. A half giggle.

Locke did the same.

Both women smiled.

After a long moment, Queen swallowed deeply. "I'm gonna help you."

"Help me how?"

"Help you get away. With Evan."

Locke wasn't sure her ears were working. "I—"

"Don't get me wrong," Queen said. "I need this job to go down. I need the money, I need . . ." She scratched at her arm.

Locke pictured the pill bottle Huang had shaken in front of her several times. "Whatever you're on, you can get clean."

Queen shook her head. "I haven't been clean since I was sixteen."

"Still, you don't have to do all this. Follow his orders. You could—"

"You don't understand. After my dad kicked me out, I drifted around. I ended up somewhere . . ." Queen paused for a deep breath. "The folks I fell in with, they wanted to make sure I was . . . agreeable. Huang found me, bought me out of all that. If I don't do this job for him, he'll send me back. Or they'll come for me." She shook her head furiously. "I . . . can't. I just . . . I can't."

"But he's using you—"

"No shit. That's what they all do. But it's not like before. You don't—just trust me. This score, this job, it pays Huang back and gets me free, all in one shot. Then I'm done."

Locke didn't believe that last bit, and didn't know if Queen did either. She shot Queen one of the sideways looks she gave Evan sometimes. "There's plenty of things you could do besides this."

Queen laughed out loud. "Girl, I'm four foot eleven, got a fourth-grade education, and my number-one skill is I can throw my feet behind my head. There's only a couple jobs this world thinks I'm qualified for. I prefer the ones I can do standing up. But you. And your boy. That's different."

After a beat, Locke asked, "So, what's the plan?"

"Huang's gonna leave Evan here—we can't bring him to the boat."

Queen's words hit like a swift kick to the stomach, and Locke tried not to double over in the chair.

From the moment they'd been kidnapped, Locke had always known that, unless they escaped or got saved, a moment would come where she'd be forced to leave Evan. And some kind of decent odds said she wouldn't make it back to him.

Until now, Locke hadn't allowed herself to think about security on the boat. She had no idea of Huang's plan, but she imagined the billionaire's guards were the best money could buy. If the crew got caught, she figured there was little hope she'd be shown any mercy, or distinguished from Huang and the others. And, even if they managed to succeed, she was still probably doomed. Huang said he'd chosen Locke for her discretion, but was it really that? Or did he want someone with as few connections as possible? A bitch no one would miss.

Her neighbors' faces flashed through Locke's mind—had any of them even noticed that she, Evan, and Constance were missing? A pandemic seemed to be just about the perfect time to commit a kidnapping.

These thoughts pressed down on Locke's chest like a barbell too heavy to lift. Suffocating her.

Unless something changed, she'd be dead soon, and Evan wouldn't last long after.

Locke felt her teeth grind together. Her muscles tensed. If she was doomed, why the fuck was she just sitting here?

Queen must have noticed. She put a hand on Locke's shoulder.

"We can do this. But you've gotta play along."

Although her heart still raced, Locke didn't move.

"After you crack the safe, once Huang gets whatever he's after, there'll be a moment. Everybody will relax, even if it's just for a second. That's when I'll make some distraction. I'll do some crazy shit that lets you sneak away. You get a head start back here. You grab Evan and get gone."

Locke drew a deep breath.

Although she'd never fully trusted Jack, he'd still found an opportunity to screw her. In contrast, Queen had now had several chances to betray her and hadn't taken any of them. Besides, what were Locke's other options? Fighting her way out? She could probably get past Queen—one good hit would flatten her. But Locke couldn't take on Huang, Jack, *and* King. Not while protecting Evan.

That meant going along, at least for now.

And, just maybe, Queen meant it. Maybe the Pink Punker was for real.

Locke extended her hand. "Thank you."

Queen seized it and squeezed. "Let's get those lips done."

*   *   *

When Locke stepped from the office fully dressed, she felt an odd energy surging through her. A raw sexual power she'd never experienced before.

From the way air coursed over her skin, she could tell the dress was barely covering her backside. Meanwhile, the bra puffed up her chest a cup size or two. Each time she looked down, she was surprised by how much cleavage she had. Sequins on the dress caught the late-afternoon sunlight— when Locke moved, she shot reflections in every direction. She was literally glowing.

Queen had brushed Locke's raven hair to her right side, copying photos of some old actress. The styling helped camouflage Locke's bad eye and gave her a bit of a shield to hide behind.

Thankfully, the shoes Queen had chosen didn't challenge Locke's balance. Her footing felt solid enough that Queen urged her to do something she called the "bad-bitch strut," a runway walk where you imagined each step landing on the head of someone you hated.

If Locke's look would turn heads, though, Queen's would set them spinning like tops. Her one-shoulder gown stretched to the floor, with a slit that rose to her hipbone. The back was equally revealing, a wide keyhole exposing everything from her shoulder blades down to dimples at the base of her spine. Platform heels gave Queen an extra four inches, and the former gymnast had no problem strutting around on the little stilts. Above it all, Queen wore an auburn wig whose reverse-bob cut framed her face and caused her eyes to pop even more than usual.

Queen had said Huang wanted them to be a distraction. Mission accomplished.

When they reached the play area, Evan's mouth hung open. "Momma, is that you?"

She did a little pirouette. "Do I look good?"

"A-ma-zing!"

As she spun, Locke noticed King standing alone near the Ticonderoga. He wore an impeccably tailored black suit with a double-breasted jacket. In an apparent act of mercy on his shirt's top button, King wore his collar open with no tie. His face and scalp were freshly shaved, the latter almost as shiny as one of her sequins. While he seemed to stare in their general direction, she couldn't be sure—King's eyes were obscured behind large round sunglasses.

"Don't you two look lovely."

Jack's brogue came from behind the women. They turned to find him a few feet away. Like King, he'd cleaned up—beard neatly trimmed, hair slicked back beneath a Union Jack bandanna. Instead of a suit, he wore a fresh set of chef's whites.

Locke's first thought on seeing the crisp, clean jacket was to wonder how fast she could cover it with his blood. Her fingers flexed instinctively.

Jack must have noticed. "Don't be mad, princess. We're all dressed up, now we get to go to the ball. Where's the boss man?"

As if on cue, Huang emerged from his office and strode to the safe. Wearing the same gray suit from the law office, he'd added a red power tie and a duffel bag slung over one shoulder.

When he reached the Ticonderoga, the crew formed a semicircle around him. Huang rocked up onto the balls of his feet. His face spread into the slickest smile Locke had seen from him yet. "I thought you all would like a glimpse of your reward before we depart."

With the oscilloscope disconnected and out of the way, Huang had no trouble swinging the Ticonderoga's door wide open so that the dark interior of the safe was visible to all.

"Assuming we are successful, each of you will have your existing debts forgiven. Some of those are . . . significant." Huang's gaze moved down the line, causing heads to dip. "In addition, this operation offers each of you a healthy profit."

Sliding the bag off his shoulder, Huang jabbed a hand inside and withdrew a block of bills that barely fit between his outstretched fingers. Locke could see they were crisp new hundreds, still wrapped in their black Treasury band.

"Each stack is one hundred thousand dollars." Huang turned and placed the block into the bottom of the empty safe. Then he pulled out another. And another. He continued until the entire bottom of the safe was lined in a layer of bills. "Three million US dollars. One for each of you."

"And you?" Queen asked.

Huang shook his head. "My reward is not financial." With that, he jabbed his hand inside the bag again. This time, he produced a small wooden box—Locke recognized it as the one she'd liberated from the Malibu safe. After holding that out in front of himself a moment, he shoved it into his suit jacket pocket.

"I notice we don't get a cut of the cash," Locke said.

"Ah, but like me, you and Evan stand to receive a much greater reward . . . your freedom. Speaking of which." Huang descended to one knee. "Evan, I do have something for you. A gift."

Locke splayed her fingers in front of Evan to keep him from leaving her side. "What *gift*? What're you talking about?"

"Things he will need while we are gone," Huang said.

"Wait . . . you're leaving?"

Locke dropped to a squat, and when she met Evan's eyes, his expression hit like a slap across her cheek. "Just for a little bit. This place we're going only allows grown-ups."

"I'm gonna be . . . alone? Here?"

His dismay at being left behind made her want to laugh as much as cry. At home, Evan was always angling to avoid errands like the grocery store.

"Yes, but you can play as much as you want. And you can stay up till we get back."

Locke tried giving Evan an *Isn't that great?* smile, but his eyes said he wasn't buying it. Not one bit.

His chin dropped to his chest. "Can I at least get the gift?"

At that moment, she probably would have let him play with a chainsaw if it would cheer him up. "Sure. Go get it."

Evan's eyes rose; his face perked up. Then he approached Huang and the safe.

"I actually have several things," Huang said. He reached into the duffel and pulled out a white plastic bag. "First . . ."

Evan drew within arm's reach and took the plastic bag. Peering inside, he said, "Wow, Snickers and Twix!"

"That should help if you get hungry," Huang said. "Can you guess what's next?"

"Uh, something to drink?"

Huang nodded. "Smart boy. Water."

When Huang pulled a large plastic bottle from the duffel, Evan took it and slid it into the bag with the candy.

"Is there anything else?"

"Evan—" Locke said.

Huang chuckled. "The boy is very perceptive—there is one more thing he will need. Do you know what it is, Evan?"

After thinking a moment, he shook his head.

Huang made a show of opening the duffel, peeking inside, then shutting it again so no one else could see.

Evan fidgeted.

Smiling broadly, Huang curled his index finger, gesturing for Evan to come closer.

The boy took one step forward, then another.

Huang held the duffel open, its mouth pointed at the ceiling, inviting Evan to reach inside without seeing the surprise.

Evan inched forward and stuck his hand into the bag. Instead of pulling it out immediately, though, he made a confused face.

When he finally began to pull his arm out, his hand was wrapped around the bottom of a metal cylinder. It looked something like a very small fire extinguisher, except its sides were metallic silver instead of fire engine red.

Locke started to ask what it was. But as the top of the cylinder cleared the lip of the bag, two things happened at once.

First, she recognized the topper to the cylinder. It bore a plastic mouthpiece, like you'd find on a snorkel or a scuba tank.

Second, Huang sprang up from his knee.

Locke barely had time to process the purpose of the oxygen tank before Huang had lifted Evan off the ground.

Her muscles tensed and she started to sprint forward.

But she was too late. Huang pivoted and tossed Evan, still holding his "gifts," into the Ticonderoga. No sooner had the boy landed inside the box than Huang slammed the door shut and spun the dial.

23

THE METALLIC ECHO of the safe door shutting beat the sound of Locke's shriek around the room.

"No!"

In that moment, Locke's vision narrowed until nothing else existed but Huang and the safe. She became a laser-guided missile—locked on target, her only mission to launch herself at Huang and hit him as hard as she possibly could.

Time slowed, allowing her to visualize the impact before it happened. Her shoulder, plowing into Huang's back. His spine, flexing from the collision. His head, whiplashing back and then forward, striking the metal door.

Locke's brain ordered her legs to accelerate. To build as much momentum as they could.

And as her right leg started to follow through, her mind continued to race ahead. Past the impact, to what would happen once she got Huang on the ground. How she'd force him to let Evan loose.

He might refuse at first.

She might not mind.

She knew ways to inflict pain on the male anatomy. Huang wasn't getting off the floor without freeing Evan.

Her right foot flew forward, ready to plant and launch her into the air.

But before it touched down, something struck Locke from the side.

She didn't see what knocked her off course. One moment Huang was an easy target, standing in front of her with his back turned; the next, his gray suit blurred to the left as her body got slammed to the right.

Locke landed on her right shoulder. A hard fall, made harder by additional weight that dropped on top of her. On contact, though, she rolled, letting whoever hit her tumble over the top.

As the world spun, Locke focused on ending up on top of her attacker. She let the momentum carry them through one complete roll, then extended a leg to stop herself. Rising onto her knees, she got her first look at who was beneath her.

The white jacket gave it away, even before the bandanna and the beard.

With Jack's arms pinned beneath her shins, she had a free shot at his face. Instead, Locke jammed her hands down against his throat. She leaned forward, digging her fingers underneath his Adam's apple.

Jack's mouth sprang open, releasing a hoarse croak. Although gasping, he somehow managed to sneak a couple of tiny breaths through the pressure her hands were exerting.

Which only made Locke's face burn hotter.

She locked her elbows and leaned every bit of weight she could muster onto her hands. Although Jack worked an arm free, lack of oxygen rendered his attempts to club her with it halfhearted. His eyes bulged and began ticking back and forth.

"Looking at the ceiling, Jack? Nothing up there's gonna save you—"

Click-clack.

Locke recognized the sound again. When she glanced up, she found Huang's gun pointed at her.

Her head dropped. She squeezed her eyes shut and let out a guttural scream.

"Please get off of him, Ms. Locke. I do not wish to kill you."

Something inside her clenched tight, like a fist. Locke jumped to her feet and stormed at Huang. "Gonna shoot me? I don't think so."

She didn't watch the gun barrel. Instead, Locke kept her vision locked on Huang's eyes. As she kept advancing, they widened ever so slightly.

"Your goons had the chance in Malibu, but I don't think they just missed. You can't *afford* to shoot me."

More steps put her within inches of Huang and the gun.

"Whoever you're robbing that safe for won't want to hear you killed your only chance to get inside."

Although the barrel was pointed at her chest, she saw Huang's index finger slip outside the trigger guard. He retreated a half step.

If she wasn't certain before, now she knew: she had him.

Huang's hand was shaking when she smacked it. With one open palm, she struck the inside of his wrist; her other hand hit the opposite side of the barrel. The simultaneous opposing blows jarred the gun from his grip, sending the barrel spinning back toward Huang himself.

He winced and backpedaled.

Locke didn't blink. She plucked the moving gun from the air and absorbed it into a two-handed, high-ready grip pointed at Huang's forehead.

"Open the safe."

Huang's hands rose to his shoulders, even as his knees bent beneath him. He ended up crouched in a kind of half cower. But his expression remained defiant. "I will not."

"Then I will blow your motherfucking head all the way back to LA."

Locke adjusted her aim, eyeing him down the sights. "Let Evan out. *Now.*"

"You cannot kill me any more than I could kill you. I am the only one who knows the new combinations to the safe."

"And I'm a goddamn *safecracker*!"

"You're also a bit too slow, princess." Jack's voice came from behind her, along with a hand on her shoulder.

Before she could look back, Huang straightened. "I'm afraid I have you outnumbered."

Huang gestured to Locke's left. King had a pistol trained on her.

Locke's eyes drifted to Queen, who stood several feet to the Giant's side. If Queen moved fast, she could knock King's aim off.

But she slowly shook her head at Locke.

A quick glance backward showed why. Even if Queen took down King, Jack had his knife pointed at her kidney.

Huang straightened and stepped forward, palm outstretched. "The gun, please."

Locke gritted her teeth but took her finger off the trigger. She raised the barrel skyward.

Huang snatched the gun from her grasp. After shoving it into a holster beneath his jacket, he gave her an ugly smile. "Now that you are properly motivated for our mission, I think we can depart."

"I am going to kill you for this," she said. "For what you've done to him."

"Thank you for reminding me, Ms. Locke. Your histrionics interrupted me before I properly finished with the safe."

Huang turned back to the Ticonderoga, squatted down, and pressed a button on the biometric sensor. When it beeped, he placed his right hand onto the scanner's black glass. A moment later, the safe beeped again and the little green light flashed.

Huang rose and spun on his heel to face her. He raised his hand and wiggled his fingers the same way Locke had done the day before. "Now my return is guaranteed."

*   *   *

Locke had expected that leaving the warehouse would provide a brief moment of joy. But the trip to the SUV might as well have been a spacewalk, it felt so foreign. One of those detached out-of-body experiences, where she could almost watch herself moving along the little path to the parking lot.

After working so hard to escape, nearly dying to determine their location, now she stood outside in broad daylight and the opportunity to look around didn't matter in the slightest. She'd run out of chances to signal for help—she'd almost certainly be accompanied from now on. Worse, Huang's use of the biometric lock meant that coming back without him would be fruitless.

What dominated her thoughts, though, was how long Evan could survive inside that safe.

The Ticonderoga would be airtight, no doubt about that. Locke had no idea how fast Evan would consume the oxygen inside the box or how much time the extra tank would provide.

Was he panicking? Huffing and puffing would use the oxygen faster.

Wouldn't you *panic, locked inside a pitch-black steel box?*

When she reached the Mercedes, Locke was glad no one challenged her for the shotgun seat. At least she wouldn't have to face anyone during the drive.

Her relief evaporated when Huang climbed behind the wheel and keyed the ignition. His proximity alone caused a physical reaction—her skin seemed to tighten, her muscles twitched.

"Evan will be fine, Ms. Locke," Huang said, as if reading her thoughts. "With the bottle, he has well over four hours of oxygen. Our mission should take no more than three. So long as we all cooperate, you should be reunited with him before his bedtime."

Locke's eyes darted to the dashboard. The clock said 4:54.

But the small comfort of having a deadline disappeared as she started to think through it.

Three hours?

That struck her as impossibly quick. As she tried to make the math work, Huang's Mercedes lurched into reverse and turned out of the lot.

After a few hundred yards down a sandy path, Huang steered onto a real, asphalt road. At that point, the sun shifted to sit squarely, uncomfortably, in her side mirror.

Blocking the glare with her hand, Locke watched passing warehouses and power stations gradually give way to small strip malls. Although the terrain was interminably flat, no buildings loomed as landmarks. Street signs proved equally useless—all the identifiers were numbers, as if knowing you were crossing Seventy-Fourth Street helped if you had no idea where the other seventy-three were located.

Eyeing the dashboard clock every few seconds, Locke was relieved to see an overpass approaching.

But as they drew closer, Huang made no move for the ramp. He cruised underneath without slowing, turning north a few blocks later.

Now Locke really began to fidget. Although only four minutes had elapsed, she'd thought the only thing south of Miami was Key West. Why would they be heading north?

A minute later, the SUV turned into a parking lot ringed by chain-link fencing. The lone building visible was a Quonset hut–type hangar with three private jets lined up next to it.

Locke couldn't contain her confusion any longer. "I thought we were going to that yacht."

"We are," Huang said. "Our transport is there."

Huang angled the SUV into a parking space and pointed out the windshield.

A helicopter stood waiting on the tarmac.

24

Locke swallowed her questions about the helicopter and went along silently. They were pretending to be rich people, after all.

Besides, whatever got them to the boat faster ought to be a good thing.

When she exited the SUV, though, Locke was surprised to find King unloading suitcases from the trunk. No one had brought bags out of the warehouse, so she had no idea where the luggage had come from or what it contained.

Locke ended up with a window seat in the helo. Queen sat next to her, with Jack and Huang filling out the back row. After dealing with the bags, King sat up front, serving as a copilot.

Aside from the better-padded seats, the start of the flight reminded Locke of CH-47 Chinooks she'd flown in as a soldier. The headset helped but didn't eliminate the deafening rotor racket. Unlike the smooth flight on a commercial jet, in the chopper you felt everything—every vibration, every little shift in momentum and position. When she closed her eyes, she could see the sunbaked hills of Iraq instead of the tropical landscape below.

Locke had never expected to hate a place more than Camp Taji, but now Miami was definitely in the running.

When she opened her eyes, the downtown skyline and bridges had already appeared. The low sun cast long shadows past the shoreline, turning the bay a deep emerald. As the chopper banked over the water, Locke felt a twinge in her gut. Consciously, she understood a water landing was better than crashing on land, but she held her breath until they reached the thin spit of Miami Beach.

Ahead she could see the glass towers Huang had shown them that first night. They gleamed in the setting sun, forcing her to squint to look for *Helios* among the heavily shadowed ships below.

She didn't see the yacht at first glance, a surprise considering how large it was. Before she could check again, the black towers flashed by her window, interrupting her view.

Assuming they'd bank back toward the marina, Locke abandoned her search. But as seconds continued to tick, the chopper maintained its heading. Soon they passed out over the water again.

Locke's muscles clenched when the land disappeared.

And that feeling worsened when the bird banked the wrong way. Instead of turning right, back toward shore, it leaned left.

Out to sea.

Below the chopper, the ocean deepened to a dark navy blue. Staring down at it and the whitecaps dotting its surface, Locke tried to swallow.

Her throat resisted.

No one had used the intercom yet, but she toggled the radio. "Where's—"

Before she finished the question, Queen elbowed her and pointed out front.

Locke strained against her shoulder straps to see around King. But quickly the chopper banked right, leaving her a clear view of *Helios*.

Painted bright white, it stood out like an iceberg adrift on the indigo ocean. The vessel was monstrous—longer than navy vessels Locke had seen and much taller, its decks stacked high like a cruise ship's. The foamy wake spilling behind the boat suggested it was steaming away from shore in a hurry.

Locke barely had time to register *Helios*'s speed before the helicopter cut altitude. Her eyes shut and stomach flipped as the chopper dived.

When she finally sensed the craft leveling, she forced her eyes open. Although she guessed the chopper was still fifty feet above the waves, it looked as if the skids were scraping the water's surface. To keep from vomiting, Locke focused on *Helios* as the copter flew alongside.

At the rear of the ship, a swimming pool was mounted lengthwise in the lowermost deck—men and women in swimsuits played and swam in the clear water while others sunned themselves on surrounding lounge chairs. The dozen or so bathers were the biggest crowd Locke had seen in weeks.

From the tans on these people, none had missed any pool time recently.

Although the decks were tapered in length, particularly toward the rear of the ship, the yacht rose almost vertically, a five-story white wall buffed to such a shine that Locke could see the helicopter's reflection in it. Each deck had a balcony, and additional passengers were gathered on every level, eyeing the horizon or pointing at the chopper.

After passing the yacht, the helicopter rose and banked back across the ship's nose. This gave Locke a full view of the forward deck, which had been converted to a dance floor. Colored lights on tall stanchions flashed across a crowd of a dozen or two gyrating before a deejay and his turntables.

The helicopter sped back along the opposite side of *Helios* until it cleared the stern. There it made a tight U-turn and approached the uppermost deck, where a landing pad was marked with a red *H*.

As a soldier, Locke had never landed on an aircraft carrier or anything like that. Watching the chopper line itself up with the moving ship and descend to its skids while both were steaming forward was awfully impressive. Although she felt a flash of sweat at the maneuver, the pilot never flinched.

Once the chopper landed, flurries of activity began around the bird. Three crewmen in yellow vests and helmets began tying her down. Another group, outfitted like hotel valets but wearing face masks and gloves, slid mobile stair-cases to the doors before unloading the luggage King had handled before departure. Finally, a medical crew appeared. Dressed in green scrubs with gloves, masks, and face shields, this bunch wheeled carts to the edge of the helipad.

Huang's voice came over the intercom. "Masks."

Having not worn one for a couple of days, Locke was jarred by the concept of donning a mask again. Quickly, though, she remembered: her *Jaws* mask was presumably still sitting back in Val Verde. She started to ask what she should do when Queen shoved a piece of fabric into her hand.

Locke checked the mask before slipping it on. It matched her dress down to the sequins.

Once the rotors were restrained, the medical crew moved to either side of the helicopter. King hopped out first and was immediately escorted to one of the carts. Locke couldn't see what they were doing to him before another crewman offered her a gloved hand.

She stepped down from the helo as gracefully as she could—with the skirt so short, she needed one hand to hold it in place. Like King, Locke was steered toward one of the rolling carts. There, a medical worker produced what looked like an elongated Q-tip and pointed at her face. "Nose."

Locke glanced around, but King had already been shuf-fled off to the side. She gestured at her mask, like she might pull it down. The crewman nodded.

Once she lowered the fabric, the medic jabbed the swab uncomfortably far up her nose. Circular motions seemed to scrape the underside of her skull—an odd feeling that both tickled and made her eyes water. Upon withdrawing the swab, he gave her a sheepish bow, then motioned for her to re-cover her face and stand with King.

Queen, Jack, and Huang all underwent an identical procedure. After the probing was completed, Huang flipped through a folder of papers with one of the medical team. Then he joined the others.

Locke fidgeted as they waited. While the air was still warm and thick, the wind was significant. All that air rushing over so much of her skin at once left her feeling . . . vulnerable.

Finally, one of the medical crew motioned for the group to follow him inside.

They passed through a steel hatch one by one. Although doors at the far end of the hallway marked entrances to the bridge, they were shown into a conference room on the right. Huang lined Locke and the others up along the windows before seating himself at the table.

A minute later, a gaunt man entered the room. Dressed in a blue herringbone suit, he carried a leather portfolio under his arm. The flecks of gray in his tightly trimmed hair, the deep furrows in his brow, and his small spectacles all conveyed that he was some kind of serious official.

He sat across from Huang and, after adjusting his shirt cuffs, folded his hands on top of the unopened portfolio. He glanced over all of them, although Locke could have sworn his eyes lingered an extra moment on Queen.

Huang spoke first. "A pleasure to see you again, Mr. Zhilkin."

Zhilkin's hairline, carved into a sharp widow's peak, left lots of room for his dark eyebrows to move, and they jumped at the words. "Have we met?"

"At the St. Petersburg economic forum. Perhaps six months ago."

"Ah, the discussion of Chinese and Russian cooperation. Yes." The way Zhilkin's dark eyes twinkled behind his glasses, Locke wasn't sure he needed to be reminded.

"A lovely evening," Huang said. "I am very happy the cooperation between our countries has been expanding as part of the Belt and Road initiative. And, given the construction projects announced so far, I imagine Mr. Glebov is pleased as well."

"Mr. Glebov always favors mutually beneficial business arrangements. Which raises the question, what can we do for you and your . . . party?"

"I have come in response to Mr. Glebov's invitation."

Zhilkin stared back at Huang silently.

Huang leaned back in his seat. "As you are doubtlessly aware, travel has become sharply restricted. I cannot return home, but with the politics of this disease, America has become significantly less hospitable. Weathering the storm aboard this vessel seemed a prudent choice. From what I witnessed from the air, it appears to be a most pleasant way to pass the time."

"Our facilities are quite comprehensive." Zhilkin gave a slight nod. "But your country's role in the current . . . situation may cause some on board to question your presence here."

Huang chuckled. "As chief of security, I understand it is your responsibility to be paranoid, Mr. Zhilkin. By all accounts, you are outstanding at your job. However, I have provided health papers for myself and my entourage. Your own men have now tested us. Have we not proven ourselves clean enough?"

Locke's heart accelerated. She had little faith that Huang would free her and Evan if the mission was successful. But if they weren't even allowed onto the boat . . .

Zhilkin smiled sheepishly, although, coming so quickly, it struck Locke again as more scripted than genuine. "You must understand, it is not Mr. Glebov *himself* who would object. His other guests . . ."

"You will recall," Huang said, "that his invitation came with two conditions?"

"Yes."

"I have provided all the medical documentation necessary to comply with the first condition. But I suspect Mr. Glebov will be particularly interested in how I plan to satisfy the second. The thing of value."

"I understood that the value would come via your group's . . . services." Zhilkin flicked his wrist at Locke and the others, but again his eyes seemed to focus on Queen.

"Partially. But I also have something Mr. Glebov has expressed an interest in obtaining."

Huang produced the wooden cube from Malibu and set it on the table in front of him.

Zhilkin reached forward. "May I—"

Huang placed his hand over the top of the box. "This gift is for Mr. Glebov. In appreciation of his hospitality. If he cannot be bothered to receive it himself . . ."

He glanced to the side, then focused back on Zhilkin. While Locke couldn't see Huang's face, she'd received enough of his sharp-eyed stares to imagine his expression.

"Perhaps I should take my entourage and depart," Huang continued. "My country has been scorned and ridiculed for centuries. Our government understands this, even as it works with others in hopes that cooperation will lead to understanding. To better treatment abroad for businessmen such as myself. When I explain how I was refused here, my contacts in Beijing will hopefully sympathize and facilitate my return."

Although Zhilkin remained stone-faced, his Adam's apple bobbed above his collar. "Mr. Glebov is engaged at the moment. Let me see if he will excuse himself."

"Thank you."

Zhilkin stood, adjusted his jacket, and departed as efficiently as he'd entered.

Once the door closed, Huang pocketed the box before standing and turning around. His smile let Locke exhale.

Jack whispered something to Huang in Mandarin—a wisecrack, from the way he snickered.

Huang silenced him with a stare. He tugged on his ear, then glanced around the room.

After two minutes that seemed more like ten, the door reopened. Zhilkin entered, followed by a shorter, heavier-set man clad in shorts and a resort shirt. From the way his bronze skin glistened and the faint scent of coconut that followed him into the room, it seemed he'd been retrieved from sunbathing by the pool. Much like his clothing, the shorter man's movements were more relaxed than Zhilkin's except for his shoulders, which he carried thrown back in rigid fashion.

Zhilkin withdrew the chair for his boss, then tucked it underneath him as he sat.

Huang took his own seat and bowed his head deeply. "Mr. Glebov, I thank you for welcoming us aboard."

"Of course." Glebov's mouth remained downturned even when he smiled; his cheeks merely pulled his lips to either side, exposing some teeth.

"I was in Malta for business several years ago," Huang said, "and saw the *Helios* docked. Among all the fine yachts, it shone like a diamond. I wondered if I would ever set foot aboard it. Now that I have, it is even more impressive."

Glebov nodded once. "We have never opened *Helios* to the public. But what is going on in the world, this plague . . . very dangerous. Every week, each day, the news seemingly grows worse. That is the reason, two weeks ago, I decided we would wait no longer. I sent word to friends and contacts, announcing our plan to anchor off the United States. I meant for people to join us. Assuming they were healthy and could contribute to our little community, of course."

"Your generosity is inspiring," Huang said. "As consideration for this favor, I have an offering."

Huang produced the wooden box again, only this time he opened the lid. From inside he withdrew a small figurine.

Glebov blinked several times. "I assume that is—"

"Oh, yes. Yes, it is."

25

Upon finally seeing the box's contents, Locke felt acid creep up her throat.

The figurine was cast from pale-green stone, the same color as a jade pin her mother had worn on special occasions, and showed a rabbit resting on its haunches. With a surface more smoothed than polished, the statue didn't shine as Huang spun it slowly in his hand.

To Locke's untrained eye, the carving looked simple and unimpressive. Had her neighbor and friend Constance really died over a stupid lump of stone?

Glebov showed no such reservations. The way his eyes narrowed on the little statue, he looked positively smitten. "May I?"

Huang passed the figurine across the table.

"At last," Glebov said, "the Rabbit raises its head. You know the story, I assume."

Huang nodded. "Yuanmingyuan is legendary."

"Zhilkin, have I explained the significance of these jade pieces?"

The security chief shook his head.

"It is quite ironic, actually, that we have just departed the United States. You studied their Revolution while at Georgetown, yes?"

"Of course," Zhilkin said. "Seventeen seventy-six."

"And yet this statue's carving preceded George Washington." Glebov lifted the figurine up to the light and gazed through it. "In 1707, the Qing Dynasty's third emperor ordered the creation of a grand garden outside Beijing as a gift to his son. He called it Yuanmingyuan, the Garden of Perfection and Light.

"Over one hundred and fifty years, the garden was expanded into one of the great wonders of the world. In 1747, extensive fountains were added to the Yuanmingyuan. The most famous of these was a water clock called the Haiyantang. Twelve bronze animal heads, each representing a sign of the Chinese zodiac, were arranged around a large pool. Depending on the hour, water would spout from a different head.

"Then, in 1860, the British destroyed Yuanmingyuan. Four thousand troops required three days to burn it completely. But the soldiers also looted countless pieces of artwork, including the bronze fountainheads. Treasure hunters and archaeologists have sought them ever since. Seven heads have been recovered and now reside in Chinese museums. Five remain missing. The Chinese effort to locate them has been quite extensive."

Zhilkin nodded at the Rabbit. "How does this piece relate to the fountain?"

"That," Glebov said, "is the interesting part. The bronze pieces are legendary, as Mr. Huang indicated. The emperor commissioned them from an Italian artist who created many works for Chinese royalty. But few know he based them on a series of jade figurines that date back even further."

"How far back?"

"The Han Dynasty," Glebov said. "Approximately 200 BC to 200 AD."

Zhilkin's eyes widened. "So that statue—"

"Dates from the time of Jesus Christ, yes. Holding this statue is a look back through two millennia." Glebov raised the figurine to his eyes, his hand flat like a platter. "Can you imagine? The artisan who carved this statue likely earned only a small wage for his trouble. Yet through it, he achieved what we all seek: immortality."

After a long, silent moment admiring the Rabbit, Glebov trained his gaze back on Huang. "I must admit, Mr. Huang, given the way Chinese artifacts have been forcibly reclaimed over the past few years, I am surprised you are delivering this to me. If anything, I expected your government to come demanding the return of its brothers at some point."

"If you are referring to the objects taken from certain English museums, those were robberies—"

"Not just England." Glebov began counting on his fingers. "Drottningholm Palace in Sweden, six pieces stolen. The Château de Fontainebleau in Paris, fifteen pieces taken in seven minutes. The Oriental Museum at Durham University; the Fitzwilliam Museum at Cambridge; the Kode Museum, twice . . ."

Huang shook his head. "The Western media suspects my country is behind everything that happens in the world. None of those crimes were tied to the Chinese government."

"Yet only Chinese artifacts were taken from large collections including countless other masterpieces. Curious, no?"

"Not everything Chinese implicates the Chinese government." Huang grunted. "And I do not work for the government, as you are aware."

Glebov gestured to the security chief, who was still standing to his right. "When you first arrived, Mr. Zhilkin worried you might be here to try to talk me out of the statues I have located. Or to take them from me straightaway."

A jolt of electricity flashed across Locke's skin.

They know.

Locke had never met a billionaire, but she figured they hadn't accumulated all that money by letting people steal from them. For all of Glebov's easy-breezy talk and relaxed clothing, he radiated power and control. And while Zhilkin looked like some kind of professor in his suit and glasses, she saw the same hardness in his eyes as she'd seen in Big Bo and other gangsters around LA.

A chill settled into her bones.

They were on a boat. In the middle of the Atlantic Ocean.

If Glebov wanted them to disappear, tossing them over the side would be about as easy as it got. She flashed back to the Malibu swimming pool, struggling for breath. And that hadn't been teeming with sharks.

Huang interrupted her thoughts with an awkward, high-pitched laugh. "Me, a thief?"

Locke had to hand it to him: it sounded authentic.

"I am flattered," he said, "but I am merely a businessman. Granted, far less successful than yourself. But what success I have enjoyed puts me in a position to be able to ask for your assistance at this difficult time. And to show my appreciation with this gift."

Glebov squinted as he rubbed his chin. "Does it not trouble you to see pieces of your homeland's history in others' hands?"

"If artifacts cannot be in their ancestral home, there is still value in knowing they are well looked after."

Glebov stared at Huang for a long moment.

Although Locke couldn't see his eyes, she imagined Huang staring right back.

"Then . . ."

Locke's heart climbed into her throat. A quick glance down the line showed the others leaning forward.

". . . welcome!" Glebov raised open arms.

Locke exhaled, and thought she heard others do the same.

Glebov replaced the Rabbit in its wooden box before standing. "I hope you find our accommodations comfortable. I will leave you in Mr. Zhilkin's capable hands."

Huang rose to his feet. "Mr. Glebov—"

"Please, call me Stepan."

"Stepan, at some point I would love to see the other members of your collection."

Glebov smiled broadly, his cheeks straining. "A wonderful idea. Now that the statues are reunited, we should find time to display them together. I will have someone see to it."

Although Locke had only the last ten minutes to judge by, she figured Glebov's offer was utter bullshit. No way he was ever letting that Rabbit out of his sight. And even less chance he'd let Huang near the other figurines.

Locke also realized something else: if Glebov was allowing them to stay despite his suspicions, that meant his security detail had already fortified the boat enough that they considered it impregnable.

Glebov clapped his palms together and left the room. As he exited, a pair of armed guards stepped in to replace him. Worse, Locke could see more uniformed men stationed outside the door. An odd way to greet honored guests.

Zhilkin remained standing. "Welcome to *Helios*. A few words of explanation to assist you with your stay.

"Everyone aboard has tested negative for the novel virus, as have you via the rapid tests we administered upon your arrival. Thus, while we are equipped with a doctor and state-of-the-art medical equipment, there is no need for masks or other PPE."

Locke tried not to let her mouth hang open. She didn't know a single person who'd been tested. News reports talked about results taking weeks, not minutes.

"Based on expert projections, we may need to remain at sea for six months."

"And you foresee no problems with that schedule?" Huang asked.

Zhilkin raised an eyebrow. "We can sail indefinitely thanks to our ability to resupply via helicopter. We have ample supplies of water, food, and other . . . necessities, but we will receive regular deliveries while observing proper contact protocols. Our chefs will provide three meals per day at standard times, but there is à la carte service between meals. If you have any food allergies or dietary restrictions, please alert our staff."

Locke thought back to her grocery runs at home, her visits to the pharmacy for Constance's prescriptions. Donning masks and gloves, sanitizing a cart, then wiping down her purchases when she returned home. *Must be nice to have everything airlifted.*

She also wondered what Zhilkin meant by "other necessities." The tone in his voice didn't suggest sunscreen or pool floaties.

Huang pointed at Jack. "I can offer additional hands for cooking."

"Running our kitchen continuously is a challenge, so your offer is appreciated." Zhilkin turned to the guards. "Please show Mr. Huang's man to the kitchen. I am sure Chef Nikolai can find a place for him."

Without a word, Jack followed the guards from the room.

Zhilkin now moved to a framed diagram of the ship on the wall behind him. He pointed with a bony finger. "*Helios* has six decks. Guests generally have run of the ship, but we have installed certain restrictions that we would ask you to observe. This uppermost deck houses the bridge, security, and certain functions like the helicopter pad that render it off-limits. Please do not visit this deck unless your presence is specifically requested."

"I have brought my own security," Huang said, jerking a thumb back at King. "I am also willing to share his services."

Zhilkin gave a narrow smile. "Thank you. My team does not require outside assistance. I will need to collect any firearms, however."

King withdrew a gun from inside his jacket and laid it on the table. Huang followed suit.

Zhilkin gestured at the next level down on the map. "Deck five is reserved for wives and children. It is completely self-contained, so a single man such as yourself should have no need to interact with them. Deck four contains the balance of our staterooms. One is being prepared for you as we speak.

"I expect deck three is where you will spend the bulk of your time. Meals are served in the indoor/outdoor dining space. Forward of the dining area is the theater, while in the stern you have likely already seen the pool and sun deck.

"Finally"—Zhilkin pointed to the rear of the ship—"our lowest deck holds our dive locker, spa, and gymnasium. A full range of equipment is available in each one, and professionals are available to assist you."

Locke recalled her trip through the wooden model and tried to determine how it aligned with the layout Zhilkin had described.

Huang pointed at the chart. "You skipped deck two . . ."

"You will not need to visit the second deck," Zhilkin said. "It merely houses the crew quarters and office space for Mr. Glebov's business ventures. Like this level, deck two is restricted to authorized personnel only."

Huang nodded.

"Elevators connect the decks fore and aft, as do interior and exterior stairs at midship. Which brings us to the women. I assume they are not your wives?"

Huang chuckled. "No. Like my security man and my chef, they provide . . . professional services."

Locke blinked several times. Queen had said *distraction*, not *prostitute*.

Zhilkin's face spread into an openmouthed grin that bared his teeth. "Several passengers have agreed to pool the services of such professionals to . . . diversify their choices.

You may of course decide whether to join that group or keep your assets private."

Huang splayed his hands out to this side. "As you have seen, I am grateful to be included among the distinguished guests aboard. I would, of course, be more than happy to share what is mine."

Zhilkin looked at Locke in a way that turned her blood to ice.

And while his eyes shifted quickly to Queen, all the power and ferocity Locke had felt back at the warehouse evaporated. Everything she was wearing—the dress, the makeup, all of it—irritated her skin. She wanted to claw at it, to scratch it all away and replace it with her coveralls and boots.

"I did not mean to suggest earlier that my gratitude extended only to Mr. Glebov," said Huang. "I appreciate your consideration as well, Mr. Zhilkin."

Without warning, Queen stepped out of line and strutted around the table toward the opposite side.

"From the functions we have attended together," Huang said, "it appears you prefer redheaded companionship?"

Zhilkin didn't answer. His eyes were locked on the auburn-wigged Queen the whole time.

To Locke's surprise, the Pink Punker was smirking back at Zhilkin. Encouraging the skinny prick. Once she stood before him, Queen had to look up to make eye contact despite the heels. She poked his chest with her index finger.

Zhilkin flashed a quick glance across the table. Huang waved back with an open palm.

Wrapping his bony fingers around Queen's arm, Zhilkin squeezed into her flesh in a way that turned Locke's stomach.

"If you're trying to search me, Mr. Chief of Security, that's not really the dangerous part." Without breaking eye contact, Queen grabbed his hand and moved it to her breast.

Other than swallowing noticeably, Zhilkin froze.

"You can squeeze harder than that," she cooed. "I'm not gonna break."

Zhilkin's fingers flexed. The knuckles grew whiter as he applied increasing pressure until Queen gasped.

"Don't leave me lopsided." She grabbed his other hand and slapped it onto her other breast.

Locke couldn't believe what she was seeing. After what Queen had said she'd been through . . . how could she let him manhandle her like this?

Finally, Queen grabbed his wrists. Her eyes flicked open and stared up at him. "More later?"

Zhilkin nodded. Then he turned back to Huang. "We have separate accommodations on deck one for employees such as these."

Huang hesitated. "I . . . I expected they would remain in my stateroom. With the wives upstairs—"

"You may certainly bring them to your stateroom whenever you like, but we prefer to have them separately quartered. Allowing the women to roam freely can lead to problems— jealousies and misunderstandings. Plus, our guests tend to desire female companionship for certain activities more than others. The ocean, the spa, that sort of thing. For that reason, we have located them on deck one, close to the gym, the dive locker, and so forth. We ask that you return them there when you are finished."

"So . . ." Huang hesitated a moment. "I have no choice in this matter?"

"I am afraid not." With that, Zhilkin stepped to the conference room door. He yanked it open and motioned for the additional guards.

"Take these two below," he said, pointing at Queen and Locke. "You know where."

CHAPTER

26

THE FOUR GUARDS were bulky guys, imposing enough that taking on any one of them would have been a challenge, even without the pistols on their waistbands. They paired up, bracketing the women front and back as they escorted them to the elevator.

When the door slid open with an electronic chime, it revealed a posh, wood-paneled interior with a brass rail and thick carpeting. But the car was tiny, barely five by five.

Before Locke could process how they'd all fit, two guards packed inside, backs pressed against the rear wall. The remaining two shoved Locke and Queen in, then squeezed behind them as the doors closed.

They stood body to body, women pinned in the center, surrounded by the men. With so much of herself exposed by the dress, Locke couldn't help but feel the stiffly starched fabric of the guards' uniforms, the hair on their arms, the sweat on their skin. It roiled her stomach. She pinched her shoulders, drew in her elbows, sucked in her tummy. Anything to make herself thinner.

But she still had to breathe.

The air inside the car was noticeably warmer than the conference room, and packing in six people didn't help.

Worse, the stale air started to take on the sour stench of body odor and bad breath.

Between the heat and the pressure and the smell, Locke felt like she might not make it downstairs. And that wasn't counting the leering looks the guards were giving her and Queen.

Locke's eyes darted to the floor indicator, desperate to see the numbers change. As they crept by slowly, though, something pressed against her hip. Glancing down, she found one of the guard's hands.

She slapped it away.

It returned, more forcefully this time.

Locke's pulse quickened—she didn't know how rough she could afford to get. Or how far these guys would insist on taking things.

Queen spoke up, wagging a finger at the guards. "Nuh-uh, boys! I don't think Mr. Zhilkin wants sloppy seconds."

At the mention of their boss, the guards' hands dropped to their sides. Their faces straightened.

"That's right. No touching." Queen spun in a slow circle, pointing at each of them. "Yet." She laughed a tipsy, drunken laugh.

The guards traded nervous looks. Finally, one of them let out a chuckle.

Then another.

Soon, everyone inside the elevator was laughing.

Everyone except Locke. She still couldn't believe any of this.

When Queen noticed her expression, she twisted up her face into mock anger. She flashed that to the guards, saying, "So grumpy."

They laughed again. Harder now.

Every cell in Locke's body wanted to rear back and slap Queen silly. To scream at the top of her lungs.

Instead, a chime sounded.

They'd reached deck one.

When the door slid open, the exterior guards backpedaled out, looking disappointed that the ride was over.

But a wild smile spread across Queen's face. She grabbed Locke's hand and dragged her from the car. As soon as they cleared the door, the Pink Punker veered to the right, pulling Locke behind her.

Locke strained to slow their progress, hoping at least to see where they were going. All she could make out ahead of them was a long, white passage. A door was approaching on the right, close enough she could read the sign mounted on it: SUBMARINE. A quick glance back showed the four guards following. They strode all tall and official, as if shepherding the women, but Locke quickly realized Queen was the one leading the way.

Suddenly, a glimmer of hope flashed in Locke's chest. Maybe this was all part of some crazy plan. It looked like a straight shot to the stern—was Queen sneaking them ahead of the guards to outrace them?

Locke stopped resisting and started moving her feet. Slowly at first, then faster. Soon she was using her long strides not only to catch up to Queen but to push her along.

Two more doors appeared: ENGINE 1 and ENGINE 2.

The women were almost running now. Another glance back showed the gap widening.

Up ahead, a series of matching doors loomed on both sides. These were packed close together, without labels.

Queen stopped and called back to the guards, "These?"

Locke, who'd been racing along, now nearly collided with Queen. Barely sidestepping the Pink Punker, she ended up with a view back at the guards. The leader shook his head and motioned forward with his finger.

Queen started and stopped again at the next pair of doors. "These?"

The lead guard nodded and jerked his thumb to the right.

Queen gave Locke's arm a final yank, pulling her closer and tipping her off-balance. As Locke stumbled, Queen opened the unmarked door and redirected Locke through it.

Once Locke regained her balance, she spun to confront Queen, who'd followed her inside. "What are you—"

Before she could finish, the lead guard entered the room, looking amused. He raised a finger. "One per room."

Keeping her eyes locked on him, Queen wrapped her arms around Locke's neck. "You sure we can't be . . . together?"

The guard's mouth dropped open.

But then a second guard burst into the room. Racing to the women, he pried them apart and dragged Queen toward the door.

She resisted, forcing the first guard to help.

Soon each man had one of her arms. As they faced the door and applied more force, Queen glanced back and gave Locke a quick wink and a smile.

And then she was gone.

Once the guards got Queen through the hatch, they slammed it shut and locked it with a loud clack.

After the echo stopped reverberating around the tiny room, Locke's heartbeat became the dominant sound. Pounding rapid-fire, it thudded in her ears like the sound a boxer made on a speed bag. She drew deep breaths, trying to slow her pulse and process what the hell had just happened.

From what Huang had said, it certainly seemed like he'd been after the contents of Glebov's safe for a long time. Long enough to have gotten the *Helios* plans and determined Zhilkin's taste in women. But aside from those details, Glebov seemed to be ahead of Huang at every turn. He'd known Huang was coming. He'd taken the Rabbit statue. And she didn't believe for a minute Jack needed armed escorts to find the kitchen—she suspected he was now locked up in some similar cell elsewhere on the boat.

Not that Jack deserved any sympathy. He could rot.

But Locke had assumed Huang and the others would protect her, at least until she opened the safe. Now they were disarmed and divided, spread all over the ship.

Worst of all, every second that passed, Evan sucked down another breath inside the Ticonderoga. The clock to free him was ticking away faster than her heartbeat, and Glebov had just tossed Huang's three-hour plan overboard. In fact, she had no idea how much time had elapsed.

Panic flashed across her skin.

Reminding herself that she'd already escaped one locked room, Locke checked the door. A flat metal sheet. Unlike the warehouse closet, this compartment seemed specifically designed to hold people captive—there wasn't even an interior knob.

She was stuck until someone opened the door from the outside.

Slowly, she spun to take in the rest of her accommodations.

Small, but clean. An improvement from the janitor's closet.

The room was built long, but narrower than her outstretched arms. Like the two decks she'd seen so far, the floor was coated in that gray, sandpapery paint they used on boats to keep you from slipping. A quick rap of her knuckles against the bare walls suggested they were fiberglass or hard plastic, nothing she could cut through easily. There were no windows, no vents. Even the fluorescent tube overhead was caged behind metal bars bolted to the ceiling.

The lone piece of furniture was a small cot pushed into one corner, a bare mattress laid over the metal frame. A steel toilet and sink jutted out from the opposite wall.

Overall, not too different from her holding cell at Camp Taji. This at least smelled better, thanks to a deodorizer cake inside the commode, although the thick pine scent didn't exactly match being on a boat at sea.

Locke's eyes returned to the mattress.

Judging from the snow-white cover, it was likely brand-new. Glebov could afford to change them out.

It still made her skin crawl.

The idea of lying on it . . . it . . . touching her. After what might have already been done on top of it. And what Zhilkin and his pigs had in mind for it now.

Locke's stomach revolted, sending a scalding mouthful of vomit up her throat.

No.

Mentally clamping a lid on her stomach, Locke stepped to the sink and spat the gob of bile out. She slurped a handful of water from the faucet, swished it through her mouth, then spat that out too.

The white mattress was still waiting when she spun around from the sink.

The mattress at Taji hadn't been as new. Or as clean.

Still, it had been a welcome sight. By the time the MPs had locked her up, all the adrenaline had faded. She'd dropped onto the cot and fallen asleep without so much as rinsing off her hands. Of course, she'd paid for that later, waking up to find her knuckles bloody, her hands swollen. She could barely flex her fingers. But at that moment, simply seeing the mattress—the prospect of laying her leaden arms and shoulders down, of closing her eyes and drifting away—had been too much to resist.

Earlier that night, Kori had woken her from a sound sleep, which was part of the problem. After a full shift at the machine shop, Locke had returned to her Container-ized Housing Unit looking forward to a few hours' rest. She and her comm tech corporal roommate were on opposite schedules, so she'd have the CHU to herself. The little air conditioner mounted on top made the perfect white noise for sleeping—despite cutting the temperature inside the modular trailer only to the mideighties, its mechanical hum had knocked her out in seconds.

She'd fallen so far under, the banging on the metal door to her CHU had slipped right into her dream. But as the noise continued, her brain registered that something wasn't right.

Locke's eyes popped open, and she rolled out of her rack into her boots. Her first assessment was whether they were under attack, but this didn't seem like the rocket fire they'd warned about in orientation. The only noise was coming from her door.

She rose and snuck to it as the banging continued.

The lock on the CHU door was merely a metal bar that slid into an eyelet on the doorframe. Locke hooked a finger around the latch and held her breath. The stories she'd heard before shipping out made it sound more dangerous for females inside the wire than out, but through thirteen months, she hadn't experienced anything unusual. Some wiseass comments here or there, ogling eyeballs from some E3s. But nothing worse than that—nothing to keep her from sleeping.

Until now.

The only light inside the CHU came from the streak of yellow spilling under the door from halogens outside. Locke could see two shadows blocking the light outside. A pair of legs.

The pace of the pounding gradually subsided. The force behind it softened.

The sound grew weak. Almost . . . desperate.

Biting her lower lip, Locke yanked the latch free and pulled the door toward her, all in one motion. She slid behind the door as it swung into the room, hoping it would shield her from whoever or whatever came through.

To her surprise, a body tumbled inside. It fell face first onto the floor, then curled into a fetal position facing away from her.

Even from behind, Locke recognized the tiny woman framed in the yellow light.

She rushed to Kori, kneeling at her back and rubbing her shoulder. For a moment, there was no reaction. Locke's fingers dug into the meat of Kori's arm until finally her chest moved.

Thank god.

"Muh . . . muh . . ."

"It's me, it's Monna. I'm right here."

She rubbed Kori's arm again. This time, Kori's whole body convulsed.

"Hey, hey." As Locke shushed her, she noticed how much of Kori's hair had pulled free of her French braid and become plastered across her face. It wasn't like Kori didn't know how to tie it—for a long time in basic, her hair had been the only thing Kori got right.

Locke swept the strands off Kori's cheek, hooking them behind her ear. The hair was damp with tears. "What's wrong, what happened?"

The CHUs at Camp Taji were arranged in groups called pods—Kori's pod wasn't far, but both their workstations lay in the opposite direction. There was no reason for Kori to be over here, unless she was seeking out Locke. Not that she'd been doing that lately.

When Locke tried to shift Kori onto her back, she resisted, curling into an even tighter ball. Her chest heaved under her BDU blouse.

Locke moved Kori's arm and took her hand. "C'mon, breathe with me."

Locke drew an exaggerated breath in through her nose, then released it through pursed lips, as if trying to blow out the world's biggest birthday cake. Back in basic, as she'd helped Kori build her endurance, there'd been plenty of times Locke had pulled them off the running track and guided Kori's breathing to keep her from hyperventilating.

Jaw trembling as if she were freezing, Kori sucked in a ragged breath.

"Now, let it out."

Kori exhaled in several short puffs.

Locke continued coaching until Kori's chest was rising and falling smoothly. "Okay, now tell me, what's going on? What's wrong?"

From her position at Kori's hip, Locke could see her dark eyes flick open. But Kori didn't look over, didn't make eye contact. She continued staring off at the far wall. "I'm . . . I'm sorry. For coming, I . . . I didn't know where else to go."

When the women had last seen each other two weeks earlier, Kori had asked Locke to stay away. To give her "space." Kori said it was what she wanted, but Locke knew the request had come from Kori's new boyfriend.

At twenty-two, Newton was nearly three years older, a living reminder of the nugget from high school health class that boys matured later than girls. A ground pounder from Iowa—or was it Indiana? one of those *I* states in the middle—he'd approached Kori at the gym. At least, that's the story he told. Knowing the talk the two women had had a few days before that, the hard questions Locke had asked Kori about what she wanted and where things were going, Locke suspected Kori had made the first move. Or convinced Newton to do it without realizing he'd just been played.

Either way, the first time Newton met Locke, he wouldn't look her in the eye. And afterward, he'd actively avoided her—getting up and leaving the table when she arrived, turning and walking away if he saw her coming. She had no idea what Newton knew, about Miami or anything else, but he very clearly didn't want her around Kori.

So, when Kori'd made her request for space, Locke had stormed off. Their first fight . . . ever, really. Now that seemed like ancient history. "You can always come to me if there's a problem."

Kori started shaking her head, tears flowing again. "I . . . you . . ."

"It's okay. But you gotta tell me what happened."

"Newton."

Of course. "What about Newton?"

"He got . . . angry."

"Why?"

"He thought . . . said I was . . ."

"Thought you were what?"

"He . . . he said he saw me . . . talking with Mandal . . ."

Mandal was another infantryman in Newton's platoon.

"But I wasn't. I swear. I told him . . . I'd never . . ."

Locke could sense Kori's breathing getting rougher again. She shushed her and debated what to say. "Newton's just . . . he's a little insecure, it seems like. Where did all this—"

Kori swallowed hard. "Wrenn's still. We were all drinking, and . . ."

Locke rolled her eyes. One of the cooks, a jovial North Carolina boy named Wrenn, had built a small still underneath his CHU. Although alcohol was technically illegal, almost everyone knew about the vodka he made from potato peelings, preferring it to the hajji juice moonshine that civilian contractors smuggled onto base. "So Newton got a little drunk. It'll blow over."

"No." Kori squeezed her eyes closed again and shook her head. "No, he said he's gonna kill Mandal. He stormed off. That's why I had to come get you . . ."

"Newton said he's gonna kill Mandal?" Locke laughed out loud. Newton was barely five eight and probably weighed one thirty after Thanksgiving dinner. Paul Mandal was six two and cut from granite. "Mandal's huge. He doesn't need to worry."

Kori turned to Locke, panic in her eyes. "That's just it. If Newton goes after him—"

"If Newton's dumb enough to go after Mandal, maybe it'll teach him a lesson." The stupid prick. Locke was half tempted to go watch.

Kori sat halfway up and grabbed Locke's shoulders. "No! Monna, you have to—"

The booze on Kori's breath was noticeable now. Locke closed her eyes and shook her head. "If you think I'm getting in the middle of those two—"

"Please!"

Locke's eyes flicked open to find Kori staring up at her. Although half her face was shrouded in shadow, the tears pooling in Kori's eyes glinted in the yellow light.

"Please, Monna! Mandal will *kill* him."

Kori buried her face in the shoulder of Locke's BDU blouse and sobbed.

Locke's muscles softened. She wrapped one arm around Kori while stroking the back of Kori's head with her other hand. "I . . . I don't . . ."

Her eyes looked up to the dark CHU ceiling, wishing she could find an easy answer up there.

Holding Kori close, Locke could feel her breathing. The rise and fall of her chest. The warmth when she exhaled. The knobby bumps of her spine, the smooth skin at her neck.

And Locke felt her own resolve draining away. "I . . . I can't promise anything."

Kori's head stirred, lifting off Locke's shoulder. "You'll go? Really?"

Before glancing back down, Locke warned herself to soak in whatever look Kori was giving her. That if she did this favor, there might never be another. After a heavy sigh, she said, "I'll try . . ."

"Oh, Monna—thank you!"

Kori's dark eyes beamed above her smile.

But there was something else.

As Kori's body shifted, the light struck her face differently. For the first time, her left cheek was illuminated, and Locke could see something dark smeared across it. In the harsh yellow glow, it looked like black mud.

Locke figured Kori's tears had blotted dirt off the CHU floor. With two fingers, she went to wipe the grime away.

Instead of gritty sand, though, the smudge felt warm and wet. Viscous.

"What's—"

Kori turned away.

"No," Locke said. "C'mere."

When she tried to turn Kori's head, the smaller woman resisted. She gathered her feet underneath her.

But Locke was faster. She bounced up off her knees, seizing Kori's wrist in one hand while reaching for the CHU's light switch with the other.

The moment the light flicked on, she knew.

The way Kori turned away. The way she tilted her head down.

"Let me see."

"No."

"Kori . . ." Locke's teeth were already locked together, the words emerging in growl.

Ever so slowly, Kori's shoulders started to turn.

"Let me see, goddamn it!" Locke used her grip on Kori's wrist to whip her around.

And that was when she saw the blood. The left side of Kori's face was caked with it.

"He didn't mean it," Kori said immediately. "He—"

Locke turned Kori's chin until she found the source, an open cut at the end of her eyebrow. Small, but deep. Enough to need stitches.

"Go see the medics," Locke said. She took a step toward the door.

"No, Monna! Don't!"

Kori clawed at Locke's sleeve, but even at full strength she wouldn't have stood a chance of stopping her. Kori's tiny fingers slid down the fabric as Locke stomped out the door with a full head of steam.

Between that moment and falling onto the dingy mattress inside the holding cell, things were mostly a blur. All Locke remembered now were flashes and feelings. How inky the night sky was as she stormed across camp. The stench of Newton's breath when she spun him around. The satisfying crunch his cheek made as it crumpled beneath her fist.

They told her later it was Mandal who pulled her off him. Him and two other guys.

Staring at the pristine white mattress now, Locke felt the same eerie calm that had crept over her that night as she headed out into the Iraqi darkness. No hot anger, no overwhelming grief. Just . . . quiet and calm. The same silence in her head she experienced when she was laser-focused on a safe dial.

If Zhilkin and those goons thought they'd have their way with her, if Huang thought he could pass her off like some cheap whore, well.

Locke stepped to the little cot and flipped the mattress up. Underneath, the framing was pretty simple—metal rods screwed together, a matrix of springs in the middle.

It would do. She just hoped she had enough time.

*   *   *

In the end, the cot legs weren't as helpful as Locke had thought.

She'd expected to use those, but the L-shaped pieces didn't sit well in her hand.

The cross braces fit better.

Each was a three-foot-long, two-inch-wide strip of metal. Flat, with holes drilled out every few inches as connection points for the springs. The eighth-inch steel plate wasn't as solid as a crowbar. But if you swung quickly, if you led with the narrow edge like it was a supremely dull samurai sword, you could get some leverage behind it.

Enough to break bones.

Locke moved to within two yards of the door.

Far enough that a guard would need to step inside to reach her. Close enough there'd only be room for one attacker at a time, and whoever came into the room would shield her from any guns out in the hallway.

Besides, if they got too close, that's what the springs were for. The first one she'd detached had served as a makeshift screwdriver to help disassemble the bed frame. Once she discovered how neatly it fit into her fist, though, she'd separated a handful more, straightening one hooked end of each spring into a wicked point. After she'd slipped the remaining hooks down through the gown fabric, they hung like fishing lures—if she needed one, she could pluck it right off.

Once she was in position, Locke staggered her feet shoulder-width apart, left in front of right. Then she hoisted the metal brace up onto her shoulder like a baseball bat.

She'd get one good swing at whoever entered first. If she raised the bar over her head and pulled it down like an axe, she could probably crack the guy's skull.

That'd make them think twice.

Seconds ticked by. Long enough, Locke started to wonder if they'd ever come.

Then the door clicked.

Lightly, followed by a louder thunk.

Locke raised the bar. Tensing her arms and shoulders, she took a cleansing breath.

As the door began to move, Locke reminded herself to be patient.

Let them rush in. Don't overcommit.

When the door started to clear the frame, Locke inhaled deeply.

Any second.

Then Queen bad-bitch-strutted into the room. Holding one pistol in her hand and another under her arm, she gave a wicked smile.

"That for me, hon?"

27

"Drop the sword, Conan. If we run into trouble, this'll hit harder." Queen offered Locke the pistol from under her arm.

Locke let the metal bar drop and took the gun. Some kind of compact semiautomatic. She didn't recognize the model, but it looked like one of the guards' guns. The firmness of the grip, the weight in her hand—all of it reminded her of her old M9 and sent a tingle up her arm. Telling herself to get over it, Locke checked the chamber and found a round. "How—"

Queen winked. "Part of the plan, sweetie. C'mon, we're on the clock."

Locke ditched the springs she'd hung off the dress, then followed her into the hallway, which stood empty in both directions. Queen relocked the cell door and started aft, away from the elevator that had delivered them. Walking quickly, she left Locke hurrying to catch up.

"You should tuck that away," the Pink Punker said, staring at the gun.

Locke realized Queen's own pistol had disappeared somehow. "Uh, where exactly?"

"Did I not tell you about the fabulous pocket I added?" Queen took the gun and wedged it down the back of Locke's dress, then beamed proudly. "I made my own leotards too."

The feel of the barrel along her spine made Locke stand up straighter. Realizing she hadn't paid much attention to the rear of the dress, she looked over her shoulder—a drape of fabric hung across the small of her back, obscuring the pistol's outline.

"If you sewed the pocket in," Locke said, thinking it through, "you were counting on all this? Us getting locked up?"

"Oh, yeah," Queen said.

"That shit in the elevator?"

Queen shrugged. "Improv. Gotta keep 'em entertained, one way or another. Now just walk normal."

Locke told herself she wasn't risking blowing off a butt cheek by having the gun wedged back there. But knowing it and believing it were two different things. To distract herself, Locke checked their progress. They'd traveled far enough down the hallway that a frosted-glass wall was now visible at the end of the passage with the letters *S-P-A* etched into it.

What concerned her more was a black dome mounted on the ceiling several yards ahead. "They're watching us."

"Hopefully," Queen said.

Locke did a double take.

Instead of explaining, Queen said, "When we get inside, keep your dress on."

As Locke struggled to understand what the hell any of that meant, the women drew close enough to the glass wall that two of its panels slid apart. The Pink Punker didn't hesitate. Heels click-clacking against the tile floor, she strutted through the door, straight to the reception desk. "Two for the sauna."

"Name on the reservation, Miss?"

"Huang."

Trailing Queen, Locke got a look at the spa's interior while the receptionist checked his computer. They stood in a two-story atrium decorated in weathered white-and-blue tiling that reminded her of a hammam, the Turkish style of bathhouse she'd seen around the Middle East. Adding to that feeling were thick stone columns that separated the desk from the area behind it. Part of her wondered whether Glebov had grabbed all this from some historical site just to jam it here.

As old-school as the reception area was, that's how modern the two open floors behind the columns looked. Downstairs, rows of computerized exercise equipment stretched back to a series of Jacuzzi tubs. Locke could see several men lifting weights and jogging on treadmills. The second level was outfitted with tables and recliners for massages, nail treatments, and haircuts. A fleet of attendants buzzed around, tending to guests.

Seeing the people—all the activity—left Locke feeling whiplashed. It all seemed so . . . normal.

Her disorientation might have lasted longer if it weren't for the view. Unlike the enclosed hallway they'd just cleared, both side walls of the spa were lined with windows. Outside, the shifting sea had turned an eggplant purple, accented by darker wavelets that jabbed and jerked in random directions. Above the ocean, the orange sky backlit popcorn-puffy clouds, rendering them a deep candy-apple crimson.

As breathtaking as the sunset was, Locke was more amazed to see the spa's curved ceiling matched it exactly. Through fancy lighting or some kind of projector, similar clouds and the earliest pinpricks of stars shimmered overhead.

The receptionist's voice interrupted her brain's effort to absorb it all. "I see the reservation, miss." He passed them each towels and pairs of individually wrapped slippers. "The sauna is upstairs, through the changing room."

When he gestured back the way they'd come, the women turned and found the frosted glass wall bracketed by curving stone staircases that met at a balcony overlooking the atrium. At the top of the steps, another automatic door led them into a circular chamber with an ornate gurgling fountain at its center.

Shower stalls lined one side of this changing area, while the other sported a series of slatted doors you might find inside a department store fitting room. At the opposite end, a door was marked SAUNA.

What was distinctly missing from the changing room, Locke noticed, was any form of security camera. The ceiling here was bare, the corners empty. No surveillance at all.

Queen grabbed Locke's hand. Despite the platform heels, she skipped across the floor, dragging Locke along while swinging their linked arms back and forth like they were little children. When they reached a pair of slatted doors that stood ajar, Queen gave a quick wink and disappeared behind one.

"Remember what I told you," she called from inside.

Locke entered the neighboring room and locked herself in. Instinctively reaching for her zipper, she caught herself and unwrapped the sandals instead. Then she unfurled the towel. Big and thick and warm, it felt like a downy blanket. Wrapping it around her back and under her arms, she found it hung to her knees, completely hiding the dress.

Queen emerged from her changing room at almost the same instant as Locke, dressed identically. Although the towel covered more of Queen's tiny frame, her shoulders and shins were bare, suggesting she'd violated her own advice and lost the black dress.

Before Locke could question that, Queen beelined for the sauna door.

To Locke's surprise, the sauna was a dead end. Unlike the bright changing room, this tiled chamber was lit in a dark shade of blue. Glass doors along a narrow central aisle provided access to small sauna compartments on either side, but she saw no other exit, no obvious way out. Feeling trapped, Locke wondered why exactly they'd come here.

But Queen offered no answers. Instead, she strutted to the far end of the chamber and entered the compartment on the right.

When she didn't immediately reappear, Locke chased after her.

Pushing her way through the glass door, Locke had to squeeze past Queen, who was standing just inside. Once she reached the middle of the compartment and got a look around, though, her heart sank. The boxy little room was its own dead end, a small square paneled in dark wood, with a bench ringing the room at sitting height.

"Why are we wasting time in here?" Locke asked.

Queen flipped what looked like a light switch on the wall. Immediately the door glass frosted over, rendering it completely opaque.

"Privacy. Now we can really get *comfortable*." Queen ripped off her wig and flashed Locke a wicked grin. Then she reached for where her towel was secured.

Even over the steamy sauna heat, Locke felt her face ignite. And as the Pink Punker started to pull the ends of the towel apart, Locke's eyes dropped to the floor.

All at once, her head was swimming. Embarrassed, but more than that, angry. Furious. And afraid. The hot, dense air made her think of Evan in the—

No, she told herself. *Don't. Not now.*

"You can look, dummy," Queen said.

Locke's eyes remained locked on her feet.

"It's not like I'm naked."

The comment caught Locke off guard. Slowly, she allowed her eyes to tick upward.

Queen held the towel splayed out behind her. Underneath, she wore some kind of black bathing suit.

"Fooled ya." Queen dropped the towel to the floor. "I built tear-away sections into the dress—told you I could sew."

Locke now saw what Queen meant—the bathing suit was what remained of her gown once the skirt and shoulder strap were removed. Still, they didn't have time for this foolishness. Evan didn't have time.

"You should lose the towel too," Queen said. Then she spun and squatted in front of the wooden bench where it met the doorframe. Reaching under the seat, she started fiddling with something Locke couldn't see.

Confused, Locke unhitched her own towel. As the plush fabric hit the floor, a loud metallic clack echoed through the compartment.

Queen exhaled sharply and stood, wiping her hands together before turning back to the door. "C'mon."

Locke exited the sauna compartment and found a section of the wall outside had swung open a few inches. Some kind of door, hidden by the tiling and dim lighting. On the opposite side, she could barely make out another enclosed hallway like the one downstairs.

Queen slipped through the opening, whispering, "Emergency door. C'mon!"

Locke squeezed though, noticing that the far side of the door was marked with red lettering and a push-bar release. Clearly, this was one of many things that Huang's plywood replica and their endless rehearsals had taught Queen.

Once Locke cleared the door, Queen pulled it closed with a metallic thud. After the sauna's warmth, the cool air here poked at Locke's bare skin in a way that helped clear the fog filling her head.

They'd sneaked onto deck two. Zhilkin had mentioned office space on deck two.

The safe.

She locked eyes with Queen, who was already wide-eyed and grinning.

"Let's go," they said at once.

Queen took off at a full sprint. Locke started after her, using her long strides to catch up.

Seconds later, Queen said, "It's the next door."

Locke glanced ahead. Like the corridor on deck one, the hallway here was nondescript—plain white walls with occasional pipes and metallic bracing. Maybe a dozen yards ahead on the right, she could see an alcove containing internal stairs. But even closer, on her left, was a simple hatch. Unmarked, it looked even less assuming than the janitor's closet back at the warehouse.

When they reached it, Queen lifted a panel next to the door that Locke never would have noticed. Behind it, a narrow horizontal slot contained a sheet of black glass. A biometric scanner like the one on the Ticonderoga.

"What's it read?" Locke asked.

"Handprints," Queen said. "Glebov's. Or . . ."

"Or who?"

"His security chief."

Locke blinked. "Zhilkin?"

Queen flashed a devilish smile. "Good thing I let that skinny prick feel me up."

The Pink Punker fiddled with the bathing suit, removing circular, sequined panels from the bustline. She tore at each of these in turn, ripping the stitches at their edges. Each circle proved to be two pieces of fabric with a paper layer sandwiched between them.

When Queen unfolded one bit of paper and held it up, Locke could see it bore a clean black-and-white handprint.

"Huang's idea," she said, placing the sheet on the glass scanner. "Some kinda special Chinese technology. Like transfer paper, but super sensitive."

A moment later, a light flashed and the door buzzed slightly.

"Ta-da." Queen turned the knob and pulled the hatch open.

Locke ducked inside quickly. The office lights were already on, and she realized they stood at one end of a long rectangular room that stretched to her left. She naturally moved that way, and as she got a better look at the space, she had to resist the urge to whistle out loud.

The office was the size of the Mule's living room, if not the whole craftsman house. No industrial nonslip paint on the floor here—rich, cherry-colored wood was draped with two expansive Persian rugs that divided the room into sections. One portion close to the door centered around a large desk flanked by bookshelves, several flat-panel screens, and a long wall-mounted mirror. The remaining two-thirds of the room contained casual seating arranged around various pieces of art. Illuminated glass cases displayed statues and pottery, while the wall at the far end bore framed paintings. Some large ones Locke recognized as famous, although she didn't know a Vincent van Gogh from a Dick Van Dyke. Others were smaller, barely the size of book pages, containing sharply angled scenes of Asian- and Middle Eastern–looking figures in front of boldly patterned and brightly colored scenery.

Despite all the treasures around the room, Locke saw no sign of security cameras. She imagined Glebov didn't like being watched, even by his own people.

Which made her wonder exactly what kind of business he got up to in here.

The most striking thing about the office, though, was the long walls on either side. Although this room lay buried in the dead center of the ship, the walls were lined with what looked like floor-to-ceiling windows akin to those she'd seen in the spa. The sky outside had darkened further now, the last gasps of daylight yielding to an indigo sky that nearly matched the churning ocean beneath it.

Locke faced the wall with the door. Although consciously she knew the hallway behind it meant she couldn't possibly be looking outside, the image out the "window" looked impeccably real. So much so that even when she pressed her face up close to it, she couldn't detect any dots or other clues that the images were being projected.

"Can you believe this?" she asked.

The voice that answered wasn't Queen's. "The video system is quite impressive."

Locke whipped around.

Glebov stood behind the desk. Over his shoulder, the big mirror had swung open like a door—he must have been hiding behind it when they entered. Zhilkin stood next to him, a pistol clutched at the end of his outstretched arm.

It was pointed at Queen's temple.

28

THE MIRROR/DOOR GLEBOV had hidden behind turned out to be one-way glass, reflective on one side, transparent on the other. Locke got to see that up close when Zhilkin shoved her and Queen into the small compartment behind it and locked them in.

Although the security chief hadn't found the women's hidden pistols, he'd zip-tied their hands tightly behind their backs. Even Queen, flexible as she was, wasn't able to reach her gun.

And, even if she had, it wouldn't have mattered much. With metal walls, floor, and ceiling, the compartment behind the mirror seemed to be some kind of panic room. Excellent for protecting someone inside, but equally effective at keeping someone from getting out. Equipped with only a cot, a desk, and a panel of monitors, you could watch what was going on in various parts of the boat, but there wasn't any way to escape.

Although Locke tried to engage with Queen, the Pink Punker sat on the edge of the cot, silently staring out the mirrored door toward Glebov at his desk. If Queen's eyes could have shot bullets, they'd have blown out the back of his head.

With nothing else to do, Locke watched security feeds on the various monitors. Cameras in public areas of the yacht—the pool, the dining room—showed guests blissfully unaware of what was happening belowdecks. Eventually, though, she saw Zhilkin and several guards escorting Huang and King toward the office.

Once Zhilkin triggered the door with his palm, Locke turned and watched through the one-way glass. A speaker above the mirror/door projected sound from the office; she could hear and see everything that happened.

Glebov rose from his chair as Zhilkin entered, followed by Huang and King. Behind the Giant were four guards, different from those who'd escorted her and Queen earlier. These bruisers looked more powerful, as did their weaponry—each carried a compact submachine gun. They steered Huang and King to the far corner of the desk. While Locke's angle only let her see the backs of Glebov and Zhilkin, she had a perfect view of Huang's face.

"Stepan," he said, bowing. "I did not expect to see you again so soon."

Glebov crossed his arms. "And I did not expect my hospitality would be repaid with thievery."

Huang cocked his head. "I . . . I do not know what you mean."

"Where is the other one?" Zhilkin asked Glebov. "The cook."

"Locked in the kitchen. They are busy preparing dinner and asked permission to deliver him after service."

"We should wait—"

Glebov waved a hand at the security chief. "We do not need him here to deal with these two."

"Deal with us?" Huang asked. "Stepan, I am at a loss—"

"Do not trifle with me." As Glebov's voice rose, the speaker over the door squelched with feedback. "We all know why you have come; you wish to take back the statues. The question is, for whom?"

Huang furrowed his brow. "I have merely come to ride out the quarantine."

Glebov's head bobbed once.

Without a word, the quartet of guards moved on King. One threw a black hood over the Giant's head while the other three rushed him from behind. Although he struggled, the fight ended quickly—after tackling him, they cuffed his wrists and ankles, then hog-tied the cuffs together with a chain. When they were done, the hooded giant lay on his belly, immobilized.

Huang's face fell as he watched King go down.

Glebov jerked his thumb back toward the mirror/door.

Zhilkin opened it and dragged the women out of the panic room. He forced them to the floor just outside the entrance, where they ended up sitting cross-legged, backs against the wall. After giving them a nasty stare, he rejoined his boss at the desk.

"Your whores were caught breaking into my office," Glebov said.

"I know nothing about—"

"Come now," Glebov interrupted. "You expect me to believe these two little mice came up with this idea by themselves? They work for *you*. *You* brought them here, *you* equipped them."

"I . . . I did nothing of the sort. They—"

"No one believes that. Least of all me."

Glebov motioned again, and the guard holding Huang's shoulder bent him over, smashing his face down onto the desk. The guard held Huang there, one hand on the back of his neck, the other twisting his wrist up in the air. The steep angle of his arm pressed Huang's cheek flat against the wood.

"I do not take kindly to thieves," Glebov said. "Your associates will pay the price for that. Your security man here, your chef upstairs—neither will see the dawn. And your two little mice who invaded my office"—he turned and gave the women a menacing look—"will wish that their end was as swift as the men's."

Locke tried to swallow, but all moisture had disappeared from her mouth. She considered speaking up, to confirm Huang's guilt and beg for mercy for herself and Evan. But Glebov's scowl left no doubt that he had all kinds of horrific tortures in mind for her and Queen. She didn't see him relinquishing those merely to hear her vouch for what he already knew.

Gathering as much strength as she could, Locke pulled against the zip ties, but the plastic had absolutely no give.

Glebov spun back to Huang, bending at the waist so their faces were on the same level. "Unlike your associates, you have an opportunity to save yourself. Because you have something I want to know."

A noise—not quite a moan, but more like muffled words—spilled from Huang's lips along with a dribble of blood.

"Who are you are working for? If it is your government, I can alert my country, and we can adjust our diplomatic relations. If it is some individual, well . . . I can deal with him. Either way, I will let you live. Simply identify your employer, and you can return to enjoying the amenities of the *Helios*."

Locke had no idea whether Glebov would actually let Huang loose. But she also didn't know how much abuse Huang could take.

"And . . . if not?"

Glebov's voice dropped to barely more than a whisper. "If you do not tell me, then my men will cut you into such small pieces it will take every fishing vessel in the Chinese fleet to catch the crabs that will feed on your carcass."

Facedown on the desk, Huang grunted, more blood spilling from his mouth.

Glebov leaned closer. "Your choice, Mr. Huang. Which will it be?"

"I—"

"Yes?"

Locke tensed, even though there was nowhere for her to go, nothing for her to do. As she did, she heard a small rumble.

Distant, like a thunderclap on the horizon.

Recalling they were off South Florida, Locke didn't give the noise much thought. A quick glance at the "windows" showed night had finished falling, leaving her with no sense of the weather.

She was ready to disregard the sound completely.

Until Glebov straightened.

He turned toward the monitors, lips pursed.

Zhilkin turned too.

Security feeds lit the flat-screens . . . all except one. That panel had gone black.

"Is that—" Glebov started.

"The kitchen feed," Zhilkin said. He pointed at the guard holding Huang down. "You, stay. The rest of you, with me."

Zhilkin jogged out of the office with the three guards in tow.

Locke thought of Jack as she watched them go. Wondering exactly what mischief the knife-wielding maniac was making upstairs. What they might do to him.

After the door shut, a nudge on her shoulder interrupted those visions.

She glanced over at Queen.

Given all the action, Locke hadn't paid the Pink Punker any attention for several minutes, and apparently, neither had anyone else. Somehow, while sitting, Queen had managed to slip her hands down under her feet. Her wrists were still bound, but now they lay across her belly instead of behind her back.

Queen raised her eyebrows, and Locke knew exactly what she wanted.

Locke leaned forward, pretending to stretch for a better view of Huang's face. As she did, she rotated her shoulders slightly, giving Queen extra cover.

When Locke felt Queen's hands down the back of her dress, her only thought was, *Hurry.*

A moment later, she felt the metal barrel of the pistol dragging against her spine.

"Now," Queen whispered.

Locke dropped onto her left side as two shots thundered from the muzzle.

With her face against the floor, Locke couldn't see the guard directly. But a splatter of red erupting above him told her that Queen's shots had found their target.

Glebov whipped around. He took a quick step toward Queen.

She fired again.

It was a gut shot. Bright-red blood spilled from the wound almost immediately.

Glebov looked down at the life trickling out of him. His expression was one of surprise rather than pain. He pressed a hand against his belly, but the blood continued to pulse outward. Leaking around and over his fingers, dripping down his shirt.

A realization spread across his face. He glanced up at Locke, then at Queen.

With his free hand, he started to reach for her again. He took another step forward.

She fired three more times in rapid succession.

Glebov's body dropped in a heap at their feet.

Locke looked to her left—Huang was already kneeling beside King, working to free him. When she turned back to Queen, she saw Glebov's face pointed in her direction.

His eyes were locked open in a glassy stare. Lids retracted, whites exposed. Enough that she concluded he was gone.

Then his lips moved.

Smacking together, like he was searching for breath.

Locke flinched, then lashed out with her foot, kicking the bridge of his nose with her heel.

By the time she looked up, King was free, rubbing his wrists and retrieving the guard's submachine gun while Huang cut away Queen's zip ties. Quickly, all three stood over her.

"Now the time has come for your handiwork, Ms. Locke."

29

ONCE FREED FROM the zip ties and back on her feet, Locke glanced around for the Ticonderoga. But she didn't see it.

"Here." Huang stepped to one of the bookshelves and gave it a tug. The shelving unit swung outward, revealing a familiar-looking metal door behind it.

Locke strode to the box, her slippers landing silently on the carpet. As she eyed the Colonial logo, her mind flashed to the duplicate safe back in the warehouse.

Evan, locked inside.

She imagined him crying in the darkness. Desperate and scared.

Is he even alive?

She pictured him again, eyes closed peacefully like when she peeked in on him sleeping. But this time, his chest didn't rise or fall. No matter how hard she focused in on it, his little torso remained completely still.

Locke drew a ragged gasp. Her eyes began to fill, and she could feel her hand start to shake.

No.

She swallowed hard, pinching her eyes closed to squeeze out the tears. Getting all weepy wouldn't help.

She needed to do this.

She was the only person in the world who *could* do this.

Locke reached her hand back over her shoulder. "Your phone."

She turned to confront Huang again. His bloodied face was blank.

"I need your phone," she said. "For the oscilloscope and my notes. Oh, and a pen."

Huang pulled the handset from one pocket, unlocking it and handing it to her along with some probe wires. Queen tossed a pen and small pad from Glebov's desk, which Locke snatched out of midair.

Armed with her supplies, Locke knelt in front of the box. She quickly connected the wires between the digital lock's power port and the phone. She also tested the pen with a quick scribble in one corner of the pad.

"Someone needs to keep time. Once I start, we've got nine minutes for all three locks."

Huang shook his heavy Rolex down below the cuff of his sleeve. "Are you ready?"

Locke nodded. *As I'll ever be.*

He paused a moment. "Go."

Locke started with the digital lock rather than the dial. She knew she needed to wake up the system to eavesdrop on the electrical signals inside the safe, and she didn't want to take any chances. She pressed a button to wake the screen, then checked the oscilloscope app on the phone.

Although the trace recorded, it took a lot of zooming and scrolling to find the five little heartbeats. She was still searching for them when Huang called, "One minute."

Locke's own heart seemed to skip, but she reminded herself she still had plenty of time. Quickly, she compared the first wave to the photograph of the chart she'd made.

The number 04—she wrote that down.

Then Locke moved to the next shape and repeated the process. 01.

Again. 91

And again. 72

She found the fifth number—65—and was jotting it down as Huang said, "Two minutes."

Locke allowed herself a breath. She was running well ahead of pace—she just needed to enter these five numbers on the keypad and she could move to the dial.

Carefully, slowly, she punched in each digit.

Then, wincing slightly, she pressed enter.

For half a heartbeat, nothing happened. Locke's breath caught in her throat.

Then a light on the keypad flashed green.

A wave of adrenaline flooded Locke's veins and she pumped her fist. Someone clapped once behind her.

"That's one," she said.

Now she switched to the manual dial. Five quick spins picked up all the wheels. Then she closed her eyes and kept turning until she felt the same little disturbance she'd noticed back at the warehouse.

She opened her eyes to note the number and allowed herself a little smile.

"Three minutes," Huang said.

Locke started twisting the dial in the other direction.

Back and forth she went like that, pausing only momentarily each time she felt the edge of a notch to jot down the number.

"Four minutes gone."

Locke glanced down at her paper. Of the ten numbers she needed to bracket the combination's five digits, she'd already discovered half of them. It didn't seem like nearly enough, but she reminded herself that she remained ahead of pace.

Still, her next spin was faster.

When Huang called, "Five minutes," she'd just reversed direction to look for the final number.

She found it a moment later, and jotted it down with the rest.

Looking over all ten, the scribblings lined up—five pairs of numbers, each pair separated by four digits on the wheel. Splitting the difference between them, she knew the exact components to the combination: 4, 6, 51, 71, and 92.

Locke's heart soared. Every hair on her arms seemed to rise.

She forced herself to draw a cleansing breath. On the dial, merely knowing the digits didn't get you all the way home.

She still had to order them correctly.

Lowest-to-highest was always most likely. She dialed all five numbers in order, then went to turn the handle.

It wouldn't budge.

That's okay, she told herself. *Highest-to-lowest next.*

Locke cleared the dial, then spun backward through the numbers: 92, 71, 51, 6, and 4.

She tugged on the handle. Again, it wouldn't move.

Her stomach twisted a little. And a moment later, when Huang said, "Six minutes gone," it cinched even tighter.

Three minutes left. Worse, she had only three more tries on the dial. After the fifth failure, the Ticonderoga would lock down completely. At that point, she'd be of no more use to the team. Even if they managed to escape—a big *if*— they'd have zero incentive to take her along.

She'd likely die here. Maybe fast, maybe slow.

But Evan . . .

No.

Locke pushed all the negative thoughts from her mind. She'd been in this position plenty of times. Never with a ticking countdown, but still. She could do this—she just needed to focus.

If the numbers weren't in order, they likely meant something to Glebov. What would he care about?

Locke glanced back over her shoulder at the Russian's body. He looked to be in his forties, at least. Likely his fifties, given the money he'd made.

People that age had spouses, kids. Maybe even grandkids. *Dates.*

Dates mattered to old people. Birthdays, anniversaries.

"How old is he?" Locke asked. The way Huang had studied Glebov up and down, surely he would know. "What's his birthday?"

"You have two and a half minutes remaining, Ms. Locke. Why—"

"Just tell me. What's his fucking birthday?"

"August thirtieth," Huang said.

"What *year*?" Locke asked.

"Nineteen sixty."

She thought through it quickly. August was the eighth month—8, 30, 60. Those didn't work with any of the combination numbers. 'Fifty-one shouldn't have been an important year to Glebov, nine years before he was born. In 1971, Glebov would have been eleven.

What happened when you were eleven?

Not much.

But he'd have been thirty-two in 1992.

People got married at thirty-two. They had children at thirty-two.

If 92 referenced the year, that would make 4 and 6 the day and month, or vice versa.

Locke dialed in 4, 6, 92, then went lowest-to-highest, 51, 71.

The handle didn't turn. Three tries burned.

"Fuck." Locke spat the word.

"Seven minutes gone."

"C'mon, you got this," Queen said. "You got this."

Although Locke couldn't see the Pink Punker's face behind her, she could hear doubt hollowing out the words.

And she didn't disagree.

As Locke saw it, one of three arrangements was most likely the combination. The first three digits exactly as she'd just entered them, but with the 51 and 71 reversed. Or reversing the 4 and 6 while leaving the 51 and 71 the same. Or reversing both pairs.

Three permutations. But she only had two tries remaining.

And only a minute of time, as she needed to leave a minute for them to trigger the biometric sensor.

Locke went with 4, 6, and 92 again, but she reversed the final two digits.

She yanked hard on the lever, but it wouldn't budge.

Sweat slicked over Locke's skin now. And while her heart raced, her stomach was doing a slow somersault in her belly.

One last try.

Locke switched up the first two digits, 6 then 4. Then 92.

Which way?

Huang's voice croaked. "Eight minutes gone."

Locke dialed 71, then 51. And she reached for the lever.

30

W HEN THE LEVER turned and the green bulb next to it illuminated, Locke felt fireworks exploding through her nervous system. She bounced to her feet.

"Quick! His hand," she said, pointing. "We need his hand!"

"Forty-five seconds," Huang said.

Locke dashed to Glebov's body and grabbed it by the wrist. Leaning all her weight into it, she began dragging him toward the safe. The carpet added tons of friction—each pull moved the body only a few inches. Then a few inches more.

Fuck, billionaires are heavy.

She turned toward the safe, trying to tow Glebov behind her. Still several feet to go.

"Thirty seconds."

Keeping her eyes locked on the sensor, Locke heaved again.

This time, Glebov moved more freely. In fact, his body kept moving even as she paused to gather herself for the next step.

Locke glanced back and saw King and Queen carrying the corpse along by its clothes.

"Twenty seconds."

Okay, close enough. She pulled Glebov's wrist toward the sensor, sliding his fingers into the slot and pressing them onto the glass with her own hand.

"Ten seconds."

Locke tried to ignore Huang while maintaining pressure on Glebov's fingers.

"Five. Four."

The light at the side of the sensor glowed green.

Locke reached over with her free hand and yanked on the main door lever.

It turned!

As the door swung open, Locke flopped flat onto her back.

Her first breath after opening the safe felt like emerging from the Malibu pool—she sucked down as much air as she could, enjoying the cool freshness inside her lungs.

Confirming she was still alive. Washing relief over her.

Huang hurried to the open safe as Locke rolled onto her knees to watch.

Unlike the hollowed-out Ticonderoga at the warehouse, this box was more like the Malibu safe. The interior was out-fitted with all manner of drawers and cabinets.

Huang seemed to know exactly where to look. Squatting, he dragged open the lowermost drawer with both hands.

The contents dropped him to his knees.

Locke leaned forward and peeked into the drawer. Like so many others she'd seen, it was lined with soft felt to pro-tect its contents. What made this drawer unique were the compartments built into it. Three rows of four evenly spaced squares.

Twelve spots, one for each of the zodiac statues Glebov had described.

Four were filled.

One spot belonged to the figurine she'd retrieved in Mal-ibu, the Rabbit.

But three other boxes were nestled in their own slots, each bearing a series of Mandarin characters.

"Glebov's success has been underestimated," Huang said. "He was rumored to have found only two."

Huang reached inside his blazer and withdrew a tightly folded canvas satchel. He shook it open and spread it on the floor at his knees. Then, ever so delicately, he lifted the familiar Rabbit box out of the drawer with both hands and placed it inside the satchel.

He repeated the process for the second box, and the third.

When Huang lifted the fourth box from its compartment, an alarm started ringing. Shrill bells, like an old-fashioned alarm clock.

So loud, Locke could barely hear anything else.

"What's going on?" Queen yelled. She and King stood by the monitors, watching the security feeds.

After placing the final box in the satchel, Huang pushed up onto his feet, drawing the bag with him. While fastening it closed, he shouted to the others, "Additional alarm. Unexpected but irrelevant."

For a moment, Locke wondered exactly how much of all this Huang and the crew had scripted out. Glebov's suspicions, Jack luring Zhilkin away—was this what they'd been practicing all those hours in the plywood model?

Huang slipped the strap over his head and arm so it crossed his chest. "Status?"

Queen gave a quick glance back at the screens. While one panel was still blacked out, the others showed scores of uniformed men running in multiple directions. "Looks like Zhilkin's bringing the whole army down here."

"Then we must move quickly." Still staring at Queen, Huang fished into his pocket and pulled out the pill bottle he had displayed several times. Once again, he shook it in Queen's direction before turning for the door.

Locke glanced over at Queen and saw the Pink Punker's lip quivering. Her eyes blinked rapidly, and she inhaled a massive breath.

Unsure what had her so emotional, Locke tried to catch her eye, but Queen seemed deliberate in avoiding it.

After a moment, Locke abandoned the effort and started after Huang. Queen's emotions could wait—right now, the only thing that mattered was making it up to the chopper before Zhilkin's soldiers intercepted them. The seconds ticked loudly in her head, even over the alarm, as Locke took a first, hurried step toward the door.

But when her slipper pressed into the plush carpet, a gunshot rang out over the alarm bells.

Boom.

Locke instinctively flinched.

This shot sounded different from the ones that had dropped Glebov. Deeper pitched. More powerful.

Strong enough that the noise hitting her ears pressed some kind of pause button in Locke's brain. All around her, things slowed to a crawl. Even her own body seemed mired in slow motion as she struggled to figure out who'd fired, and at what.

Her eyes locked first on Huang, directly in front of her.

He'd almost reached the office door, his back facing her and the others. His hands were empty.

Locke's eyes ticked to her right as fast as the elongated seconds would allow.

The far end of the office beyond Huang still stood empty except for its sofas and statues.

The virtual windows, rendered empty by the moonless night outside, had been reduced to black mirrors, reflecting hazy shapes of the office interior.

Locke's eyes swept farther right. Over her shoulder.

The landed on Queen, standing at the opposite side of the desk.

In particular, they focused in on Queen's hands. Held out in front of her, at shoulder height.

Clutching her pistol at high-ready.

Aimed directly at Locke.

The gunshot's echo, having traveled to the far end of the room, now boomeranged back. It reached Locke's ears at the same moment her eyes locked onto Queen's gun barrel. Much as the original sound had slowed things for Locke, the echo now accelerated them. Back to normal speed, if not faster.

So fast that Locke noticed a whole host of things at once.

No brass casing had spat from Queen's gun.

The slide on her pistol hadn't moved.

All of Locke's extremities reported in—she didn't seem to have been hit.

Finally, her vision widened outward. She got a look at Queen's face behind the gun.

Queen's baby blues were as bright as ever, wider than Locke had ever seen them. Unnaturally open, and glazed over. Like a doll's eyes, locked in a look of complete confusion.

Then Locke saw why.

The blood gave it away first—Queen's right shoulder was covered in it.

Her body crumpled to the floor. As she fell, Queen's neck and head twisted, giving Locke a perfect glimpse into the exit wound.

Queen's ear, scalp, the entire side of her throat were missing. An ugly mess of red, white, and gray was exposed underneath. Locke's eyes darted even farther right, following the path the shot must have taken.

Several feet away, Locke found King. Holding the submachine gun at arm's length. Pointed at the exact spot where Queen's head had been.

Locke's heart fluttered as her brain struggled to make sense of what had just happened.

She was still trying to process it when something seized her arm.

Locke looked down and found King's massive hand wrapped around her bicep.

Her first instinct was fear—she started to pull away, but his grip only tightened.

She checked his face, expecting one of his scary, teeth-baring scowls. Instead, he directed her with his eyes. He looked toward the door, nodding that way. When she turned and followed his gaze, she saw the door was open.

And Huang had disappeared through it.

Something clicked inside her, and Locke started after him in a dead sprint. Regardless of what had just happened, she couldn't let Huang reach the helicopter alone.

Not if she wanted to get back to Evan.

She dashed to the door, but upon entering the hallway, her eyes were immediately assaulted by flashing white strobes. Evenly spaced down the corridor, the lights throbbed together even as the shrill bells continued to ring.

Trying to ignore afterimages the strobes left in her vision, Locke searched up and down the hallway for Huang.

She spotted him a few yards to her left, making for the internal staircase. Out past him, near the end of the hallway at the nose of the ship, the first of Zhilkin's troops were coming into view.

Locke kicked off the slippers—more of a liability now than anything—and sprinted after Huang in her bare feet. Using every inch of her legs, Locke reached the stairs in only two strides.

As she made the turn, the guards started shooting.

31

Locke managed to duck into the stairway alcove as bullets began plinking and plunking against the metal walls and floor. One at a time, then in rapid succession.

As Huang climbed the stairs above her, Locke stole a glance backward. King emerged from the office, and the hail of fire shifted toward him.

King retreated momentarily but extended the submachine gun out the office door. He ripped off two blind bursts to halt the incoming fire, then used short, controlled sprays to creep back into the hallway. After two quick steps forward, he looked to the stairs.

Their eyes met.

King blinked once, then jerked his head upward before resuming fire at the guards. Laying down a longer spread, he backpedaled away from her, retreating toward the sauna.

Locke checked up the staircase again. Above her, Huang had just reached deck three.

Although she felt a pang of guilt at leaving King, Locke knew she couldn't help him. Especially unarmed. She had no way of taking on the guards, and at this point, catching Huang was everything. If King could draw away some pursuers, all she had to offer was gratitude.

Gathering her strength, Locke launched herself off the first riser and bounded up the stairs three at a time. She reached the top of the staircase in four quick strides, emerging on the left-hand side of a small, wood-paneled anteroom with doors that led fore and aft. A stylized sign over the aft door immediately in front of her said the bar and dining room lay in that direction. A matching sign over the forward door to her right identified it as the entrance to the theater and kitchen.

Locke spotted Huang in her peripheral vision. Near the theater and kitchen door, he'd reached the base of the next staircase and was starting upward.

She started to follow him, but a bullet ripped into the wood just above her shoulder.

The near miss still felt like getting punched. She winced and ducked and struggled to hold on to her breath.

Retreating down two steps, she could see multiple guards amassing at the threshold of the forward-facing theater/kitchen door. While she'd need only two or three strides to catch Huang at the next staircase, it would require running straight toward the guards' field of fire—their guns would rip her to shreds.

Of course, they'd eventually do the exact same thing to her here if she stayed put.

Locke checked back the way she'd come, but shadows were gathering below on deck two. Those troops would be starting upward any moment.

That left her only one way out.

Locke drew a quick breath and sprinted forward in a crouch, cutting through the door immediately to her left.

Expecting a hail of bullets would follow her, she was shocked when none came.

The metal flooring gave way to varnished wood that felt slick beneath her feet. When she finally lifted her head, she quickly saw why the guards had held their fire: she'd entered a posh, dark-paneled lounge. At least a dozen male guests were spread between stools on her right and high-backed booths on her left.

Although she'd hoped she might slip through the room unnoticed, she rapidly realized there was zero chance of that. The alarm noise and gunfire was blunted here, but still audible. As soon as she straightened to her full height, every head in the place turned her way. In the corner of her eye, she caught one of the bartenders speaking into his jacket cuff. Summoning the gunmen behind her, or some other form of security.

Keep moving.

At the far end of the bar, she spotted another doorway. Marked as the entrance to the dining room.

Locke lowered her head and sprinted for it.

After several steps, a loud clatter erupted behind her. She guessed it was the guards colliding with one of the servers, but she didn't dare look back. Instead, she focused on building speed, her bare soles squeaking against the wood. Thankfully, the dining room doors slid open as she approached, allowing her to maintain momentum.

Even before she cleared the doorway, the change in air hit her. Thicker, warmer. She was moving outside.

Quickly, she saw the dining "room" was actually a kind of patio, open on three sides to the tropical night but shielded overhead by the deck above it. Recessed LEDs shone down from the ceiling like extra-bright stars, their light gleaming off the top of a polished-stone banquet table that stretched toward the rear of the ship.

At least half the thirty-odd seats around the table were filled. Mostly by men wearing relaxed, resort-style clothing like Glebov's. The few women were elegantly dressed plus-ones, heavily made up and hanging on whoever had brought them. The noise from indoors hadn't disturbed these guests yet—insulated by the hiss of the ocean and the whistle of the breeze, they continued their conversations, oblivious. None of them even looked up as Locke emerged through the doors.

Still, she could feel her pursuers closing in behind her. She couldn't slow down or risk getting trapped. To catch Huang, she needed to get upstairs *now*.

But her paths to the stern were blocked. A bar on one side and a carving station on the other pinched the aisles on either side of the table. Servers delivering food and the guests themselves left Locke no way to get through.

She never broke stride.

Instead, Locke rushed at the guest closest to her, a balding man seated at the closest corner of the table. Although he was looking away when she emerged from the bar, he turned at the same moment she planted her right foot hard on deck and launched herself toward him.

The man recoiled, raising his hands to protect his face.

Which exposed the armrest of his chair.

Locke's left foot landed on it squarely, letting her bound back to the right.

When her right foot landed on the tabletop, she felt the cool, slick stone and smiled. For a fleeting second, she was seventeen again, making mincemeat of the Fort Jackson obstacle course.

The view ahead of her snapped Locke back to reality. Diners turned, mouths agape at the tall, barefooted woman sprinting past their place settings. Behind her, dishes and silverware clattered. Chairs groaned and tumbled against the wooden deck.

She didn't have time for any of it. To maintain her speed, each foot placement had to land perfectly, avoiding a wineglass here, a serving dish there.

She covered half the table in three strides and allowed herself a glance to the end, now rapidly approaching.

Several yards beyond the table, a glass railing marked the edge of deck three. Two umbrella-covered seating areas framed a staircase leading down to the pool.

That did Locke no good—wrong direction.

Glancing to either side, she found what she needed: open chrome-and-wood staircases stretching back toward the nose of the boat, leading up to deck four. With no diners on the table's right-hand side, her choice of staircase was clear.

Locke took one more step with her right foot, steering herself that way. Then she stretched out her left leg, planning to plant that foot near the edge of the table and launch herself over the empty chairs.

But instead of eyeing her foot placement as she'd done the whole way along, Locke let her vision rise. Up and over the chair backs to the open floor beyond. Her mind started to plan how she'd make it to the stairs, how close behind her the troops might be.

When the ball of her left foot landed, it caught the corner of a place mat.

The fabric slipped sideways like it was on ice.

Locke pitched forward into the air.

CHAPTER

32

BY THE TIME Locke realized what had happened, the world had already turned topsy-turvy. Her feet were above her head and her body was rotating through the air. The wooden deck was rushing up at her, fast.

She did the only thing she could think of: she turned into the rotation as hard as she could.

When Locke hit the floor, her back took the brunt of the blow. She rolled several times, ending up on her belly, head pointed toward the stairs only five yards away.

Fifteen feet that might as well have been forever.

Rising onto her hands and knees, Locke launched herself forward with a kind of track-style start. Her back throbbed, but the real problem was dizziness. All that spinning had left her woozy—she didn't get two full strides before the horizon tipped on its side and the floor slipped out from under her.

She hit the wooden deck with an extra-loud thud.

Allowing herself a glance back, she realized the guards had cleared the diners from their field of fire—one had his pistol up and had let off a round.

Falling had probably saved her life.

Locke scrambled faster now, returning to her feet but staying low. Three more shots split the air as she sprinted for the staircase. One bullet ricocheted off the chrome railing ahead of her with a sharp ping.

Rather than slowing to turn for the stairs, Locke flew by the railing at full speed and hooked it with her hand. That torqued her body back around, letting her start the climb without losing any speed.

Now the guards really started to unload.

Through the open risers, she counted three gunmen firing simultaneously. Sparks flew across the underside of the stairs as the hail of bullets struck metal and wood. She pumped her knees furiously, praying none of the hot lead would catch her through the gaps.

In four strides, Locke reached the top of the staircase and scanned for where to go next.

With the trailing edge of each deck tiered to overlook the one below it, from the stern you could gaze to the top of the boat as if it were an angled mountainside. Locke could see all the way up to the helipad, where the chopper's tail rotor was visible.

There's still time.

But how to get up there?

Here on deck four, one of the open walkways along the side of the ship stretched forward all the way to the bow. Lights spaced every few yards illuminated the path, and maybe a third of the way along, she could see an external staircase leading upward.

That would take her to deck five, maybe even to the top.

As tempting as that was, though, Locke hesitated. Looking at the sight lines, she pictured herself getting picked off going that way. Shot in the back by whichever guard climbed the stairs first and drew a bead on her.

Much closer, on the wall to her right, a hatch led indoors. Hoping that would offer more protection, she dashed for it.

When she slipped inside, however, noise assaulted her ears. Gunshots, dozens of them. This was the deck with the staterooms and curving hallways—she couldn't see who was shooting at whom. With echoes coming from both directions, it seemed that no matter which way she went, she'd end up on one side of the firefight or the other.

But she couldn't go back outside. The downstairs guards would arrive any moment.

Desperate, Locke searched for some other option.

She considered breaking into a stateroom, but that would only trap her, and she couldn't waste time hiding.

Then she remembered.

The two sides of the boat were roughly symmetrical. If there was a door on this side of deck four . . . there might be one on the opposite side too.

Hoping the carpet and the gunshots would mask her footsteps, Locke followed the passage to her right. She passed a handful of stateroom doors on either side until finally, she saw it.

Another hatch!

She dashed over and pressed her face to its tinted window. As she'd hoped, on the opposite side of the glass, a corresponding walkway stretched along this side of the ship. Everything—the lights, the railing, the stairs—was a mirror image of what she'd seen before coming inside.

As she was about to duck out, though, Locke heard hurried footsteps behind her. She whipped around in time to see a figure come into view around the curve.

Jack.

Running as fast as he could but limping severely. One leg was doing almost all the work, making it look like he was hopping.

And it wasn't just Jack's leg. His chef's coat, smeared with blood and soot, was torn open, exposing a bullet wound in his side. A gash across his forehead had spilled even more blood down the side of his face and forced one eye closed.

Still, he smiled when he saw her.

The strain on his face melted away and his white teeth flashed, as if she represented the finish line of a long, painful race.

Until a four-shot burst sliced through the air.

The shots came from his pursuers, still mostly out of sight around the corner. Locke heard the gunfire first, then saw Jack's body jerk as the bullets ripped through him from behind.

He fell face first onto the carpet.

Locke's hand flew to her mouth, but her eyes quickly rose to the far end of the passage. The first guards had come into view, and from the shadows bouncing on the wall, plenty more were following.

She backpedaled, stumbling through the hatch before turning up the walkway toward the bow of the ship.

The external staircase loomed a couple dozen yards ahead.

Although her heart hadn't stopped pounding and her back was tightening from the fall off the table, Locke forced herself forward as fast as she could go. Her quads complained as the stairs grew closer, but she ignored them, launching herself at the risers.

Her feet landed squarely and she grabbed for the railing with her outside hand. It wasn't much more than a stainless-steel cable, but she used it to help pull herself upward even as the woven metal dug into her palm.

Shouts rang out behind her, and she knew bullets wouldn't be far behind.

Two flights of stairs, twenty-four steps.

To the chopper . . . and Evan . . . and freedom.

In seconds, Locke reached the top of the first flight. Deck five coming into view made her heart swell. She could feel vibrations behind her—the guards were gaining. But at least this level looked clear.

Once again, Locke hooked the railing with her hand and used it to whip herself around toward the next upward flight.

Her feet were moving so fast, they almost flew out from under her on the varnished wood deck. Somehow, though, she steadied herself and kept running.

Sweat was pouring off her by the time she mounted the final set of stairs. The wind had also picked up—it whipped her hair into her face. Realizing how high she must be, Locke deliberately avoided looking out past the railing. She kept her eyes locked on the white steps at her feet.

She ran until none remained—only then did she allow herself to look around.

Locke had emerged on one side of the helipad. Off to her right sat the hatch they'd entered hours earlier, and beyond it, the conference room and bridge. Large spotlights mounted on the roof shone back across the white decking, making the helipad so bright, she almost had to squint.

And there, exactly in the middle of the pad, sat the helicopter. Still strapped down, exactly as they'd left it.

When Locke realized she'd beaten Huang up here, a wave of relief washed over her. For the first time since the guards had escorted her and Queen to the elevator, Locke felt she might stand an honest chance of escaping. And while she didn't believe in any kind of religious hocus-pocus, she squeezed her eyes shut and tried to send a thought to Evan. In case there was some way he could hear it.

I'm coming.

Loud footfalls on the stairs below snapped Locke back to the moment at hand. Leaning over the railing, she could see a handful of guards progressing upward from the lower decks. They'd be on her in a minute.

But a quick glance around showed nowhere to hide.

No sign of Huang either.

Locke ran for the only cover she could see—the chopper itself. Circling to the far side of the fuselage, she took up a position next to the pilot's door. From there she could keep an eye on the hatch leading to the bridge, while glass insets in the helicopter doors let her peek back toward the stairway she'd just climbed.

The guards appeared first.

One, two . . .

She kept counting until she reached a half dozen. Each carried the kind of submachine gun King had commandeered in the office. They formed a semicircle at the top of the external stairs and began shouting at one another.

Although Locke couldn't make out their words, from the way the men pointed in all directions, it seemed that her hiding place had worked.

At least for the moment.

But she could sense time moving and wondered where Huang could be. The thought registered that he might have ended up like Jack, a corpse sprawled somewhere below.

Locke swallowed hard. If Huang was dead, then she really stood no chance. She couldn't fly a helicopter. She imagined there were likely smaller boats on board—lifeboats, landing craft, something—but that would require fighting all the way back down into the bowels of the ship.

She doubted she could make it that far. And, even if she did, without Huang's handprints, there'd be no freeing Evan from the Ticonderoga.

The wind whistled furiously across the deck, tousling her hair and biting at her skin. Her hands started to shake.

Locke wondered how long she could hold out up here. As if to answer the question, the guards divided themselves into two groups of three that started advancing toward the front and back of the helicopter.

She looked over her shoulder. The external staircase on this side of the boat ended a few yards away. Reachable in a few strides.

Glancing back and forth between the guards and stairs, she debated how long she could wait. The front squad had almost reached the chopper's nose. Locke realized they might spot her through the cockpit windows even before they rounded it.

Her pulse accelerated, her leg muscles tensed.

But then she heard a commotion. Gunfire, shouting.

She checked the advancing guards—they must have heard it too. They glanced at one another, then one pointed toward the hatch that led to the bridge.

A moment later, Huang burst through it.

His hair was disheveled, his blazer gone. But the satchel strap remained visibly taut across his chest. And he carried one of the submachine guns in each hand.

He sprayed a long burst of automatic fire at the three guards near the nose of the chopper, dropping all three. Moving as he fired, he sidestepped along the wall toward the side of the chopper where Locke was hiding.

Once he'd cleared the nose, Huang started for the helicopter door. He took two strides forward before spotting Locke.

The sight of her stopped Huang in his tracks.

They locked eyes and he blinked several times.

Finally, Huang shook off whatever had stalled him. He raised one of the guns and pointed it at her.

Locke's heart froze, and when a shot rang out, she flinched.

But it was one of the guards who'd fired.

Huang must not have noticed the squad back by the tail. That group of three had circled up to the nose to outflank him. And now they unleashed all their firepower on the man who'd killed their colleagues.

As bullets started ripping into him, Huang turned away from Locke to face the guards.

The force and frequency of the shots staggered him as he got hit again, and again. One step back. Two.

Bullets tore into his chest, his legs, his head.

Finally, Huang's body began to fall backward. Lifeless and limp, he seemed to tip over in slow motion, like a tree after being sawed through.

The problem was, Huang had been standing only a few steps from the helipad's edge when the shooting started. By the time his body bounced against the deck, his entire torso extended over the side. Almost immediately, gravity grabbed hold of the corpse and pulled it over the edge into the inky night.

Nothing left behind except a bloody smear where Huang's body had been.

33

DESPITE THE WARM Miami night, a deathly chill seized Locke when Huang's body slipped over the side. She sprinted to the external stairs and scanned below.

As she'd seen from the air, the decks were virtually all the same width, so she found herself staring straight down. The yacht's hull must have had some sort of lighting built into it—the waterline around the ship glowed a neon purple. That backlighting let her see waves churning, along with a dark silhouette drifting down the length of the ship.

Huang's body.

Facedown, but floating.

For now.

He looked so small, it was a stark reminder that she was standing on the roof of a five-story building.

A visceral twinge in Locke's gut urged her to jump over-board. She had eyes on the body—who knew how long that would last? How long he'd stay afloat? The *Helios* seemed to have stopped motoring for now, but if it resumed its course, she might never find him again.

She couldn't let the body disappear. Without Huang's handprint, Evan was dead.

But the churning sea below liquified her knees. The con-tents of her stomach came halfway up her throat. She'd almost drowned in a backyard pool—did she really believe she could play Navy SEAL and jump off the equivalent of a cruise ship?

The two emotions left her body torn between them. While her arms and legs tensed to make the leap, her hands clamped onto the wire railing with white knuckles.

Locke glanced back over her shoulder. After taking Huang down, the three remaining gunmen had spent a moment admiring their aim. Now one of them spotted her at the stairway railing and pointed.

This was her moment: she had to choose.

Her grip on the railing tightened.

And she yanked herself sideways, ducking as she darted down the stairs to the next deck.

The guards must have thought she was going to jump, as no gunshots followed her immediately. She moved her feet as fast as safety allowed, since skipping risers on the way down was a lot trickier than on the way up.

She'd just reached the bottom of the flight when gunfire crackled above her. Bullets ripped the wooden floor of deck five inches from her feet as Locke whipped around the railing to make for the next set of stairs. While that bought her a moment's cover, she now saw even more guards making their way up from below.

Locke spun on her heel and sprinted away from the stairs, toward the rear of the ship.

She made it several yards before shouts rang out, more words she couldn't understand. But by then her eyes were locked on the end of the deck. Out beyond it, she could see the trailing edges of the additional decks below—the stateroom level, the dining terrace, the pool.

And, even farther out, the black ocean, where Huang's body was waiting.

The problem was, unlike on deck four, no stairs led downward from the end of this level. A wire railing marked the end of the line.

A sudden idea caused Locke to glance to the ceiling. She wondered what exactly it was made from—drywall, fiberglass, something else? To support the helipad, was it reinforced differently than the other levels?

With no way to tell, she would need to take the chance regardless.

Two strides from the wire, the first shot rang out.

The bullet whizzed by on her left, an invisible buzz she felt as much as heard.

Locke willed herself to go even faster. She launched herself at the railing, letting her hands hit the wire first, then using its resistance to help swing her body up and over it.

Now gunfire really started to erupt.

As her feet cleared the railing, she let them fly forward. Once they got out in front, she settled her hips in behind them. Locke landed on the slanted overhang in a reclined seated position, praying it might hold her weight.

Somehow, it did.

As she started sliding down the smooth incline, Locke leaned back, pointing her toes and crossing her arms over her chest.

The ride didn't last long. Two seconds and she was airborne, flying at the floor of deck three feet first.

On impact, Locke let her legs compress before dropping into a forward shoulder roll. That bled off most of the force, and she emerged from the somersault on her feet with some forward momentum.

The gunmen up on deck four had reached the railing now and resumed firing. With their angle straight down on her, Locke didn't have time to cut over to the stairs—she sprinted straight for deck three's railing and hurdled it the same way.

Again she landed on her bottom and started to slide.

But the bullets were closing in on her now.

One slug struck a few inches to her left. Close enough she felt the impact.

Her eyes darted to the bullet hole as it slid past her. She was thinking how lucky she'd gotten when a slug grazed her right thigh.

The wound stung sharply. Instinctively, she rolled to that side.

While that presented a narrower target to those aiming at her from above, Locke realized as she started to slide off the inclined overhang that she was now facing the side of the boat instead of the stern. Rolling off a fall like this would be nearly impossible.

At the last second, she spun onto her belly. She grabbed at the overhang, hoping to catch hold. To stop and dangle before dropping to the next deck.

But the fiberglass was too slick, and the smear of her own blood only made it worse.

Her fingers slid off.

Locke tumbled through the air and landed in an awkward heap next to the long dining table. Pain shot through her in all directions, a throbbing echo of the impact.

She lay there for a heartbeat, or two.

Until a voice in her head warned her to get moving. It forced her up onto her feet and sent her staggering toward the stairs to the pool deck, even as she was still groggy from the fall. In her mental fog, she lost track of all the guards—she was having enough trouble putting one foot in front of the other. She could still hear shooting, but the noise sounded far away. Echoes of distant thunder.

Somehow, she managed to start descending the steps without losing her balance. Knowing Huang's body was drifting alongside the ship to her right, she steered that way, mostly by leaning and letting gravity pull her in the proper direction.

As Locke continued moving, though, bullets kept plink-plink-plinking closer and closer. One shattered a tile next to her left foot, and that helped snap her back to attention.

She scrambled downstairs faster now, scanning the deck as she went, searching for some way out—some way to reach the ship's waterline. The rectangular pool, set perpendicular to the boat, consumed most of the real estate on this level. On either side, a row of chaise longues, umbrellas, and other furniture for the sunbathers adorned the deck, leaving only a narrow aisle along the waist-high wall that surrounded this level.

Gunfire from behind her intensified as Locke reached the halfway point of the stairs. Thinking she might not make it to the bottom, she took two more quick steps and then leapt forward.

This staircase was longer and flatter than some of the others around the yacht. Once she was airborne, Locke worried that she'd jumped too soon. To wring every last bit of momentum she could from the jump, she frantically cycled her arms and legs.

In the end, she cleared the bottom step. Barely.

Her left foot struck first, but the speed she'd built up immediately plunged her forward.

The pool's edge lay only a yard or two ahead. Lit from below, its shimmering water lapped at ornate tiling along its edge. Locke imagined those tiles would be slick as ice—if one of her feet hit them, she was done.

Even worse, bullets continued creeping up behind her. She could sense them landing closer and closer, driving her toward the water.

Shifting her weight, Locke managed to turn sideways. Even as she slid toward the pool, she started to the right, ending up on tiptoes, tightrope-walking the lip where the wooden deck and tile edge met.

The string of bullets trailing her didn't adjust so quickly. They continued straight ahead, ripping the surface of the water.

Locke's next breath came slightly easier, as she figured she'd bought herself a few seconds while the guards on the upper decks adjusted their aim. Even better, she was nearing the corner of the pool—if she could round that before the guards locked back on her, shadows from the ship's sidewall might give her some cover.

She swung wide to the make the turn, bearing down and accelerating to cover as much ground as she could.

When a muzzle flashed off to her left, though, it caught her by surprise.

Worse, the bullets struck directly in front of her. At least one ripped through a chaise cushion, sending a cloud of feather stuffing into the air. Another struck the fiberglass sidewall, kicking up splinters that dug into her side.

Locke's eyes darted to where she'd seen the flashes—across the pool, at the back corner of this deck on the opposite side. In the relative darkness, she spotted a guard down on one knee, drawing a bead on her.

All at once, thoughts flooded her mind—whether the chairs could provide any cover at all, whether she should jump over the side. Nothing seemed to be a good option, given the way he had her flanked at close range.

But then she realized: that guard had to have come from somewhere.

Widening her focus, she saw a shadow beyond him at the far corner of the deck. Part of the wall that was darker than the rest.

Glancing ahead, she saw a similar shadow in the corner on her side.

The longer she looked, the more she realized it was roughly rectangular.

Some kind of door or passageway.

But the opening sat nearly twenty feet away.

Could she reach it before getting cut to ribbons?

Another set of shots rang out. Ahead of her, a red-and-white lifesaver mounted on the wall exploded into a million pieces.

Locke dropped to the ground behind the next chaise longue. While she doubted the chairs would stop any rounds, they'd at least make her harder to spot. Huddled in a crouch, she darted to the next chair in the row.

The corner guard must have realized her strategy. Instead of short, controlled bursts, he unleashed a hail of bullets on full auto.

Locke collapsed to the deck, spreading herself as flat as she could. Bullets slashed through the chair backs above her, nearly deafening her while burying her in an avalanche of snowflake-like stuffing.

Her pulse on overdrive in her ears, she listened for the shots to stop and prayed no rogue bullet would catch her. Hyped on adrenaline, her senses were overwhelming—she could feel every seam in the wooden deck, smell every singe in the cushions.

After seconds that seemed to last an hour, the shooting paused.

Locke knew that was her chance.

Before the flanker could reload, before the guards up top could lay eyes on her, she popped off the deck and sprinted forward. As she drew closer to the opening ahead of her, she saw a darkened set of fiberglass stairs leading downward.

Gunfire erupted again as she dived for the opening.

CHAPTER

34

A LTHOUGH LOCKE SPARED her face by turning her head at the last minute, the steep fiberglass stairs battered her chest, belly, and thighs as she bounced her way down from deck two.

She landed sprawled across a broad platform that floated on the waves rather than being rigidly attached to the hull. The rubberized surface felt damp against her cheek and reeked of salt. The purplish glow she'd seen from above touched everything here, shimmering as the waves rose and fell.

Locke knew she only had seconds before the gunman followed her down. Scrambling to her feet, she was considering jumping into the water when a large, rounded shadow toward the middle of the platform caught her eye.

A Jet Ski.

Several of them, actually—parked in U-shaped depressions on the platform.

She'd ridden a Jet Ski once, here in Miami, all those years ago with Kori. It hadn't been . . . horrible. And this would whisk her away from the gunmen a hell of a lot faster than she could swim.

Winch cables secured the skis at their noses, so Locke quickly unhooked the nearest one and shoved it backward into the water. Jumping aboard, she snatched the key from where it dangled off the handlebars, jammed it into the slot, and pressed the ignition.

Hope this is like riding a bike.

As the ski's engine roared to life, the guard from the opposite side of the ship appeared. He raced to the center of the platform, raising his gun.

Instinctively, Locke clamped down hard on both handlebars. That pegged the throttle, causing the ski's nose to rear up out of the water.

Although the guard let off two shots, they plunked against the bottom of the ski.

Locke managed to loosen her grip, settling the ski down. Then, with a more controlled squeeze, she accelerated again. Cutting a sharp turn in front of the platform, she sprayed the guard with a wave of wake while steering sharply to the port side.

By the time the guard recovered from getting doused, Locke was fifty yards away and flying.

She beelined perpendicularly away from the ship, traveling several hundred yards before finally feeling safe enough to ease off the gas.

The *Helios*'s lights reflected off the ocean between her and its hull, allowing her to scan the surface for Huang's body. She spent a good minute looping back and forth, trying to spot anything unusual on the surface.

When that failed, Locke decided to circle back behind the yacht. That was the way Huang had been drifting. Plus, from the way the *Helios* was moving, it seemed they might have restarted the engines. If it was motoring forward, approaching from the rear would be safest, and the yacht's lights would hopefully help her spot the body before anyone aboard spotted her.

Locke opened up the throttle and cut a wide arc to a position several hundred yards behind the *Helios*. Then she cut power and began weaving back and forth across the line the boat had traveled.

The longer she swept behind the yacht, though, the more difficult searching became. The wind blew stronger, whipping her hair and kicking up more spray. The waves themselves had grown larger, their faces constantly changing. Meanwhile the water itself was an oily black that, if not reflecting the light in a harsh yellow glare, seemed to swallow every last bit of illumination.

Locke was also starting to feel the effects of being on the water. Guiding the ski up and down over the waves roiled her stomach, while the wind began sucking heat from her wet skin. All the while, salt water stabbed at her thigh wound, making Locke grit her teeth.

The only upside to the discomfort was that it allowed her to forget how deathly afraid she was of being adrift on the ocean. She'd successfully ignored her nerves this whole time, and while they flared now, she silenced them by reminding herself that, as long as she had the Jet Ski, she was fine.

Locke had trimmed about half the distance to the *Helios*. That left her close enough she could see men moving on deck. With no idea if they could see her, she prayed the sequins on her dress and the reflective front of the ski wouldn't give her away.

Suddenly, she saw a flash of white among the waves.

It disappeared almost instantly, leaving her wondering whether she'd merely seen some kind of fish, or a dolphin. Or if she'd simply imagined it—if her eyes, stinging from the salt, were playing tricks.

But Locke goosed the Jet Ski forward. Little bursts of power that pushed her to the spot where she'd seen it.

She saw it again.

Just below the surface. Solid white.

And it wasn't moving.

She slid the ski in next to it, reaching one hand below the surface to grab whatever it was.

Without warning, a wave surged, rocking the ski backward. It also lifted what she'd been feeling for, revealing it in the light.

A man's shirt.

A black strip cut diagonally across it.

Huang's body—with the satchel still strapped across him.

Locke reached forward again, but missed when the ocean tossed the ski in another direction. She added some throttle, cutting through the chop until she pulled up alongside Huang. This time she managed to snake her fingers underneath the satchel strap.

Yes!

If she hadn't worried about earning the attention of the *Helios*, Locke might have let out a joyous squeal. As it was, her insides were screaming. She squeezed her eyes shut and sent another mental message to Evan.

I'm coming for you. I'm really coming this time.

After projecting those words into the universe, Locke looked around and realized she didn't have a great plan for what came next. Retrieving the body had been such an emergency, she hadn't considered how to get it back to the warehouse without the helicopter.

Turning the ski away from the *Helios*, she scanned the horizon.

Thankfully, lights were visible onshore. If she steered for them, she could haul Huang back herself. It would be a slog, but what other choice did she have?

As she added power and steered for the shore lights, Locke wondered how much gas remained inside the Jet Ski's tank and how best to utilize it. Cutting through the waves required lots of throttling up and down, which she imagined chewed through fuel. Plus, she now had a much heavier load to haul—it took a decent amount of arm strength to keep a grip on Huang's soaked body and clothes each time a wave lifted the ski and tried to pull it away.

But she wasn't about to let go.

Someone would have to amputate her arm before she'd release her grip on the satchel strap.

Gradually, Locke built up speed on the ski. Although she kept her eyes focused primarily on the shore lights, periodic glances back at the *Helios* showed she was making progress. Even better, her senses gradually numbed to the sensations that had threatened to overwhelm her during the search. The cacophony of the engine, waves, and wind receded to the background. Her eyes stung less. The ache from her leg wound seemed to dull.

The only thing that worsened was the cold. She felt the chill down deeper than her skin now. In her bones. When her teeth started chattering, she clamped her jaw shut.

She continued that way for several minutes. Enough distance that the shore lights grew into larger shapes. Enough time that the glimmer of hope that had sparked in her chest flashed again.

Now when she thought of Evan, trapped in the box, she pictured herself freeing him. He'd cough, he'd sputter. But he'd be breathing.

He'd fall into her arms *alive*.

That image warmed her. Not all the way through . . . not enough to combat the cold.

But enough to offset it, just a little.

As if to deny her even that small moment, the noise around Locke swelled into a tremendous howl.

She smiled at the sky and shook her head. This too would pass—she wasn't going to give up, no matter how hard the wind blew.

But this noise didn't abate.

If anything, it grew louder.

As it continued to overwhelm Locke's ears, she noticed something about the sound. It was different than before. Along with the wind's roar and the waves' thundering, she heard something else. Something . . . different.

Locke looked back for the first time in a while, hoping her progress from the *Helios* would buoy her.

She did a double take when she saw the lights.

Not on the yacht, which had slipped even farther away.

No, these lights were above it.

A pair of them. One constant, the other blinking.

Only these lights didn't bounce with the waves or shift with the wind.

They were growing steadily larger, speeding right for her.

And that was when she recognized the noise.

The helicopter.

CHAPTER

35

Locke opened the throttle, even though she knew it was little use. Her glances back showed the helicopter gaining every second.

She could feel as much as hear the rotors now—a steady, thundering vibration that echoed through her. More than anything, it reminded her of machine gun fire.

The pitch of the rotor noise deepened as it drew closer. Downwash from the blades intensified, swirling like a burgeoning tornado around her, until finally the lights zoomed past overhead.

To Locke's surprise, the chopper didn't turn around immediately. As it continued its course and the lights shrank again, she wondered if it was racing ashore for some other reason. Not searching for her but ferrying wounded, or something else.

Her insides clenched, silently urging the helicopter on its way.

But, after a moment, the lights hesitated.

They flipped around, and Locke immediately knew what that meant.

The spotlight confirmed it.

Pointing down from the chopper's nose, it cast a bright circle onto the water's surface. A bit of light also leaked backward, reflecting off the rounded canopy, making it look even more insect-like.

Locke steered the Jet Ski to her right. If the chopper didn't have an exact visual on her, maybe she could veer around the spotlight and slip past, leaving the pilots searching in the wrong direction.

But the spotlight beam moved with her.

She leaned even harder to the right, and again the chopper matched her course. The beam kept advancing, its bright circle closing on her.

Although Locke laid on the throttle, the Jet Ski's little engine was no match for the helicopter. After a quick surge ahead, the spotlight quickly caught up.

And that was when the gunfire started.

She didn't even hear it at first, the shots lost in the noise of the engines and the waves and the wind. But when a bullet smacked her ski, Locke felt the impact. Glancing back, she saw not only the entry hole in the rubber seat behind her but more muzzle flashes coming from the right side of the chopper above.

She immediately banked the Jet Ski left, nearly pulling a full one-eighty. While holding on to Huang's body through the hairpin turn felt like it might rip her arm out at the shoulder, the maneuver caused the helicopter to overshoot.

Once it zoomed past her, Locke gunned the engine.

Although she hoped to gain some separation, the spotlight was back on her in seconds. This time, the circle of light swallowed her completely—from inside it, she couldn't see where to steer. Everything beyond the spotlight was reduced to a flat black curtain.

Locke tried everything she could think of to escape. Alternating speeds, juking this way and that, spinning around. None of it helped.

And now the gunfire came again.

Bullets ripped the water to her left, forcing her to lean right. But the illuminated circle simply wasn't wide enough—the hail of bullets turned quickly and walked directly toward her.

She knew they wouldn't miss this time.

Sucking down the biggest breath she could, Locke plunged off the Jet Ski to the right.

Once she was underwater, the deafening noise disappeared. Between the odd silence and her eyes clenched shut, she felt completely disoriented.

Still clinging to Huang's body via the satchel strap, she pulled herself underneath it, hoping it might shield her from the bullets.

But after what seemed like a thousand frantic heartbeats, her lungs demanded another breath.

Locke hung there in the water for a moment, blind and deaf, wondering what to do.

Finally, when her lungs couldn't take it anymore, she started pulling toward the surface.

The climb took longer than expected, and when she didn't find air where she believed it should be, a shock of panic hit. Instinctively, her eyes popped open.

Seawater stabbed at them, allowing Locke nothing but a quick glimpse of shadowy murk.

She clamped her eyes shut again, her brain racing to divine the direction to the surface.

Suddenly, a wave seized hold and swept her upward. A moment later, she felt air on her face. She wasted no time in sucking down several breaths, even before trying to gain her bearings.

Reopening her eyes, Locke saw a blurry mix of lights and darks. She'd somehow reached the edge of the spotlight circle, the water around her churned to a boiling froth by the rotors overhead.

Her Jet Ski bobbed several yards away. Black smoke poured from it.

Gunfire ripped the air again, and Locke forced herself back under. This time she kicked and pulled and clawed, desperate to get deeper while keeping a hold of Huang's body. Deprived of her other senses, she had only the solidity of the satchel strap as security.

Again, Locke stayed down as long as she could. This time she waited until her lungs burned and the back of her brain screamed at her to get moving.

Several powerful kicks pushed her to the surface. As she emerged and started to inhale, though, a wave smacked her square in the face. Seawater flooded her mouth and nose, leaving her sputtering and even more desperate for breath.

When fresh air finally tickled the inside of her lungs, Locke cracked her eyelids open.

Things had grown dark but incredibly loud.

She whipped her head around until she located the spot-light circle—it lay maybe a half dozen yards behind her, still focused on the Jet Ski. Looking up, she saw the helicopter hovering nearly straight overhead.

Locke flinched when more gunshots erupted from the side of the chopper. But she quickly saw these were aimed at the Jet Ski. Round after round struck the ski, until finally the thing burst into flame.

That seemed to satisfy the chopper, which stopped hov-ering and started sweeping its spotlight around.

Drawing another, exhausted breath, Locke dropped her chin and submerged again.

Her lungs began complaining almost immediately. Her sides ached, and the pain in her thigh returned. Still, she tried to count as high as she could before allowing herself to surface.

When she finally came up after twenty-one, darkness had settled over the sea. The spotlight had disappeared; the helicopter lights were speeding away. The only illumination nearby now came from the burning Jet Ski, yellow flames lapping at the sky and casting shimmering reflections on the waves around her.

Locke leaned back, pointing her mouth to the sky and allowing her lungs to make up for lost time. Once she'd stopped panting and her heart rate slowed, she used Huang's body as leverage to straighten herself in the water and look around.

Lights on shore were visible, but distant. She guessed they were a mile away, maybe two. A minute's drive on the freeway, but forever to swim.

Especially if you didn't know how.

Other than the neon reminder of a far-off Miami Beach, all Locke saw was water and stars. She was completely alone now—the *Helios* had disappeared, and no other boats were visible. Overhead, Locke had the kind of uninterrupted view of the stars that she normally loved back home. The kind where you could see the bright band of the Milky Way, maybe make out a satellite passing by.

After all the noise she'd endured during the chase, the night had grown eerily silent. The wind had died down to a low whistle, leaving only the rumble and hiss of the waves as they rhythmically lifted her up and lowered her down.

Despite the merry-go-round feeling, her seasickness had disappeared. The cold remained, though. Even though she was frantically churning her arms and legs to stay afloat, she couldn't keep her jaw from trembling. She felt as if all the heat in her body had drained away.

From the throbbing in her thigh, that probably wasn't far from the truth. She didn't know how much blood she'd lost, but it was enough.

And that caused a new discomfort to settle over her.

A dark, hollow feeling—the fear that she was now waiting to see what would happen first: whether she would tire and sink or the sharks would show up and rip her to pieces. Didn't they say on the Discovery Channel that the sound of shipwrecks attracted them?

Blood certainly did. She knew that.

Locke checked the Jet Ski again. The fire had mostly burned itself out, only gray wafts of smoke and a few glowing embers remaining. Clearly the thing wouldn't run, but would it give her some shelter? Could she haul herself up onto it?

Deep down, she questioned whether it would matter. No one would see her in the dark, and night had only recently fallen. Hours and hours remained till dawn.

She wouldn't survive that long.

Still, she struggled her way over to the ski and grabbed on with her free hand. Its buoyancy helped her float, and Locke rocked her head back to gaze up at the stars again.

She'd felt this type of solitude, this kind of hopelessness once before. Staring up at the night sky.

Granted, a different set of stars. A half a world away.

When she'd accepted the plea deal in the Camp Taji brig, the terms hadn't sounded so bad. Decreasing from aggravated to simple assault got her a general discharge. Her lawyer had said that was important for benefits and not having to answer too many questions out in the real world. A few more weeks' confinement, okay. The pay forfeiture hurt, but it was only three months. The reduction in rank didn't matter if she was getting out.

And she was getting out, no question. After all this, she was done with the army.

What had worried her most was the Mule.

Going into the military, skipping the end of high school—that had been his suggestion. "This place has nothing for you," he'd said. "You need a career. A way to support yourself."

"Don't be a Marine," he'd advised her. "Not like me. The corps wants to make everyone an infantryman—you don't need that. You're good with tools, with machines. The army's got the best ones. Go let 'em teach you something you can do after you get out. Then stay outta trouble and collect paychecks till you're ready to be done."

"Sounds simple," she'd said, not knowing any better.

"It can be," the Mule said. "If you let it."

Realizing she'd have to confess what she'd done, how she'd mucked up the Mule's plan, alternately scared her and broke her heart. Sitting in that Camp Taji cell, Locke had no idea the Mule had already passed. That she'd never see him again.

His presence when she rotated home was a given—in her mind, the Mule was a constant. Just like Kori, the other fixture in her life.

Except it turned out she wasn't, either.

When Locke settled on leaving the military, she figured Kori would be done too.

With the army. With Newton.

Locke and Kori had enlisted around the same time, so both their contracts were coming to an end. Locke figured they'd head back to the world together. She'd bring Kori back to Val Verde, introduce her to the Mule. Those two would like each other—their senses of humor would dovetail. Hell, Kori might take the edge off how disappointed he'd be. Then Locke and Kori could figure the rest out from there. Together.

The way they'd always done it.

Locke never questioned it. She'd simply assumed.

There'd been a little scare when the new commanding officer took over the base. Because the outgoing CO had come up with the punishments, Locke worried the incoming guy might flush her deal. Not to worry, her lawyer said. He could reduce sentences, but he'd find it almost impossible to raise them.

And, sure enough, when her scheduled release day arrived, the MPs opened the cell door and she strode out. Her very first stop was Kori's CHU.

They hugged, and she told Kori about the deal.

Kori's eyes said it all. The way they dropped to floor, then slid to the side.

Locke knew the answer before Kori's lips ever got to "reenlistment."

That wasn't even the worst part, though.

The real kick in the gut was Newton.

Back when she was pleading, the JAG prosecutors had told Locke that Newton's career was over too. Defending Kori was a mitigating factor for Locke—Newton's drunken assault had no excuse. They'd receive the same punishment, even though Locke's fists had inflicted so much more damage.

Locke decided she could live with that. And that was why, when Kori's eyes narrowed instead of glimmering with excitement when she spilled the news about re-upping, Locke managed to fight off the pain in her chest.

She told herself that Kori forging her own path was a good thing.

An independent thing.

But then Kori told her the rest.

How Newton had . . . apologized. How she felt bad for him, all those injuries.

How the new CO had reduced Newton's sentence. Reinstated, with time served and a note in his file.

After everything that happened, the army had picked Newton over Locke.

And Kori had too.

When Locke spun around and marched out of Kori's CHU into the Iraqi night, she'd felt more isolated, more . . . alone than ever before. Even after her mother died, it had been different. That was a good thing, almost. That was freedom. Independence.

Not having the army or a job or Kori anymore?

That was . . .

Empty.

The best word she could find for it. Standing outside, Locke had looked up at the Iraqi stars, feeling as cold and barren as the space between them.

When she got home and discovered the Mule was gone too, well . . . .

Locke chuckled now, a weak laugh escaping her chattering teeth. Back then, she'd steeled herself by declaring that learning about the Mule was the bottom. That she'd never feel worse than that moment. Promising herself she'd never be that cold or alone again.

It wasn't long after that Locke had found the Alpine safe in the shed. The one from shop class, the one she'd cracked open. Like one last message from the Mule: *Go do this. You're good at this.*

Except.

Except now, she'd fucked that up too. The Mule and Kori had both left pieces of themselves with her, and she'd been too stupid and careless to protect them.

Taking hold of more than her jaw, the shiver came from inside Locke now. Deep down. All her muscles starting to tremble and shake.

Her right arm was especially struggling. Her hand had managed to keep its grip on Huang through the chaos, but now her muscles ached unbearably.

Evan's face flashed in her mind.

Not just the preschooler he was now, but as a baby. The day he was born. The day Kori died. The faces of his different ages bled together, so she saw all of them at once.

Her last words to Kori had been a promise. That she'd care for him, that she'd protect him.

And she'd tried desperately to keep it. The last five years hadn't been easy. She hadn't always enjoyed it. But she'd done her best. Whenever she'd faced the choice of doing something for herself or being with him, she'd chosen Evan every time. Out of respect. Out of obligation.

Then all this.

Locke had grown accustomed to Evan surprising her by now. Things he'd say that would make her laugh, or think.

Stuff he'd accomplish that left her scratching her head, wondering whether she could have done the same at his age.

But the last few days.

The bravery he'd shown. The times he'd tried to protect her, when that was supposed to be her job.

All the doubts in Locke's mind over how Evan felt—whether he would have preferred his real mom, or saw Locke as the pretender she so often felt like—this whole crazy kidnapping had erased them.

Evan didn't love her partway. His feelings weren't some debt to Kori.

They were *real*.

And so, Locke realized, were hers.

Which made this failure so much worse.

When Evan needed her, when Locke was supposed to be there for him, where was she?

Stuck out here. No help at all.

And, as with the others, Locke would never get to apologize. To say goodbye.

Her eyelids trembled, but not from the cold. All the tears she'd held back over the last forty-eight hours, all the sadness and the worry, came spilling out.

And along with it, so much more.

Locke threw her head back and screamed. Not in hopes someone might hear, not even voluntarily. But because she had to. The rage, the sadness, the fear. She had no control over it anymore.

Finally, after several minutes that left her lungs panting, her throat sore, her eyes raw, it all stopped. She blinked away the last of the tears, and her sight cleared. Locke saw the Miami lights on the horizon and knew what was happening. And that she had no more power to change it.

Although she'd held on to the Jet Ski the whole time, now Locke pushed it away. She leaned back in the water and closed her eyes. In her mind, she focused on two little words.

A final message to her little boy that she prayed he'd somehow hear.

I'm sorry.

Every instinct told her to curl up into a ball to keep from freezing, but Locke spread out her arms and legs, hoping to accelerate the process. She hoped Evan managed to fall asleep. That he dreamed. That the last images in his mind would be happy ones.

And she wished the same for herself, that she'd fall asleep before the sharks came.

Listening to her own breathing, her own heartbeat, was peaceful. It calmed her. Took away the fear.

So much so that when the loud bubbling sound began, her first emotion was anger.

What on earth could possibly disrupt my final few minutes on the planet?

As the noise grew louder, she found she couldn't ignore it. The bubbles hissed and popped—they even tickled their way up her legs and her back.

Locke raised her head and saw she was surrounded by a wide circle of bubbles. Her imagination, she figured.

She was hallucinating a hot tub or something.

But then the biggest bubble of all appeared. A life-sized bubble that reflected the starlight.

Locke had absolutely no idea what the giant bubble was. And when she saw King's face inside, that only added to her confusion.

My final hallucination, she thought.

When her eyes closed, she still didn't understand.

CHAPTER

36

LOCKE FELT HER body jerk to a stop. Her head rocked forward.

With her eyes still closed, she imagined a massive shark had come and seized her. Any second, it would shake her in its mouth and rip her to pieces.

Her eyes squeezed shut even tighter—she didn't want to see.

But nothing else happened.

No pain. No more motion.

She cracked one eye open, enough to get a blurry view of her surroundings.

When she saw car headlights against the green warehouse wall, she assumed she was dreaming. Or already dead. Maybe some shark had done its toothy best, and now her personal hell would be reliving the past few days over and over.

Something grabbed her upper arm, and Locke recoiled at the heavy grip. Her head spun to identify it.

A monstrous hand, wrapped around her bicep.

Although she recognized it immediately, her eyes slowly traced upward from the fingers to the wrist, arm, and shoulder.

King.

The Giant was wedged into the driver's seat next to her. Head bowed, knees pressed up against the steering column, the wheel cutting into his massive chest.

The sight was almost funny. But it brought Locke back to the question of where she was.

King leaned toward her, giving her an imposing stare. He removed his hand and pointed through the windshield.

Her eyes followed it, and slowly her brain began to catch up.

They were in the warehouse parking lot, same as that first night. King was motioning toward the path that would lead around the side.

Evan!

Locke had the car door open in an instant, clumsily trying to climb out before realizing a seat belt restrained her. She struggled to unlock it, but once the latch popped free, she was out the door like a shot.

She made it only three quick steps before stumbling. Her right leg wasn't completely cooperating, and suddenly she remembered the bullet wound. Looking down, she saw someone—King?—had bandaged her quad. Blood no longer spilled from it, but the muscle wouldn't bear her full weight either.

Relying almost exclusively on her left leg, she hop-limped the rest of the way to the warehouse door. When she pulled on it, it was locked.

Locke glanced back toward the lot, and King appeared, carrying a heavy load over his shoulder. He dropped it at her feet.

When she realized it was a body, she instinctively hopped back a step. Then she saw it was Huang. King grinned at her, then crouched down to fish through Huang's pockets. In a moment, the Giant drew out the key ring Huang had displayed several times and used it to unlock the door.

She held the exterior door open while King dragged the body inside. At the interior metal door, King needed several tries to find the correct keys, which led to Locke bobbing up and down on her good leg. "C'mon . . ."

Finally, the locks clicked and he hauled the door open with a loud screech. Locke bolted through it, dragging her bad leg as fast as she could.

The floor of the warehouse stood darkened, much as it had the night she'd snuck out. But the lack of light didn't slow her—Locke hopped around the wooden structure to the back of the floor. Even in the dark, she could see the Ticonderoga looming.

"Evan!" Locke screamed as loud as her throat would allow. "Evan, we're here!"

As she reached the face of the box, overhead lights began to glow, reflected in the shiny chrome.

"King, *hurry*!"

Locke glanced toward the front of the building and saw the Giant jogging her way with Huang's body over his shoulder. While waiting, she hauled the big oscilloscope over, connected it to the safe's power port wires, and retrieved her notepad with the original chart of signal shapes.

By the time King reached her workspace and set Huang down next to the safe, she had everything she needed. Locke looked King squarely in the eye. "Ready?"

He flashed her a thumbs-up.

She drew a deep breath and went to work. Starting with the digital lock, she woke the keypad and then compared the shapes on the oscilloscope trace to her hand-drawn chart. After converting the shapes to their corresponding numbers, she entered the combination on the keypad. When its light glowed green, she exhaled—that was the fastest she'd ever finished with that lock.

Next, she turned to the manual dial. Spinning and feeling for the notches, Locke found the combination digits quickly: 1, 7, 8, 14, and 21. But, like before, the issue was the order of numbers. And she only had five tries to get it right.

Her eyes dropped to Huang's body at her feet.

While low-to-high and high-to-low were almost always her first two attempts, something about Huang's face told her those wouldn't work. That he would have worried about her cracking the safe. And, counting on her trying those patterns first, he would have deliberately chosen something different.

Locke tried to put herself in Huang's shoes. Knowing he needed to retrieve the money from the safe, he'd set the combination while the crew was dressing. He would have been in a hurry—that suggested something obvious. Something easy, right at his fingertips. But the combo also needed to be simple to remember. Ideally, you wanted it to be like your name—an arrangement you'd never, ever forget.

For Huang, what was as basic as his name?

Wait a second.

The combination had five digits. Huang's name had five letters.

It couldn't be that easy, could it?

Which letter of the alphabet was *H*?

Locke counted on her fingers and got to eight.

U took a minute to count out, but she found it was letter twenty-one. *A* was obviously one.

Quick counts showed *N* and *G* were fourteen and seven. All the numbers matched.

Locke drew a deep breath and then spun them out in order, 8, 21, 1, 14, 7.

When she grabbed the lever under the dial, it didn't budge.

She pulled on it again but found the same result: the combination was wrong.

Locke's heart climbed into her throat. Had she really just wasted one of her only chances?

Reaching for the dial again, she saw her hand shaking.

She couldn't afford to panic. Lowering her arm, Locke closed her eyes and took a deep, cleansing breath. She reminded herself she'd been in this spot before. Heck, a few hours ago.

As she reopened her eyes, Locke took another look at Huang's face. He wasn't smiling now, but she thought of all the smug grins she'd wanted to wipe off his face. The way he'd mansplained testing the safe, even though he'd been completely wrong about the way the digital lock worked.

Locke reached for the dial and spun the name numbers again, this time in reverse order: 7, 14, 1, 21, 8.

She reached for the handle.

It turned!

Locke's mouth hung open, even as tears started to fill her eyes. But, as happy as she was, she warned herself that Evan wasn't free yet.

She signaled King, who lifted Huang's body to make his hand accessible. When Locke took it, she assumed the dead flesh would turn her stomach. But it was so cold it didn't feel real. She was able to jab it into the scanner straightaway.

As she waited for the biometric sensor to beep, every second that ticked by made Locke worry. She had no clue whether the exposure had affected Huang's handprints— he'd certainly taken on a ton of water.

Finally, though, the green light flashed.

She reached immediately for the main handle. When she pulled the door open, Evan tumbled out.

Locke caught him before he hit the floor.

37

Unlike Huang, Evan's skin was flushed and warm. With limp muscles and eyes closed, he looked like he was sleeping. She could feel his chest moving, so she dragged him away from the box, stretching him across the floor on his back even as the oxygen bottle clanged against the concrete.

Once Evan was laid out straight, Locke noticed his arms and legs twitching slightly. She pressed her ear to his chest. His little heart was beating, but it sounded faint.

King, who'd moved to Evan's feet, gave her a quizzical look.

She threw her hands out to the side. "I . . . I'm no nurse. I don't . . ."

A noise interrupted her. A soft puff of air.

Then another.

She turned back in time to see Evan's shoulders twitch as he coughed.

Locke ran her fingers over his forehead. "Evan?"

He sputtered, his body rocking to each side. He ended up facing her.

"Muh . . . Muh . . ."

"I'm right here, baby!"

When his eyelids cracked open, Locke's throat clamped shut. Tears began pouring from her eyes as her head dropped to his chest and she sobbed against it. While she tried to be gentle, she squeezed him in a hug that she didn't want to release.

"Momma . . ."

She lifted her head and looked at him. "Yes, baby. I'm here."

"You smell fishy." He smiled weakly, then coughed.

Locke laughed through the tears.

"They messed up your pretty dress."

She shook her head. "That's okay. Getting back here was what mattered."

King circled to Evan's other side, kneeling next to him.

Evan's head lolled over. "Hi, Henry."

King smiled at the boy, then patted his shoulder.

"Henry?" Locke asked King. "That's your real name?"

He nodded, then pointed between himself and Evan. With noticeable effort in his face, he forced out a word. It sounded like *sense*. Or *cents*.

Locke tried to understand, but couldn't. When she shrugged, King held up one finger, then rose to his feet and jogged off.

While he was gone, Locke traced her fingers through Evan's hair. Some of the red had already drained from his face, and he seemed to be relaxing.

He looked up at her. "The dark was really scary."

"I bet," she said. "I'm so sorry you had to go through that."

"I told myself you'd be back soon. That if I just went to sleep, it would happen faster."

Locke smiled. She said that every Christmas Eve, not that it seemed to help. "Did you fall asleep?"

"Yeah. But I'm still tired."

"It's been a very long day."

King returned, carrying Locke's bags from the janitor's closet in one hand and the air mattress in the other. Over his shoulder, he'd slung one of the heavy towels Queen had purchased. He flopped the mattress next to Evan, then gently scooped the boy onto it before draping the towel over him. King patted his head with one of his huge mitts.

Locke nodded at King, then smiled at Evan. "Rest now. Sleep if you can, okay?"

Evan didn't argue. He simply shut his eyes and said, "Oh-kay."

Once Evan's breathing deepened, Locke jerked her head toward the front of the building. King nodded.

As they started walking, he pulled a pad and pen from one of the bags. He wrote something and turned the paper to show her: *Evan and I are friends.*

Friends.

That was the word King had been trying to say. Not *sense.*

Locke thought back through the times she'd found King near Evan. She'd assumed the worst, but with the Giant's problems speaking and the way the others had mocked him, his openness to Evan made sense. And, of course, Evan would have reciprocated.

When that all clicked, a pang of guilt rang in Locke's chest. "I . . . I didn't know," she said. "I'm . . . sorry."

King nodded. He gave her a thumbs-up, then wrote some more. *Change clothes. Eat.*

When they reached the front, King handed her the shopping bags before beelining into his office. Locke made her way gingerly to Queen's room and shut the door.

When she flipped the lights on, they glinted against the rhinestone makeup case.

In addition to the bags, traces of the Pink Punker were scattered throughout the tiny room—a makeup brush sitting on the chair, clothes piled in the corner, her phone lying on the desktop.

Locke decided to ignore all of it for now and extinguished the lights. After stripping off the dress in the dark, she donned the denim shorts and blouse she'd set aside earlier. An extra benefit of the dark—it helped her resist the temptation to check her thigh wound. Leaving the bandage in place, she slipped into her flip-flops. It had been hours since she'd worn shoes.

When Locke emerged from Queen's office, King's door was still closed. While her outfit provided more coverage than the dress, it still wasn't enough to calm the gooseflesh that covered her arms and legs. So she went looking for extra layers.

Having never searched Huang's office, she checked there first. The room itself was identical to the others, but inside he'd stored a suitcase and a small leather handbag.

A quick check of the suitcase revealed nothing useful, only slacks and golf shirts that smelled of tobacco and wouldn't have fit anyway. The handbag's contents were slightly more interesting—US and Chinese passports bearing Huang's name and picture, a few hundred dollars in both countries' currency, business cards written in Mandarin, and a set of airline boarding passes. While she expected the tickets would be routed to somewhere in China, Mexico City was listed as the destination.

Not knowing whether any of that might be useful, Locke shoved it all into her pockets.

As she debated whether to search Jack's office, the chill still ringing in her bones convinced her it was worth it. He had no carry-on bag, only a suitcase splayed out next to his cot. Locke rummaged through the case, finding an extra, unused chef's coat and a pair of baggy chef's pants that would fit over her existing clothes.

Happy about the extra warmth they provided, she left Jack's office at almost the same moment King emerged from his own. He'd ditched the suit and was once again clad in sweatpants and a jersey. He waited for her as she limped over, smiling at her new outfit.

Locke shook her head. "You like this, huh?"

King nodded vigorously, releasing one of his deep chortles.

With King's office door still ajar, she was able to peer inside as she passed it. She saw the same suitcase and hanging bag she'd searched before. But the floor was different. The book she'd seen earlier now rested on the carpet, with no sign of the air mattress.

Locke did a double take back to Jack's. And then to where Evan was resting.

"Wait . . . is that *your* mattress Evan's been sleeping on?"

King nodded. He raised the pad again and pointed at the *Evan and I are friends* note.

Locke's head fell back against her shoulders. She'd assumed Jack had given Evan the mattress, but now she remembered King exiting the closet as she'd voiced her thanks. Evan had tried to correct her, but she'd shushed him, too busy to listen.

After a long look at the ceiling, Locke grabbed King's elbow. "I am . . . so sorry." She took a hard swallow. "You were sleeping on the floor for us—for him—and I didn't even realize."

King's gaze dropped to the floor.

As best she could on her weak leg, she bent down to maintain eye contact. "Really, thank you. For the mattress. For Queen. For . . . rescuing me."

Locke pictured the Giant, leaving her on the staircase to return to the sauna. He'd likely drawn some of the guards away from her as she chased Huang. Moving farther into the bowels of the ship had seemed like suicide at the time, but now, thinking about the bubble he'd arrived in when she was adrift, Locke recalled the door she'd passed with Queen on the way to the spa. "How on earth do you know how to drive a submarine?"

King's face cracked into a slight smile.

She returned it. "Seriously, I don't know how you got out of there, or what else to say. But . . . just . . . thank you for getting me home to him."

King nodded once. Then he made a note on his pad: *FOOD.*

When they reached the round table, King steered Locke into a chair. Then he lifted her bad leg and stretched it across to another seat.

"I'm okay," she said, starting to rise. "I can help—"

King pushed her back down with one of his heavy hands. Circling to Jack's refrigerator, he dug out some containers. In a matter of minutes, he was scooping a frypan's contents onto two plates and delivering one to her.

Just the smell of the scrambled eggs and vegetables energized Locke. She waited for King to sit, and once he dug into his pile of food with a plastic spoon, she took a bite.

Not as refined as Jack's cooking, but the warm calories were exactly what her body needed. She and King both ate silently for several minutes until their plates were nearly empty. Heat radiated from her full belly out to the rest of her body. Her muscles were relaxing now—she noticed her eyelids growing heavy.

But there were still things to do.

When Locke looked over at King, his eyes were closed. That made what she had to say a little easier. "I don't know where you're headed next. But . . . if you need a place . . . you could come back to California. With us."

She held her breath. The offer was the least she could do for the man who'd saved her, twice, and by extension, her son.

King's eyes flicked open. He thought a moment, then scribbled something. *Going to Switzerland. Need my surgery.*

"Surgery?"

King scribbled some more. *Cancer.*

Locke blinked blankly. She read the words three times before looking up.

King must have noticed her expression, as his mouth opened in a goofy grin. He wrote, *Don't I look like a cancer patient?*

She chuffed. "No, not at all."

Tumor made me this way. Who knew cancer made you big and strong? King raised his arm and flexed his bicep.

Locke shook her head—it was easily the biggest muscle she'd ever seen, even among some of the 'roid heads in the army. "I don't get it. If it's good for you, why remove it? How do they even do it?"

King's brow furrowed as he wrote this time. *This is second time. First one, when I was a kid. Made me big. They found later, took it out.* He rubbed the scar on his scalp. *Now, another one. Gotta remove it.* King bent his index finger and made a twisting motion by one nostril, as if miming how a kid picked their nose. Then he yanked the hand down suddenly.

Locke giggled in spite of herself. "They're gonna go up your nose to pull it out?"

King nodded and chortled.

Locke took a breath to cleanse that image from her mind. Then she decided she had to ask the question that had been eating at her. "Queen."

King grunted.

"Was that always the plan? I mean, did she know Huang wanted her to . . ."

The Giant scribbled something, then showed her the pad with a raised eyebrow. *Do you really want to know?*

Locke swallowed but didn't answer.

After a silent moment, King took their plates to the trash. Then he disappeared for a moment. He returned carrying the shrink-wrapped cash from the safe, the satchel Huang had used on the yacht slung across his shoulders.

One at a time, he separated the bricks of money into two piles on the table, one-for-you/one-for-me style. He slid one stack to Locke, then dragged the other to his place.

"Huang said you owe some kind of debt," she said.

He nodded, then reached for his pad. *When doctors found first tumor, football coaches didn't want me anymore. Worried I'd die or something. Not easy to get job like this.* He pointed to his mouth.

"So, you've never . . ."

King shook his head. *Tongue too big. Got in way. With no football, needed money. People hired me for this.* He flexed his mighty arm again. *Huang bought me away from them.*

His words echoed the story Queen had told. Remembering Queen's fear of having to go back to her previous life, Locke pushed her stack of money toward him. "You should take all of this. Get your surgery, and pay off whoever you need to."

King closed his eyes and shook his head. With his hand, he sliced the air in front of him.

"Even Steven? No."

The Giant nodded, then cut the air again.

"Won't whoever it is come looking for you?"

King scribbled something quickly. When he turned the pad toward her, his face narrowed into a sinister grin. *Let them come.*

After a moment, King retrieved the satchel from across his shoulders. One at a time, he withdrew each of the four wooden boxes from the bag and set them on the table. Then he looked at Locke and gestured toward them with an open hand.

She pulled herself up onto her feet and hopped over. She removed each of the box tops and looked at the statues inside.

The figurines left her cold. With all the trouble they'd caused, she wasn't sure she wanted to have anything to do with them. Besides, with that story Glebov had told, it didn't seem right. They belonged elsewhere, in China, wherever they'd been made.

Locke looked at King. "I don't . . . You should take them."

He shook his head. He pointed two fingers at her, then at himself.

Turning back to the table, she looked over the figurines. If King was going to insist that she take a pair, maybe she could find a way to turn them in or something. Recognizing the one from Malibu, the Rabbit, she plucked it off the table.

"If it's okay, I'll take this one. Otherwise, you pick."

King nodded and moved two of the statues over with his money, a rooster and a dog. That left her with the final figurine, a small monkey. She placed that with the rabbit and quickly replaced the tops on both her boxes.

As the two figurines disappeared from sight, the jade glinted one last time in the light.

Locke felt a bit of relief once the stone figures were covered, and she smiled at King. He grinned back. A moment later, a yawn forced its way to her lips.

He made a sleeping sign, tilting his head over his hands pressed together.

"That sounds wonderful."

They made their way back to the offices. Wanting to be close to Evan, Locke decided to move the cot from Queen's room out to the edge of the workspace. When King saw her trying to move it, he gently nudged her aside, then lifted the folding metal frame like it was nothing.

After he placed it next to the sawhorses for her, Locke mouthed *thank you*. Evan was snoring lightly, but she didn't want to risk waking him. Finally, she raised a hand in a silent good-night wave.

Henry smiled and returned the gesture before trudging back toward the front of the building and disappearing inside Huang's office.

When Locke stretched herself across the cot, she assumed fatigue would knock her right out. But each time she closed her eyes, all she saw were Queen's baby blues.

Opened extra wide, like in Glebov's office.

Locke's own eyes popped open, leaving her staring at the rows of girders on the ceiling.

In her mind, she pictured Queen's expression just before pulling the trigger. Quivering lip, tears welling up.

Despite the clear implication in King's nonanswer, Queen hadn't seemed like she'd wanted to kill her. And Locke really didn't want to think otherwise. Because if Queen hadn't felt torn, if everything she'd said and done had just been some cynical lie to gain Locke's trust . . .

No.

King was right. In Locke's mind, Queen was a victim of Huang's plan, and that was true no matter what else had happened. She didn't need to know anything more than that.

She realized she owed Henry yet another debt of gratitude.

She could tell him so in the morning.

With that settled near her mind, at least for tonight, Locke began to relax. And when the blackness finally hit, there was no stopping it.

It seemed only seconds later that she heard Evan saying, "Momma."

Locke bolted upright. To her surprise, he was standing at the side of her cot, wearing a slight smile. Behind him, out on the floor, she could see daylight filling the warehouse.

"Morning," Evan said.

As her heart rate slowly returned to normal, she smiled. "Morning. Sleep okay?"

He nodded. "I just woke up. Henry's gom."

"Gone?"

"I looked for him, but he's mot here."

Pulling herself up to her feet, Locke found her right leg offered slightly more support than the night before. She shuffled toward the offices, rubbing the sleep from her eyes.

Sure enough, the door to Huang's office stood ajar. A glance over to the round table showed King's half of the loot missing.

Locke turned back to Evan and shrugged. "Last night, he talked about a trip he had to make."

"I wish he'd said goodbye."

Images of the Mule and Kori flashed through Locke's mind. Even her mom. Not saying goodbye was the worst. "Maybe he had an early flight or something," she said.

Then, recalling that King had been the one who'd knocked her out in Val Verde, she added, "He knows where we live. He'll probably find us when he's ready."

Evan's eyes dropped to the floor.

"You fell right asleep last night. Are you starving?"

He glanced back up and nodded eagerly. "Will you tell me what happened last might? At the fancy party?"

Locke felt a pinch in her gut, wondering which parts she could actually share. "Uh, sure. It's a long story."

"It's a long way home," he said.

She took a deep breath. Figuring out how to get there would be her next challenge. It wouldn't have been easy in normal times, but she expected that traveling into California when it was locked down would make it extra tricky. Her mind started reeling through all the different pieces of how it would work.

Evan interrupted her thoughts. "I love you, Momma."

She smiled, enjoying the sound of that.

And realizing she never needed it to change.

ACKNOWLEDGMENTS

UNLESS YOU'RE WRITING an autobiography, you're writing from someone else's point of view, but the further that character strays from your own experience, the more work you have to do to try and make that perspective true and believable. And that necessarily involves consulting more people and enlisting more readers during the early drafts. Here, because Monna Locke is further away from my own life than other characters I've written, I owe a tremendous amount of thanks to huge number of people thanks for contributing their views and opinions to help round her into shape.

Kim Lim, Sarah Marshall, Jude Mercer, Maddee James, Jennifer Sarja, and others provided invaluable insight into what it's like to be a mother, a businesswoman, a lover, and a friend from a female perspective. Evan Day, TJ Buttrick, Heath Marcus, Joshua Westbrook, and Anthony Toreson all helped me shape Monna's military career and its end. Michael Gorges provided some key plotting insights. Dr. Monna Hess contributed a fabulous first name and the priceless line, "like Donna, with an M" that I've been meaning to use somehow since I met her twenty-five years ago. Despite the input of all of these people, any errors you find in here are mine and mine alone.

I'm extremely grateful to Matt Martz, Terri Bischoff, and the entire team at Crooked Lane Books for welcoming me with open arms and for working to make this book the best it could be. Once again, Dana Kaye and her team at Kaye Publicity helped me land this book in your hands, and as an author, that's what it's all about. Ed Stackler remains the sherpa without whom I'd be out lost, wandering aimlessly around on the mountainside.

More than ever, I owe a huge debt to my literary agent, Cynthia Manson, for her tireless efforts on my behalf. Writing this during COVID, and including COVID in it, made her job all the harder, but she believed enough in me and in the book that she wouldn't rest until it made it into the world. For that, I am beyond lucky.

Finally, special thanks to my wife Molly and my daughters Makela and Charlotte. Having three such wonderful, complex women in my life provided special inspiration for this one, so I hope I did it justice and gave you someone to root for.